AMONGST OUR WEAPONS

BEN AARONOVITCH

ORION

First published in Great Britain in 2022 by Orion Fiction,
an imprint of The Orion Publishing Group Ltd.,
Carmelite House, 50 Victoria Embankment
London EC4Y 0DZ

An Hachette UK Company

5 7 9 10 8 6 4

A CIP catalogue record for this book is
available from the British Library.

ISBN (Hardback) 978 1 473 22666 1
ISBN (Export Trade Paperback) 978 1 473 22667 8
ISBN (eBook) 978 1 473 22670 8

Typeset by Input Data Services Ltd, Somerset

Printed and bound in Great Britain by Clays Ltd, Elcograf S.p.A.

www.orionbooks.co.uk

AMONGST OUR WEAPONS

For John, Stevie, Anne, Genn and Liz without whom nothing would get done.

Wednesday

Surprise . . .

1

Airsoft

As a rule, we don't get to see the bodies when they're fresh. It's drilled into every modern copper that our first duty, after protecting life and limb, is to preserve the crime scene from contamination. That means the first plod on the spot doesn't want to let anyone in but the murder team. And the murder team, when they get there, don't want anybody else except the forensics people getting close.

They certainly don't want to call in yet another specialist team until they're absolutely certain they need to. Especially not us – on account of us being the Special Assessment Unit, famed throughout the Met as purveyors of weird bollocks, sudden violent upsets and, worse, poor detection rates. Especially if they've worked with us before.

DI Stephanopoulos being a notable exception to that rule.

She was waiting for us outside the entrance to the London Silver Vaults on Chancery Lane on a cold wet Wednesday morning in April, a hefty-looking white woman with sharp blue eyes and resting scowl face. At least I assume that was her habitual expression – certainly it was the one I saw the most. And she was definitely scowling when I tooled up with the Folly's latest trainee in tow.

'Who's this?' she asked.

'This is Danni Wickford,' I said. 'She's on the course.'

That being the Basic Falcon Management Course, an intensive one-on-one jaunt around the world of magical policing with yours truly, so that me and DCI Thomas Nightingale, my governor, could get time off for bad behaviour.

We refer to magical gubbins as Falcon in the police – all the better to draw a veil of comforting euphemism across the disturbing face of supernatural policing.

Danni Wickford was a DC from Kingston CID whose Performance Development Reviews contained phrases like 'utterly reliable' and 'completely dependable'. Dependable and reliable being the qualities that the Falcon Recruitment Committee – that is, me and Nightingale – had decided were what we wanted in a Falcon-capable officer. Physically she was a no-nonsense white woman, skinny, shorter than me with dark brown hair tied up in a French braid, blue eyes and a pointy chin. Born and raised in Dagenham, she had a proper East London accent but, like me, could cycle through various degrees of middle-class, cockney and Multicultural London English as the situation required.

Stephanopoulos favoured Danni with a nod.

'Try not to pick up any bad habits,' she said.

'I'll do my best,' said Danni.

The London Silver Vaults were originally built as just that – as vaults for valuable items. Shopkeepers used to store stuff there at night, safe inside metre-thick,

4

iron-reinforced walls, and then bring them up to stock their shops during the day. At some point some lazy git asked why they had to schlep all this expensive – but, above all, heavy – metal up and down the stairs each day. Why not just invite the punters downstairs? Safer all round.

So the vaults were converted into shops and, *voilà*, London gets its first ever underground shopping mall. Amazingly, I'd never heard of it and Danni had had to look it up on her phone while we drove over.

'The original surface building was bombed during the Blitz,' she'd said.

Which explained the neoclassical pile that was sitting on the site, now complete with faux-Georgian windows and rusticated masonry façade of the ground floor.

At least it was an easy crime scene to secure, with a marble reception desk guarding the main staircase down and the lifts. The cordon officer had simply strung a line of blue and white tape across the doorway leading from the atrium and turfed the vault's security guard out from behind his desk. The cordon officer now sat behind it in his noddy suit, looking like a doorman from a dystopian future. Once he'd signed us in the log, we proceeded down half a dozen flights of stairs to a lobby with a coffee machine and a stack of crates with police labels.

DS Sahra Guleed was waiting for us at the inner cordon in a low-ceilinged waiting room with a black and cream coloured floor and a couple of blue sofas that looked like rejects from the 1990s. At one end, a pair of grey metal and glass cases displayed artfully arranged collections of silver.

5

In the opposite corner was a huge old-fashioned safe with a maker's plaque proudly welded onto its front: JOHN TANN — RELIANCE.

'Is this the new trainee?' asked Guleed when she saw us.

I introduced Danni.

'Try not to pick up any bad habits,' said Guleed.

'Yeah,' said Danni giving me a questioning look. ''Course.'

Guleed waved us over to a storage box half-filled with packets of paper noddy suits. She was already kitted out with her hood up, drawn tight so that she could keep her expensive hijab tucked away in her jacket. We shed our coats and struggled into our suits and gloves, and I had to rifle through the cellophane-wrapped packets to find one in XXL size. You nearly always have to go one size up to fit them over your street clothes, and if you're late to a scene you can end up squeaking round in something too small.

As we wrestled our way into our suits, Guleed filled us in.

'Just after nine o'clock this morning an unidentified white male entered the vault, made his way down here, then proceeded to one of the shops and threatened the proprietor. The proprietor hit the silent alarm, but before anyone could respond something happened – we don't know what – and the male was killed.'

'Something happened?' I said.

'Want to guess how much CCTV there is in this place?' asked Guleed. 'Want to guess how much of it is still working?'

Strong magic damages microprocessors – one of the telltale signs of a Falcon event tends to be the local CCTV getting knocked out. Us police like our CCTV. It makes our job easier, and our only complaint about the surveillance state is that it's not nearly as seamless as everyone seems to think it is. Just ask anyone who's had to sit through five hundred hours of grainy video on the off chance someone in a hoody looked the wrong way at the right moment.

Once we were kitted out and as anonymous as stormtroopers, we waddled off to see just what 'something' had happened to our victim.

The vault proper was guarded by a door forty centimetres thick, with the John Tann maker's mark embedded into the header. The weight of the door and the building above me gave me a queasy moment as I followed Guleed through.

Beyond the *Tron* door we turned right into a brightly lit and blindingly white corridor which infinitied off into the distance. It was lined with vault doors and display cases filled with silver. At the far end I could see blue and white tape and forensic types swishing around with cameras and collection kits. As we walked down the corridor I saw that John Tann's name was on every header, but the name of each shop was displayed on the inside of the door so you could see them when the shop was open.

And inside each shop was the *most* silver. It was crammed onto shelves and free-standing display cabinets. Ranks of cutlery, salvers and gravy boats. Lines of dogs and cats and bears and eagles and intricate galleons under full sail. All of it glittering in the bright white tungsten light.

And in each shop, standing or sitting amongst the splendour, was the proprietor or salesperson watching us slither past in our noddy suits.

'We offered them a chance to wait outside the perimeter,' said Guleed. 'But they refused to go.'

Most of the shops had been owned by the same families for over fifty years, and so it was with Samuel Arnold & Co, two thirds of the way down the main corridor.

Samuel Arnold & Co was a double-width shop, which meant it had two John Tann doors, which was just as well because one of them was blocked by the body which lay sprawled across the threshold, legs sticking out into the corridor. The SOCOs backed off as we approached, I like to think out of deference to my expertise but more likely because they didn't want to be associated with the kind of weird bollocks that doesn't look good when making a court appearance. Me and Danni went in through the second door and picked our way down the narrow aisle between packed display cases until we could get a good look.

I'd noticed as I passed them that some of the shops seemed very specialised. One was all silver cutlery, salvers and plates; another specialised in silver figurines or candelabras. Samuel Arnold & Co was mostly jewellery, the display cases showing lines of rings, chains and pendants, while delicate spun silver necklaces hung around the necks of headless busts.

By the standard of murders most gruesome, this was

not particularly bad. I've seen headless, faceless and dismembered bodies. Not to mention the one that was cooked from the inside out. And it's not that you get used to it, but you do feel a little wash of relief if the injury is small and neat and the corpse hasn't yet started to smell.

He was a white man, looked to be in his fifties, with thinning brown hair cut short, regular features, pale grey eyes staring at the ceiling, thin-lipped mouth now slack with death. He was wearing jeans, trainers and a plain purple sweatshirt under an olive Patagonia jacket. A hole, about a hand's width across, had been burnt in the sweatshirt just below and to the right of the label; it was perfectly circular and the edges of the fabric were charred black. Through the hole a huge wound was visible but its exact nature was obscured by congealed blood and unidentifiable bits. I'd have said it was a shotgun wound, except I couldn't see any pellet holes surrounding the main injury and it seemed too deep.

'Does that look strange to you?' I asked Danni, pointing at the wound.

'Yes,' said Danni in a slightly squeaky voice. And then, in a normal register, 'Yes, yes, it does.'

I called out to the hovering forensic techs and asked whether I could pull back the sweatshirt and have a look.

'No!' came the unanimous reply. 'And get a move on.'

'We're going to do an Initial *Vestigium* Assessment,' I told Danni.

Magic, including the everyday magic that permeates the world, leaves behind it a trace – an echo, if you like. You've probably felt it all your life – that sense of familiarity when you walk into a strange room, that shiver you felt for no reason on a particular stretch of pavement, the sense that someone just whispered your name. These can all be *vestigia*, or they can be random misfiring of neurons, a memory or even a daydream. Separating the two takes training and practice, and is the first step in becoming a Falcon-capable officer.

'Don't worry if you don't feel anything,' I said. 'If you're unsure don't hesitate to ask me. Remember, that's part of the training process.'

We were already squatting down by the body, so that seemed a sensible place to start. I leant over and got my face as close to the corpse as I could. I smelt sweat, fabric softener and, underneath, the first sweet, creeping hints of decay.

But nothing else but the random tick-tock of my brain.

I pushed myself back onto my heels and looked over at Danni.

'What can you sense?' I asked.

Danni closed her eyes and slowed her breathing. It was hard to tell behind the glasses, mask and hood, but I think she frowned before looking at me.

'There's nothing there,' she said. 'Is there?'

I was impressed.

'No,' I said. 'No *vestigia* down here at all.'

'You said there's nearly always something,' said Danni.

'There's some things that can suck magic out of the environment,' I said, and heard Guleed groan from her position in the doorway.

'Not that again,' she said as we stood up.

'Not what again?' said Danni.

'I'll brief you when we've finished evidence collection,' I said. 'You need to get hold of a crime scene map, locate all the CCTV cameras, electronic cash registers, phones and laptops, and mark where they were when the incident happened. If we track the level of damage they've sustained, we might be able to triangulate the epicentre of the effect.'

Danni nodded and swished off to get the job done. Another phrase used in her reviews was *efficient*.

'Look at you,' said Guleed. 'Ordering people about.'

'Better than the alternative,' I said, and we went and found the SOCO to make sure all the CCTV cameras and the rest were bagged and tagged.

'That's going to cost money,' said Guleed.

'We'll let Nightingale argue the toss with Stephanopoulos,' I said – that being, in my opinion, what senior officers were for.

'I love that you still call them by their last names,' said Guleed.

'When I'm a skipper like you I'll call them Thomas and Miriam,' I said, but I wasn't sure I ever would – at least not Nightingale. 'I think I need to have a word with the witness.'

Phillip Arnold was a third-generation silver trader. He was proud to inform us that his family had owned a shop in the London Silver Vaults for fifty years.

'Although I've got to say I worry about the future,' he said.

Phillip was a young-looking forty-year-old white man with black hair and light brown eyes. He was dressed in a well-cut but, deliberately to my eye, old-fashioned pinstripe suit complete with embroidered waistcoat and matching yarmulke. His movements were nervous and he kept making repetitive little gestures with his hands. In normal policing it's usually better to wait a bit before you conduct a second interview, but with Falcon cases you wanted to get in quickly. Faced with the supernatural, witnesses tend to rationalise away things they didn't understand. So it's better to get a statement before they can convince themselves they didn't see what they actually saw.

And Phillip wasn't at all sure about what he'd seen.

'A light, he said. 'Only not like a real light but . . . Have you ever been hit in the head?'

'Occupational hazard,' I said.

'Did you ever get that flash of light?' he said, making exploding gestures in front of his eyes. 'It's not really a flash of light but that's what it looks like?'

'Definitely.'

'It was like that,' he said and clutched at the bottle of water we'd provided.

I was conducting the interview on the blue sofas in the lobby by the safe and the display cases. I was still in my noddy suit, which was not ideal, but I wasn't sure that I wasn't going to have to go back into the crime scene.

'Like that, really,' said Phillip, and he took a swig from the bottle. 'Really. Like being smacked on the back of the head.'

Which hadn't happened – at least according to the paramedic who'd had a look. He had worried about concussion all the same, and had wanted Phillip to take a quick ride to A & E. But Phillip had refused to leave until his dad or one of his brothers arrived to keep an eye on the shop.

I led him through his initial statement. How the victim had entered his shop shortly after opening time and asked about rings.

'He seemed totally normal,' said Phillip. 'A little intense, maybe, but normal. I showed him some rings, but he was after a particular style.'

'What was he after?'

'That's difficult to say,' said Phillip. 'I'm not sure he knew exactly himself. A puzzle ring, or possibly a gimmal ring.'

A gimmal ring being two rings joined together to form one – very popular with romantics and suspicious husbands from the Middle Ages onwards.

'He said it "opened up" and had "symbols" on the outer and inner surfaces.'

In the old days I would have made a *Lord of the Rings* joke about the Black Speech of Mordor, but now that I'm almost a father I'm trying to adopt a more professional attitude and set a good example for trainees like Danni.

'Did he say what kind of symbols?' I asked.

'Well, I did ask him if he meant Elvish,' said Phillip. 'I've heard that was popular fifteen years ago – on gold rings, anyway.' He obviously misinterpreted my expression because he continued, 'Because of the hobbit films.'

Not Elvish, replied the man, but mystical symbols, alchemical symbols.

'I said we didn't have anything like that in stock,' said Phillip. 'And he said I was lying. He said that his ex-wife had sold it to us and, when I asked when, he said years ago. I said I'd look it up in our inventory, but there was nothing like that in the shop and he could look around if he didn't believe me.'

The man was getting agitated and Phillip wondered whether he should activate the silent alarm, only you weren't supposed to do that unless it was a real emergency and Phillip wasn't sure it was – right up until the moment the man pulled out a gun.

'At first I couldn't believe it,' said Phillip. 'It didn't seem real.'

And you'd have to be meshuga to try and rob the vault. Shop policy was to give them whatever they wanted and let them run out into the arms of the police.

Only Phillip couldn't give the meshuggenah what he wanted, because Phillip had never heard of this particular ring, or the man's ex-wife, and definitely didn't have it in stock.

'Wait,' I said, because some of this was missing from his earlier statement. 'Did he give the ex-wife a name?'

Phillip paused.

'Anthea?' he said, 'No it wasn't that – older, old-fashioned . . . Althea. Like the woman in the poem.' I must have looked blank. '"To Althea, from Prison"? "Stone walls do not a prison make, Nor iron bars a cage"?' He sighed. 'It's a poem by Richard Lovelace.

Fairport Convention did a famous version. You lot are making me feel old,' he said, and chuckled. He flexed his shoulders and neck and became noticeably more relaxed.

Contrary to what people think about police interviews, we like relaxed. People are more likely to blurt out the truth when they're relaxed – even incriminating truth – so I smiled and said that we get that a lot.

And then I asked whether the man had given his ex-wife a surname.

'Moore,' said Phillip. 'Moore with an *e* – he was very definite about that. Wanted me to check our records.'

'And did you?' I asked.

'Of course I did,' said Phillip, tensing up again. 'He was pointing a gun at me. Or at least I looked it up in the book.'

This was an old-fashioned account book which Phillip's family still used, mainly because it added an air of mystery and style to the shop. Their true stock control system ran off a laptop.

I was willing to bet money that the laptop had been sanded along with everyone's phones and the CCTV cameras. Still . . .

'Do you have off-site backup?' I asked.

'Of course,' said Phillip, and I added searching that database as an action to pass on to Guleed.

'Was Althea Moore with an *e* in the book?' I asked.

'I never got a chance to find out,' said Phillip. 'I was looking it up when . . . it happened.'

The flash of light that was like being brained with a plank of wood.

'And then he was just lying there,' said Phillip. 'Brown bread.'

'The pistol was a fake,' said Stephanopoulos once we'd reconvened in the upstairs lobby for post-crime-scene coffee. 'The firearms guy knew it as soon as he looked at it. It's an Airsoft replica – shoots pellets.'

'When are they going to move the body?' I asked.

'This afternoon,' said Guleed, and I made a note to let Nightingale know so he could wangle the PM for Dr Vaughan and Dr Walid.

'Do you think this is a Falcon case?' asked Stephanopoulos with the merry tone of a senior officer hoping to make a tricky-looking case somebody else's problem.

I was pretty certain it was indeed Falcon, but it's the policy of the Special Assessment Unit to discourage other units from foisting their cases on us. Even if it's Stephanopoulos.

We call this *encouraging operational self-sufficiency.*

'I don't think we'll know until we have a cause of death,' I said.

So, after I'd briefed Nightingale over the phone I commandeered the vault's meeting room, conveniently located just off the lobby, and used it to finish up our Initial *Vestigium* Assessment. With the aid of Danni's crime scene map we collected a representative sample of phones, cameras and laptops from the SOCOs. Or, more precisely, we prised them out of their reluctant fingers by promising that everything that needed logging or signing would be logged and signed, and that the chain of custody would be maintained yea, even unto the end of days, or the first court appearance – whichever came first.

We started with Phillip Arnold's iPhone 6, since that was most likely the closest affected item. You need a special screwdriver for the pentalobe screws, but apart from that, the 6 is less hassle to open than previous models. I'd known just by shaking it by my ear what to expect, so I made sure to put down a white sheet of paper to catch the sand that dribbled out when I lifted out the motherboard. Unfortunately the protection plates were soldered on, so I had to pry them loose to show Danni the chips.

'This is what happens when someone or something does serious magic around modern microprocessors,' I said. 'It's basically just silicon sand with trace impurities from metals and quartz.'

'Is this why I'm wearing a crap wind-up watch, then?' said Danni. 'And why my lovely phone, which has my entire life on it I may add, is locked in the safe back at Russell Square?'

'We got tired of replacing people's phones,' I said.

'And you get the Airwave handsets cheap,' said Danni.

'Not that cheap,' I said. 'I prefer to use the burners.'

I'd issued one to Danni when she'd started the course. Experience had taught me that it's much easier to get a copper to do something if you throw in some free kit.

'Do I get to keep it?' she asked. 'After the course is over?'

'If it's still working,' I said, 'be my guest.'

The shop's laptop was easier to open and, like Phillip Arnold's phone, just as buggered. The whole chipset had basically disintegrated, leaving nothing but the connector pins, the cables and the motherboards behind. It had a physical hard drive, which at least meant that the Arnold family might be able to recover any crucial data off it. Although I had no doubt Sahra would be trying to winkle any mention of Althea Moore out of their off-site storage.

We checked a CCTV camera that had been two metres from the body, then a cash register that had been four metres away, another camera at six, and so on at two-metre intervals until we found one, another iPhone, at twelve metres that showed no visible damage.

'Still "inoperative",' said Danni, reading off the evidence label.

'It doesn't take much to knock out a chip,' I said, and used my jeweller's glass to spot the tiny pinprick-sized craters in the surface of the silicon.

Once we'd established the probable radius of visible effect, we went back and checked the items we'd picked up within that circle. It was a laborious process because we had to take pictures of the damaged components, then relabel them and package them up neatly for the forensic guys. Once we had everything plotted, it was clear that whatever magical happening had happened to our victim had happened just outside the door to Samuel Arnold & Co.

'There's a shock,' said Danni as we started packing up. 'What I don't get is if there was enough magic to knock out all cameras and stuff, why didn't it leave a *vestigium*?'

Points, I thought, *for correct use of the singular.*

'I've got a theory,' I said. 'Do you want to hear it?'

'Is this like the one about the sentient tree?' she asked.

'This one has a bit more data behind it,' I said.

'Data?'

'Verifiable data,' I said. 'All carefully noted down and ting.' As my cousin Abigail would say.

Danni sighed and finished the label she was working on.

'You know, when I volunteered for this course not one person warned me that a science background would be an advantage,' she said.

'What were you expecting? Ouija boards and tarot cards?'

'Yeah, actually,' she said. 'Something like that.'

'I think I saw a crystal ball in one of the labs,' I said. 'But we are modern go-ahead police officers. We stick to the facts and operate in a rigorously empirical environment.'

'It's been a long time since your last foot patrol, hasn't it?'

'Do you want this theory or not?'

She made me wait, carefully folding over an evidence envelope and putting it in the plastic travel box with the others.

'What's the theory?' she said.

'I'm glad you asked,' I said, and explained while we carried the boxes back to the forensic staging post and signed them back over to the SOCOs.

'We think when you cast a spell you're doing two things,' I said. 'One, you're sucking in magic. And then, two, using that magic to create an effect. Like the were-light I showed you on day one.'

'That was a bit of a shock, I can tell you.' she said.

'When you cast a spell, as well as the magical effect, you are also putting out excess magic,' I said. 'The same way that when you turn on a light bulb you get heat as well as light.'

'So the heat bit is what leaves the *vestigium*,' said Danni.

'Correct. So the magic is drawn from yourself and, for some reason, microprocessors,' I said.

I didn't add that possibly it was a boundary effect caused by our universe rubbing up against parallel universes. Because, A, that's an even more unproven theory than the first one. And, B, it makes me sound like an episode of *Doctor Who*.

Danni frowned.

'So that's what does the damage,' she said. 'The same way it damages brains?'

'You did the brain tour with Dr Walid?'

The Folly's chief cryptopathologist liked to emphasise the dangers of practising magic by displaying the results of *hyperthaumaturgical necrosis* – or cauliflower brain syndrome, as those of us without medical degrees call it. We've got quite a collection sitting in jars back at the Folly.

'Yeah,' she said. 'Right after breakfast, too.'

'So we also know that there's some things that can draw magic from the wider environment,' I said. 'They suck up everything magical around them, including *vestigia* – so no trace is left behind.'

'Some *things*?'

'Yes.'

'Not people, then?'

'Depends on your definition of people.'

'Only I've heard stories . . .'

'Like what?'

'Like there was a thing, like a ghost, that got inside people's head and made them do stuff,' she said. 'And that's what caused the Covent Garden riots. And when it was finished with you, it would rip your face right off the front of your head. And that happened to some poor sod in the Belgravia MIT.'

And her name was Lesley May, and we came up from Hendon together and her face was broken and destroyed by just the thing that Danni was talking about. Her face wasn't ripped off, but the bones, cartilage and muscles that held it together fell apart.

Happened right in front of me, and there was nothing I could do.

'You said you'd brief me once we'd finished evidence collection,' she said. 'So brief me.'

'The thing you're describing is called a revenant,' I said. 'You can think of it as a super-ghost.'

'You said ghosts were harmless,' she said.

'Well, that's what makes them super,' I said. 'They can't get in your head unless you let them. They try and play on your weaknesses.'

'That's not reassuring,' said Danni. 'I have a lot of weaknesses.'

'As far as we know, there's only one confirmed revenant,' I said. 'And he's been dealt with.'

Sort of.

I actually had written provisional guidelines for

encounters with that particular revenant. Admittedly they amounted to *Run back to the Folly as fast as you can and hide under Foxglove's bed.*

'You're sure about that?'

'If Mr Punch had been here we'd know about it,' I said. 'He doesn't like to do his work anonymously.'

'Mr Punch?' said Danni.

'It's in the briefing material I gave you,' I said, and Danni gave me the bright, interested look of a trainee who has skipped a vital bit of reading but doesn't want to admit it.

'Of course,' she said. 'I remember.'

We were stripping off our noddy suits when the undertakers wheeled the body bag out of the vault.

'What next?' asked Danni once it had clattered past.

'Now we find out what happened to that poor sod,' I said.

2

Scalpel

If you're dead, in England and Wales you belong to the local coroner. Invested with powers that predate the Magna Carta, they're the ones that are charged with finding out what exactly did you in. Originally this was to determine whether the Crown had a right to hoover up your estate – royalty always being short of cash in those days. Nowadays, their job is to separate the accidents and illnesses from the acts of malice or despair. A combination lawyer and doctor, the job is a West African parent's wet dream, and it amazes me my aunties never bring it up when discussing their plans for their kids.

My mum was different – she would have settled for jazz musician.

So, anyway, the coroner decides when, where and under whose scalpel you get unzipped. Which is why we let Thomas Nightingale, gentlemen wizard, war hero and posher than an afternoon tea at the Savoy, do the negotiating. He has an arrangement with the Westminster coroner and, as a result, Dr Abdul Haqq Walid and, more importantly, his better-qualified assistant, Dr Jennifer Vaughan, get first dibs on potential Falcon cases.

In addition, the Westminster coroner, who obviously

has a thing for the macabre, has an agreement with the other London coroners that she, the coroner, gets first dibs on any Falcon cases that would normally fall outside her jurisdiction. Her colleagues are usually happy to surrender what often proves to be a complicated and frustrating case.

There are several ways into the Iain West Forensic Suite, and while our victim went in feet first via the loading bay, Guleed, Danni and me – after stopping off at Joe's café round the corner for refs – went in via the back and trooped up the stairs to the observation room. This looks like every other institutional meeting room built since the 1990s, with magnolia walls and a genuine wood-effect conference table, except for the big flat TV screen upon which is broadcast a live feed from the lab below. There's a little joystick thing so you can move the camera around, but if you wiggle it too much Dr Vaughan starts making sarcastic comments.

You are not allowed to record anything off the TV, on pain of the coroner's displeasure. And given that she's actually a judge, as well as everything else, that displeasure can be manifested in many legally prolonged ways.

Still, we were perfectly happy to sit upstairs drinking our coffees and working our way through our baguettes while watching Dr Vaughan do her work at one remove.

I should have known it wouldn't last.

About half an hour in, Nightingale stepped away from the table and spoke in a voice loud enough that he could be sure it was picked up by the CCTV's mic.

'Peter, I'd like you and Danni to come down and see this directly.'

Danni pulled a face, but Nightingale wouldn't have called us down if it wasn't important.

'Can I have your doughnut?' asked Guleed as I quickly finished up my coffee.

'No,' I said and dropped it into my bag.

'What does he want us to see?' asked Danni as we changed into our PPE.

The big hole in the victim's chest where his heart should be.

Cleaned up, I could see that it was the size and depth of my fist and smashed right though the ribcage. White shards of bone poked through red and grey tissue. No, not smashed . . . because the ends of the bone looked sheared rather than broken, and the sides of the wound cavity were horribly regular. It looked as if someone had cut out the man's heart with an enormous ice cream scoop.

'What the fuck,' said Danni when she'd had a look, 'does that?'

'Nothing, in my experience,' said Nightingale. 'It would be difficult for a practitioner to cast a spell that would so overwhelm the human body's defences that you could excise a portion of a victim's chest.'

'What defences?' asked Danni, who'd been due to do that particular class next Friday. Part of the *Identifying Falcon Incidents Unit III: Physical Injury.* I'd been planning to finish writing it Thursday night – honest.

Still, nothing beats on-the-job training.

'It's hard to affect the human body directly,' I said. 'Anything with a central nervous system seems to generate a sort of anti-magic shield. You can knock people down or throw things at them, but you can't reach inside with magic and mess with their guts.'

'That's a relief,' said Danni.

'At least not this crudely,' said Nightingale, gesturing at the horrible gaping wound.

'It makes sense from an evolutionary point of view,' said Dr Walid. 'Any species that couldn't resist magic would be at a survival disadvantage over the long run.'

Danni shrugged.

'But obviously,' she said, 'you *can* mess with someone's guts.'

'We're sure there wasn't some weapon involved?' I asked – slightly desperately.

'We did find a foreign object in the wound track,' said Dr Walid.

He produced a stainless-steel specimen tray. On it rested something that looked like a short ceramic tube, just wide enough that I could get my little finger inside. It was an iridescent blue-grey colour, and one end had clearly snapped off leaving irregular shards, but the other looked like it had been fashioned into a hollow point, like that of a bamboo spear.

I assumed that it was this, rather than the hole in the chest, that Nightingale wanted me to sense.

'Shall I?' I asked, and extended my hand towards the tray.

Nightingale nodded and I let my gloved fingertips rest on the tube. Even through the nitrile the surface felt rough and gritty. At first I thought it was as devoid of *vestigia* as the empty space back at the Silver Vaults. But then, like a coin at the bottom of a well, I felt it.

I stood back and let Danni have a go.

'Nothing,' she said after touching the tube. 'The same nothing we felt at the scene.' Despite the mask and safety goggles, I could see her frowning. 'No, wait – there's something very faint, like a sort of light or a musical note.'

I looked over at Nightingale, who was nodding.

When you train someone, I thought, *you don't muck about.*

A light like what you get when you hit your head, Phillip Arnold had said.

'I believe the object is a piece of worked fulgurite,' said Dr Walid. 'Otherwise known as lightning glass.'

Which happened when lightning struck sand and fused it into a glass tube. Although, Dr Walid pointed out, if it was the same then the exterior had been smoothed or polished in some fashion.

'I've heard of something like this,' said Nightingale. 'But I can't remember where. I'll need to check the libraries at the Folly.'

Guleed was waiting for us in the changing room.

'We've found the ex-wife,' she said.

Danni was due a training session with Nightingale back at the Folly so, after clearing it with Stephanopoulos, me and Guleed headed over to Richmond to have a chat. While me and Danni had been fondling lightning glass, Stephanopoulos had persuaded Samuel Arnold & Co to access their sales records and this got us an address.

'She only came in last week,' said Guleed, as we

walked out to the nasty Hyundai she'd snagged from the MIT pool. 'And she didn't sell any rings, just some antique candelabras.'

It had started to rain as we negotiated the traffic on the Brompton Road. Shoppers and tourists were hunched under umbrellas, heads down and walking quickly. As we passed it, I saw that the Harrods windows were tastefully minimalist displays of bicycles and dummies dressed in what looked like 1920s flapper dresses.

I wondered if they'd fixed the consumer electronics hall. It had been over a year, and the management hadn't sued the Met yet, so I figured the damage must have been covered by their insurance. We never had figured out how Lesley May had rigged her iPhone to create the magical explosion which sanded every up-market plasma screen TV and ruinously expensive Bang & Olufsen entertainment centre within twenty metres.

That had been easily as powerful as whatever had knocked out the CCTV in the Silver Vaults, but hadn't been nearly so clean.

'I wonder where she is?' said Guleed, and I knew she was thinking about Lesley, too.

'Somewhere without an extradition treaty,' I said. 'Probably with better weather.'

By the time we'd crossed the Chiswick Bridge, the inside inquiry offices had texted us some of the results of their integrated intelligence platform (IIP) check. I summarised for Guleed as we picked our way through the leafy backstreets of Richmond looking for the address.

Her maiden name had been Althea Emma Synon, born 1984, married one David Moore at Camden Town Hall in August 2005.

'Aged all of twenty-one,' said Guleed. 'How old was he?'

According to his side of the marriage certificate, David Moore had been forty-four, having been born in Handbridge, Chester, wherever that was, went to Manchester University and described himself on his social media as a social entrepreneur, whatever that was.

'Professional freelance charity worker,' said Guleed.

'Does that make us Social Cohesion Entrepreneurs?' I asked.

'Depends on the shout,' said Guleed. 'Doesn't it?'

Althea Emma Moore, née Synon, lived in the basement flat of a semi-detached Victorian villa on Onslow Road, whose owners, like most of the local residents, had concreted over the front garden the better to create off-road parking for their 4 × 4. Guleed mercifully found a space one house down and we parked up while the inside inquiry office finished texting us the remains of the IIP report.

We'd only been there for five minutes when an IRV pulled up beside us – which was a record even for me and Guleed. Now, personally, I just flash my warrant card, give a 'we're all comrades together' grin, and let them drive on. But Guleed always feels the need to make a production out of it. I reckon it's because she's a sergeant and feels beholden to set an example.

She was thwarted this time because, before the PC on the passenger side got a chance to ask Guleed why she was loitering while wearing a hijab in a built-up area, the driver leant forward to get a look at us and recognised me.

'Is that you, Peter?' she said. 'You on a job?'

Her name was, I kid you not, Tiffany Walvoord, and she had been part of the emergency response team that helped extricate me from that unfortunate business in Kew.

'Don't worry, Tiff,' I said. 'Just a notification and statement.'

'Promise?' said Tiffany.

'That's it,' I said. 'If it gets interesting, do you want me to call you?'

'No,' said Tiffany. 'I want you to wait half an hour until I'm off shift.'

I said I'd see what I could do, and Tiffany drove off. Which was a lucky escape for her mate.

'You're far too easy about this sort of thing,' said Guleed, but she left it there while we pieced together Althea Moore's life from the random driftwood of her electronic presence. Once we thought we had enough for an interview strategy, we climbed out of the Hyundai and headed for the steps down to the basement.

As we did, I caught site of a pale face in a first-floor window of a neighbouring house. This was probably the person who'd reported our presence earlier, but they pulled back before I could get a good look.

Because it was a Victorian town house it had a half-basement, which meant that the original denizens, usually servants, could have a bit of a view. Although, in this modern enlightened age, that view was of the recycling bins and the rear end of a Toyota Land Cruiser. It also meant that the occupant got a good view of us clambering down the narrow tradesman's steps to the front door, so it wasn't too much of a surprise when it was opened as soon as we arrived.

'Have you heard the good news about Jesus?' she asked.

She was a tall, hippy white woman in a green tracksuit bottom and black T-shirt with an anthropomorphised half-peeled banana in dark glasses on the front. Her blonde hair was half hidden under a red and white polka-dot scarf. She had wide-set blue eyes and a big, patently fraudulent, smile. We both recognised her from her social media pictures as Althea Moore.

'No,' I said as I showed her my warrant card. 'I am the servant of a higher power.'

'You're police?' asked Althea cautiously.

'Yes,' said Guleed, and she gave me a dirty look. 'I'm DS Guleed. I work at Belgravia Police Station, and this is DC Grant. Are you Althea Moore?'

'Yes,' she said. 'I'm sorry, but I thought you were Mormons.'

'May we come in?' said Guleed. 'I'm afraid we have some bad news.'

Althea remained steadfastly in the doorway and narrowed her eyes.

'What kind of bad news?'

'The kind you might want to sit down for,' said Guleed.

'Oh dear,' said Althea, and she turned and led us inside.

The basement flat was a bog-standard London conversion, with what had once been the kitchen and the servants' quarters knocked through into two rooms separated by a wooden shutter screen, kitchenette in one corner, bathroom and toilet in an extension out into the back area.

'Watch out for the carpet,' said Althea.

The non-kitchen area had been carpeted at some point in the Neolithic, but it was impossible to tell what colour the shag pile was because it was smothered in foam. A three-piece suite had been piled up against the wall with a coffee table, TV, cheap turntable, amp and speakers piled on top.

Guleed was about to say that Althea might want to sit down, but it was obvious that wasn't going to happen in the front room.

'Yeah,' said Althea, looking around. 'You've kind of caught me doing a bit of a spring clean.'

And not a bad job for an amateur, I thought, although she needed to get into the corners with a J-cloth on a stick. We ended up in the bedroom with Althea perched on a bare and, I guessed, recently flipped-over mattress. She had to move a roughly folded pile of freshly laundered bedding and a plastic bag full of jumble to make enough room. Me and Guleed tried to stand back so we wouldn't loom. As police, we have nothing against looming in principle. But you're not supposed to do it during a notification.

'I'm afraid we have some bad news,' said Guleed again – just to get us back on track.

'Oh,' said Althea, and because she'd watched the same police dramas as everyone else, 'Who?'

'David Moore,' said Guleed. 'Who we believe is your former husband.'

Althea stared up at Guleed and repeated, 'Oh.'

You never know how someone is going to react to a notification, so we gave her about a minute of staring blankly before trying to move the conversation on.

'I'm afraid he was found dead this morning at the London Silver Vaults,' said Guleed.

We were watching carefully for a reaction, but not a sausage.

Althea shook her head as if trying to clear her thoughts.

'How?' she asked.

'He was murdered,' I said.

I've done my share of notifications. I've been shouted at, cried on, and on one memorable time a relative broke into song. But this was the flattest response I'd ever seen. I wasn't sure the news had sunk in yet.

Or, said the little policeman in my head, *she's trying to work out what lies to tell.*

Althea told us that they'd separated ten years ago, and got divorced largely by post. There weren't any kids or property worth talking about, so nothing to fight over.

'He went his way and I went mine,' she said in the same tone she'd described moving into the basement flat – which she'd inherited from her grandmother.

It wasn't until Guleed asked her when she'd last seen her ex-husband that Althea reacted. Not much of a reaction, just a bit of a start and quick look around as if checking to see if we were being overheard.

'He came over last night,' she said.

Given that she hadn't seen him for years, it had been a bit of a surprise to find him ringing her doorbell – Althea hadn't even been sure that he had her address.

'How did he seem?' asked Guleed.

'What?'

'Was he upset, happy, calm?' said Guleed. 'What was his mood?'

'He started calm,' said Althea. 'At least, calm for David, which was never very calm. Don't get me wrong, I don't mean he was neurotic, but he always had plenty of spare energy. A sort of boundless enthusiasm. It was one of the things I fell in love with.'

Her face had grown more animated as she spoke and I saw the moment when the reality of David Moore's death hit. The mouth pinched in and the eyes squinted and moistened. It looked genuine, but I've been wrong before.

We gave her a moment and then Guleed asked a few routine questions to calm her down: When did he arrive? When did he leave? Do you know whether he drove or came by foot?

Once we had those, she asked Althea if she knew why David had chosen to visit her that evening.

'He wanted his silver back,' she said, and her lips twisted. 'Not that he said that straight away. No, he was all, "I've been thinking of you and I was in the neighbourhood, why don't we have a drink and we can catch up." And I fell for it because I'm stupid that way.'

They'd had a glass of wine – he'd brought a bottle with him – and he had sat on the sofa and leant forwards and asked Althea where his silver was.

'Just like that, he looked me in the eye and said, "What have you done with my silver?"'

'And what did you say?' asked Guleed.

'I told him I'd sold it,' said Althea. 'Said I'd taken it down the Silver Vaults and cashed it in years ago.'

'Is that true?' asked Guleed. 'Because according to the shop, you were in last week.'

'I wanted him to think he was ancient history,' said Althea.

'How did you know about the Silver Vaults?' I asked.

'I'd been there loads of times,' she said.

Back in the good old days of the 2000s, when she'd being working as an intern for a PR firm.

'A friend of Dad's got me the gig,' she said.

She'd been sent there with one of the partners to vacuum up a tonne of antique silver as gifts for valued clients. It had been fun randomly selecting things that took her fancy.

'I remember one time we gave everybody silver animals – foxes, owls, bears, tigers. It was like being a kid again.'

'How did he take the news?' asked Guleed. 'Was he angry?'

'No,' said Althea. 'Not really. He sort of . . . I don't know, crumpled . . . Like his face crumpled and he started to cry.'

'What did you do?' asked Guleed.

'I moved away,' said Althea and shrugged. 'I thought

35

he was angling for a pity fuck and I didn't want anything to do with that.'

Guleed asked what happened next and Althea said that David had asked whether she'd sold the ring as well.

'And I told him I had,' she said.

And David Moore had looked at her for a long minute before standing up and leaving the flat.

'He was walking strangely,' said Althea. 'As if he was drunk. But we hadn't even finished the wine. I made sure to bolt the door after he'd gone.'

Guleed glanced at me and narrowed her eyes, which meant I was playing, if not bad cop exactly, then definitely insensitive male cop with a side order of plodding.

'But you didn't sell the ring, did you?' I said, and stepped forward so I could loom a bit.

'What makes you say that?' she asked.

'We have the sales records from the shop,' I said.

'It's mine,' she snapped. 'He gave it to me.'

Me and Guleed exchanged looks.

'We're not disputing that,' said Guleed.

'He gave it to me on our first anniversary,' said Althea.

According to our checks, the marriage had lasted less than two months more.

'May we have a look at it?' asked Guleed.

'Why?' asked Althea.

'We think it may be the target of a robbery attempt,' I said. 'We need to determine whether it is your ring that was targeted, or whether a different ring was involved.'

She bought it, but it took a bit more coaxing to bring out the ring, which she kept on a silver chain around her neck. She even dropped it into my palm after I promised not to throw it down the nearest volcano.

I felt it even before it touched my hand – old and complex and faint, like an orchestra playing in the distance. There was the scent of lemons and dust and a sad lament sung in a language I thought I should recognise but didn't.

It was heavy and ornate and obviously sized for a larger finger than Althea's.

'It opens up,' said Althea, who had relaxed once she realised I wasn't about to bolt for the door with it. I removed the chain and under her direction opened the ring until it formed a tiny armillary sphere with symbols incised on every surface. Some I recognised as alchemical symbols, others as Greek. Some I wasn't sure about.

'Is that Arabic?' I asked Guleed.

'Yes,' she said. 'And that's Hebrew, but they don't seem to make out any words.'

'It's not valuable,' said Althea. 'You can buy them on Amazon for thirty pounds.'

I doubted that. I wasn't sure it was silver, either.

While Althea fretted, I used the back of my notebook to provide a neutral background while Guleed took pictures with her phone. Once we were done I handed it back and she quickly restrung it on the chain and hung it around her neck, making sure it was tucked out of sight under her T-shirt.

Guleed asked some winding-up questions and asked Althea if she could come in and make a formal identification of the body and record an official statement. She didn't want to do either, but we said nobody else was available for the identification and that the statement was just routine. We arranged to have a car pick her up in the morning and then, before she changed her mind, we made our farewells and left.

'Now I lack your extensive erudition,' said Guleed once we were out of sight of the basement, 'but that struck me as being just a little bit *Lord of the Rings*.'

'Nah,' I said. 'She didn't call it her precious – it doesn't count if you don't call it your precious.'

'But there was something weird about the ring,' said Guleed. 'I saw it in your face.'

'It was definitely enchanted,' I said, 'but that doesn't mean that's the cause of her behaviour.'

Although I bet it is, I thought. *Just like the lightning glass.*

'Let's hope she brings it to the identification tomorrow,' I said, 'so Nightingale can have a look.'

'Oh, she'll bring it all right,' said Guleed. 'I'll bet she wears it in the shower.'

Since it was past six by the time we'd written up our notes, I had Guleed drop me off at Richmond Bus Station and caught the 65 back to Kingston, where I changed to a 57. Starting at the bus station meant I got to sit down on the long crawl down the Richmond Road and read up my OSPRE sergeant's material, which I kept on my Kindle for just these occasions.

When I got back to Beverley Avenue there was an unfamiliar Range Rover sitting in the driveway. I gave it the automatic police once-over as I passed – tyres, index, lights, back and front seats. Unusually for a Chelsea tractor, it was splattered with mud up to its wheel arches and there were dings and scrapes along the underside of the doors. It actually looked like it might spend some time off road – perhaps it came from upstream, where they laugh at roads and pour scorn on the very notion of indoor plumbing. But it seemed a bit posh for Ash, Oxley rode a Triumph sidecar combination, and on the rare occasions that Father Thames drove himself, it was in a Morris Minor Traveller estate.

So I wondered who it could be.

It turned out to be a white woman in late middle age, dressed in a tan tweed skirt and matching jacket. She had a cap of iron-grey hair, small hazel eyes and a severely thin mouth offset by a mischievous smile.

She was wearing a pair of stethoscopes which she was using to take Beverley's blood pressure in the old-fashioned way, with a manual pump and a stopwatch. I felt a sudden wash of panic – we weren't due any medical bollocks until the big day, which was any time now. And that, I knew for certain, would not involve tweed.

Or a mischievous smile.

'Ah,' said the woman, turning the smile on me. 'You must be the father.'

Beverley, the love of my life, languished on the sofa, the bulge naked and proud and serving as a convenient pedestal for a small bowl of something red and crunchy. Curried shrimp, by the smell.

'Hi, babes,' she said when saw me. 'This is Dr Crosswell. The Old Man of the River asked her to pop by.'

'Haven't done a house call for yonks,' said Dr Crosswell.

'How is the old man?' I asked.

I collected up the trail of plastic food containers, bowls, plates and empty Jaffa cake boxes. The twins were obviously going through an eclectic craving phase. I dumped them on the kitchen table for later,

'Oh, you know him,' said Dr Crosswell. 'As wonderful as ever.'

She let the cuff deflate and Beverley lifted her arm so it could be unwrapped.

'Well?' asked Beverley.

'Oh, you're just perfect,' said Dr Crosswell. 'As, of course, you should be. Although if these two wait much longer you might want to consider induction.'

'They'll be along soon enough,' said Beverley. 'They're just arguing about who gets to go first.'

Dr Crosswell had rounds in Oxford first thing the next morning and so, after packing her gear away in a very modern black nylon carryall, she bid us farewell.

'Senior Consultant Obstetrician at John Radcliffe,' said Beverley after I'd shown Dr Crosswell out. 'I expected Mum to go wavey . . . but Father Thames?'

She patted the sofa next to her. But, before I could sit down, she changed her mind and sent me back to the kitchen for another bowl of curried prawns. I took the opportunity to ensure the backup rice cooker was filled and ready to go and check the dishwasher was properly loaded before turning it on.

'We're starving in here,' called Beverley from the living room.

I opened the fridge and sorted through the contents.

'We're out of prawns. Do you want the jellied eels instead?'

'Yes please,' said Beverley in what was practically a growl.

This was another 'gift' from the fishmongers of Billingsgate. And while I'm willing to assert, through my dad's family, my claims to honorary Cockneyhood, there are limits . . . however much hot sauce you cover them in. Still, Beverley liked eels even before she hit the weird craving stage, and part of a successful relationship is learning to live with your beloved's questionable taste. I decanted the horrible mess into a bowl but took the bottle of God Slayer chilli sauce separately – Bev preferring to add it to taste.

While I was at it, I microwaved a mountain of rice topped with my mum's famous bone-free beef knuckle soup, put the whole lot on a tray and carried it into where Beverley languished, weak from lack of food. She had a pained expression, and by the way she held her hand on the bulge the twins were kicking up a fuss.

Before I could sit down, Beverley grabbed my hand and placed it on her belly. I felt a kick against my palm.

'Tell them to be quiet,' she said. 'They're not listening to me.'

'Shush, you two,' I said. 'Give your mum a rest.'

I got an extra-hard thump and then the bulge was quiet, although not the owner of the bulge, who loudly demanded her jellied eels and a glass of milk. Once she was nomming her way through the gruesome mass, I sat down beside her and started on the rice and soup.

Once she'd finished the eels, she sequestrated my leftovers.

'So, could you rip someone's heart out?' I asked.

Beverley finished chewing and swallowed before asking, 'Literally or metaphorically?'

'Literally,' I said.

Beverley held up her free hand and made an experimental clawing motion. I thought of the neat hole in David Moore's sweatshirt and the ice cream scoop smoothness of the wound tract.

'Not like that,' I said. 'With your . . .' I paused to try and think of a phrase that wouldn't make me sound like I was in a superhero film – and failed notably. 'Your power.'

'My power?' said Beverley, her lips twitching.

'Yes, your power.'

'Don't know. Never tried,' she said. 'It'd be hard work. Much easier to shoot them or something.'

'Could any of your sisters do it?' I asked.

I strongly suspected that Bev's older sister Lady Ty had killed a would-be assassin from across the street by thrusting a metre of ghostly sword through his heart. Hard enough that it left a hole in the assassin's shirt – front and back.

'Again,' said Beverley, 'why would you? Is there something you're not telling me? Is one of my sisters a suspect?'

'Not really,' I said, and explained about the death of David Moore, the hole in his chest and the lightning glass.

'I'm not saying Mum couldn't do it. And if Mum could do it then Father Thames could do it, but . . .' She dragged out the 'but' and then burped. 'It's not their style, it's not how we work. At least not these days. We're thoroughly modern goddesses, aren't we?'

An old god, maybe? I was thinking.

I doubted it, but it was, as they say, a line of inquiry. And it wasn't like we was overrun with those. Bev passed me the empty plate to put next to her bowl on the coffee table, and I lay down beside her and put my arm around her shoulders.

She sighed and rested her head on my shoulder.

'Don't get too comfortable,' she said. 'I'm going to need a wee in about sixty seconds.'

Thursday

Fear . . .

3

Harsh Language

Modern police inquiries are all about information management – extracting it, processing it, and using it to gather even more information and then repeating the process. Unlike response officers, who get to spend their shifts being attacked by drunks, chasing pickpockets and trying to stop members of the public tearing lumps out of each other, detective officers like me spend their shifts asking questions.

Occasionally this involves being physically or verbally abused, but mostly it involves paperwork.

A homicide with no obvious suspect is an automatic Category B inquiry, which means it gets a code name and a senior investigating officer who manages a mixed bag of detective sergeants, detective constables and wannabe PCs in plain clothes: in this case, OPERATION MURGATROYD, DCI Alexander Seawoll, and the long-suffering members of the Belgravia Major Investigation Team, including DS Guleed and DI Stephanopoulos. They gather the information, which is fed into the maw of the HOLMES computer system, which then showers its lucky acolytes with further 'actions' which usually involve gathering more information.

When the Special Assessment Unit is involved, some

of these actions will be marked with an *F* for *Falcon*. And these end up with my name on them in the in-tray on the desk I share with Guleed. I used to squat at that desk with a third DC called David Carey, but since he went on long-term sick leave I've got his place and Danni has mine.

Although I wasn't sure we should be dropping Danni into a case this serious.

'She won't thank you for underestimating her,' Nightingale had said when I broached it at the morning Falcon assessment. Which was basically me and Nightingale grabbing a coffee for five minutes outside Belgravia nick before we went in for the MIT briefing.

'She won't thank me if something bites her leg off either,' I said.

'Do you think that's likely?' said Nightingale. 'David Moore's death could be an isolated incident – we don't even know if there was a third party involved.'

'You think he did it to himself?'

'Possibly,' said Nightingale. 'It's much easier for a practitioner to affect their own body than somebody else's. But there's also the possibility that he either carried an enchanted artefact in with him, or he encountered one already in the Silver Vaults.'

Or even that he was simply in the wrong place at the wrong time.

None of those choices seemed likely, but if I've learnt one thing on the job, it is that a coincidence can kill someone just as easily as malice. Was David Moore a practitioner? Did he have access to other enchanted items, and was the whole business with the ex-wife and the ring actually relevant to the case?

We needed more information, which was why Danni and me were heading for Poplar to check out David Moore's gaff while Nightingale would sit in on Guleed's interview with Althea Moore and see if he could cop a feel of her ring. We'd conduct an initial Falcon assessment and then call in search teams and forensics if necessary.

'And I mean necessary,' said Stephanopoulos. 'Unless you want to pay for it.'

The government were in their sixth year of trying to cut crime by reducing the number of active police officers. So management were getting shirty about expenses.

David Moore had owned an ex-council flat in a brick-built workers' housing estate in Poplar. Built in 1937, it was finished just in time to suffer a bit of light bombing during the Second World War. This close to Canary Wharf, and with the dull uninspiring bulk of One Canada Square looming over it, many council tenants had exercised their right to buy in the 1980s – followed by selling on to posh provincials exercising their right to gentrify in the 2000s. As a result, I wasn't surprised to find an eclectic mix of low-end hatchbacks and impractical compact SUVs crammed into every available parking space.

We'd driven over in my orange Ford Focus ST, the one with the mileage and the dent in the bonnet where something had thrown a deer at me in Richmond Park.

The deer was startled, but fine – I never did find out what had thrown it.

Looking worse for wear as it did, the orange Asbo had the double advantage of being weirdly inconspicuous and unlikely to be TDA'd by local ruffians – not even the ones on six-figure salaries.

We parked by the bins and trotted up the stairs to the first-floor balcony, where David Moore had the last flat on the left. All the flats had brand-new composite wood doors with continuous locking and anti-ram bolts. The kind being installed by many councils to save local drug dealers from having to install steel reinforcements themselves. David Moore's door had a large sheet of un-varnished plyboard covering an area from knee height to just below the spyhole. It looked like the sort of thing the council put up to cover racist or other abuse until they can replace the door.

The doorbell wasn't working and the knocker, which should have been below the spyhole, was missing, so I gave the door a sharp rap with my knuckles. When that didn't get an answer, we quickly escalated to the open palm slap combined with shouts of 'Open the door, we're the police!' But fortunately, because it was covered by plywood, we didn't have to resort to the vaguely de-meaning shouting through the letterbox stage.

Stephanopoulos had wangled a section eight PACE warrant from a magistrate, so now we'd established that the flat was uninhabited I used a spell called *clausura-frange* to slice the bolts on both sides of the door. Danni was gratifyingly impressed.

'You never said we could do shit like that,' she said,

and after a moment's thought, 'What on earth do you record as your method of entry?'

'I put "authorised Falcon entry method",' I said.

'And they let you get away with that?'

'So far.'

I pushed the door open and squatted down to check there wasn't a demon trap or other, more mundane, booby trap on the threshold. This is not something you usually have to worry about entering a suspect house, but I've learnt to be careful. Once my healthy paranoia was satisfied, we stepped inside.

The flat was painted in various shades of blue, ranging from indigo in the kitchen to a vaguely turquoise tinge in the hallways. The floor was fake parquet effect lino but, as Danni said, it was *expensive* fake parquet flooring. The bathroom, straight ahead from the front door, was tiny – barely big enough for a shower cubicle, toilet and basin. There were two bedrooms, but interestingly David Moore had used the larger of the two as an office.

Inside the smaller bedroom the queen-sized bed had been stripped to reveal a memory foam mattress and a pair of hypoallergenic pillows. A large rectangular section of the wall above the headboard had obviously been repainted recently – the fresh paint not quite matching the sky blue of the rest of the wall. When I crouched down to look underneath I got a strong whiff of bleach, which of course made me instantly suspicious. Even my mum, who practically drinks bleach, doesn't use it that much in a bedroom.

'Forensic countermeasure?' said Danni when I pointed it out.

I thought of Althea and her busy spring cleaning and wondered if there was a connection.

'Don't know,' I said.

We both slipped on our plastic booties just to be on the safe side. In my experience, the bleach usually only comes out when members of the public want to shift those troublesome incriminating bodily fluids.

Especially if they've been watching a lot of *Silent Witness*.

The desk in the office had a space for a missing laptop and the shelves were mostly filled with rows of box files with hand-lettered labels. Fewer books than I expected, and none seemed to be fiction. Hefty tomes on development economics, environmental activism and the like, with titles such as *Lean Startups for Social Change* and *How to Save the World*. There was a brand-new desktop Spanish dictionary sitting on top of its Amazon packaging next to an A4 ring-bound notepad. I could see the little remnants left on the rings where several sheets had been ripped out.

'This man had a boring life,' called Danni from the living room.

I joined her and immediately saw what she meant – it was hard to tell that anyone had spent time in the living room. A couple of Billy bookshelves were half empty, the TV was five years old and stood in splendid isolation without so much as a Blu-Ray player or cable box. The sofa looked brand new and there were no photographs anywhere.

'It's weird, isn't it?' said Danni. 'These charity types usually have lots of pictures of themselves doing good deeds – you know, holding starving refugees and the like.'

The gateleg table didn't have so much as a coffee ring on it.

'Also, who did he work with?' asked Danni. 'There must have been charities or something helping him do good.'

'Sahra's looking into that,' I said. 'Our priority is checking for Falcon before we call in a search team.'

'Are you waiting for me to make suggestions?' asked Danni.

I said I was, and she pointed out the patch of fresh paint in the bedroom and said we should check that.

'And then we should lever off the board on the front door and see what's underneath.'

'Good idea,' I said, but not before we'd run through the potential practitioner checklist – if only because it had taken me a sodding day to compile it.

So starting with the bookshelves – any genuine Newtonian magic books like what I might find in the Folly library? None. Any occult or secondary works by known Newtonian authorities such as Richard Spruce, Samuel Erasmus Wolfe and Charles Kingsley, but not counting *The Water Babies*. None. Any general occult or other religious books that show a serious interest in spiritual topics but don't generally show up in the Mind, Body, Spirit section in Waterstones. Possibly – a couple of books that looked like Catholic theology. I made a note of the titles in the box provided.

Then you check for paraphernalia, always bearing in mind that the line between cosplay, magic practice and niche sex play can get pretty blurry. The only ritual item we found was a large wooden and silver crucifix mounted in the hallway. We hadn't noticed it on entry because it was hidden behind the open door, and it was definitely unusual. The wooden cross was made of varnished mahogany, while the Christ figure was silver and abstracted to the point where the face was a drooping featureless blob and it was impossible to tell where his flesh ended and his loincloth began.

'It's melted,' said Danni, and I saw it was true.

When I got close I caught a hint of the same concussive light I'd got from the fulgurite tube. Now that I knew what I was looking for, the trace was getting easier to spot. I had Danni confirm before we moved on to the bedroom.

The first thing we did was pull back the bed, to check underneath as well as get better access. This revealed splatters of blue paint at the base of the wall. It had been painted over in haste and without any protection for the floor. I did the first assessment, letting my gloved hand rest on the middle of the patch, and felt nothing except maybe a persistent salt tang which I reckoned as an old *vestigium* from when the London docks were still in operation. I made a note of the sensation while Danni confirmed – although she thought the *vestigium* was more fishy than salty.

I left Danni on guard while I popped down to the Asbo to grab my hooley bar to carefully lever off the plywood sheeting. It was only held in place by the sort of masonry nails you might use to hang framed pictures on a wall, and they mostly spanged out when I put my weight on the bar.

Gouged so deeply into the door that it had penetrated past the surface laminate and into the compressed hardwood beneath were three marks. The centre design, despite being made of only three lines, was unmistakably a Christian cross. To its right another three lines made a smaller, inverted cross, while on the left three gouges of different length branched out in jagged lines from a single point – like lightning.

When I touched it, it was indeed like being hit in the back of the head by an angry maths teacher. Once Danni had confirmed the *vestigium* I called Stephanopoulos and arranged for a search team and a forensic sweep, starting with the painted patch in the bedroom.

'My money's on blood,' said Danni. 'What's next?'

'Some initial house-to-house,' I said.

Danni was not happy going door to door.

'I signed up for Falcon to avoid this shit,' she said.

I knocked on the next door along.

'Some things are unavoidable,' I said, and was proved right when a white man with no neck, tattoos and a Rottweiler opened it and demanded to know what the fuck we wanted.

The Rottweiler was huge and snarling and straining at its lead. I could see the man was having to exert some pressure to hold it back. His expression indicated that he was perfectly willing to let go if we gave him an excuse.

Nightingale's got this spell that can make a dog go to

sleep, but unfortunately he hasn't taught it to me yet. Fortunately, to my amazement, Danni crouched down and stuck her face out at the forty-odd kilograms of solid muscle.

'Who's a beautiful girl?' she said.

The unlovely, flat-faced lump of genetic killing machine immediately lurched forwards, tail wagging so that Danni could stroke its head, all the while telling it what a beautiful, lovely, happy baby it was.

Danni looked up at the owner, who was looking as amazed as I felt.

'What's her name?' she asked.

'Beatrice,' he said.

'Who's a lovely girl, Beatrice?' said Danni, flinging her arms around the dog's neck. 'Yes you are, yes you are.'

After all that, the only logical next step was being invited in for a cup of tea.

The interior of the flat contained more chintz than I was expecting, given its owner, so I wasn't surprised to find out that he'd only recently moved in with his nan. His name was Craig Sandwell and, judging from how scrupulously clean he kept the flat, I was guessing that he'd spent most of his life being institutionalised. Prison or the armed forces? I was reluctant to ask because he was being so co-operative, and in any case someone in the inside inquiry office could look him up later.

His nan was asleep in the main bedroom. Craig had moved in after she'd had a stroke, and acquired Beatrice the throat-ripper to keep her company while he was at work. He worked nights as a security guard at the

Crossrail works at Canary Wharf and worried about burglars.

'Some of the kids round here are well out of order,' he said.

When we steered him around to it, he told us David Moore had been quiet and standoffish.

'Typical posh leaseholder,' said Craig. 'He'd nod if he met you on the walkway but he wouldn't get in the lift with you.'

When we asked whether he'd shown any recent changes in behaviour, Craig said he hadn't noticed any but his nan had.

'She said he'd started singing in the middle of the night,' said Craig. 'Said it sounded like hymns to her.'

Craig wasn't about to let us wake up his grandmother to confirm, so we moved on to the next flat for even more hearsay.

We were kept on the doorstep by a cheerful, angular, middle-aged white woman with ex-blond hair, unseasonable shorts and a green sweatshirt with 'Fuck Off I'm Busy' written across the chest. The colour and lettering had faded enough for me to think that this was a relic of an enjoyably misspent youth.

The sweatshirt lady didn't have much to do with her neighbours, apart from next door, where she would check on the old lady and take Beatrice for a quick spin. She wasn't even sure if she could pick David Moore out of a line-up, although she was willing to try. She hadn't seen or heard anything unusual recently but her daughter, Megan, had said she had. She was at school at that moment but we could come back later if we liked.

'She said she saw an alien,' said Megan's mum. 'Last weekend. If that's any help?'

'Did she say what it looked like?' I asked.

'She might of,' said Megan's mum, 'but to be honest I wasn't paying attention.'

We were saved from further house-to-house by the arrival of forensics and some hand-picked bodies from Belgravia who'd been designated the H2H team. Hand-picked, that is, by Stephanopoulos on the basis of who'd irritated her the most recently.

I did say I'd personally come back and interview Megan the alien-spotter when she was back from school.

'Are there aliens?' asked Danni as we climbed back into the orange Asbo.

'Out there?' I said. 'Very likely. Down here? Not so far.'

We were going to head back to Belgravia for tea and paperwork but Stephanopoulos called us before we could pull out.

'We've been going through David Moore's phone logs,' she said, 'and we've found something you might want to get on to.'

David Moore had made no less than twenty-three calls to the mobile phone of one Preston Carmichael between six in the morning and seven in the evening on the same day he'd visited his ex-wife.

Two days after Megan had allegedly seen an alien.

The outside inquiry team had tried his number, but it went straight to voicemail. Preston Carmichael's address was listed as in the village of Skirmett in the Chilterns, but when they tried his landline his wife told them he was spending the week at their flat in London.

'Ability Place,' said Stephanopoulos. 'Down by the Millwall Docks.'

Less than a kilometre away from our location.

'That's convenient,' I said.

'That's what I thought,' said Stephanopoulos.

Back when London was the largest port in the world, Millharbour had once circled the Millwall Docks, where timber and grain were shipped in to feed the ferocious furnace that was London's industry – back when we had industry. Now it is yet another development canyon lined with shapeless postmodern apartment blocks, and the grain all comes through Tilbury, further up the estuary.

Ability Place was your classic speculative luxury housing development, a twenty-two-storey concrete frame filled up with identical rows of luxury flats built to the lowest specification that you could get away with and still appeal to Chinese investors. It had twenty-four-hour concierge services, a gym, a spa, three storeys of underground car parking, and looked like a laboratory storage rack for giant mutant rabbits.

The concierge lived behind a desk at the end of an orange corridor lined with postal boxes. I assumed this was convenient for the postie and the absentee tenants alike – although the layout reminded me of the computer core in *2001: A Space Odyssey*. I half expected a calm voice to suggest that it still had great enthusiasm for the mission.

Because we hadn't had our dinner yet, me and Danni

had our warrant cards out before the concierge had a chance to speak and hustled him up to the first floor to let us in.

The thing about *vestigia* is you get better at spotting them the more you spot them. And this includes particular types of *vestigia* as well. So it wasn't surprising that even Danni felt the same stunned musical silence we'd sensed from the fulgurite tube and the melted crucifix at David Moore's flat, before we'd even reached Preston Carmichael's front door. I sent the concierge down the corridor and took the opportunity to run through Falcon entry procedure with Danni.

There's such a thing as being overcautious, even in policing, but I still had a fresh memory of the hole in David Moore's chest to keep me paranoid.

We stood either side of the door as I unlocked it and carefully pushed it open with my extendable baton. Most plain clothes officers don't routinely carry their ASP with them, but then most plain clothes officers aren't called upon to face down unicorns, sentient mould and the occasional carnivorous tree. I waited for a count of ten to see if anyone came rushing out or opened fire before crouching down and peering around the door jamb.

I did this partly because it makes you less of a target, but mostly because I was already in position to check whether the floor just inside the door was clear of magical booby traps.

Since it was a studio flat, the door opened straight into the bedroom half, which was screened from the reception area by a half-wall. Beyond that I could see that the curtains were drawn and the lights were out. The air inside the flat was cold and I could see the curtains rippling from the breeze outside. But the chill couldn't disguise the sickly tang of decay, urine and faeces that every police officer gets to know as the harbinger of overtime.

'Shit,' said Danni.

I slipped on my booties, my nitrile gloves and, leaving Danni to guard the door, I stepped gingerly inside. It had a real parquet floor polished up to a bootie-sliding sheen and the walls were painted a characterless white with a hint of peach. The bed had been made up in the bachelor style, with the duvet thrown haphazardly over the mattress, and there were a couple of thick paperback books on the bedside table.

I saw the body as soon as I rounded the half-wall. It was stretched out on a red and green diamond-patterned rug in front of a leather sofa. It was covered in a yellow cotton fitted bed sheet that matched the duvet cover. There was a circular red-brown stain on the sheet about where I judged the chest to be.

You're supposed to do two things when you discover a body – double-check they're dead and protect the locus of the crime. I squatted down at what I hoped was the head end and resisted the temptation to uncover the chest – forensics would want to do that.

The face matched that of pictures we'd lifted from Preston Carmichael's social media pages. His skin was pale and, when I checked his neck for a pulse, cold to the touch. Even through the gloves. I fished my last disposable face mask out of my jacket pocket and put it on so I could get closer to the corpse without breathing my DNA all over it.

The *vestigium* was identical to that I'd sensed from the fulgurite and crucifix, only this time widespread – affecting the whole bedroom. With that connection established, I checked the bathroom, just in case, and then retraced my steps to the corridor, closed the door behind me and called Stephanopoulos.

While we waited for the full weight of the Metropolitan Police to arrive, Danni stayed to secure the flat and I went and talked to the concierge. He hadn't seen Preston Carmichael recently, but also wasn't sure he'd recognise him if he had. CCTV was limited to covering the garage ramp, the main entrance and the fire doors. I told him that we were going to need the footage from at least the last seven days. He said he wasn't sure he was allowed to do that, and I explained that he was legally obliged to hand it over.

To my surprise, the first officer on the scene was Detective Chief Inspector Alexander Seawoll. Vast, profane, northern and suspiciously clever, he played at being an old-fashioned governor, but in real life he was something far more modern and effective.

He stared down at me and narrowed his eyes.

'What have you done with your trainee?'

I explained that she was guarding the scene while I secured the CCTV, and it pained him that he couldn't find any fault in that.

'You're probably wondering why I decided to grace you with my presence,' he said.

Which was true, since DCIs spend most of their life

in their offices or, worse, in other people's offices and conference rooms. 'Playing,' Seawoll once said, 'pin the fucking buzzword on the sodding flow chart.'

'You have a secret love nest in Canary Wharf,' I said.

'Chance would be a fine thing,' said Seawoll. 'I'm here on my tod because once again your lot have managed to spread my team over half of bloody London. Poor Pam is going to divorce our Miriam for neglect and it will all be your fault.'

I've met Pam, and as far as I could tell, her and Stephanopoulos were more doting than the last page of a Jane Austen novel. Still, I've learnt never to interrupt Seawoll when he's ranting. Apart from anything else, my therapist says that this is obviously the way he expresses affection. I doubt that, since she's never heard him swear at an illegally parked car.

'Where's the nearest coffee?' he asked suddenly.

'Tesco Express,' I said. 'Round the corner.'

So he sent me out for refs, but not before making sure I phoned Danni and asked her what she wanted.

'Always look after your people,' he said as I noted down the order. 'The way you treat them sets an example for the way they treat others.'

By the time I got back, I found Seawoll intimidating a thin nervous white man with thinning sandy hair and an almost bespoke medium-grey pinstripe suit. He was from the property management company and, having softened him up with some strategic looming, Seawoll was now killing him with soft words and kindness. Officers past the rank of inspector normally never get to interview anyone except other police, so Seawoll likes to dust off his famous 'Don't make me angry, you wouldn't like me if I was angry' technique at every opportunity.

Including to use it on, rumour has it, senior officers up to and including the rank of deputy assistant commissioner.

'So we're going to need the names and contact details of all your tenants,' said Seawoll, and the man in the pinstripe suit promised Seawoll the sun and the moon, a USB pen and anything else he might need.

Which turned out to be coffee – which I provided once Pinstripe had scuttled off.

'The list for the whole building?' I asked.

'You never know what we might find once we've run all their names,' said Seawoll. 'Could be a couple of fortuitous clear-ups hidden in a place like this.'

This is the sort of thing that upsets money launderers and Liberty alike – although for different reasons, obviously. We were still divvying up the snacks when Guleed arrived and forced us to start again. She'd brought an advance guard of officers who, having just finished one house-to-house sweep, were not overjoyed about being launched into another. While Guleed got them organised, Seawoll asked me about Beverley.

'Any day now,' I said.

'Do you think it's going to make a difference to you?' asked Seawoll. 'Professionally speaking?'

I said I didn't know.

'Come on, Peter, you're about to become a fucking father,' said Seawoll. 'You need to start thinking about the implications. One of which will be an obligation not to die suddenly in the line of duty.'

64

'Thanks, sir,' I said. 'I'll take that on board.'

'More to the point, am I going to be invited to the christening?'

'Might not be a christening,' I said. 'They're still arguing.'

'It's not going to be one of those hippy New Age things, is it?' said Seawoll.

'If it is, do you still want to come?'

'Will there be anything to drink?'

'At the ceremony? Maybe.' I said. 'Afterwards – definitely.'

'Then count me in.'

Guleed returned with Danni in tow, and we had one of those al fresco policy meetings that occur whenever police find themselves hanging around at an active crime scene waiting for forensics or prisoner transport to arrive and there's no pub or café to slope off to. On the TV they either cut to the next scene, or the meetings are conducted while the SIO strides in or out of the locus, but in reality we mostly stand around because there's nowhere to sit.

Seriously, the first clever sod that invents a combination extendable baton and shooting stick is going to be minted.

'We're not going to get the scene processed before this evening,' said Seawoll once we'd briefed him as to David Moore's flat. 'And we're not going to get a PM before tomorrow. Where's Thomas?'

'Heading out to liaise with TVP for the notification of Carmichael's family,' said Guleed.

And no doubt taking the opportunity to have a sniff

around his house to see if there were any signs that Preston Carmichael was a practitioner.

Seawoll asked me whether I needed further access to the flat, and I told him I'd done the IVA but I would want to know if there was an obvious cause of death.

'Like what?' asked Seawoll.

'Like a great big hole in his chest,' I said.

Seawoll checked his watch.

'Why don't you and Danni action the statement with the little neighbour girl,' he said. 'Sahra can suit up and check the body when the forensics go in. If nothing immediate comes up from you or Nightingale, we'll have a briefing at 6.30.'

And with that we separated like a bunch of teenagers in a slasher movie.

4

Misdirection

The smell of death is insidious. Spend any time close to a corpse, especially when they're not fresh, and it gets into your clothes. Which is why I keep a spare jacket and shirt in a dry-cleaning bag in the back of the Asbo. I've got quite good at changing in the car, and I only nearly elbowed Danni in the face once getting into the spare shirt.

By the time I was finished the schools were out, and we headed back to Poplar to talk to Megan about her alien. I let Danni do the charm offensive and it worked almost as well as it had with next door's dog. Soon we were in the living room sitting around the homework table with Megan, aged nine and three quarters, cups of tea, and Megan's mum hovering in the role of appropriate adult.

'I normally make her do her homework as soon as she gets in,' said Megan's mum, who worked nights as a cleaner for the DLR. 'That way I know it's done before I go out.'

She was quick to reassure us that Megan's big sister would be home from work soon enough to keep an eye on her.

'It was an alien,' said Megan – she sounded quite

definite and looked quite pleased to be getting out of doing her homework.

'How did you know it was an alien?' I asked.

'It felt like an alien,' said Megan, and slurped her tea.

Felt, I thought, *not looked*.

I looked at Danni. She had caught this, too, because she followed up by asking Megan if she could describe how the alien felt.

'Glowy,' said Megan. 'As if she was giving off radiation, and there was a noise.'

'What kind of noise?' asked Danni.

'Like this,' said Megan, and opened her mouth and sang 'La' in a perfect high G. She kept going until she ran out of breath.

'So like someone singing?' said Danni.

'Yeah,' said Megan. 'But only if you was an alien.'

Danni asked a few more questions to nail down the time frame and then we left Megan to get on with her homework.

'She really seems to think it was an alien,' said Danni once we were out on the walkway.

It had started raining while we were doing the interview and the clouds were low enough to obscure the tops of the dull glass boxes of Canary Wharf.

'That's the zeitgeist, isn't it?' I said. 'Back in medieval times she would have described it as an angel or a devil or a fairy. Nowadays everything is aliens.'

One of the forensic techs was taking a breather outside David Moore's flat. She had her hood down and her mask off. Short brown hair was plastered to her

68

forehead with sweat. I gave a friendly wave and got a nod in return.

'So if it wasn't an alien?' asked Danni, who was running through her notes.

'Maybe a fae of some kind,' I said. 'Some of them can have pretty strong *vestigia*.'

My cousin and fellow apprentice, Abigail, wanted to call a *vestigium* attached to a living creature an 'aura', but I was resistant. I wasn't about to start talking about people's auras in public, and definitely not in any official document with my name on it.

'Could it be an actual angel?' asked Danni. 'Or a devil?'

'I don't know,' I said.

The original Society of the Wise, which was your actual official name for the Folly, had been proudly part of the Enlightenment. God, if he existed, was the ultimate master craftsman who had set the world in motion, with fixed immutable laws, and then left it to get on with things. They saw angels and devils as abstract concepts and held that anything wandering around with a halo, wings or a pitchfork was either an uppity fae, a con man or a mountebank. This attitude had persisted even into the most strident periods of muscular Victorian Christianity, and devout wizards espoused that angels, as manifestations of god, were as above the fae as man was above the beasts that crawl in the dust. Such matters were best left to them, as was ordained by the Church to deal with them.

I was going to have to ask Professor Postmartin, our archivist, to do a sweep of the literature.

'I don't know if such things exist,' I said.

'You're not religious?' asked Danni.

'Nope,' I said.

'You're an atheist?' asked Danni, who obviously wasn't going to get off this topic however hard I hinted.

'Yes,' I said. 'What about you?'

'I believe in something but I'm not sure I'm religious.'

Danni snapped her notebook shut. I took the opportunity to saunter over and ask forensics how they were doing.

They thought that there was something written under the fresh paint on the bedroom wall, and they were consulting with friends at the National Gallery as to how to strip the paint without damaging the evidence underneath. I asked them to let me know if there were any symbols hidden under the paint, and they said they would.

I'd hoped that Danni had moved away from the tricky subject of comparative theology, but we hadn't even got as far as Shadwell when she asked what my parents believed. Luckily I've been asked this a lot – not least by Bev – so I've got my answer down pat.

'My mum is game for any branch of Christianity that involves singing and hellfire,' I said. 'She likes churches so much she switches to a new one twice a year.'

'And your dad?'

'My dad is a practising jazzman,' I said. 'He's eagerly awaiting the true rapture when Duke Ellington rises from the grave and leads a band that will unite Louis Armstrong with Charlie Parker, and Sun Ra lands his flying saucer in Wembley Stadium to lead all the cool cats to the promised land.'

Danni snorted.

'You're taking the piss,' she said.

'Swear to God I'm not,' I said. 'My dad truly believes that if you played a set with Miles Davis, Bill Evans, John Coltrane, Philly Joe Jones and Betty Carter on vocals, the dead would be rising up by the first drum solo, when Philly hit the hi-hat.'

'Jazz heaven,' said Danni.

'Or a jazz zombie apocalypse,' I said. 'You decide.'

'Funny, right,' said Danni. 'But if you don't think it was an alien, what if it turns out to be an actual angel. Proper angel. A messenger of God.'

'Then I expect you to get their details when you take the statement,' I said.

'I'm serious,' said Danni.

'So am I.'

Danni probably would have persisted but I got a call from the duty officer at Richmond Borough, who notified me that there'd been a break-in at Althea Moore's house and did I want to attend. I said I did and, foolishly, turned right across Southwark Bridge in the hope that the traffic would be less awful on the other side of the river.

It probably was less awful. It's just that it was still pretty awful.

It took us over an hour to get Richmond to find the response officer, PC Tiffany Walvoord again, standing outside Althea's house, tapping her feet and checking her watch.

'My mistake,' she said as we approached, 'was coming back on shift the next day.'

'Shifts,' said Danni. 'I remember shifts. Do you remember shifts, Peter?'

'Luxury,' I said. 'In my day we had to scavenge our refs off whatever was left at the crime scene.'

'Funny,' said Tiffany. 'Is this one of your cases?'

The answer was yes – judging by the hole in the door where Althea Moore's Yale lock was supposed to be.

'Someone knocked out the lock with magic,' I said, and let Danni have a look.

'Is there a *signare*?' she asked.

You can often tell who's done a spell by the distinctive *vestigia* they leave behind – this is called their *signare*. It's a bit like handwriting, and just as prone to misinterpretation if you don't pay attention.

While there was definitely still a *vestigium* clinging to the hole, it seemed confused, murky and very noisy. I'd have said it was done by a newbie if I hadn't known that that particular spell wasn't something you picked up overnight. Not if you want to pop the lock neatly. Otherwise, you might as well knock down the door with a battering ram or an *impello* spell – which is the magical equivalent.

I said there wasn't one I could recognise, and we went in to interview Althea.

'They stole my ring,' she said as soon as she saw us.

The spring cleaning was obviously finished, and Althea was sitting cross-legged on her bed dressed in a pink satin pyjama top and blue tracksuit bottoms – her hair falling loose around her face.

'Why don't you tell us what happened?' asked Danni, and readied her notebook to show she was serious.

'Well I'd just said goodbye to that other policeman, the posh one,' said Althea. 'And I'd knackered myself getting the flat ready.'

'Ready for who?' asked Danni.

'For me,' said Althea. 'I wanted a clean flat.'

Obviously, I thought, *but why now? Why just after your ex's visit?*

'Did David leave you feeling dirty?' I asked.

Althea flinched at the question and gave me a nasty look, but sometimes being socially transgressive is what policing is all about.

'No!' she said. 'No, God, no. What are you thinking?'

'I think what my colleague is trying to ask,' said Danni, slipping smoothly into the role of reasonable female cop, 'is whether David Moore's visit led to your decision to spring clean, or had you already planned to do it previously.'

Althea gave us a very understandable *What the fuck?* look, but answered anyway.

'I was always planning to do it,' she said. 'But it was such a disgrace when David came round that it kind of pushed me over the edge. What has this got to do with someone stealing my ring?'

Danni left me to answer that question.

'We're just trying to clarify the timeline,' I said, because *I was wondering whether you were displaying an instinctive reaction to a supernatural something that I refuse to call an aura* is not something I want taken down in evidence.

Danni leant forwards, angling slightly away from me to make clear her disapproval of her strangely rude and irrelevant colleague.

'So you lay down for a nap,' she said. 'Was the door locked?'

'Yes,' said Althea, as were the back door and the windows, because she had been living in London for the last ten years and knew better than to leave her flat unlocked – thank you very much.

'So the ring was stolen while you were having a nap?' asked Danni. 'Was anything else taken?'

'No,' said Althea. 'Just the ring. There's two hundred quid in the kitchen drawer and . . .' She looked around her flat for potential valuables – it was a meagre haul. 'My laptop. So they must have come here specially for the ring – right?'

'It seems so,' said Danni. 'So where was the ring?'

Althea instinctively put her hand on her chest – just below her throat.

'It was on a chain,' she said.

'Around your neck?' asked Danni, to be sure.

'I always wear it,' she said. 'Even in bed. Silly, really.'

'So whoever stole it took it from around your neck?' said Danni. 'While you were asleep.'

Althea nodded glumly.

No, she hadn't taken a sleeping pill, or had a drink or three. She'd had a cup of tea, read for a bit, drawn the curtains and gone to sleep.

Getting the chain over Althea's head without waking her seemed unlikely, but if the thief had cut the chain

– wouldn't they leave the chain behind? Especially if the ring was the main target.

'I have trouble getting it off sometimes,' said Althea. 'The chain gets tangled in my hair.'

'Why do you wear it all the time, then?' I asked, although I probably shouldn't have.

'I don't know,' said Althea. 'I just always do.'

Danni turned and frowned at me before turning back to Althea and asking if she remembered anything unusual happening.

'Like what?' asked Althea.

'Like your sleep being disturbed, dreams, nightmares?' said Danni, showing that she had been paying attention to Nightingale's 'witness perception displacement' lecture. Otherwise known as the 'weirdness filter', in which witnesses and victims of Falcon events often rationalise things that they don't understand into things they do. Even if, like little Megan, what they understand is shape-shifting aliens. I blame *Doctor Who* for that.

'I had a nightmare,' said Althea brightly.

'What was it about?'

'I don't know,' said Althea. 'It was a nightmare – I woke up in a fright but I don't know why.'

'Was that before or after you noticed the ring was missing?' asked Danni.

'Before, I think,' said Althea. 'I woke up and went to the loo and then back to bed.'

Something in the rote way Althea said the phrase 'and then back to bed' caught my attention.

'I know this sounds strange,' I said. 'But memory,

especially between sleeps, can be a bit funny. So do you remember anything odd about your trip to the loo?'

'Like what?'

'Like anything unusual,' I said.

'Like what?' she asked again.

I didn't have a good answer, so I suggested that we reconstructed her journey from her bed to the loo. I think she would have liked to have told us to piss off but had concluded that humouring us was the fastest route to getting us out the door.

So she lay down on the bed and then, like a child in a primary school play, mimed waking up, pulling back an invisible duvet and rolling out of bed. She headed for the bathroom at the back of the flat.

'Hold it there a moment,' I said.

Basement flats were gloomy at the best of times, but this one had heavy curtains – the kind used by people who could only sleep in complete darkness.

'Did you turn a light on?' I asked.

Althea thought about it and said she was pretty sure she didn't.

'I think it was already on,' she said.

'Do you often go to sleep with the light on?'

Althea chuckled.

'Not when I'm sober,' she said. 'Even at night I have to draw the curtains to keep out the light pollution.' Althea stopped and stared at me for a moment. 'Oh shit,' she said. 'You think they were already in here, with me, when I went to the loo.'

I said it was a possibility, and after we'd got Althea calmed down again we walked her through her movements. But she was adamant that she saw or heard nothing amiss. That she had gone back to bed unmolested. Although she admitted that she couldn't know for sure whether she was still wearing the ring around her neck.

I made a note to point forensics at the light switches in case the intruder had got careless and left a print.

We assured Althea that we were taking her safety very seriously and asked whether there was someone she could stay with for a few nights.

'You think they might come back?' said Althea, getting alarmed again.

'Best to be sure,' said Danni.

I left Danni to organise that while I went outside and called Nightingale.

'And you're sure about the lack of a coherent *signare*?' he said.

It had started drizzling again so I was sitting in the Asbo.

'Yes,' I said. 'Do you think it was deliberately obscured – as a forensic countermeasure?'

'It's a possibility,' he said. 'But some practitioners can have a confusingly murky *signare*. Particularly if they had a varied magical education.'

He hadn't seen anyone lurking on the street either, coming or going.

'I like to think I haven't got so old that my basic counter-surveillance training has atrophied,' he said.

I asked him whether he'd had a chance to handle the ring that morning.

'It was most definitely enchanted,' said Nightingale.

'And I agree with you about Miss Moore's reluctance to part with hers, although as Abdul would no doubt say, "correlation is not causation".'

'Could you tell what it was enchanted to do?'

'No,' said Nightingale. 'But then my contact was brief. Miss Moore was quite insistent that I hand it back. One thing of interest – the ring was far too heavy to be made of silver. At a guess I'd say it was platinum.'

'Does that have any magical connotations?'

'Not that I know of,' said Nightingale. 'Iron, steel and silver were always preferred for enchantment. I understand that platinum is a difficult metal to work with, but that doesn't mean it's impossible. Merely beyond my skills – such as they are.'

'Could this be something to do with the Sons of Wayland?' I asked.

They'd been the metal-bashing arm of British wizardry since before the Folly was founded. I had one of their World War Two era battle staffs and Nightingale had taught me basic enchantment. I'd been working on an armband, less conspicuous than a staff, when I'd been suspended the year before. Perhaps, I thought, I should start the project up again.

'Peter?' said Nightingale.

'Sir?'

'I said that we have to do some digging in the library,' he said. 'And, Peter?'

'Yes?'

'Try not to get distracted.'

'No, sir,' I said.

We wrapped up so I could concentrate on my notes.

I was about halfway through those when the duty officer from Richmond Borough marched up and rapped on my windscreen. Being an inspector, she didn't have to wait for me to answer and instead she immediately opened the passenger door and slipped inside. Her high-viz jacket was beaded with moisture and she had resources on her mind.

'When am I getting my people back?' she asked, gesturing at where PC Walvoord and a couple of response officers were loitering in the half stairwell – out of the drizzle. Response officers being such a rare commodity these days that there were bound to be shouts she needed them for piling up.

I sighed and started negotiating. Her name was Samantha Milocab and she was one of those fast-tracked graduates that had arrived at their rank already well versed in management-speak. So when I told her that I was waiting for Belgravia MIT to deploy the appropriate personnel to secure the scene in accordance with standard procedure, she just gave me a weary look.

'Tell your boss,' she said, 'if he wants my officers here any longer he's going to have to cough up the overtime money himself.'

See, this is what happens when these graduates fall under the influence of the rank and file. They start getting ideas below their station – worst of all possible worlds. Luckily, at least from my point of view, detective constables – however ambitious they may be – do not make these kind of administrative decisions. So it was with a light heart that I called up Nightingale again and made it his problem.

'I see,' he said after I'd explained. 'Please inform Inspector Milcocab that we're taking budgetary responsibility for her team's deployment outside the scene, but ask her if she could supervise until I can get there.'

I was stunned – Nightingale had just used the phrase *budgetary responsibility*. Talk about bad influences. I was going to have to start watching my language around him.

'When will that be?' I asked, knowing that that would be the first thing Milcocab asked me.

'We've removed the body and I've finished my supplementary sweep,' he said. 'We can leave the routine actions here to Stephanopoulos. You and Danni might as well go off duty and we can have an early start tomorrow.'

I came home to a candlelit dinner – which was unexpected.

Beverley had cleared all her coursework off the gate-leg table in the living room and laid it out with napkins, two types of knife and fork, the china plates that Tyburn had given her for her birthday and had stayed in their box since then and, of course, a pair of candles mounted in carved wooden candlesticks.

Beverley hustled out of the kitchen with her hair wrapped in a scarf and wearing one of my barbecue aprons over the bulge. She shooed me back into the living room – claiming that she didn't want to spoil the surprise. More likely, she didn't want me to see that she'd managed to use every single pot and pan we owned, as well as spreading a fine layer of ingredients over every single flat surface. Including the pages of whatever cookery book she happened to be using.

'It occurred to me,' she said as she thrust a bottle of Special Brew into my hands, 'that I hadn't cooked you a dinner for a while.'

'You did beans on toast last week,' I said, and then wished I hadn't when Beverley scowled at me. 'It was very nice beans on toast – you added butter to the beans and everything.'

Which went down as well you might expect.

I went to have a shower and change. As soon as word got around that Bev was pregnant I'd received a lot of unasked-for advice – much of it from people who'd only ever experienced the process from the inside. But amongst all the things I'd been warned to expect – food cravings, mood swings and visits from earlier incarnations – dinner for two had not featured.

Since Bev was making an effort, I dressed smart casual and stayed calm when the kitchen smoke alarm sounded. I heard Bev swearing, the back door opening and then the smoke alarm's ear-splitting pips doppler down the length of the garden, followed by a crack as it hit a planter and went silent.

Beverley once extinguished a five-appliance fire at Covent Garden. She did it in under sixty seconds while me and a terrified German family watched. Apparently she got a bollocking from her older sisters Tyburn and Fleet, but I always got the impression they were secretly proud of her.

She still gets Christmas cards from the German family.

I didn't know what she was cooking but it smelt good.

It was good, cajun steak with butter, and much better than I would have made. I'm a utilitarian cook, bish-bash-bosh meals made with minimum fuss. And presentation . . . what's that?

Beverley had taken the opportunity to slice the steak, rare enough to send to a vet, rub in spices and then marinated it in a butter peppercorn sauce. It was hot enough that neither of us felt the need to break out the Tan Rosie's hot sauce – actually I wouldn't have suggested that anyway, because I don't have a death wish.

'We should go,' I said after I'd chased the last slice around the plate.

'Go where?' asked Beverley, and burped loudly. She leant back in her chair and folded her hands on the bulge.

'New Orleans,' I said and belched back. 'Go pay our respects to the Mississippi – see if anyone's at home. Sample some cooking – listen to some jazz.'

'You don't like jazz,' said Beverley.

'I don't mind the old-fashioned stuff – in the right venue.'

'What if the twins don't like jazz?'

'We could take Abigail to help with the twins.'

'Oh yeah, because that's not a recipe for disaster in any way whatsoever.'

'Or something,' I said.

'You know I appreciate you don't bring your work home,' she said. 'But what the fuck is going on?'

I sighed and cleared the plates. We were having fruit for pudding – which was just as well because I didn't think the kitchen could have survived anything more complicated. I brought out the fruit bowl, another Special Brew for me, and the jug of tomato juice that had been chilling in the fridge for Bev.

'It's not work,' I said. 'Not exactly anyway. It's about aliens.'

Beverley gave me an incredulous look and started to laugh.

'You think aliens are funny?'

'Yes, no, maybe,' she said. 'But that's not why I'm laughing. I was expecting a different conversation, that's all. Aliens, right. What about them?'

'If we define "alien" as something that has evolved separately from earth's biosphere,' I said, 'rather than grey guys in flying saucers, do you think it's possible something like that might be active here, right now?'

'"Here" meaning London?'

'"Here" meaning the world.'

'What brought this on?'

Standing in a room where a mechanical computer did weird shit to the fabric of space-time and thinking, just for a moment, that something huge and alien was looking at me.

Before we blew it up.

And today a little girl was adamant she'd seen an alien visiting David Moore's house and I'd dismissed it as a modern interpretation of the ordinary supernatural. But should I have?

And when did the supernatural become so ordinary?

'The whales think there's something living in the North Sea,' said Beverley. 'But it might be a giant squid.'

83

I'd seen Beverley talking to whales before, or rather shouting at them in an attempt to warn a pair of bottle-nose whales from swimming too far up the Thames and getting themselves stranded. When I asked why the pair wanted to swim up the river, Bev said they were looking to launch a social media career. But I don't think she was serious.

'Aren't they sure about whatever it is in the North Sea?' I asked, because I figured if anyone would know what was lurking under the sea it would be the whales.

'They might be,' said Beverley. 'But my spoken whale is not that brilliant. I'm mostly limited to basic noun–verb combinations – "food here" "danger there". Abstract concepts like "alien" and "non-alien" are a bit beyond me. And that's assuming a non-tool-using aquatic mammal is going to have the same language equivalencies as we do.'

I love it when Beverley talks science – it gets me all hot and bothered.

'Giant squids are pretty alien,' I said.

'Not to another giant squid,' said Beverley.

I helped Beverley up the stairs to the bathroom and made sure she had her tea and her waterproof Kindle on the bath table and then sat on the footstool to watch her. You could see the water rippling as she altered its temperature to suit herself. Her bulge rising like a mythical island from the surface of the water.

'What do you see when you look at me like that?' she asked.

I didn't have a good answer, so I went for honesty instead.

84

'I don't know,' I said. 'Everything. That's what I see – everything.'

'You think I'm that huge, then?' she said. 'I am *woman*, I contain multitudes. All shall look upon me and despair.'

'Shall I compare thee to a giant squid,' I said. 'Thou art more lovely and less tentacled.'

Bev smiled and shook her head.

'Go and do the washing-up.' And when I hesitated, she said, 'I cooked, you wash up.'

So downstairs I went, leaving my beloved with *Gravitational Systems of Groundwater Flow* by József Tóth, to tackle the kitchen. Which was even worse than I'd imagined.

I mean, how do you get an egg whisk covered in grease while making butter sauce? After all, it's not a butter whisk.

I'd just got the surfaces regulated and the small stuff in the dishwasher when I heard scratching at the kitchen door. I opened it to find a talking fox waiting for me on the patio with an envelope in its mouth. When it saw me, it trotted forwards and dropped the envelope at my feet.

'Special delivery,' it said. 'Handed in at the Seven Sisters dead drop.'

I popped back into the kitchen and picked up a pair of nitrile gloves.

The fox sat back on its haunches and waited expectantly while I pulled on my gloves and opened the envelope. I always open strange packages from the bottom or the side. There's only so many ways you can booby-trap a letter and in most of them the trigger mechanism relies on you opening the flap. This piece of fox post was a flat white standard envelope of the type used to send birthday cards. Inside was a single sheet of printer-quality paper with a message written across it in familiar handwriting. There were no foreign substances coating the edges, and when I gave it an experimental sniff it smelt only of paper with a hint of fox.

I read the message by the light from the kitchen, then I went back inside and placed it carefully on a clean plate. I opened the fridge and found one of the emergency snack containers, marked with a fox sticker. The fox perked up as I brought the container out with me and crouched down in front of it.

'What's your name?' I asked.

'Jigsaw Alpha,' said the fox. 'But most people call me Sally.' It eyed the container in my hands. 'Cheese puffs?'

'Was the dead drop under observation?' I asked.

'That's an operational matter,' said Sally. 'And need to know only.'

'Oh,' I said and went as if to stand up. 'No matter.'

'No,' said Sally quickly. 'It's not monitored – it's only an emergency drop and checked once a day.'

I settled back down with the container displayed to its best advantage.

'When was the letter found?'

'Halfway through the first prance,' said Sally. I knew better than to ask for a clock time, and in any case I had a rough translation primer pinned to the fridge with a magnet. 'It was there when we made the routine check. No smell or spoor, so definitely not a fox or fae.'

I opened the container and gave Sally a cheese puff, which she ate in a couple of happy bites. I closed the container and she gave me the big eyes, but I'm made of sterner stuff.

'I want you to stick around. I may have a message for you to take back,' I told her, and waved the container for emphasis. Sally nodded enthusiastically.

'Roger that,' she said, and then after a hesitation, shyly, 'Can I go see the Bev?'

'Yes,' I said. 'But don't annoy her.'

Sally scampered past me and into the house. I followed her in, closed the door and hunted out my scene-of-crime kit and a plastic evidence bag. While I did that I speed-dialled Nightingale.

'We have a problem,' I said when he picked up. 'Lesley just sent me a message.'

Friday

Ruthless efficiency . . .

5

Knowledge

A surprisingly large number of London's most famous institutions started in coffee shops. Unless he was labouring for a living, eighteenth-century Man liked nothing more of an afternoon but to jam on his wig, adjust his garter and hie himself down to the coffee shop of his choice. There he could sit all day inhaling second-hand tobacco smoke, getting a buzz from a cup of truly vile-tasting coffee, reading the latest newspaper and shouting at his fellow patrons. What they shouted about depended on the coffee shop. Politics, philosophy and science in the 'penny universities' like Don Saltero's or the Grecian near St Clements. Or maybe the price of maritime insurance in Lloyd's of London, or even if some poor inmate might be mad or nay at a Hoxton coffee house *inquisition of insanity*.

And in one particular coffee house – how to do magic.

Or, at least, during the reign of George II and his slightly brighter wife Caroline of Ansbach. This was the Folly of the Thames, basically a coffee house built on a barge that was moored off Somerset House. The rent was low and, as its clientele were less refined, it became the favoured meeting spot of those who would practise magic.

Sir Isaac Newton, in between dreaming up a workable theory of gravity and reforming the coinage, had gone looking for the principles that underlay the existing hotchpotch of folklore, rituals, cunning knowledge and Renaissance magic, and created what Postmartin calls 'The Newtonian Synthesis'. Unlike his first *Principia*, published in vast numbers, bought by the multitude, actually read by like six people, Newton's second *Principia* – the *Philosophiæ Naturalis Principia Artes Magicis* – was a strictly limited edition. There was no second edition while he lived, and it's clear that if he'd had his way, he would have suppressed the first.

There is literally a bookshelf of books written about why Newton, so gung-ho about taking credit for calculus and gravity, wanted to keep magic on the down-low. My personal theory is that he never found a satisfactory mathematical underpinning for magic, and that irked him.

So while Newton swanked around as President of the Royal Society and conducted long bitter feuds with Hooke and Leibniz, the students of the second *Principia* spent their days in a coffee house on the Thames.

But there's a kind of freedom that comes with official neglect, especially if you're someone who's usually the subject of official disdain. So to the Folly came Jews and Nonconformists, foreigners and criminals and, of course, women.

There, driven by the same caffeine-fuelled intensity as everything else in the capital, they took the principles laid down by Newton and by trial and error forged the forms and wisdoms that power magic today. And this was perilous work, because magic is dangerous stuff and plenty of the early pioneers ended up in the ground, mysteriously vanished or, occasionally, floating down the Thames.

But this was the eighteenth century, when life was cheap and ambition unlimited. The secrets of the universe were there for the taking. And if you could separate some wretch from their ill-gotten gains – so much the better. They took their cues from the apothecaries and the physicians, because if they could make money selling arsenic and bleeding the rich, what couldn't a body who conjures light out of nothing do?

But as their skills grew, so did their notoriety and it was only a matter of time before they attracted the attention of the great and the . . . well, the rich and powerful anyway. Even a state as lacklustre and disorganised as the British couldn't allow such power to continue uncontrolled.

Enter Victor Casterbrook, born on the wrong side of the blanket in Mayfair, a butcher's boy by trade and a young man on the make. His official biography glosses over his introduction to magic, but I reckon he wandered onto the Folly one evening looking for a good time and found a way out instead. I'm not sure he ever learnt a single spell, but our boy Victor was good at organising, and while his peers studied the interplay of *formae* and *inflectentes* he studied the business of wizardry. We know he visited the Académie Royale de Philosophie Occulte in Paris and saw what a little bit of royal patronage might buy in the way of wealth and status.

By 1775 Casterbrook had an in at the court via Queen

Charlotte, and he must have done some kind of deal with the Duke of Bedford because he moved off the boat on the Thames and into an actual folly on the duke's estate.

But no such elevation comes without a cost, because when the newly formed Society of the Wise met in their new headquarters it was notably an all-male affair. Amongst themselves they were 'wizards', but to the public they were 'practitioners', and if that respectability meant jettisoning the women – that was a price Victor Casterbrook was willing to pay.

Especially when in 1801 our butcher's boy on the make ligged a brand-new purpose-built headquarters on the south side of the newly developed Russell Square. It had a grand front entrance and over the double doors carved into the Portland stone pediment were the words *Scientia potentia est* – Knowledge is power.

It also had a mews in the back, which is where I parked the Asbo first thing the next morning. I put it in the converted coach house between the Ferrari and the backup Asbo, and as far from the haunted Bentley Speed 6 as I could get. Nightingale's Jag was missing – he'd gone early to Westminster Coroner's Court to oversee the post-mortem on Preston Carmichael.

As I closed the garage doors behind me, a small white and brown mongrel terrier came up the steps from the kitchen door. This was Toby, the ghost-hunting dog, who was either pleased to see me or pissed off that I hadn't been round to visit for so long. Barking continuously, he followed me up the spiral stairs fitted to the outside wall to give access to the top floor. Once a hayloft and tack store, then servants' quarters, then a den for gay young wizards in the 1920s and, finally, where I keep all my job-related tech, widescreen TV, Airwave charger and my old PlayStation 3. It had to be here because according to Nightingale the Folly proper was surrounded by powerful mystical defences against unspecified threats and running fibre optics inside might create a weak spot that could be exploited by malignant entities.

I had my doubts, but since Nightingale swore that it couldn't be replaced without a full cadre of qualified wizards he didn't want to take any risks. I kept meaning to ask whether it could be temporarily deactivated but had never got round to it. Beverley says that secretly I like having a corner of the Folly that is my domain, and she may be right.

And inside the Folly the Wi-Fi works in most of the rooms on the ground and first floors.

The master power switch for the Portakabin is kept safely in a locked metal cabinet bolted to the wall. Toby watched with bright eyes as I unlocked it and threw the master switch – he knew what this meant. Unlimited leftovers – small dog heaven.

I walked into the Folly proper through the scuffed oak splendour of the rear corridor, with Toby scampering at my heels, and out into the main atrium. Waiting for me was a supermodel-tall white woman with a narrow oval face, hazel eyes and a cascade of black hair down her back. This was Foxglove, and today she was dressed in an orange tie-dyed kaftan and yellow and black striped leggings and clutching an A3 artist's pad to her chest.

As Toby did an excited circle around her, she bounced up and down on dainty bare feet and smiled – showing slightly too many teeth.

I was about to ask where Molly was, when the prickling of the hairs on the back of my neck informed me that she had crept up behind me. Four years of practice means I no longer jump when she does that, although Beverley says I should at least pretend to be terrified for Molly's sake.

'You want to keep her happy, after all,' said Beverley.

So I winced and said, 'Please don't do that.'

Molly was as tall as me, thin and sinuous even in her Edwardian maid's outfit, with the same waterfall of black hair as her sister, that framed a long narrow face with a sharp chin and black almond-shaped eyes.

When she smiled at me she showed even more teeth than Foxglove.

I told her that we were opening up for an operation and we were going to need operational feeding for ten to twenty, plus coffee and snacks. She nodded gravely and glided off towards the kitchen stairs. I wasn't fooled. She was practically skipping when she vanished into the gloom.

'It's sausage heaven for you, Toby,' I said, and the dog scampered off after Molly.

I turned back to Foxglove, but she, too, had vanished. No doubt to stock up her art bag in anticipation of a fresh wave of artistic subjects.

Where possible, the Special Assessment Unit attaches itself to an existing police operation. In the past this was because of Nightingale's cavalier attitude to procedure. But these days it's because it allows us to pass unremarked outside what we now call the policing community. Inside said community it gets remarked on quite a lot – some of it in words even I have to look up.

'Don't pay any fucking attention,' Seawoll once told me. 'Coppers like to fucking moan. It's when they stop you've got to worry.'

But the Folly is on the books, through a complicated leasing arrangement, as a proper police station complete with a recently installed and PACE compliant custody suite. I spent a very dull hour downstairs in the suite going through the checklist to make sure all the appropriate first-aid kits, prisoner-need essentials and approved microwave dinners were present and correct. When I went back upstairs I found Seawoll and Stephanopoulos lounging in a pair of overstuffed green leather armchairs, drinking tea and enjoying what I suspected was a second breakfast. Before I could join them Nightingale returned with Guleed and we were off to the races.

There are three types of police briefing. The one you see on the TV where people stand around pointing to things on a whiteboard. Or, more often, the one where we sit around like we're at a particularly dull book club meeting while the SIO goes through a list of the actions we're supposed to have done but haven't got round to yet. The third is when a clique of senior officers sit around a table and thrash out what the hell they're going to do about . . . in this case, Lesley.

I try to avoid these, but for some reason they keep

dragging me in. I don't know what Guleed's excuse was. At least this time we got tea and halal sandwiches.

Stephanopoulos held up a copy of last night's letter – the original was at the lab.

Across it written in black pen was *Something powerful and strange is doing these killings. Watch your back.*

I'd recognised the handwriting immediately. God knows I'd copied out her notes for forms and paperwork enough times.

'First things first,' said Seawoll, who was staring up at a point on the balconies above. 'Do you think she's doing the murders herself?'

'No,' I said. 'If that was so, why would she tip us off?'

'I'm hesitant to say she doesn't have the capability,' said Nightingale. 'She obviously learnt some questionable skills from the late Martin Chorley.'

Otherwise known as the Faceless Man mark two, an ethically challenged magician responsible for murder, death, kidnapping and serious property fraud. Lesley May had worked for him once, before they had a theological falling-out and she shot him in the head.

'But?' said Stephanopoulos.

'The manner of the killing seems too extravagant for Lesley,' said Nightingale. 'She always struck me as being a great deal more straightforward than that.'

The others looked at me and I nodded.

I'd been standing next to Martin Chorley when Lesley had 'straightforwardly' dealt with him.

'They never did find her source,' said Stephanopoulos.

Even after her 'retirement' from the Met, Lesley had obvious access to the kind of information that only

98

came with log-in privileges to the Met's IT system. The Directorate of Professional Standards had gone looking for the scrote or scrotes unknown that had been feeding her information, but without success. Despite the best efforts of the government, the Met still employed over 43,000 people – which was a lot of needles to find a paper clip in.

Seawoll sighed.

'In that case, what *is* her interest?' he asked.

'I think she stole the ring,' said Guleed. 'Perhaps there's a connection between the ring and the attack.'

'Perhaps it's supposed to be a protective charm,' I said, and Seawoll winced.

'Magic rings,' he said. 'God help us.'

'The ring *was* enchanted,' said Nightingale.

'And according to Althea Moore's statement, David Moore's main concern was recovering the ring,' said Guleed. 'Perhaps he felt threatened. Perhaps he thought the ring would protect him.'

'Threatened by what?' asked Stephanopoulos.

'I'll bet it's related to the markings on his door,' said Seawoll. 'And whatever is under the paint in his bedroom.'

Seawoll's theory being that either or both were a threat or a warning, followed by a visit from Megan's alien.

'Unless that was Lesley,' said Stephanopoulos, and everyone looked at me for some reason.

'Maybe,' I said. 'She can disguise her face and she can obviously use the glamour. But I think she'd go inconspicuous – not glowing like an alien.'

'Little Megan is not a good witness,' muttered Stephanopoulos.

'Do we know if Preston Carmichael had a bloody magic ring, too?' asked Seawoll. He obviously caught something in my expression because he went on, 'Yes, I'm using the m-word, Peter, because it's traditional with rings. Don't get used to it.'

'I asked his wife,' said Nightingale. 'She said he had an antique silver puzzle ring that he wore on a chain around his neck. That certainly sounds familiar.'

'Do we have any other connection between the two men?' asked Seawoll. 'Beyond the possible ring and the phone calls?'

Stephanopoulos grinned and flourished an iPad at us. On it was the scan of an old photograph showing a group of six figures lined up for a group picture. Two white women, four white men in front of what looked to me like the kind of low wooden stage you found in church halls and library annexes. That familiar patina of dark varnished wood and dusty corners. One of the men was older than the rest of the group, and you didn't have to squint to recognise Preston Carmichael. Particularly since the team had acquired an old photograph of him from his wife and inset it into the frame.

'We texted a copy to his wife, but she didn't recognise the place or the people,' said Stephanopoulos. 'The original was in a frame, but piled in with some old books in a storage box at Ability Place.'

One of the other faces was familiar, although he was looking much younger and less dead than when I'd met him.

'That's David Moore,' I said.

'And that's Jocasta Hamilton,' said Guleed, pointing at one of the women. 'I think.'

'Oh, good,' said Seawoll. 'Now we can blag some free smellies.'

'You're sure about this?' asked Stephanopoulos. 'She doesn't look like that now.'

I knew Jocasta Hamilton from the Nice N' Pure chain of shops selling organic make-up, perfume, soap and the kind of skin creams used by white people who've never heard of half-kilo tubs of Palmer's Cocoa Butter. Even when your eyes were shut you'd know when you'd walked past one of her shops on account of the smell. But I wouldn't know Jocasta herself if I passed her in the street.

Guleed said she was pretty certain about the woman in the photo and called up some old publicity pics of Jocasta Hamilton on her phone. The 1990s entrepreneur did resemble the woman in the picture – although there was a definite spark in the later photographs. She seemed brighter somehow, more animated. But then it *was* a publicity shoot.

'Fine.' Stephanopoulos made a note in her daybook. 'You can confirm that once we've finished here.'

'So we have a definite connection between Moore and Carmichael,' said Seawoll. 'But do we have any hard evidence that the attacks were related?'

'Same modus operandi,' said Nightingale. 'An identical mortal injury, a similar fulgurite tube in the wound track – each carrying the same *vestigia*. One very similar to that we found at Preston Carmichael's flat.'

'Could it be two similarly trained . . .' Seawoll paused a moment before soldiering on, '. . . wizards?'

'No,' said Nightingale.

'You're sure?'

'I knew twin brothers who passed through Casterbrook together and received their staffs in the same ceremony,' said Nightingale. 'And there was as wide a difference between them in their *signare* as there was between them and their classmates. No, this was the same person.'

'Or same *thing*,' I said, thinking of little Megan's alien sighting and Lesley's warning.

'Just because I'm using the m-word doesn't mean we're doing the full *Star Trek*,' said Seawoll. 'Let's keep this as close to normal policing as we can manage.'

Which meant looking at the differences between the victims as well as the similarities.

'There's no doubt that Preston Carmichael was tortured before he was killed,' said Nightingale.

There had been damage to all four fingers of both hands. His fingernails had been torn out, and there were what looked like cigarette burns to his thighs and genitals. A full report was being prepared, but Dr Walid and Dr Vaughan estimated that the torture had continued for at least four hours.

'The *coup de grâce* being delivered shortly afterwards,' said Nightingale.

'Do we know when that was?' asked Seawoll.

'The last sighting we have is by the concierge at Ability Place, who saw him when he came in through reception last Friday morning,' said Guleed.

Five days before David Moore was murdered, two days before Megan saw her alien.

'Given that he was tortured,' said Stephanopoulos, 'is it possible that the perpetrator was looking for information that led on to David Moore?'

'Anything's possible,' said Seawoll. 'And the timing would fit.'

'The torturer can't have known David Moore's identity then,' I said. 'He wasn't hard to find on social media – he was a public figure of sorts.'

'Or it was torture for torture's sake,' said Stephanopoulos.

'Apart from the photograph,' said Seawoll, 'do you have any other connection?'

The inside inquiry team had David Moore's background all but done. These days even the older generation seemed determined to self-document on social media – or, as we might say, 'open source intelligence'. It didn't half make our job easier.

Our David Moore had been born in Handbridge, Chester, gone to his local Catholic school, then Manchester University before going on what he called, in a 1992 article about him in *The Observer*, a 'secular pilgrimage' around the world. 'Charity doesn't need to be dull,' he was quoted as saying. 'That's the real lesson of Live Aid.'

There were lots of pictures of him looking interesting and moody against a variety of London backgrounds. We'd checked where his hands were visible, and we were pretty sure he was wearing the silver puzzle ring on the index finger of his right hand. Not totally sure, because there's only so much you can do with an early scan of a photograph from a pre-digital magazine.

He'd been active in a load of charitable organisations, including biggies like Shelter and Christian Aid, and small community projects like one that built a park on wasteland in Stamford Hill.

For the last ten years he'd been running a consultancy in which he advised wannabe charities, NGOs and government agencies on how to deal with social problems the trendy entrepreneurial way. The work for the smaller NGOs was at token mate's rates, but he was coining it from HMG, who never saw a consultant they didn't want to overpay.

'What was he spending it on?' I asked. 'Because it wasn't his flat.'

'He gave most of it away to charity,' said Guleed. 'More than sixty per cent of his gross income.'

'Fuck me,' said Seawoll. 'That sounds like guilt to me.'

'Guilt for what?' asked Guleed.

And again, for some reason everyone turned and looked at me.

'He's not a practitioner,' I said. 'Or a special person, or anything else.'

'We're definitely missing something,' said Seawoll.

'That makes a change,' said Stephanopoulos. 'What have we got so far on Preston Carmichael?'

Guleed checked her notes.

'He's got a sizable social media presence, lots of YouTube where he offers courses in spiritual healing backed by a ton of self-published books and merchandise,' she said, and showed us an example.

It had a strangely dated Californian hippy mood, although Jesus and God definitely got namechecked at regular intervals.'

'Nice,' said Stephanopoulos. 'Anything on his actual background?'

'We've heard back from the DVLA and Carmichael first registered a vehicle in 1977, a Mini no less, at what we think is his parents' address in Hexham, Northumberland.'

'That's funny,' said Seawoll. 'The concierge thought he was American.'

'Geordie, American – who can tell the difference,' said Stephanopoulos.

'He doesn't register another vehicle until 1985,' said Guleed. 'This time with an address in Fallowfield, Manchester. This one a six-year-old Ford Cortina.'

'Classic car,' said Seawoll. 'Didn't David Moore go to Manchester University at around that time?'

'It's a big city,' said Stephanopoulos.

'Ah, but Fallowfield is where all the students live,' said Seawoll. 'Especially back then.'

'We need to reach out to the GMP,' said Stephanopoulos, and Seawoll said he'd do that.

'All friendly northerner, like.'

And, just like that, the investigation expanded to encompass our friends in the North. It's not unusual for a major inquiry to balloon out in the first couple of days as the inquiry team desperately squeezes every teat it can grab looking for anything useful.

Like I said, information management.

Which was what Seawoll and Stephanopoulos were

paid to do. And they couldn't even claim overtime.

We spent half an hour dividing up our actions and lines of inquiry before Seawoll slapped his hands on the table and declared that it was time for elevenses.

'And while your elders and betters are having cake,' he said to me and Guleed, 'you two can see if you can liberate us some smellies.'

I never wanted to be Falcon Two. When I'd drafted the document that went on to become the *Interim Falcon Operational Procedures Manual* I'd tried to get everyone to use Foxtrot or Zulu or Kilo or anything other than bloody Falcon. But they refused.

'Life's too fucking complicated already,' Seawoll had said.

So I stayed Falcon Two while Nightingale, obviously, was Falcon One. And Guleed was Falcon Three and Danni was Falcon Four. When I went on paternity leave, any day now, Guleed would move up to Falcon Two and be seconded to the Folly as paternity cover.

I don't think the prospect filled her with glee, but she was a professional and knew it had to be done.

Since Lesley had made her presence known, Nightingale as Falcon One became our mobile reserve. Since he was stuck on call at the Folly, he decided to take the opportunity to start Danni's Countermeasures Training. Otherwise known as how to deal with magic when you can't do it yourself.

'Why not train up more wizards?' Stephanopoulos had asked when we'd started the scheme.

'That will come in good time,' said Nightingale. 'In

the meantime we need magic-aware officers to deal with problems in the short term. When we have a suitable structure in place we can graduate to full apprenticeships. Eventually we'll have a cadre of officers who are in a position to make an informed choice about further training.'

So it was that me and Guleed, Falcons Two and Three, headed down to Spitalfields to talk to Jocasta Hamilton. Or, more properly, Dame Jocasta Hamilton DBE FRSA – for services to making tons of cash and donating it to the right political party.

'Or all her charity work,' said Guleed as I negotiated the Asbo down the joy that is Great Eastern Street.

'That too,' I said and made a mental note of the index of a Mercedes A-Class that cut us off at the junction to Shoreditch High Street. Chances of that driver ever coming to my professional attention were slim. But if they did, things would go very hard on them indeed.

Dame Jocasta Hamilton had her offices in a surprisingly stylish converted warehouse on Middlesex Street. On approach the clean lines fooled me into thinking they were 1920s art deco, but as I got closer the brash white-brick pilasters that shot up two storeys topped by Corinthian capitals gave it away as late Victorian. There was a double door sandwiched between a barber's shop and an Argentinian cantina, on which a tasteful brass plaque announced *Jocasta Hamilton Holdings*.

Spitalfields had once been the heart of London's rag trade, where subsequent waves of immigrants had crowded into sweatshops turning Indian and Egyptian cotton into clothes for the burgeoning English middle class. That might have explained the strange babble of voices I felt as I brushed my fingers along the pale cream brick.

But not the weird sensation like a cold breath on the back of my neck.

Guleed felt it, too, because she paused and, like me, turned to scan the street behind us.

It had been raining on and off all morning and the cars parked outside were beaded with moisture. Pedestrians scuttled past with their heads down or hidden under umbrellas. The chattering of pneumatic drills floated through the damp air from further down the street, where yet another uninspired office building was going up.

I saw nothing suspicious – which is unusual. A copper can usually find something suspicious if they look hard enough. Nobody was loitering in the doorway of the Indian restaurant opposite or covertly watching us from any of the parked cars.

The cold feeling had evaporated, but its memory remained.

I exchanged looks with Guleed, who shrugged and turned to press the button on the gunmetal grey intercom box.

'Detective Sergeant Guleed,' she said when an indistinct voice squawked at us from the box. 'To see Dame Jocasta.'

The offices on the first floor were definitely from the Lidl school of office furnishings. There weren't even cubicles, just rows of dark wooden tables that looked like they might have been bought at a garden centre, with lots of extension cables snaking up between gaps so that the minions could plug their laptops in. Either everyone was an intern or nobody over thirty could stand to work there. I judged them to be typical London office jockeys, mostly white, mostly from affluent suburbs in the Midlands and the North. Lots of skinny jeans, checked shirts and noise reduction headphones. Their posher counterparts were all working in publishing, PR or advertising and subsidised by Mummy and Daddy. This lot would be sharing with four others in a three-bedroom house in Zone 4 or living in narrowboats on the canals.

Surprisingly, Dame Jocasta didn't have a separate office, but instead she sat amongst her underlings at one of the tables near the windows that looked out onto Middlesex Street. In the flesh she looked nothing like the young woman in the Manchester photo – not just older, but more animated. Her face was in constant motion, expressions flickering almost too fast to read. Her eyes were bright and a proper cornflower blue. She was still too young to be a bohemian granny, but with her long greying hair pulled into a ponytail, multicoloured cardigan and a sheath of bracelets on both wrists, she was obviously heading in that direction.

When she looked up and spotted us, I saw surprise, puzzlement, and then what almost seemed like genuine pleasure. This is not a normal reaction to having a pair of plods turn up in your office and I was instantly suspicious.

Guleed introduced us and a couple of minions were booted off their hot desks so we could be offered seats – and coffee. We declined the coffee because Guleed is getting increasingly finicky about her coffee ever since she was promoted. And generally you don't accept a beverage without an ulterior motive. Like having a chance to poke around in someone's kitchen.

'Is this bad news?' asked Dame Jocasta. She spoke with a low, throaty contralto. A natural voice for the blues, my dad would have said.

'We believe you're acquainted with a man called Preston Carmichael,' said Guleed.

We'd agreed to hold back David Moore's name to see if she volunteered it herself.

'*Was* acquainted,' said Dame Jocasta. 'Quite a long time ago.'

There'd been no hesitation, so not a very casual acquaintance. Her hands were in constant motion, making it hard to see whether she was wearing a platinum ring amongst the five or six bands that adorned both hands. I thought I saw a flash of silver but I couldn't tell if it was a puzzle ring.

'Wait,' she said, her eyes flicking from Guleed to me and then back. 'Has something happened to Preston?'

'I'm afraid Mr Carmichael died last week,' said Guleed.

'How did he die?' asked Dame Jocasta.

'We're treating it as a suspicious death,' said Guleed.

'That's not exactly an answer.'

'I'm sorry,' said Guleed. 'That's all I can reveal at the moment.'

Dame Jocasta would have insisted further, but this was my cue to ask a question and break her chain of thought.

'When did you know him?' I asked.

'What?' Dame Jocasta blinked at me.

'You said "quite a long time ago",' I said. 'How long exactly?'

'Oh.' She paused to count it up in her head. 'At least twenty-five years ago, when I was at uni.'

We already knew that Dame Jocasta had attended Manchester University at roughly the same time as David Moore – that was one of the reasons we'd pushed up this interview. 'Just in case something effing horrible happens,' Seawoll had said.

Guleed asked where Dame Jocasta had gone to university, in order to keep the rhythm going, and then I asked what kind of an acquaintance Preston Carmichael had been.

'That's a good question,' said Dame Jocasta. 'I suppose you might call him my spiritual advisor. That was before I learnt that it was better to forge your own relationship with the cosmos rather than rely on other people.'

'What was the nature of the spiritual advice?' asked Guleed.

'Oh,' said Dame Jocasta. 'We did everything he told us to. It was a cult, darling.'

6

Spear

'Or can you call something a cult when it's a rec-ognised part of the Catholic Church?' said Dame Jocasta. 'Actually, I'm not sure it was that well recog-nised – certainly I don't ever remember anyone particu-larly churchy turning up. Not a dog collar in sight. I was nominally raised a Catholic, so the absence of official priests might have been part of the appeal.'

According to my therapist, attaching conditionals to your past is a classic distancing technique indicating an unwillingness to face your memories directly. Or, I pointed out, it could be a rhetorical device designed to add a humorous note to enliven a story. To which she said, 'Or both.' You can't win with therapists, you know. And even if you do, they just tell you it's part of the process.

Guleed showed Dame Jocasta a copy of the group photograph.

'Oh my God, oh my God,' she said, taking the picture from Guleed and holding it close to her face.

'Just to clarify,' said Guleed. 'The woman on the left is you?'

'Don't I look young?' said Dame Jocasta. 'And the hair . . .'

'Where was this taken?' asked Guleed.

'In Manchester,' said Dame Jocasta. 'In Fallowfield. At a church hall near my digs – about 1989, judging by my clothes. I can't believe I was such a frump.'

'Were these your fellow cult members?' I asked.

'I suppose so,' said Dame Jocasta.

'Can you remember their names?' asked Guleed.

'Let me see,' said Dame Jocasta, and she pointed at the only other woman. The same age as young Jocasta, but tall and thin with blonde hair cut into a Lady Di style. 'That's Jackie, who was so stuck-up you'd think she was related to the queen.'

She stabbed her finger at a young man with dark curly hair, thick eyebrows and a strong jaw. He was dressed in a denim jacket and loose jeans and leering at the camera as if daring it to make something of it.

'That's Alastair, the randiest man on earth. The girls used to call him the octopus.' Dame Jocasta paused and, looking up from the picture, laughed. 'If he'd been at university now, you lot would have had to arrest him. Terrible groper, although I heard he did reform.'

Since Guleed was a skipper and I was but a lowly constable, I was the one scribbling this down in my notebook. I'd just written *Alastair – groper* when I had a sudden cold sensation as if someone had opened a window. It was strong enough that I looked over at the windows, but they were all still closed.

I glanced over at Guleed, who gave me a slight head tilt to show she'd felt it, too. She flicked her eyes over at the entrance and I stowed my notepad and went to have a look.

'So who's this here?' said Guleed behind me.

Another garden table facing the entrance served as a reception desk. As I passed it I caught flashes of hot sunlight, lemon-scented dust and what sounded like a choir singing something medieval and off-key in the next room.

The nervous young white man with floppy hair who served as receptionist gave me a worried look as if he sensed something, too. When the phone on his desk rang it took him a moment to remember it was his job to answer it.

All my mobiles and Airwave handsets are rigged to have a hard on/off switch. It's a pain to get them retro-fitted, but if there's no power running through them, the chipsets don't get damaged by nearby magic. I took a moment to thumb off my mobile before cautiously making my way to the entrance and out on to the land-ing. But I left my Airwave on, just in case and because it came out of the Folly's budget, not mine.

Whoever had converted the warehouse into offices and flats had obviously done it back in the carefree sixties, when lifts were for wimps and people with disabilities hadn't been invented. This explained the long steep staircase, minus handrails, stretching straight down to the double doors at the front. Halfway up, climbing the stairs towards me, was a small white woman in a grey zip-up hoody.

'Lesley!' I shouted, because she was about the right size and shape and you never know.

The woman looked up and her eyes literally flashed – a white light in both sockets like a pair of camera flashes. Bright enough to make me flinch but leaving, I noticed, no after-image. A magical effect, not a real one. The light faded to reveal brown, widely spaced eyes in a smooth tanned face with a straight nose and an oxbow mouth.

Lesley can change her face but this woman's response was all wrong. She'd hesitated, and after the flashes the eyes looked puzzled – no hint of recognition at all. Not Lesley but, potentially, the person who had scooped the hearts out of two men's chests.

'Sahra!' I shouted. 'Code Zulu, IC1 female on the stairs. Bring in Falcon One. Call in Zulu One.'

Or translated, major Falcon threat on the stairs, looks like a white woman, get Nightingale quick. Since there was a good chance Dame Jocasta was the next target, Guleed would have to stay with her. So that just left me on the landing and little Ms Code Zulu on the stairs.

Policing dilemma. Do I let her come up and get closer to her potential target? Or do I go down the stairs and greatly increase the risk of both of us falling down and breaking our necks? I figured if she started coming up I could use *impello* to knock her feet backwards so she'd fall safely on her face. Then see if I couldn't get a restraint in before she could recover. *Impello*, with its variants, was the second spell I'd ever learnt. So it's something I can cast fast and accurately when I need to.

The woman gave a long-suffering sigh and, neatly solving my dilemma for me, turned and started walking back down the stairs. I started down after, keeping my distance and trying to not look like Scooby Doo sneaking after a ghost.

She paused at the bottom and turned to look back up at me when I was halfway down. I kept going but in as friendly and non-threatening a manner as I could.

'Hello,' I said. 'You wouldn't mind answering a few questions, would you?'

Her brow furrowed and she squinted at me for a moment and then she turned and went out the door.

I went down the remainder of the stairs three at a time, and just managed to avoid tripping and planting my face on the wall at the bottom. I yanked open the door, looked both ways and caught a flash of grey hoody heading north on the right-hand pavement. I went after her at a lope in the hope of closing the distance before she noticed me. But before I'd got a couple of metres she looked back, spotted me and took off in a sprint.

Running while yelling into your Airwave is a skill you pick up the first couple of weeks into your probation.

'All units, all units, Falcon Two chasing suspect on Middlesex Street towards the market. IC1 female, slim build, grey hoody, blue jeans and white trainers. Possible Falcon – report only, do not approach. Repeat, do not approach.'

Once I'd got that out of the way I could concentrate on narrowing the gap. She was fit, but I was fitter and taller, and I was less than three metres behind her when she did an abrupt right turn into Wentworth Street. This is the street where Petticoat Market runs six days a week, and despite the rain it was choked with stalls and people out for a lunchtime shop.

As I rounded the corner she turned to face me and

suddenly I heard the crash of cymbals and a brass note so deep it rattled my fillings. Around us there were yells and screams as stallholders and punters scattered.

I skidded to a halt like a cartoon character and showed my hands.

Her hood had fallen loose to reveal curly dark brown hair falling in ringlets to her shoulders, and behind her head blazed a circle of white fire. Light sprang from her back and spread like wings to either side. Where they brushed the tops of the stalls, the tarpaulin awnings snapped and rippled like flags in a gale.

In her right hand she brandished a spear of burning gold.

Fuck me, I thought, *she's the Angel of Death*.

I lifted my hands to make sure she could see they were empty.

Her eyes were wary, her mouth a thin determined line.

The spear, I couldn't help but notice, was pointing at my chest and I remembered the hole scooped out of David Moore's chest, the shattered ribs pale amongst the glistening remains of his viscera.

'Hello,' I said. 'My name's Peter Grant – what's yours?'

The angel's expression didn't change. No response – nothing.

But nothing is good when you're a copper. Nothing means nobody's getting stabbed or shot. Nothing means time is passing, and time is the police officer's friend. Time for support to arrive, time for members of the public to clear the area, time for . . . whoever it might be . . . to sober up, come to their senses or realise that, really, he ain't worth it, Tracy.

'Would you like a cup of tea?' I asked, giving her my best reassuring smile. 'Nice cup of tea? Coffee? Latte? Chai?'

The mouth lost a bit of its firmness and the eyes widened. The tip of the spear dipped, although that wasn't as reassuring as it might have been, given it was now pointing below my belt buckle.

'We can sit down,' I said. 'Sort things out. I'll even throw in a croissant.'

The eyes snapped up to meet mine and the spear came up again – obviously she didn't care for a continental breakfast.

'Full English?' I offered, but even as I said it I was lining up the *formae* for my shield.

She lunged, spear darting, the wing-like sheets of flame sweeping forwards. I jumped back and got my shield going – angling it so any trouble would be deflected into the air.

The world in front of me went white, the cymbals crashed again, and when the light was gone so was the angel.

I ran forwards but there was no sign of her.

Bollocks, I thought.

Guleed arrived beside me with her extendable baton ready and held, sword-like, in an overarm position that she definitely didn't learn on an officer safety course.

'What the fuck was that?' she said.

'That was an alien, bruv,' I said. 'Believe it.'

'Oh yeah?' said Guleed. 'Looked more like an angel to me.'

We even had CCTV of the incident from a camera that was outside the area of immediate magical effect, and thus still had its chips in one piece. In it you can just make out, in the middle distance, me and the angel facing off. Just for once, it was a modern camera with enough resolution to get a clear image of her face.

What it didn't show were the fiery wings and the halo. That some magical phenomena that seem visible to the naked eye don't register either on chemical film or a photosensor array is something we've known for some time. Our current theory – that is, mine and my cousin Abigail's – is that no photons are being emitted or bouncing off the ghost, or the unicorn or the burning spear of a vengeful angel. What we think we see is, in fact, our brain's interpretation of input from different senses – the one with which we 'sense' *vestigia* and ghosts, et cetera. We've even run up a tentative experimental protocol and one day, when we have time, we might even get to carry it out.

Dr Jennifer Vaughan thinks this is bollocks. If it was merely our individual interpretation of magical sensory input, she reasons, why is there such a strong correspondence between separate witnesses? Answer that or get the next round in.

And it's true. There were a dozen witnesses to my confrontation with the angel and all but two of them agreed about the wings and the halo. Although one of them thought there was a tail as well, and another was adamant that there were no wings but was sure she had a whip.

The uniformity itself was suspicious – usually you canvas three witnesses and get five versions.

Fortunately for my finances, Jennifer doesn't have an explanation for why the wings didn't show on the camera footage, and so we had to pay for our drinks separately like normal civilised people.

Except for Beverley, of course, who never has to pay for her drinks – not even when it's a Sprite.

All that came later.

'An angel?' said Nightingale after he'd arrived on scene.

'Wings, halo, burning spear,' I said. 'All she was missing was a chariot of fire.'

'And you think it was truly a messenger of God?' he asked.

'An angel wouldn't have run away,' said Guleed, with the conviction of someone who actually paid attention during Saturday School at her mosque and had taken a GCSE in Religious Education to boot.

'Whatever it was,' said Nightingale, 'it seems from your account both powerful and capable. And I'm worried by this apparent ability to disappear. I've never heard of anything that could do that – not even during the war.'

'Do you think it's teleporting from place to place?' asked Guleed. 'Like in *Star Trek*.'

'It could have been a trick,' I said, 'but it would explain how she got into the Silver Vaults to kill David Moore.'

This possibility was why we were having our little strategy meeting on the landing outside Dame Jocasta's office while her underlings stole glances at us and occasionally offered us decaffeinated fair-trade macchiatos.

'We need to finish the interview,' Guleed had said, 'before anything else happens.'

'And ask whether she has a ring,' I said.

Because to my mind it was obvious David Moore thought, at least, that the ring would protect him.

'Are you talking about this?' asked Dame Jocasta when we resumed the interview. She held up her left hand to display the silver band on her ring finger. 'What's so interesting about it?'

I wasn't about to say it was enchanted, so I explained that the theft of a similar ring may have had a connection to Preston Carmichael's suspicious death.

'We'd like to rule out that line of inquiry.'

Getting it off Dame Jocasta's finger involved removing three other rings – including one carved out of black shale that she admitted was literally an archaeological find – and, finally, Vaseline. When I held out my hand, she hesitated.

'You will give it back?' she said.

I assured her I would and she deposited it in my hand.

Nightingale had been right – it was too heavy to be silver and was definitely enchanted. As I opened it up it took the form of an astrolabe. I smelt lemon-scented dust and heard, as if a distant call to prayer, a lamentation in a foreign tongue. This time I got a greater sense of age, and over that a sharp crimson tinge like drops of blood in clear water. I put it down on the back of my notebook and took some pictures with my phone.

'For comparison purposes,' I told Dame Jocasta when she got restless.

When I was finished she didn't snatch it out of my hand – but only, I got the impression, through an act of will. She pushed it back on her ring finger, wincing as it went over the knuckle.

'I don't dare have it adjusted,' she said. 'In case they break it.'

Guleed switched the focus back to the photograph. Dame Jocasta identified David Moore, but only knew his first name. She did know the surname of the last figure in the picture – Andrew Carpenter. Short, plump, with straight black hair cut into an untidy fringe, black-framed NHS specs and a surprisingly engaging smile. He was wearing a quilted blue bomber jacket over a white shirt with big lapels. Flares would have fitted that ensemble but the picture cut off at his knees. To me. for some reason, he looked out of place amongst the others but I couldn't work out why. Certainly it was all very eighties.

'I don't remember very much about him – except his name, of course,' said Dame Jocasta.

'Why his surname in particular?' asked Guleed.

'Carpenter?' said Dame Jocasta – as if the answer was obvious. Obviously me and Guleed looked blank because she said, slowly, 'As was Jesus's father – a carpenter, I mean.'

'Got it,' I said.

'Who took the photograph?' asked Guleed.

Dame Jocasta hesitated, her brow furrowed in memory.

'It must have been Brian Packard,' she said. 'He sent me an eCard from America a couple of Christmases ago. I didn't reply, though – I try not to look backwards.'

'Did you keep the email?' asked Guleed.

'No, of course not,' said Dame Jocasta. 'I deleted it at once. One must otherwise one drown in long-lost acquaintances.'

Guleed gave her a bland smile.

'Tell me about the cult,' I said.

'We were charismatics,' she said.

Which, it turned out, meant that they believed that the Holy Spirit imparted special gifts, called *charism*, to believers in order to build up the Church and, by building up the Church, improve the lot of all humanity.

'What kind of gifts?' I asked.

'There were lots,' said Dame Jocasta. 'I doubt I can remember them all. Let me see . . .' She tilted her head to stare up at the ceiling. 'There were gifts of grace . . . prophecy, speaking in tongues – which is not what you think it is.'

'No?' I asked.

'It's not babbling and making random noises,' said Dame Jocasta. 'It's about being able to preach the word of God beyond the constraints of your own tongue.'

'The better to spread the word,' said Guleed.

'Precisely,' said Dame Jocasta. 'Then there were the gifts of service, which I seem to remember were all about being able to discern God's wisdom or something.

You're probably going to have to ask somebody else about them.'

I was thinking Professor Harold Postmartin – this seemed his sort of thing.

Then there were the gifts of work – which was the good stuff. Miracles, healing and the faith needed to recognise these things as God's works.

'Wouldn't want the credit to go somewhere else, would we?' said Dame Jocasta.

'Did you receive any of these gifts?' asked Guleed.

'No,' said Dame Jocasta, but there was an edge in the way she said it. 'I was far too lazy to do God's work on earth. Barely managed my coursework as it was.'

'So how did you come to join this cult?' I asked, and Dame Jocasta winced.

'You shouldn't call it a cult,' she said. 'I know, I know, I started it, but it wasn't a cult, not really. There's a difference between being enthusiastic in how you express your spirituality and a . . .' She groped for a definition but didn't find one she liked. 'A cult,' she concluded.

'So when did you join this group of like-minded religious enthusiasts?' I asked.

Dame Jocasta gave me a long look and then smiled.

'I'll bet you're a hoot down the station, aren't you?' she said. 'I met Preston after Mass in Manchester.' She could remember the date because it was All Saint's Day, 1 November 1988. 'He was handing out leaflets,' she said. 'He looked at me and said, "I'll bet you can't be bothered to believe in anything." And before I could think of anything to say he said, "If you turn up I'll stand you a pint." So I took the leaflet. Don't laugh, I

124

was a student – a free drink was not to be sneezed at.'

She shook her head.

'Mind you, I had no intention of going,' said Dame Jocasta. 'It's just that I couldn't be bothered not to.'

It had started much like she'd expected. They sat around in a circle of chairs in a community hall and talked about Jesus. When we asked if she could re-member who had been at that first meeting, she named the subjects in the photograph but admitted that there had been a couple more whose names she couldn't remember.

'But I don't think they came back,' she said.

Which was strange, because Preston Carmichael was very compelling.

'One of those quiet preachers,' she said. 'None of that gesticulating and yelling nonsense. He spoke softly, but with this huge weight behind his words, as if God himself was sitting behind him with his hand on his shoulder. It was irresistible.'

And what he talked about was the power of the Holy Spirit, and how many Christians had tried to push that aspect of God into the background. Preston believed that by embracing the Holy Spirit as fervently as they embraced God and Christ their saviour, Christians could not only strengthen their faith but also get cool superpowers.

'Wait,' I said. 'He actually said "cool superpowers"?'

'Like Superman,' said Dame Jocasta. 'He actually said that – "God wants you to be a superhero for Jesus."'

'Was he serious?' asked Guleed.

'No,' said Dame Jocasta. 'Not serious serious. He was

making a point with a kind of knowing wink behind it. But he was serious about his faith and the power that faith brings.'

'So did you get any superpowers?' I asked.

Dame Jocasta hesitated, glanced out of the window and then back at me.

'Of course not,' she said. 'But it did renew my faith in God and my Church.'

There hadn't been any mention of religion in our background report – all her charitable foundations and organisational affiliations had been defiantly secular. If she went to church, it didn't appear in any of her PR.

'So you're still a practising Catholic?' I asked.

'Oh, I don't need to practise any more,' said Dame Jocasta. 'I've got that good at it.'

'So how long were you with the group?' asked Guleed.

'Not that long,' said Dame Jocasta. 'Until Easter the next year – 1989 that would have been, I think.'

'Why did you leave?'

Again the hesitation – this time Dame Jocasta frowned down at the rough blue wood of her trestle table desk and idly rubbed the surface with her fingertips.

'I suppose I drifted away,' she said without looking up. 'Besides, I felt it was time to concentrate on my studies.'

'So there wasn't a particular incident that decided you?' asked Guleed.

'Like what?' asked Dame Jocasta, sharper than I think she meant to.

'We're trying to establish whether you're at risk,' said Guleed.

'Am I at risk?' asked Dame Jocasta.

'We think you might be,' said Guleed.

'Should I be worried about my safety?' asked Dame Jocasta.

I thought of the angel and its spear of burning gold.

'Yes,' I said.

'You never went to university, did you?' said Guleed as we walked down the long stairway to the entrance. Nightingale was waiting at the bottom. She didn't wait for me to answer.

'The thing is,' she said, 'it's like school – you make friends there that you keep for ages and even if you never see them again you remember their names.'

'Maybe she's crap at names,' I said.

'And that was not the only thing she was keeping back,' she said.

'Something definitely happened at her not-really-a-cult,' I said.

'We need to TIE the rest of them,' said Guleed.

As we reached the tiny hall at the bottom, Nightingale held up his hand to halt us.

'Just a moment,' he said, and then, louder to someone on the other side of the closed door, 'Have you finished, Allison?'

'All done,' said a muffled voice on the other side.

'Splendid,' said Nightingale and, opening the door with a flourish, said, 'Observe.'

Scratched into the paint on the outside of the door was a series of horizontal, diagonal and vertical lines. Despite being obviously fresh, I could still see curls of paint on some of the edges. They were faint enough that me and Guleed had walked right past them. In our defence, we'd been more worried about securing Dame Jocasta.

It was the same design we'd found on David Moore's front door and it hadn't been there when we'd first arrived – that much was certain.

7

Intelligence

Sometimes we police believe a member of the public might be at risk of serious death and/or injury but we're not in a position to arrest the person or persons we believe to be a threat. This might be due to lack of evidence, the intended victim being unwilling to give a statement or, as in the case of Dame Jocasta Hamilton, having no fucking idea who might be trying to kill her.

Beyond the possibility that they were the Angel of Death. Or at least *an* angel of death.

In these cases the police are obliged to issue a 'threat to life' warning, otherwise known as an Osman letter, named after a famous case which established that members of the public had a right to know when someone was out to kill them. The counterpart of an Osman letter is a 'Disruption Letter', which is what gets sent to whoever we suspect is thinking of murdering someone in the hope of making them think twice.

'Bugger,' said Seawoll, when me and Guleed returned to Belgravia to brief him and Stephanopoulos. 'Who the fuck are we supposed to say is after her?'

He held up a hand to stop me from speaking.

'And you better not be just about to say an angel of bloody death,' he said.

'I was going to say person or persons unknown,' I said.

'Liar,' said Stephanopoulos.

'What's Dame Jocasta's level of security now?' asked Seawoll.

'Nightingale has stayed on site,' said Guleed, which pleased Seawoll.

'Good,' he said. 'If anyone can twat an angel it's going to be him.'

'What do we do if she asks for protection?' asked Stephanopoulos.

It was a good question. Contrary to what people think, the Metropolitan Police are not in the habit of stashing potential victims in safe houses. For one thing, we don't have any safe houses, and for another, we don't have the manpower to protect everyone who's vulnerable. But if you want an entertaining hour of shouting, get Stephanopoulos started on the subject of the underfunding of women's refuges.

'It would have to be at the Folly,' I said.

'Good,' said Stephanopoulos. 'Problem solved.'

Me and my mouth, I thought, and headed back to the Folly to tell Molly to prepare a guest room just in case.

I'd parked up the Asbo in the coach house and was crossing the atrium when Professor Harold Postmartin, MA, DPhil (Oxon), FRS, AFSW came bounding in from the front lobby. He stopped when he saw me and caught his breath.

'An angel?' he said. 'Really?'

'No,' I said. 'But that's what she looked like.'

He threw himself down on one of the green leather sofas and waved at me to join him. He was a tall thin man in, I guessed, his seventies, with a stereotypical shock of white hair and a vast collection of tweed jackets, all with suede patches on the elbows. When I first met him he'd seemed physically older, slower – but recently he'd seemed full of energy.

Being the suspicious type, I'd asked him whether he'd been consorting with fairies or collecting mystic portraits in his attic, but he insisted it was Molly's cooking.

'Nothing motivates a man like a proper suet pudding and custard,' he'd said.

Toby ran up to Postmartin and barked twice, turned to give me a reproachful look and scampered off in the direction of the kitchen stairs. Postmartin gave me a less reproachful look. I shrugged. Now that I lived full-time with Bev, I'd lost track of the intricate weirdness of life in the Folly.

Postmartin wanted details on my encounter.

'It's hardly likely to be an actual biblical angel,' he said when I'd finished.

'Why not?'

'In a world chock-full of murderous blaspheming bastards,' he said, 'why would an omnipotent and omniscient deity pick a couple of obscure Brits to do away with in such a public manner.'

'Maybe they did something particularly bad?'

'Have you looked at the news recently?' said Postmartin. 'It would have to have been something truly magnificent to get that manner of personal attention.'

'So you're ruling out religion?' I said, and then started

as Molly materialised beside my seat and placed a tea tray on the coffee table in front of me.

'Ah, lovely,' said Postmartin. 'Thank you, Molly.' He leant over to pour the tea. 'I've been wrestling Hatbox for rare books and that always gives me an appetite.'

Elsie 'Hatbox' Winstanley was a senior librarian at the British Library, and frequently feuded with Postmartin over his attempts to acquire rare books for the Folly archive in Oxford.

'It could be religiously inspired, though,' I said. 'A *genius loci* or High Fae that thinks they're an angel.'

Postmartin dunked a biscuit and took a bite before answering.

'Or something we've never encountered before,' he said.

'There's been a lot of that recently,' I said.

I was thinking of that moment when *something* had scrutinised me out of the shadows as the Mary Engine spun magic out of nothing in a warehouse in Gillingham. I'd had a definite sense of it being vast, aware and not very friendly.

'We've long known that early folk traditions practised ritual magic,' said Postmartin. 'Why not Christianity as well?'

Ritual magic, in which a single practitioner could lead untrained participants in a ritual which generated a magical effect, was Postmartin's passion. It was his contention that early religions, particularly those of the ancient world, regularly employed such magic to boost crops or aid hunting or get their orgies off to a really good start.

He asked me for a detailed description and when I got to the wings of flame, the halo and the burning spear, he smiled and shook his head.

'Traditionally,' he said, 'angels are not described that way. According to Ezekiel, the cherubim had the face of a man, the face of an ox, the face of an eagle and that of a lion. Also, if I recall, four sets of wings and the hooves of a bull.'

Then there were the angels composed of interlocking wheels covered in sparkling eyes, and the seraphim who had six wings and spent their days circling God's throne, bigging him up through song.

'There are human-shaped angels in the New Testament,' said Postmartin, 'who act as the messengers of God. They're described as shining, but no wings were involved.' The wings first turned up in the sixth century with *De Coelesti Hierarchia*, written by the strangely named Pseudo-Dionysius the Areopagite. 'And, of course, they're all over the late medieval annunciations.'

'Of course,' I said. 'The annunciations.'

'This manifestation,' said Postmartin, 'strikes me as being very late medieval. I think I may have to see what the library upstairs has about angels. I seem to remember a number of the early Victorian practitioners getting rather exercised on the question.'

With Postmartin hitting the books for mentions of angels, Belgravia MIT looking to trace the people in the 'cult' photograph, and Nightingale hanging around Dame Jocasta on the off-chance the Angel of Wentworth Street returned, I was left sitting in the atrium wondering what do next.

The twenty-third rule of modern policing is *don't duplicate the efforts of your colleagues*. Not only are they probably better at whatever it is than you, but chances are you won't get the credit if you do get a result. Instead, work out what you've got that nobody else has. In my case – lots of friends amongst the demi-monde.

Well, I say friends, but what I really mean is potential informants. Only these days CHIS, Covert Human Intelligence Sources, are supposed to have a separate controller. The idea being that if you segregate intelligence-gathering from operational policing, there will be less of the quid pro quo or tactical grassing that was a feature of the 'good old days' and led to the many exciting miscarriages of justice that enlivened the television documentaries of the 1990s.

It was time to get seriously old-fashioned and do some community outreach in a completely non-covert open and accountable manner.

I took Danni with me because I figured it would be educational.

'She's back,' said Zach, when we caught up with him behind the bar in the Quiet Saloon at the Royal George Pub off Charing Cross Road. He spoke quietly because down here in the basement the clientele preferred whispers.

He didn't say who 'she' was.

'She sent me a letter,' I said, keeping my voice low. 'How did *you* know?'

Zach sighed. He'd been Lesley May's on–off lover while she'd been working for Martin Chorley.

'Your lot came round to see me this morning,' he said. 'I don't know where she is and you'd have to be fucking stupid to think she's going to come see me.'

My 'lot' would have been officers from the Directorate of Professional Standards or DPS – who were still, technically, the lead branch in the hunt for Lesley May. They liaised with Nightingale but they tried to keep me out of the inquiry as much as possible. It's not that they suspected I was colluding with my former friend, but they weren't about to take any chances either.

'I'm not here about that,' I said. 'I want to know where the Goblin Fair is today.'

'What makes you think I know?' asked Zach, who, if questioned, would deny his own existence out of sheer habit.

'Because you always do,' I said.

'What's in it for me?' he asked.

'I'll get you an invitation to the christening.'

Zach squinted at me.

'What if there isn't a christening,' he said. 'It's not like either of you are Christians.'

'There'll be something,' I said. 'You know it's inevitable. It will be loud, go on for hours and involve a fuckton of food and drink. What it's called isn't really important, is it?'

'Oh, that's deep, innit?' said Zach. 'Also a bit reductionist.'

I wasn't sure that meant what Zach thought it meant, and I made a mental note to ask Bev that evening.

'You want to come or not?' I asked.

'Lloyd Square,' he said, and gave me a house number.

Demi-monde is French for half-world and, according to Abigail, is an abusive misogynistic term coined in nineteenth-century France. For us in the Society of the Occasionally Wise, it refers to the subculture that exists amongst the magical, the supernatural and others who have drifted into their orbit. They have their favourite pubs, clubs and hotels – the Quiet Saloon at the Royal George is one. You might well have drunk or stayed the night in one and never known it. You might have thought it had an 'atmosphere', been strangely serene or you might have had a strange urge to run screaming into the street – that's the demi-monde.

Then there's the Goblin Fair, where like-minded people gather together to chat, exchange gossip and sell each other the sort of things that you don't want getting into general circulation. Since the Folly really doesn't want some of these things being sold to unsuspecting members of the public either, we don't try to shut them down. It's that famous discretion that police are supposed to exercise in the course of their duties – plus it means we can do our community outreach all in one place.

Lloyd Square was a late Regency square in Islington that had the distinction of being neither square nor flat. The address we were looking for was part of a terrace that was staggered to cope with the slope. They were typical two-storey mansions – three, if you counted the basement – but missing the rusticated stucco and columns that were usual for the time. Instead, their flat faces were made of London brick in an unmistakable Dutch bond and fitted with deeply recessed sash windows.

'You're a bit of an architectural trainspotter, aren't you,' said Danni when I pointed this out.

I could only surmise that the actual address we were heading for matched its neighbours, because it was wrapped up in the kind of serious boards, scaffolding and Monarflex sheeting that indicates major structural surgery was under way. If any of the interior features survived the operation, I would be surprised. On the human-sized door in the hoarding had been spray-stencilled the words THE CIRCUS – AUTHORISED PERSONAL ONLY.

'Why here?' asked Danni as we approached the hoarding.

'They pick a location,' I said, 'usually one that's being renovated or left derelict, and move in for a couple of days. I think there's some underlying pattern to the locations but I'm not sure I've figured it out yet.'

I did the police knock, a series of hard slaps with the palm of my hand, on the word CIRCUS and it opened by ten centimetres to reveal a teenaged white girl dressed incongruously in a blue knit twinset and pearls and a blond pageboy wig.

'George sent me,' I said.

'Fuck off,' she said. 'We're rammed.'

'Alice,' I said, 'why do we have to do this every time I come to the fair?'

The girl shrugged.

'One – you're the filth,' she said. 'Two – you're still barred from that time in Kentish Town, and three . . .' She held up three fingers but managed to give the effect of two. 'I'm not joking, we're fucking rammed in here – come back later.'

'You don't want us to come back later,' I said. 'Let us in and I promise nothing will get broken. Promise.'

'Swear?'

'Swear.'

'Swear on your about-to-be kids' lives,' she said.

Christ, I thought, *does everybody in the demi-monde know about the twins?*

'I swear I won't start nothing,' I said. 'Unless you don't let me in.'

The door opened and Alice stepped aside to let us in. Once inside, I glanced down into the basement area and was surprised to see it full of punters. As was typical of the demi-monde, they were mostly white and dressed as variedly as any London street crowd. Maybe more hats than you might see normally – three or four pork pies, some baseball caps and one operatic topper, the last belonging to an elderly gent in a cape and black three-piece suit. Despite the drizzle, they were standing around chatting with drinks in their hands like a bunch of smokers outside a pub.

The actual front door was completely missing, as was the door frame and the exterior casing. Beyond, a generously proportioned hallway ran into the house, with a staircase a third of the way in. This, too, was so crowded that it reminded me of the pound parties I went to in my teens – all that was missing was a massive sound system vibrating our ribcages and clouds of ganja smoke. I asked Alice where the stalls were and she pointed down.

'Hallo, darling,' said a white person with an androgynous face, blue-black hair and a raven perched on their shoulder. The bird gave me a suspicious look, although I think the 'darling' might have been for Danni. 'Fancy a drink?' they asked brightly.

'Maybe later,' I said, and squeezed past.

'Fair enough,' they said.

Downstairs was much bigger than upstairs, and I realised that house must have been undergoing one of those super basement extensions beloved of all those rich people who think living in London as nothing more than a shopping opportunity. This was obviously going to be a combination gym and swimming pool – making it modestly sized by oligarch standards – and since I nearly once drowned in a basement pool I was quite glad that the builders hadn't finished it yet. Instead, the pool area had been dug out and lined with cement but not painted or filled. A wooden ramp extended down to the bottom, where half a dozen full-sized market stalls were arrayed. Builders' lights in metal cages hung from the ceiling and patches of what looked like red sound-proofing material had been attached to the walls at random intervals.

At the front of the house, still with its original door out into the area, a makeshift bar had been set up on trestle tables and was keeping a crowd suitably lubricated. I could smell spilt beer and wet coats, but underneath was the piping grind of a fairground automatic organ murdering something baroque by Handel. I knew it was Handel because the older Thames girls are very big on his music for some reason. To fit a decent-sized pool in, the builders had been forced to butt one side right up against the wall. But the other side had what I assumed was going to be a lounging area. Along that area smaller stalls had been arranged and one, near the far end, I recognised. It seemed a good place to start.

I told Danni to check down in the pool area and see if she could see if anyone was selling jewellery.

'I see someone I know,' I said.

The stall was tall and narrow, with a miniature proscenium arch elaborately carved with small birds, branches, grinning theatrical masks and frowning moon faces, all painted metallic silver or gold. The stall was topped with a black pointed witch's hat of a roof made from pleated black canvas. The whole thing looked like a gothic Punch and Judy booth. The sign above the opening read *Artemis Vance: Purveyor of Genuine Charms, Cantrips, Fairy Lures and Spells.*

I slapped my hand on the side of the booth and called 'Shop!'

A young white man popped up from somewhere in the recesses of the booth. He had silver-white hair cut short at the sides and gelled up into spikes at the top. He was wearing a blue and red pinstriped jacket over a ruffled white shirt. This was Artemis Vance. I saw, from the widening of his eyes, that he recognised me straight away.

'No refunds!' he said loudly.

'No refunds for what?' I asked.

In fact, come to think of it, the last time we'd met he'd sold my cousin Abigail a completely worthless charm.

But then, had it been truly enchanted I wouldn't have let her keep it.

'Just no refunds in general,' said Artemis – deflating somewhat. 'As a general principle.'

'You remember me, right?'

'I'm not going to forget the Isaacs, am I?' he said. 'So what can I, in my humble capacity as purveyor of quality enchantments, do you for?'

'What do you know about jewellery?'

'And in what form does your desire for adornment find its expression?'

'Enchanted jewellery,' I said. 'Rings, in particular.'

'Aha!' said Artemis, and dropped briefly out of sight before popping up again with a pair of blue jeweller's trays. He laid them out before me, each with six rings gleaming amongst the velvet. Most of them were gold and half of them had stones. Of the non-gold rings, none appeared to be platinum.

'Are they enchanted?' I asked.

Artemis straightened up, puffed out his chest and made a theatrical gesture at the rings.

'They are as puissant as they are required to be for the purposes for which they have been wrought,' he said.

'So no,' I said.

'Not so you'd notice,' said Artemis.

He watched, frowning, as I brushed my fingertips over each ring in turn – it always pays to be thorough. None of them were enchanted, though, and I'm pretty certain half of them were costume jewellery.

'Got anything with a bit of zing?' I asked, and Artemis gave me a bland look.

'Define "zing",' he said, and I gave him the police stare. The aim of the stare is to convey cynicism combined with weary patience. *I know you're about to lie to me but because I am a hugely magnanimous agent of state power, I'm willing to give you a moment to think better of it.* Seawoll probably gave his midwife that stare just after she smacked him, but it took me years to perfect it.

Artemis licked his lips.

'Not rings,' he said. 'Alas, nobody seeks to enchant jewellery any more.'

Apparently enchantment, as it was practised in these 'degenerate modern times', was confined to low-level protective charms cast on door locks, bicycles and family shrines. So I asked who used to enchant jewellery.

'The Sons of Wayland,' he said without hesitation.

Of course, I thought. *Them again.*

'And where can I find these sons of Raymond?' I asked, because know-it-alls can never resist ignorance.

'The Sons of Wayland,' he said, and gave me a suspicious look. 'I thought you Isaacs knew all about them.'

'I'm just a lowly constable,' I said, which made Artemis laugh.

'You're the Herald of the Dawn,' said Artemis. 'The harbinger of the new world.'

I've been getting this a lot recently and since nobody seems to have a clue about what it actually means, I try and not let it get in the way of work. So I asked about the Sons of Wayland again, but Artemis didn't know any more than I did.

He did try and sell me another charm – this one against cockerels. I declined.

I looked down into the empty pool – in time to see Danni being handed a small package wrapped in black paper which she quickly stuffed into her bag. The stall wasn't one I'd seen before, and seemed to specialise in T-shirts and studded leather accessories. When I met her at the top of the ramp she did a little guilty start.

'I need to check it,' I said.

'Check what?'

'Whatever it was you bought.'

'Why?'

'In case it's cursed,' I said, which got a sceptical look.

'Really?'

'Really,' I said. 'I need to make sure it's safe before you take it away.'

Danni sighed, pulled the packet from a shoulder bag, unwrapped it and handed over what looked, to me, like a small mop head made of leather. It had a handle fashioned of wood wrapped in leather and the strands were neatly stitched. When I held it up and let it unfurl I saw it was a small flail whip.

I looked at Danni, who gave me a defiant grin.

It wasn't magical but it was beautifully made.

I handed it back and Danni put it away.

I didn't ask what she wanted it for and she didn't volunteer the information.

Danni hadn't found any jewellery on the stalls down in the pool, just T-shirts, whips, death masks, books and candles.

I was about to suggest we head upstairs to see what else we could find when someone poked me in the back. I turned to find Alice, the teenaged door warden, looking up at me.

'My old man wants to see you,' she said.

This was new. We had intelligence that Alice's family ran the Goblin Market but never any confirmation. Even Nightingale admitted that he'd never had an audience.

'Oh yeah?' I said, trying to keep the eagerness out of my voice. 'What's he want, then?'

'I don't know,' said Alice. 'I think maybe you should ask him yourself.'

She led us back out the front of the house and pointed us at where a Ford Transit with a Luton box body was parked across the road by the park. It looked like a typical removal van, except stencilled down the side were the words BACK OF THE LORRY DELIVERIES and the silhouette of a bird. It might have been a sparrow, a crow or a blackbird for all I knew. There was a door on the left side just behind the cab. Placed on the pavement before this door was a beautifully carved set of mahogany steps. Alice skipped up the steps to open the door for us and, hopping down, gestured for us to enter with an oddly formal half-bow.

As I stepped through, I smelt old paper and beeswax – things I associate with the mundane library back at the Folly, especially after Molly had been cleaning. The source was obvious as soon as we entered – both sides of the interior were lined with bookshelves from floor to roof. The upper shelves were crammed with large leather-bound volumes, but the lower shelves were filled with neat rows of modern box files.

Not books, I realised – ledgers.

Halfway down the length there was space for an antique mahogany writing desk – an *escritoire* Postmartin would have called it – with a fold-down work surface and a double bank of small ebony box drawers behind. On a matching leather upholstered swivel chair sat a short slender white man in a blue shirt and tan trousers held up by red braces. His hair was cut long to hang down to his shoulders and was that dull brown colour that blond hair fades to in middle age. He snapped shut the MacBook he'd been working on and rose to greet us. He had a narrow chin, widely spaced grey eyes, a long straight nose and a wide mouth that, when he smiled, seemed weirdly familiar.

'Good afternoon,' he said, and shook our hands. His grip was dry and firm. 'Please have a seat.'

He gestured at a low green leather sofa that sat opposite the desk. I sat down and Danni followed – her eyes curious but her mouth shut.

Me and Nightingale had drilled this protocol into her on the first day of training. When meeting a supernatural power, watch, learn, follow your more experienced partner's lead.

And this was a supernatural power and then some, for all that he lacked the flashy burst of *vestigia* that some give off. Instead, there was a sense of an enormous depth, as if an entire age had been wrapped up in his skin and set in motion.

'My name is Robin Goodfellow,' he said. 'You must be the famous Peter Grant – and this is . . .?' He inclined his head at Danni.

'Detective Constable Danni Wickford,' I said.

He didn't, I noticed, offer us a cup of tea or any small talk.

'I have a problem I need your help with,' he said.

'If I can,' I said. 'What's the problem?'

'Numbers,' he said. 'Too many punters, not enough floor space.'

The number of people visiting the Goblin Market had been steadily increasing since Robin Goodfellow took over the family business in the late 1970s. According to his grandfather's records, which went back to the 1950s, they were now attracting quadruple the punters they did in 1963 and the trend was upwards.

'You've seen it,' he said. 'It's like the Tube in there.'

They needed to operate from bigger premises.

'A permanent site?' I asked.

'If that's what it takes,' said Mr Goodfellow.

'You'll have to go official,' I said. 'That's a lot of paperwork.'

Mr Goodfellow chuckled and pulled a box file from a nearby shelf. Opening it revealed it was filled to the brim with paper. The top page was titled 'Royal Borough of Kensington and Chelsea Health and Safety standards for market operators, market stalls, mobile caterers and street food sellers'.

'I have three more boxes of this,' said Mr Goodfellow. 'Mundane bureaucracy I can cope with.'

'So what do you need us for?' I asked.

'We need to make a change to the Agreement,' he said.

The relationship between the Folly, the demi-monde and the other powers, such as the Rivers, was governed

146

by a series of informal traditions and agreements. According to Postmartin, it was a typical British mixture of archaic tradition, handshakes between gentlemen, and a stubborn refusal to engage with anything that might smack of dangerous continental legalism.

Still, I sensed an opportunity to inject a bit of rationality into the demi-monde, and after a moment I detected a more immediate advantage as well.

'I'm sure it can be done,' I said, channelling my inner Del Boy. 'But it will cost you.'

'Oh yeah?' he said. 'What do you want?'

'Information.'

'How much information?'

'Let's start small,' I said. 'By way of down payment.'

'I'm listening,' said Mr Goodfellow.

'What do you know about the Sons of Wayland?'

The trouble with foxes is, if you let one into your house they don't half take the piss. Although Abigail is quick to point out that with the talking variety, at least they don't literally mark their territory.

'Come on, I need to do some washing,' I said.

The fox currently curled up inside my washing machine gave me an appealing look.

'Do you have to now?' it asked. 'Only this is so nice.'

'Yes, now,' I said, but, because I am weak, I added, 'You can climb back in afterwards.'

'Hooray,' said the fox.

It slunk out of the machine and watched, stretching and yawning, while I loaded my laundry and carefully selected the correct cycle. I'm no expert, but I've been around these foxes long enough to recognise one or two. This was Indigo, who was my cousin Abigail's right-hand vixen.

And if she was hanging around the house . . .

'Where's Abigail?' I asked.

'She's off with Maksim acquiring a diggy thing,' said Indigo.

'What's a diggy thing?' I asked.

'You know – a big thing,' said Indigo. 'For digging.'

Maksim already had shovels and spades racked neatly in the garden shed. A horrible thought occurred to me.

'How big is this big diggy thing?' I asked.

'Big!'

'As big as me?'

'Bigger.'

'As big as a car?'

Indigo gave this some thought.

'As big as a big car,' she said.

'And what are they planning to dig with this big digger?'

'That is beyond the scope of my need to know, fam,' said Indigo. 'But it would be nice to have a permanent den here – with cushions.'

'What's Beverley doing now?' I asked.

Indigo raised her head, her ears twitching back and forth like radar dishes.

'She's in the TV and snack room watching *Crazy Ex-Girlfriend*,' she said, and jumped up on top of the washing machine as it started its churn cycle. 'This is nice,' she said, and lay down flat on top of the machine.

'Which do you think it was?' asked Beverley when I returned to the living room. 'An angel or an alien?'

She muted the TV and looked at me expectantly.

'Are there angels?' I asked.

'I've never met one,' said Beverley.

'Before I met you, I didn't know there were river goddesses,' I said.

'But you did believe in rivers,' she said. 'The existence of angels – the traditional messengers of God – implies a god. Which is a significant claim.'

'What's the digger for?' I asked.

'Maksim's going to do some work on the garden,' said Beverley. 'But leaving aside the existence or otherwise of a monotheistic god, is it possible that our conceptions of angels are based on something else?'

'What kind of work do you need a big diggy thing for?'

'Focus, Peter – this is important,' said Beverley. 'I don't like the idea of you having a beef with someone who might be connected.'

'Connected to who?'

'Or what?' said Beverley. '*What* worries me more than *who*.'

'Well, *what* will have trouble finding me, then,' I said. 'I'm going to Manchester tomorrow.'

Saturday

Nice red uniforms . . .

8

Manoeuvre

We caught the morning train to Manchester Piccadilly. Seawoll upgraded us to first class.

'I'm too fucking large for economy,' he'd said, and paid for me and Danni out of his own pocket. Even with the upgrade, he barely fitted into the gap between the table and the seat, and had to raise the armrest to sit comfortably. The seat next to him had been marked reserved, but when the designated passenger arrived – a flustered-looking white man in a business suit – he took one look at Seawoll and hesitated.

'Plenty of room,' said Seawoll with a friendly smile, but the man said he'd see if there was a free seat further up.

Going first class meant we got free beverages and a choice of microwaved mini-meals. But, despite this bounty, Seawoll plonked an M&S bag on the table and started pulling out two weeks' worth of snacks – some of them, like the grapes, even vaguely healthy.

As we divided up the goodies I briefed them on the Sons of Wayland.

'They were the engineering branch of the Folly,' I said. 'They claimed to be part of a smithing tradition

153

that goes all the way back to prehistory. They made all the battle staffs and other enchanted stuff.'

'Like what?' asked Seawoll.

'Like the statue in the Smithfield Garden – that was one of theirs,' I said.

And the battleship steel doors that guarded the Black Library in the Folly basement, which I didn't mention.

'And you think they made the rings?' said Seawoll.

'I don't know,' I said. 'But Mr Goodfellow said that if anyone in Britain made enchanted rings, it would be them. And if they didn't make them, then they would know who did.'

Seawoll turned to Danni.

'That's good policing, that is,' he said. 'Don't make any assumptions, check everything. Even if it is weird bollocks.' He waved half a large-sized sausage roll at me. '*Especially* if it's weird bollocks.'

Danni looked at me and raised an eyebrow. I shrugged back.

'Why doesn't your boss know about them?' asked Seawoll.

'He knows about them,' I said. 'He even trained with them before the war.'

I saw Danni react. The fact that Nightingale was born in 1900, had fought in World War Two and then started getting younger again in the early 1970s had, strangely, been omitted from Danni's briefing material.

'Once your trainees are up to their neck in magic,' Guleed had said, when I'd canvassed her for advice on writing the briefing, 'Nightingale won't come as such

154

a shock – it'll just be one more thing in the mad, mad world of magical policing.'

'After the war—' I said, but Danni interrupted me.

'This is like the Second World War, right?' she said.

'I'll explain later,' I said. 'The Folly never recovered from the losses during the war and the Sons of Wayland disbanded.'

Many of the smiths, who were also practitioners in their own right, had taken part in the abortive attack on Ettersberg, and subsequently been killed in action or grievously wounded. The Sons of Wayland's main headquarters on the outskirts of Manchester had been destroyed by German bombing shortly before the operation took place. There had been an archive and a repository of valuable artefacts, but that, like the contents of the Tate and the British Museum, had been moved to a safe location at the start of the war.

When I asked Nightingale where it was now, he said he didn't know.

'I wasn't told,' said Nightingale. 'Nobody who went out into the field was given that sort of information. What we didn't know we couldn't reveal under interrogation.'

'And after the war?' I asked.

'Things were confused,' said Nightingale. 'I spent a great deal of time in hospital and by the time I was back on duty nobody could tell me where it had gone. The official position of the new government was that magic belonged to a bygone age, and good riddance.'

The reports from the camp at Ettersberg – what the raiders had found, what they had fought on the ground that night – had only reinforced the conviction that the world was better off without modern magic.

But Mr Goodfellow had been adamant that the smiths' evacuated archive still existed, and that somebody had access to it.

'I hear things from time to time,' he'd said. 'I have factors at the horse fairs and conclaves in Cumbria and both borderlands, and they pass on information. Rumours, mostly, of enchanted items that have nothing to do with the fae or the spirits. Things of cold iron.'

Seawoll sighed and split open a packet of corn chips.

'To be honest,' he said, and unscrewed a jar of salsa dip, 'I don't like the fact that all we have so far is that somebody did something to somebody at some time which may or may not have some fucking connection to some other people who we're not sure still exist.'

'We have Preston Carmichael's ex-wife's home address,' said Danni.

'Let's hope she's in,' said Seawoll.

Our GMP liaison was waiting for us on the concourse. She was a dark-haired white woman with sharp features, blue eyes and narrow shoulders which she hunched forwards when at rest. She was instantly recognisable from her smart but dull black trouser suit, her sensible shoes and her look of narrow-eyed suspicion. She might as well have been wearing her warrant card on a lanyard around her neck.

She'd obviously been given a good description of Seawoll, because she had him spotted before he cleared the ticket barrier and marched over to introduce herself.

'DC Eileen Monkfish,' she said.

We shook hands, exchanged pleasantries, and Monkfish led us to where her car was waiting illegally in the taxi drop-off area. It was raining hard and we all dashed to climb into what turned out to be yet another battered Hyundai. Judging from the state of the interior and the fact that the heater had stopped working, this was probably Greater Manchester Police's least loved pool car.

'We followed up your query,' said Monkfish, aggressively pulling out in front of a black cab, which honked. 'Seeing as our last known for Samantha Carmichael was from all the way back in the eighties, I've got to say we weren't hopeful.'

So imagine their surprise when it turned out that, according to the electoral register, Sam Carmichael was still living at that address thirty years later.

'That's a long time to live in Fallowfield,' said Monkfish.

Once we were away from the station, Manchester became a city of wide straight roads with low-rise terraces, urban parks and shopping arcades sweeping past us in the rain. It could have been an inner city suburb anywhere in Britain, except that it was much flatter – even than South London.

The address was a two-storey plus an attic conversion on a street running back from the high street. One of a row of late Victorian red-brick terraces with orthogonal bay windows and vestigial front gardens given over to recycling bins and rusty un-stealable bicycles. Our address was neat and well maintained in contrast with the scruffy frontages and neglected front doors of the rest of the terrace. The area had the unmistakable signs of multiple-occupancy rented accommodation. Short-term tenancies at that.

'Students,' said Monkfish.

'Hasn't changed, then,' said Seawoll and, ignoring the doorbell, he banged on the front door.

A small slim white man dressed in a pair of green tracksuit bottoms opened the door and immediately took a shocked step backwards. Having four police turn up unexpectedly can have that effect – Seawoll can have that effect all on his own.

'Hallo,' Seawoll said brightly. 'I'm looking for Samantha Carmichael.'

'What for?' said the man, recovering a bit of his Englishman's castle and straightening up.

Seawoll showed his warrant card.

'My name is Detective Chief Inspector Alexander Seawoll from the Metropolitan Police,' he said. 'And why we're here is her business. Is she still living at this address?'

'Yeah,' said the man and chuckled. 'Samantha is my dead name. I haven't used it for twenty years.'

'In that case, we'd like to ask you some questions about your ex-husband,' said Seawoll.

'Which one?' he asked.

'How many have you had?' asked Seawoll.

The rain was definitely trickling down the back of my neck, but Seawoll's stance was relaxed but implacable. It indicated that he was willing to stand there forever if need be – whatever the weather.

The man hesitated and then shrugged.

'Just the one, actually,' he said, and eyed the four of

us looming in his doorstep. 'Some of you better come in.'

We left Danni and Monkfish in the car, although we could certainly all have fitted in what was definitely not a multi-occupancy home. Instead, the whole ground floor had been knocked out so that the living room segued into a dining room, which became a big kitchen conservatory complete with breakfast bar and ceramic island hob. Yellow and red covers were thrown over a big and slightly saggy sofa and armchairs, and the flat surfaces not covered in knick-knacks and framed photographs supported potted plants. This was not a room that had been decorated; rather it had accumulated over time around someone with a yen for comfort and a wicked sense for colour.

Instant coffee arrived in a set of rainbow-coloured mugs.

Seawoll did the notification. Like many large men, Seawoll can come across as sympathy itself when he exerts himself. He sat on the edge of the sofa, leaning forwards to make himself a comforting bulk as he notified Sam Carmichael of his ex-husband's death.

'I'm a bit shocked by my response,' said Sam, after he'd blown his nose. 'It was a fair time ago.'

'We never truly put our loved ones behind us,' said Seawoll. 'We think we move on, but we carry our baggage with us.'

Sam bustled off to make a second cup of coffee, despite the fact that we'd barely touched the first, and I took the opportunity to look at the photographs scattered around the room. They looked like holiday snaps, groups or individuals set against foreign backgrounds – beaches, palm trees, ancient ruins and a handful with snow and mountains. Sam only appeared in a few of the pictures – perhaps because he'd been behind the camera for the others. It was hard to tell what decade they were from. Some were definitely old-fashioned printed film images, while others had the 4K sheen of modern hard copy.

Nobody stood out as being a partner or significant other.

Sam returned with more rainbow-coloured mugs and noticed the originals still sitting fussily on their coasters on the glass coffee table.

'Ah,' he said. 'I'm getting senile.'

He scooped up the old cups and took them away.

'You obviously like to go on holiday,' I said when he came back.

'As much as possible,' said Sam. 'I'm trying to visit every country in the world.'

'Even the war zones?' asked Seawoll.

'Nowhere stays a war zone forever,' said Sam primly.

Seawoll cued me and I extracted my tablet and showed him the group picture. Sam sighed.

'He was a good-looking bloke,' he said.

We asked after the other figures in the photograph but Sam claimed that he'd never met them.

'We were drifting apart by then,' he said. 'We got on fine, but it's difficult when one of you has a passion the other doesn't share. To be honest, I was never what you would call an enthusiastic spouse – I'm not very roman-tic, you see. Or religious.'

Seawoll asked when Preston had become more interested in religion.

'Preston had always been very spiritual,' said Sam. 'We were both raised as Catholics, and you know what they say – once you're a Catholic you stay a Catholic no matter what you actually believe in.'

But Sam and Preston had very much been lapsed Catholics when they bought the house in Fallowfield. Sam was teaching at a local comprehensive and had met Preston when he came in as a supply teacher.

I asked what he taught.

'Any subject that needed cover,' said Sam. 'He had a degree in theology.'

Our information on Preston Carmichael had remained maddeningly scarce, and so we took a couple of minutes to establish that Preston had read theology at Durham University and had, in fact, gone on to Ushaw College, a Roman Catholic seminary, but had left before taking any vows.

'He always said that priest was really too limited a role to appeal,' said Sam. 'He was very eclectic in his interests, read widely and was extremely popular as a supply teacher.'

'With the schools or the kids?' I asked.

'Both,' said Sam. 'The kids loved him. He had that way with them that the best teachers have – strict but friendly – not an easy balancing act.'

He'd also had a bit of an American accent that young Sam had thought really sexy.

'He'd spent time in San Francisco,' he said. 'I found him quite irresistible.'

They'd bought the house in the spring of 1986 and got married the same year at St Kentigern's – it was just down the road.

'Is that the same church where Preston attended mass?' asked Seawoll, and he gave me a look. Jocasta had said she'd met Preston at a special mass.

'Yes, it was,' said Sam.

Seawoll asked me to tell Danni and Monkfish to run up to the church and see if anyone remembered Preston in his mass-going prime.

'Oh, I doubt anyone from that time is still there,' I heard Sam say as I stepped outside to pass on the instructions.

The rain had slackened to a drizzle and the pair asked if they could grab some refs while they were at it – I said yes, but to canvass the church first.

'And text us if something startling turns up,' I said, knowing that it probably wouldn't.

As I went back inside it was obvious that Seawoll had circled back to Preston's religiosity. In an interview, even a non-confrontational one, you always look to cover the important facts from several directions at once.

'In any case, it wasn't sudden,' said Sam. 'Like I said, Preston had always gone to church on Sundays. Then he started going in for special masses as well – remembrances, All Saints', Ascension Thursday. I remember over breakfast one morning he told me he was running a prayer group with some students, but I didn't really pay attention.'

'Do you know whereabouts he was running the prayer group?' asked Seawoll as I re-entered the living room.

'In a community hall around the corner,' said Sam, and he gave an address which I noted down. 'It really was just a weekly prayer meeting.'

Until suddenly something happened.

'He didn't come home one night,' said Sam. 'I thought he'd gone out to the pub at first. But by three in the morning I was getting angry. By six I was getting worried, and I was wondering whether to call the police when he turned up on the doorstep.'

Manic is the word Sam used. Manic, demented . . . he would have said hyped up on uppers, except that Preston never took drugs.

'"I've been one with the Holy Spirit!" he said. "And he has shown me so many things."' Sam shook his head. 'I thought it was rubbish. And then he turned to me and asked me why I wasn't living as a man.'

And then he passed out on the living room floor – Sam had considered calling an ambulance, but his breathing seemed natural and even.

'We separated less than a month later,' said Sam. 'He announced it one morning over breakfast as if we were discussing the shopping. It was like he was a different person.'

'What exactly changed?' I asked.

'This is going to sound weird,' said Sam, and I saw Seawoll perk up at the word *weird*. 'But he used to be much angrier.'

'At you?' I asked.

'Not at me,' said Sam. 'At the world, at society, at things he couldn't change like Margaret Thatcher and Section 28 and the miners' strike.'

'The poll tax,' said Seawoll.

Sam rolled his eyes.

'Oh God, the poll tax,' he said.

But when I asked whether Preston had been political-ly active, Sam laughed and shook his head again.

'Not active,' he said. 'Just angry and shouty. I didn't mind because he used to be funny about it. I used to tell him that he should do stand-up. If he'd taken my advice he'd be on *Mock the Week* by now.'

And then after the first manic phase, it changed. He'd become eerily calm.

'I mean, I like mellow . . . but suddenly I was living with the Buddha,' said Sam. 'If the Buddha was a Roman Catholic.'

In mundane policing, such a sudden change in per-sonality might lead to thoughts of drug use or coercion. But in my line of work I had to consider the possibility of sequestration or the glamour.

The glamour, in which magic was used to influence someone's mood or intentions, was usually short-lived. Sequestration was our technical term for possession by an entity or entities unknown and could last longer, but was nearly always fatal.

'Did he ever experiment with drugs?' I asked.

'I thought it was drugs, too,' said Sam. 'But I think in the end it was religion. He said that he had been charged to go out and do God's work. I asked him what he'd been doing all this time and he said "messing about". But now he could see clearly what he was supposed to do.'

'Did you stay in contact?' asked Seawoll.

'No,' said Sam. 'The next time I had any contact at all, it was ten years later and he was asking for a divorce. Which was just as well really, because I'd transitioned by then and was looking to divorce him in absentia.'

'Did you want to marry someone else?' I asked.

'No,' said Sam, and he made a face. 'But I did want to be legally unencumbered – he signed over his stake in the house as part of the settlement.'

'Generous,' I said.

'Not really – I'd been paying all of the mortgage for a decade. It was mostly mine already.'

Sam stared gloomily into his coffee mug, Seawoll caught my eye and tapped his ring finger.

'Did your husband have a puzzle ring?' I asked. 'In silver or platinum?'

Sam gave me a surprised look.

'More than one,' he said. 'Were they stolen – is that what this is all about? No . . . that was thirty years ago. They can't be important – can they?'

'We think they may be connected to Preston's death,' I said.

'He had seven,' said Sam. 'I remember because he kept on quoting Tolkien – "Seven rings for Dwarven kings, one ring to rule them all."' Sam frowned. 'That's not how it went . . .'

'When did he acquire these rings?' asked Seawoll, before I could correct the quotation.

'He didn't steal them,' said Sam, straightening up. 'He was a very honest man – at heart.'

I assured him that we didn't have any reason to think that Preston had stolen the rings, but were interested in when and under what circumstances they came into his possession. Sam relaxed a little. That's the purpose of that kind of long-winded police speak – it lulls witnesses into a false sense of security.

'It was February 1989,' said Sam. 'And he found them inside a book.'

Literally inside a book, an old one with a leather cover – a hole had been cut into the pages to make a space.

'Like they use to hide booze,' said Sam. 'Only smaller.'

'Do you remember the name of the book?' I asked.

'No, sorry,' said Sam.

And I thought, *Shit, dead end.*

But Sam jumped up and shook his finger in the air.

'I might still have it,' he said, and we watched him scamper up the stairs.

'After thirty years?' I said to Seawoll.

'You'd be amazed what you end up keeping,' he said.

Sam was gone for fifteen minutes, in which time I took the opportunity to rifle through his Blu-Ray and DVD collection, stick my nose in his kitchen cupboards, read all the notes stuck to his fridge and, because I'm a nice guy, rinse and put the used rainbow mugs in his dishwasher.

What I learnt, apart from the fact that he had a fondness for Wes Craven and Wim Wenders, was that Sam was neat, organised and self-contained.

I was about to push my luck and start exploring on the next floor up, but Sam came down with a book-shaped Co-Op bag held out before him.

'Found it,' he said. 'It was in the attic.'

After dithering between me and Seawoll, he handed

the bag to me and I removed the book. It was much smaller than I was expecting, smaller than a modern hardback, but it did have a cover made from scuffed brown leather. If there was a title on the front it, and the lettering on the spine, had worn away. I briefly closed my eyes but there were no *vestigia*. I opened it to the title page: *Principia Prima Formarum: lux et impello* by Victor Casterbrook.

By now my Latin was getting quite good, proof positive that if you bang your head on a copy of Pliny the Elder eventually the Romans will seep in. In any case I recognised the title – *First Principles in Formae: Lux and Impello* – a magical textbook published in limited edition by Ambrose House Press. Halfway down the page was their compass and pyramid logo, and below that the publication date of 1924.

'Inside,' said Sam.

I opened the book to a middle page and found, as advertised, the hollowed-out space. Cylindrical and quite small – just large enough for seven or eight rings, if packed in neatly.

Written in pencil at the top of the title page were words – *Portico Library, Manchester*, followed by a nine-digit alphanumeric sequence. When I showed this to Seawoll, he said he knew where the library was.

'Thank you, Mr Carmichael,' he said, getting ponderously to his feet. 'You've been very helpful.'

The Portico Library was on the top floor of a grandiose Regency building built in what I was beginning to recognise as the solid monumental Manchester style.

Obviously the city had been feeling its oats at the end of the eighteenth century and, between all those displaced agricultural workers in the mills and the slaves on the plantations in the Caribbean, it had money to burn.

Danni did the googling on her phone as DC Monkfish drove us back from Fallowfield.

I'd have liked to do a *vestigium* assessment at the old church hall, but that had gone the way of all gentrification in the teens and was now a featureless faux Edwardian terrace of affordable housing. Whatever had happened there would probably have been bulldozed along with the hall.

Danni continued her report from the back of the car.

'It was set up by some local bigwigs in 1802 because Manchester didn't have a private lending library,' she said. 'It's a Grade II listed building and has a loggia, whatever that is, and four Ionic columns. What's an Ionic column, Peter?'

'Like you get in Greek or Roman temples,' I said.

And originally it had been a temple of learning, but unfortunately the library had fallen on hard times and had to lease the ground floor to a pub chain. Now the grand façade with its three-bay pedimented loggia leads to a selection of real ales, and speciality pies, fish and chips or burgers served on a slate.

Or possibly a plank of wood – we never did get to find out, despite Seawoll calling up the menu and eyeing it speculatively.

The Portico Library proper was reached via a modest side door which led to a staircase with sandy-coloured walls and brown carpet that wound up to the top floor.

Each landing had a folding chair and a leaflet rack – presumably so visitors could pause and take a rest on the long slog up.

It was worth the walk. The main reading room took up almost the whole of the top floor, with a beautiful flattened dome ceiling with an oculus, and radiating skylights in subtly coloured stained glass depicting coats of arms and the red rose of Lancaster.

Black varnished bookcases lined the walls from floor to ceiling, and there was a counter island right in front of the entrance. Seawoll, after pausing to catch his breath, threw himself into one of a pair of chairs to the left of the counter and grabbed an *FT* from the nearby newspaper and magazine rack.

'You do the Falcon stuff,' he said. 'And I'll supervise from over here.'

We showed the nice librarian behind the counter our book and asked if it was theirs.

'You need to talk to Bob,' she said, and called him over.

Bob the librarian was a short round white man in a navy V-neck jumper, with big black-framed Malcolm X glasses and greying brown hair that, while thinning at the top, was long enough to pull into a respectable ponytail at the back.

He took the book and examined it with the same careful briskness with which vets handle pets. When he found the hollow cut out of the pages, he frowned and looked back up at me.

'This wouldn't have been on the shelves,' he said. 'It would have been in the store in the gods.'

Bob went over to his computer terminal and typed in the number pencilled onto the title page.

'According to our records it belongs in a box upstairs,' he said.

Seawoll waved pleasantly at me and Danni as we followed Bob into the back room, where an extendable ladder took us up through the ceiling and into the attic. It was, I decided, exactly what you'd expect from a library attic – clean, untidy and filled with random paper. The walls were lined with wooden and metal-framed bookcases. Some held box files, some piles of stationery or random piles of books. I was reminded of Robin Goodfellow's van full of ledgers – this was where the Portico Library kept its memories.

And quite a lot in the way of random bric-a-brac. Some rather tasty oak library ladders, old picture frames with curlicue edges leaning against a bookshelf filled with old doorknobs, coat hangers and modern metal bookends. The air was close and filled with the woodsmoke smell of old books. I was getting continuous flashes of *vestigia* – sunlight, rain, the scratching of pens – all as faint and delicate as spiderweb. We followed Bob around a U-turn, ducking to get under the slope of the roof, and into another corridor filled with the same mixture of shelves and junk. Bob reached up and pulled down a white cardboard storage box, cleared a space on the top of a chest of map drawers, and plonked it down. He lifted a cover to reveal that it was full of books.

I recognised the titles *The Principia*, Cuthbertson's *A Modern Commentary on the Great Work*, and the bloody unavoidable Charles Kingsley – both his magical work

On Fairies and Their Abodes and an 1863 edition of *The Water Babies* that looked like it had gone for a swim itself at some point.

This was obviously the box for Folly-related books. Postmartin would want to know, so he could pop up north and deprive Manchester of its cultural heritage.

'This was the box where your book was supposed to be,' said Bob.

He pulled out a manila folder that contained two sheets of A4. The first held a list of titles printed by a dot matrix printer that was probably coming to the end of its ribbon. Despite the fading, Bob could easily point out the listing for *First Principles in Formae: Lux and Impello*.

'According to this,' said Bob, 'it was inventoried twenty seven years ago – February 1989.'

The same month that Preston Carmichael had discovered them. We'd have to follow up and see if Preston had either worked at, or been a member of, the library – he must have gained access somehow.

'Does it give the provenance of the books?' said Danni, winning double librarian score for use of the word *provenance*.

The second sheet of paper was thin and almost transparent, like tissue. I recognised it as a carbon duplicate from the time I had dug bombing reports out of the London Metropolitan Archive. The faded typewritten note identified them as books handed in by dependents for return to SOW ARCHIVE, Volcrepe, Milltown, Glossop, Derbys. It didn't say whose dependents they might have been, or why they had handed them in.

But I had a good idea of why they had to go to the Sons of Wayland Archive.

Preston Carmichael must have found the book and the rings hidden inside, and taken them off to his prayer group. I had no idea what had happened next, but I was willing to bet it had involved some form of ritual magic.

Something that had drastically changed Preston's personality – a sequestration, perhaps, or something more subtle. Had they conjured Our Lady of the Burning Spear? And, if so, why had it taken thirty years to come to our attention? It was hard to believe that something so powerful had eluded detection for so long. Nightingale admits that he took his eye off the ball, but flaming wings and a halo are pretty fucking hard to miss.

Not to mention the whole heart-reduction surgery.

'Where's Glossop?' asked Danni.

'It's a town up by the moors to the east,' said Bob. 'It's the start of the Snake Pass. Last town before Sheffield.'

'Seawoll's from there,' I said.

We checked the rest of the box, but all the other books on the list were accounted for. One of them, a 1911 copy of the Second *Principia*, had a yellow bookmark sticking out the top. It turned out to be a Post-it Note. Somebody had written a couple of lines . . . I recognised the handwriting. Somebody who just couldn't resist a bit of a gloat when she got ahead of me.

Obviously, Lesley had written, *Nightingale don't know everything*.

9

Air Support

Glossop is in a different force area, so we bade farewell to DC Eileen Monkfish and the Greater Manchester Police and, pausing only to stock up on snacks, caught a local train from Manchester Piccadilly.

'I have a car in Glossop,' said Seawoll. 'My dad's going to drop it at the station for me.'

It was raining heavily as the train headed back out over the massive railway viaduct that feeds Manchester Piccadilly. Dirty grey clouds were low enough to drag their skirts across the tower-block-studded plain of the city. As the train peeled off to climb through the outer suburbs, me and Danni fired up our phones and got updated on the course of the investigation. Seawoll stayed strangely quiet and stared out the window.

At one point we shot across a valley on an extraordinarily high viaduct – one of those constructions that seems too ambitious to be made out of Victorian brick and wrought iron.

'There's a story,' said Seawoll, still staring out the window, 'that the mist came down once and the train stopped on a signal on this viaduct, and half the passengers alighted thinking it was the station and fell to their deaths.'

Glossop was the end of the branch line and a single-platform station – a low-slung, single-storey structure built of sandstone. Outside was a brick-surfaced car park, and waiting amongst a clutch of nearly new Peugeots, VWs and Toyotas was a battered Ford Escort that had, I estimated, last passed an MOT before the turn of the millennium. It was a sun-faded red, with a mismatched panel and white patches where dents had been beaten out.

'This brings back memories,' said Seawoll.

The doors were unlocked and the keys were hidden behind the sun visor. There were still drink bottles and food wrappers in the back seat's footwell. Left over, Seawoll, said, from his leaving party. I've been in better-maintained pool cars and it creaked alarmingly when Seawoll levered his bulk into the driver's seat. But when he turned the key in the ignition the engine started smoothly – that, at least, had been properly maintained.

Seawoll must have sensed my surprise.

'I use it when I come up to see my dad,' he said. 'You need a car to get around up here.'

But not to get to the Volcrepe Mill – we could have walked it in fifteen minutes. Down a high street of sandstone terraces that crowded against the pavement. Small shop fronts with local brands, an Esso petrol station, a flat-roofed leisure centre that looked as if it was a prefab but was probably too modern. More terraces of the same sandy brick, and then we turned down a narrow lane which dipped down to what I knew from the map on my phone was the Glossop Brook.

On our left reared a derelict factory with boarded-up windows, and on the other side was a hoarding festooned with hard hat signs and hazard warnings. A building site – more housing, according to Seawoll, Glossop having gone from grimy industrial town to a 'charming community' set amongst the borders of the Peak District.

'More lawyers, architects and financial advisors than you'd find in Maida Vale,' he'd said as we passed multiple estate agents on the High Street.

Seawoll parked up next to the bridge, where a grey metal palisade gate blocked off the access road to the factory. Seawoll rattled the chain and padlock that held it shut and scowled.

'We could climb over at the side,' said Danni.

The ugly modern gate was fixed between the original sandstone posts – these were low and smooth enough to be climbed. You could even use the parapet of the stone bridge to start you off.

'You can if you want to,' said Seawoll, and he turned to me and held up the padlock. 'Peter, come here and make yourself useful.'

I have a number of spells that can make short work of a lock, providing you never want to use it again. But when I gave the shackle a pull it proved to be open already.

'Excellent,' said Seawoll. 'That makes it almost legal.'

I looked at Danni, who shrugged. Given that Seawoll held the exalted rank of detective chief inspector, we were both totally prepared to abdicate our responsibilities re: proper powers of entry procedure to him, as our senior officer. Lower rank, as I have often noticed, can have its privileges, too.

Beyond the gate was a cracked asphalt road that ran between the factory building and the river. The windows were all boarded up, but there was a door at ground-floor level that had been left hanging open. The rain, which had been fitful up until then, grew suddenly heavy, so rather than follow the road we ducked inside.

'I used to come down here as a kid,' said Seawoll. 'Mind you, there was a lot more of it left in them days.'

We were in a room twenty metres long, where the first floor had obviously been allowed to collapse onto the ground. Piles of rubble and structural timbers were heaped in a ridge from one end to the other. The rain was pounding on the remains of the roof and pouring through a great gash that ran its length.

It smelt of mould, old stone and decay.

It was remarkably light on the *vestigia* – nothing more than a whiff of sulphur. I pointed this out to Danni.

'Should there be more?' she asked – raising her voice over the din the rain was making on the roof.

'A working factory this old,' I said. 'Should be tons.'

'Where to next?' asked Danni.

Seawoll pointed to where an open doorway led to what appeared, from where we were, to be a more intact area.

'Let's try through there,' he said.

'It's not here,' said a voice behind us.

We turned to find a young white girl standing on one of the piles of rubble. She looked to be about ten or eleven, with a mop of sandy hair over a round freckled face and dark blue eyes. She was dressed for mischief in a pair of blue denim dungarees, a red and black chequered shirt and red Converse.

'What's not here?' asked Seawoll – raising his voice to be heard above the rain banging on the remains of the roof.

'What you're looking for,' said the girl, and I noticed that she didn't need to raise her voice at all.

'And what are we looking for?' asked Seawoll.

'Don't you know?' said the girl.

Then she skipped down the pile of rubble towards us. She did it without hesitation or looking down to see where she was putting her feet, the heels of her red Converse kicking up dust but never slipping.

As she got closer, I heard the rush of water and the creak of gigantic wheels and, over it all, the long lonesome cry of a falcon high over the moors.

'As it happens,' said Seawoll, 'not really. Why don't you stop fucking around and tell us?'

'Alexander!' said the girl with mock severity. 'Do you kiss your mam with that mouth?'

'Who are you?' asked Seawoll.

'She's the Glossop,' I said.

'You can call me Brook,' she said. 'Or Glotti – depends on how old-fashioned you want to be.'

'Do I know you?' asked Seawoll.

'No, Alexander,' said Brook. 'I was asleep for a long time, but I watched you and your friends playing in my dreams so perhaps I was in the middle of waking up. I loved your games – all those Daleks and Drashigs and other monsters. It reminded me of when the world was young and we still had dragons.'

I must have reacted to the last, because Brook fixed me with her dark eyes.

'Oh yes,' she said. 'We had dragons back then, breathing fire and crawling on their bellies – or were that the wyrms? I couldn't keep them straight then, either.'

'You were going to tell us what we're looking for?' said Seawoll, who obviously wasn't going to let meeting the ancient spirit of his home town's river get in the way of the police work.

'First you've got to introduce me to your friends, Alexander,' said Brook. 'It's only polite.'

'This is Danni,' said Seawoll. 'And this is Peter.'

In a spirit of inquiry, I stuck out my hand for Brook to shake. She took it in her small hand, her grip firm, and for a fleeting moment I was up in a high place under a clear night sky – the stars wheeling over my head.

A wide, disturbing grin spread across her face.

'*That*, Peter,' she said, and let go.

When Danni put out her hand, Brook childishly faked her out and thumbed her nose at her.

'You're not ready for awesome yet,' she said. 'Shit will get real soon enough.' She looked at me and winked. 'Isn't the internet wonderful,' she said. 'Better than dragons any day.'

'So what is it you think we're looking for?' said Seawoll. 'That's assuming you actually know what you're talking about.'

'The Sons of Wayland,' said Brook. 'Those mad romantics in iron and steel – keeping alive the ancient traditions but not above knocking out a decent steam boiler if you asked them nicely.' She looked from Seawoll to me.

178

'You're looking for the storehouse what was brought here in 1939,' she said. 'But they moved it out again in 1946. I wasn't there, of course. I was asleep and I didn't awake for another forty years. There were only fitful dreams of bombs and fires in the night.'

'Do you know where it is now or not?' asked Seawoll, who doesn't take lip from a witness – no matter what they say they're the god of. 'Because I'm getting that desperate for my tea.'

'Come with me,' said Brook.

She led us out the back of the building. As we approached the rear door the sound of the rain faded and daylight lightened, so that when we stepped outside it almost felt like sunshine.

It was still overcast but it felt like a bright spring day. Ahead I could hear children laughing.

'I remember this,' said Seawoll. 'This was our adventure playground back in the day.'

What it *was* was a health and safety nightmare. A big orthogonal open space bounded on all four sides by the sandy-coloured ruins of the Volcrepe Mill. Small hills of brick rubble mixed with rusting girders and the remains of gantries twisted into gallows shapes by time and neglect. Weeds and scrubs pushed up through broken asphalt and concrete slabs strewn with broken glass and jagged metal shrapnel.

Anyone looking to film a low budget post-apocalyptic movie need look no further. A Young Adult dystopia at that, because a dozen or more kids were playing amongst the ruins.

'God, I hope they've had their tetanus jabs,' said

179

Danni as we watched a pair of boys sled down a rubble heap on a piece of rusty corrugated iron.

'Don't be such a mitherer,' said Brook. 'If you don't bloody your knees when you're a kiddie, what kind of a childhood would that be?'

'One without septicaemia?' said Danni.

'Nobody's going to get septicaemia or tetanus or crippled or the like,' said Brook. 'Not while I'm here.'

'Swear,' I said, and the light faded a bit.

Brook turned on me, her face a stern adult mask.

'You dare?' she asked – her voice deceptively pleasant.

'Swear,' I said.

I felt her power then, and it went all the way back to a time the Glossop was a mad unchannelled stream that ran free and wild down from the moors. A time when bears and wolves patrolled her banks and bison drank from her pools.

What was I in the face of all that geological time?

And then Brook was eleven again and smiling a mischievous smile. The sky brightened and I took another breath.

'The Starling,' she said. 'Just what the doctor ordered.'

'And the kids?' I asked.

'Yeah, yeah,' she said. 'I swear on my power and all that. Satisfied?'

I looked at Seawoll, who was looking impatient, obviously having missed all the mystical stuff.

'And the archive?'

'I can help you find it,' said Brook. 'But first I need your help with something.'

'Oh great, a bloody side quest,' said Seawoll.

But in policing, like in open-world RPGs, you get used to chasing after collectables in the hope they'll help you move things along.

'This way,' said Brook.

We followed her around the remains of a brick shed. In front of us was an area where the rubble had been cleared away. On it, bits of scrap metal had been cemented together with what looked like papier mâché to form the shape of a plane – a big plane, at least fifteen metres long and with a wingspan to match.

Not just any junk either, but what appeared to be actual bits of aircraft fuselage. As we watched, a couple of older kids held a curved section in place while a younger child pushed papier mâché into the crack between it and the next section along. I could see patches of untarnished aluminium and structural spars with the distinctive lightening holes drilled through them to save weight.

I had a friend at school who was mad keen on Airfix models, who probably could have told me the make of plane, but I knew enough to guess it was a Second World War bomber.

It was a patchwork anyway – some fragments were painted khaki, others showed bare metal or scraps of camouflage patterns. I thought I saw at least one white USAF star and part of an RAF roundel.

'It's like a cargo cult plane,' said Danni.

It was just that. As if the children of Glossop were hoping to attract planes to bring them cargo – although given that the town seemed entirely built on a slope, I wondered where they thought they would land.

'I slept for fifty years,' said Brook, 'and woke up to find you lot had made a right mess of things. Now down here in the valley I was used to that, but up on the moors?' She shook her head. 'I expected better.'

Seawoll nodded towards the front of the bomber, where a seven-year-old girl was drawing a stick figure reclining under the broken edge of the cockpit windscreen.

'Are you talking about the crash sites?' he asked. 'Most of those were cleaned up.'

'Not the planes, not the metal,' said Brook. 'That's not what I'm talking about. It's the poor dead sods left cruelly behind that plague me. Sad shadows condemned to walk the moors like a bad Morrissey song.'

'I don't know what you expect us to do about that,' said Seawoll.

'Not thee, Alexander,' said Brook, and she nodded at me. 'The Starling is the man I need.'

On the afternoon of 18 May 1945, a Royal Canadian Air Force Lancaster bomber out of RAF Linton-on-Ouse was doing bumps and circuits – a training manoeuvre where the plane circuits an airfield, comes in for a landing but after the wheels make contact with the tarmac they accelerate again and take to the air. At some point the crew got bored – after all, they were young men in a strange country currently in possession of a go-anywhere machine. And so they went for a sight-see around the beautiful English countryside. Because they were supposed to be sticking close to their airfield, they didn't have a navigator on board. Perhaps this is why they got themselves lost, and after circling Glossop for a while they crashed into a hillside on the moors to the east. Seawoll said that he'd visited the site as a boy. You could still see the scar the plane made when it hit and read the memorial plaque that marks the spot. The crew were all buried in the Canadian section of the military cemetery at Brookwood.

The crash took place ten days after Germany surrendered. It wasn't the first aircraft to crash in the Peak District, and it wouldn't be the last.

According to Brook and Seawoll, there were biplanes out there, single-engine fighters, transport planes and at least one Superfortress. Even a Meteor, the first British jet fighter, and a Vampire – which I thought was a cool name for the second.

And some German bombers, too – having got lost while attempting to flatten Manchester and hit the hills on their way out. Brook advised me to Google translate some phrases while I still had Wi-Fi.

All these crashes was why I found myself sitting on a stile built into a drystone wall on top of a ridge a couple of thousand metres east of the ruins of the Volcrepe Mill and its cargo cult bomber. Behind me, the sun had fallen into a golden gap between the clouds and the horizon. Ahead, the moors rose up as darkening shadows vanishing into the mist. To the south of me, down a steep slope, the traffic on Snake Pass passed by in a fitful distant grumble. Sensibly, the cars had their headlights on and I watched their rear lights vanish into the low cloud like will-o'-the-wisps. Which is totally a real thing, by the way, and not to be messed with.

I chose this location because by the stile was a large boulder that had been incorporated into the wall – something I could enchant to serve as a beacon. I'd spent the last couple of hours enchanting it to do just that. Me and Nightingale had once used a similar approach to create a ghost attractor at Harrow-on-the-Hill Tube station. I'd done some experimentation since then, seeing if I could get more attraction for my magic. The *lux* variant I was using didn't even radiate in the infrared, but it did imbue objects with power.

Ghosts feed off the ambient magic that accumulates around human activity. Why? Don't ask. We don't know. One day someone much cleverer than me might, but I probably won't understand the maths. That ambient magic is what we call *vestigia*. Stone, metal and some plastics retain *vestigia* better than wood or other organics, which is why old houses tend to be haunted and old horses hardly ever are.

I reckoned that the ghosts of the airmen, if there really were any, would have been subsisting off the little *vestigia* retained by the metal components of their crashed aircraft. Up on the moors, with no human activity to renew them, they must be getting pretty thin. Brook thought one good point source of magic should be enough to draw them down.

'Most of them, anyway,' she'd said. 'Some will not come however loud we call.'

We'd named the ghost attractor at Harrow the Hangover Stone, because it was set up early in the morning. But this was more of a beacon.

There were small enchanted stone beacons every two

hundred metres down the slope to the west and along the valley down into Glossop proper. I'd enchanted a section of the cockpit of the cargo cult bomber directly – it was steel rather than aluminium, and thus a good receptor.

It was a lot of magic to expend in one day, even with such a low stress spell as my *lux* variant. For the first time in years I felt it necessary to log my magic use. Overdo magic and you can end up with a brain like a diseased cauliflower. Doctors Vaughan and Walid's latest theory is that, under stress, the magic starts to open little holes in your brain.

'Like microscopic singularities,' Abigail had said, with far too much enthusiasm for my liking.

Beverley has made it clear that she loves me for both my body and my mind and expects me to keep the latter intact.

I slapped the side of the stone and gave it a last zap for good luck.

Gondor calls for aid, I thought.

Since there was bugger all for them to do, Seawoll and Danni had sloped off for dinner at Seawoll's father's place – although Danni had popped back up with a flask and a home-made bacon roll at half six. I'd eaten the roll while it was still hot, but I waited until I was done before opening the flask. It was tea – milky and sweet.

While I waited for the ghosts to arrive I moved away from the beacon, turned my phone on and called home.

'Hi, babes,' said Bev. 'What you up to?'

In the background I could hear muffled voices, then

a thump and then Maksim yelling, 'No, no, the lining goes over there!'

'I'm up on the moors fishing for ghosts,' I said. 'What's going on?'

'It's just Maksim making some last-minute preparations,' said Beverley. 'He's worse than my mum and your mum combined.'

I heard the distinctive sound of a diesel engine starting up and thought of Indigo's big diggy thing.

'Is that a JCB?' I asked.

A door closed nearby and the sound became muffled. Beverley putting some walls between her and Maksim's 'preparations'.

'Are you coming back tomorrow?' she asked.

'I hope so,' I said.

'You'd better,' she said. 'Or there'll be trouble.'

'I'll do my best.'

'I'm on my way,' said Beverley to someone at her end, and then to me, 'I've got to placate the neighbours.'

'OK,' I said. 'Laters.'

'You've got to say it – before you go,' said Beverley.

I sighed.

'Say it!' she said again – with emphasis.

'I love you,' I said.

'I should hope so,' said Beverley, and she hung up.

I shut down my phone and went back to the beacon.

The setting sun briefly turned Manchester into a glittering city of gold and then it was dark. Just to maintain the mood, it began to drizzle.

The first ghost arrived just as I finished my tea – he didn't seem happy.

'I say,' he said. 'Where the devil am I?'

He'd started as the barest impression of movement in the mist, but as he approached the beacon he took on form and colour. A sandy-haired young white man with a cheerful open face that looked all of fifteen but probably wasn't. He wore a deflated yellow life jacket over a sheepskin jacket, but under that I saw he'd gone up with his tie neatly done in a Windsor knot.

'You've been in a crash,' I said. 'You need to get to the debriefing.'

'Prang, eh?' he said. 'That explains . . .' He faltered. 'I must have hit my head because I feel like I've been waiting forever.'

'It'll all be explained at the debriefing,' I said. 'Over the wall – follow the beacons.'

'Jolly good,' he said, and vaulted over the stile. 'Good to see you West Indian chaps getting involved,' he called over his shoulder. 'Wouldn't want you to miss out on the fun.'

And then he vanished.

The next lot were Americans, who arrived mob-handed and silent. They seemed thin and attenuated, even when close to the beacon. They didn't speak but the leader, possibly the captain, nodded gloomily when I gave him his instructions and led his companions down the hill towards Glossop.

That was a mood – as Abigail might say.

There were many more – Australians, Canadians, British. More Americans. A white guy in flares and a polo shirt who wanted to ask too many questions. They came in groups, in pairs and on their own.

Something passed me as nothing more than a chill in the air.

I lit a paraffin-fuelled hurricane lamp, guaranteed magic-proof, against the darkness. But amazingly, as night drew on, the sky cleared and a sliver of a moon chased the vanished sun down towards a smudge of light that might have been Merseyside.

I waited, sitting on the stile, for another half an hour but no more ghosts appeared. I was about to pack it in when I spotted a figure briefly silhouetted on the horizon. Unlike the ghosts, this one didn't glow with pseudo-phosphorus but stayed a shifting patch of shadow until she stepped into the circle of lamplight.

It was a small white woman with blonde hair cut short and a pop-idol-beautiful face. She was dressed as I remembered her from when we were probationers – high-viz jacket over a Metvest, Airwave clipped to her shoulder, tactical belt full of CS spray, speedcuffs and an extendable baton. Blue uniform trousers and DM lace-ups. All she was missing was the uniform cap with its badge and checkerboard band.

'Hi, Peter,' said Lesley May.

I lunged to grab her, using the stile as a brace to push off with my right foot. We've had magical fights, me and Lesley, and I couldn't say who was better. Especially now when she's been off learning fuck-knows-what from Christ-knows-who. But I was physically bigger, stronger and, in any case, she wouldn't be expecting a grapple.

It was good tactics and it might even have worked if I hadn't jumped right through her body and landed flat on my face.

I rolled over to find Lesley staring down at me. My hurricane lamp was still sitting on the wall behind her and her face was in shadow.

'Good trick, isn't it?' she said. 'Picked it up in America.'

'I'm assuming you're not dead,' I said, rolled over and got to my feet.

'Nope,' she said. 'Still alive.'

I passed my hand through her torso and she stood still and let me. There was no resistance but there was a faint *vestigium*, like the smell of salt and a gentle surf breaking on a beach.

And children singing in what I recognised as German.

'Is this astral projection?' I asked.

'Not quite,' she said. 'I'm sort of piggybacking on this ghost.'

I lunged suddenly at her eyes with my left hand – she flinched.

'And, yes, I can see and hear you,' she said.

'This could revolutionise telecommunications, though,' I said. 'What's the range?'

'Nice try, but I'm not anywhere near you,' she said.

But you are, I thought. *Close enough to know I was attracting ghosts and then waylay one poor soul on his way off the moors. If I fire up my phone, can I persuade Derbyshire Police to put a helicopter overhead, bring in search teams? Probably not.*

'Peter,' said Lesley with a note of exasperation so familiar to me that it made me smile. 'Focus. Even if you had the army on standby you couldn't get a cordon around me in time to catch me. This spell isn't going to last that long and I have stuff I need to tell you.'

'Where have you been?' I asked.

'Mostly in the States,' she said. 'They're mad over there, by the way, and it's wide open. I feel sorry for Kimberley, I really do, if she's all they've got. But that's not important. I was hired to nick something but I think there might have been some unintended consequences.' She pulled a face. 'Which were totally not my fault.'

'Did you steal something from the archive?' I asked.

'Yes, but—'

'Where is it?'

'Close by,' she said. 'You'll be there tomorrow – and are you in for a surprise! I know I was.'

'What did you steal?'

'A lamp,' she said. 'A magic lamp. A collector in the States wanted it.'

'Did it have a genie in it?' I asked. 'Did it grant you wishes? Did it sing?'

'Christ, and I was starting to miss you, Peter,' she said. 'But, yeah, there was something trapped inside and I don't think it grants wishes. Unless you're feeling suicidal, that is.'

'The Angel of Death?' I asked – thinking of the way she had just vanished into thin air like a genie might.

'So you've met her, then?'

'And she was in a lamp?'

'It was a very fancy lamp, definitely enchanted, definitely old, definitely not to be fucked with.'

'And yet you obviously fucked with it.'

'Not on purpose,' said Lesley, looking defensive. 'The archive was a little bit more defended than I was led to believe. There was a bit of a scuffle. But because it was me, not you, the place was still standing at the end.'

You know that really shouldn't have annoyed me as much as it did. But even as I knew I was being manipulated, I was getting angry. And I couldn't afford angry – not when I was dealing with Lesley. Not even when she was a ghost projection or whatever.

'I think the lamp got damaged in the fight,' said Lesley. 'And I was halfway back to my bike when there was a magical discharge and everything goes white and then black.'

I sat back down on the stile and fished in my coat pockets for the emergency Mars bar I was sure I'd left in there.

'Real or magical explosion?' I asked.

'Magical, I think,' said Lesley, and she came over to lean against the stone wall as if we were just two friends having a chat. 'The lamp was intact but it had lost its sparkle – something had escaped.'

'Our angel?' I asked, coming up empty on the Mars bar front.

'Yeah,' said Lesley. 'Maybe, but I didn't see her and I was too busy running away to hang about and make inquiries. I did wonder who'd killed Carmichael, but it wasn't until the guy in the Silver Vaults that I put two and two together.'

I didn't see an obvious connection, which meant Lesley knew more than I did.

But if she'd only been after the lamp, why had she been visiting the dead Preston Carmichael in the first place?

'Are you after the rings as well?' I asked.

'Is that the time?' said Lesley, and she stood away from the wall. 'This guy's got a plane to catch.'

There was no transition – one moment it was Lesley and the next it was a German airman. He was dressed in a Luftwaffe flight suit, complete with leather helmet and quilted yellow life jacket. He seemed ridiculously young – maybe twenty – and his eyes were large and scared.

I looked around to see if the rest of his crew were with him, but there was nothing.

'*Wo ist die Einsatzleitung?*' he said. '*Ich muss doch Meldung machen, aber ich fürchte, ich komme zu spät.*' I pointed down the hill.

'*Geh den hügel runter,*' I said in my best Google Translate German. '*Folge den Leuchtfeuern.*' Follow the beacons.

'*Danke,*' he said, and slipped past me to half-walk, half-glide, down the hill.

I pulled out my notebook and by the yellow light of the hurricane lamp wrote up my encounter with Lesley. The only possible connection between the archive and David Moore and Preston Carmichael was the rings. And the only connection between the two men was Preston Carmichael's prayer group. And fellow member Jocasta Hamilton had a ring, too. Were there more rings? Did any other member of the prayer group have rings? Were they in turn in danger from the Angel of Death? And was Lesley using us to locate them so she could steal their rings?

Whatever else I did, tonight I was going to have to brief Seawoll and Nightingale so they could take steps.

I'd let Nightingale explain to the DPS about Lesley's new astral projection thing.

I was finishing up when something started fluttering around the beacon stone. I might have thought it was a moth, if moths were invisible and the size of seagulls. It was a very faded ghost – what I would call a one on the 'annie' scale of spectral solidity. My brain was latching on to the sensation of movement and interpreting it into the flapping of wings. I made sure my phone was still off and cast another werelight, using a second forma, *scindere,* to fix it into place on the other side of the stile.

Instantly the fluttering movement darted over to the fresh source of magic and landed on the railing. It solidified, so quickly that if I'd blinked I would have missed it, into a large black bird. Beverley has taught me some basic bird stuff so I recognised it as a corvid – too big to be a crow, I thought, so probably a raven.

I stayed still and watched for a bit while it preened itself. Then, satisfied with its comfort, it lifted and turned its head to regard me first with one eye and then the other,

Animal ghosts are rare. Abigail insists that the foxes believe that animals are too sensible to hang around after their death.

'They say that any animal ghost stupid enough to hang around will be gobbled up by evil vampire cats,' she said.

The foxes tend to blame most of the ills of the world on cats.

According to Enoch Corkenhale's equally unreliable

An Animal Phantasmagoria (1857), 'the spirits of animals are most often associated with the presences of man. As a faithful hound may refuse to leave its master's grave, so may its ghost refuse to leave its master's abode.'

'Were you on one of the planes?' I asked. 'The debriefing is that way.'

I pointed down the hill – the raven continued to eye me suspiciously.

'*Geh den hügel runter*,' I said, and the raven reared up, spreading its wings and cawing at me.

'*Guten tag*,' I said when it settled, and it cawed again – twice.

Perhaps this had been in one of the German planes – a not so lucky mascot.

Just on the off-chance, I repeated the German for 'follow the beacons'. The raven took off and, beating the air over my head, turned and flew down the valley.

I waited a couple of minutes and then, turning to look up the valley again, I shouted, 'Last call for ghosts! Time, gentlemen, please!'

Then I turned back and followed the beacons down the hill.

It took me a whole hour, on account of having to go slowly down the rough side of the hill. Then along the A57 as it changed from Snake Pass and became the High Street. Past neat rows of modern semis with their televisions flickering and muttering behind net curtains. The front gardens shrank down to nothing as I reached the Victorian end of town, turned left at the roundabout, hopped a fence and pushed through the bushes until I reached the ruined courtyard of Volcrepe.

Where Dennis the Glossop had recreated the last scene from *Casablanca*. The cargo cult plane was up on its wheels and whatever scrap had gone into its making – it looked like a Dakota to me. And I've watched *Band of Brothers* and *A Bridge Too Far* so I know what I'm talking about.

The moon was down, and it should have been pitch-black, but the scene was lit by the silver shimmer that seemed to roll off the plane like mist. The same mist which covered the rubble and broken metal of the courtyard.

'Play it again, Sam,' I said.

'That was a Lockheed L-12A,' said Brook. 'And this is a Dakota.'

'How do you even know about *Casablanca*?' I said. 'I thought you were asleep.'

Brook shrugged.

'Maybe I dreamt it,' she said. 'Or maybe I saw it on TV – after the first thousand years you stop worrying about these things.'

She slipped her hand into mine like I was her older brother.

'Watch this,' she said. 'You might learn something.'

Brook began to sing, starting with the child's soprano you'd expect for her apparent age. It was an old song, in a language that hadn't been spoken for thousands of years, a sad song in a minor key full of loss and longing and the silence of the high places.

It swept me away, picked me up and whirled me into the sky so that I went pinwheeling south until I was high above my own modest little town. Where Beverley was shifting uncomfortably in her sleep, and Dad was dreaming of that time he played with Joe Harriott and Mum dreamt she was grooving in the audience.

Suddenly they were all below me. The good, the bad and the merchant bankers. The mob and the gentry, the Rivers and the foxes. And I saw the delicate intaglio of their lives traced in gold and silver and blue.

And for a moment I thought I saw a pattern – one I might understand if I could just lose myself in it first.

Brook squeezed my hand hard, much harder than a child should be able to.

'Come back, Peter,' she said. 'Don't get lost on me, lad.'

I was suddenly standing beside Brook with the Dakota in a wide flat field at dusk, the sun a bright line on the horizon, hangars behind me like shadowy caverns, and beyond the plane a tower, a squat two-storey block with its windowed control room blazing like a lighthouse.

I could see movement in the cockpit as the flight crew made their last-minute checks. At the rear, the young men in American, Commonwealth and German uniforms lined up patiently to board, and as they waited they sang the sad refrain of a people long lost in history. A raven flew low over my head, circled and cried out twice before settling on the nose. When I looked again, it had become a picture of itself painted below the cockpit window.

The last of the lost pilots boarded. The port and then the starboard engines stuttered into life and roared. The plane taxied around to face away from us; imaginary prop wash made my coat flap. Before he closed the rear door, one of the young men waved goodbye – I couldn't tell which uniform he was wearing.

The engines revved, the Dakota picked up speed, the rear lifted, and then it was rising and banking towards the west. It levelled its wings and climbed out of sight.

The real world returned as darkness. I lit my hurricane lamp and its yellow light illuminated rubble, scrub and scrap metal.

'Where did they go?' I asked.

Brook looked up at me and gave me a lopsided smile.

'How should I know,' she said. 'Perhaps they went nowhere.'

'Are we done?' I asked, because frankly I was knackered and wanted my dinner.

'Yeah,' said Brook, and we picked our way through the rubble to the gate and onto the road.

Brook gave me an address that I hoped meant something to Seawoll, and walked me out of the ruined factory and onto the old stone bridge over her river.

'You want to watch yourself when you visit,' said Brook. 'They're a right fearsome lot in that house.'

And with that unhelpful statement, she jumped over the parapet and vanished without a splash.

Sunday

Hampstead wasn't good enough
for you . . .

Summary

10

Logistics

Seawoll's dad turned out to be a painter. Quite a well-known one, if you listen to Radio 4 or hang around at the right kind of soirée. Obviously me and Danni had never heard of him, but this didn't seem to worry him at all.

'I like to paint,' he said. 'I'm not doing it for the fame or the fortune.'

'Certainly not the fortune,' muttered Seawoll.

His dad lived in a small brick two-up, two-down terrace in the mini-suburb of Dinting, within view of the famous viaduct. The one Seawoll had told us about in his story of foolishly alighting passengers falling to their death. From the valley floor it was even more impressive, and I certainly wouldn't have wanted to be first on the scene at that particular fatal accident.

This wasn't Seawoll's ancestral seat. That had been further up the road in Glossop proper, but his dad had downsized ten years earlier, after Seawoll's mum had died of ovarian cancer. This was all news to us lower ranks who, while we'd theoretically known Seawoll had parents, had always assumed that he'd been assembled in a factory somewhere outside Wakefield. I was making sure I remembered details, because Guleed and Stephanopoulos were bound to want to know.

Half the small back garden was occupied by Seawoll's dad's studio/man shed. His dad slept on the couch in that, Seawoll got his dad's room, Danni the spare, and I got the sofa in the living room downstairs. Since this not only opened directly onto the street but also the kitchen and the stairs, there was no chance of me sleeping through Seawoll and his father arguing about the best way to fry bacon.

Looking at Seawoll's dad, you could see where his son had got his height. But he himself was rake-thin. Age had shrunk him further, until the cuffs on his denim shirt had to be rolled up to stop them slipping down his arms. He had a big forehead, thinning grey hair and a stubborn chin which jutted out when he fought with his son.

They were still arguing – this time about whether a collective should be allowed to win the Turner Prize – when I came down from my turn in the bathroom. Danni joined in the discussion over breakfast – Seawoll had warned us that police work was not to be discussed under his father's roof.

Seawoll father and son were civil, but there was a definite coolness. From my long experience dealing with the internecine conflicts within my mum's vast extended family, it was clear that some deadly past grievance had not been so much resolved as locked in a box and then walled up – never to be spoken of again.

My therapist says that repressing such feelings is counterproductive, but she probably hasn't seen as many family fights as me.

While the others discussed whether sticking a tree outside a petrol station really constituted a work of art, I wrote up my notes on my encounter with Lesley. She'd been commissioned to steal an item, but it had been damaged during the theft and 'something' had escaped. A *something* that Lesley believed was responsible for the murders of Preston Carmichael and David Moore. A *something* that was probably the Angel of the Burning Spear that I'd run into on Middlesex Street.

For something that had been stuck in a lamp, she'd looked pretty solid to me. And, more importantly, she'd showed up on CCTV . . . so what kind of container could she have been trapped in?

We knew that there were other dimensions of existence – what one of Nightingale's old school friends had labelled *allokosmoi*. I'd even spent time in one, the land of Faerie, twice now. We also knew that they brushed up against our world and created weird boundary effects like invisible unicorns and localised private weather systems. The *genii locorum* seemed to be able to attract them to a locality – the suddenly uncluttered airfield of the previous night was an example, as was my beloved's ability to swim like a dolphin in a river that's less than a half a metre deep.

However, I would be reluctant to suggest that the stolen lamp may have been a bit like a Tardis even in the confidential Folly files, let alone on CRIMINT.

Still, if we could narrow down the date and time of Lesley's lamp theft, then we might be able to track Our Lady of the Weirdly Glowing Halo from Glossop to London. The more we learnt about her and her origins, the easier she would be to deal with . . . this chain of reasoning being bloody optimistic even by my standards.

Disputes over the role of the individual artist aside – the breakfast was delicious.

After eating, we threw our overnight bags back in the Ford Escort and Seawoll headed back towards the address Glossop Brook had given me. This was across town and off the A57 on a turn-off I'd walked past in the darkness on the way back down from the beacons.

'This goes up to the quarry,' said Seawoll, wrenching the Escort's steering wheel round and revving it up the slope. 'I didn't know there was anything else up here.'

'Down there,' said Danni who was navigating – pointing down a narrow lane completely overshadowed by old trees. We rounded a curve, following the contour of the hill, and suddenly we were pulling up in front of a gleaming white modernist tower. It was built into the hillside so that the drive terminated in a sunken entrance/garage with vertical concrete revetments rising diagonally with the slope. Mature trees overshadowed the approach, the damp green canopies dripping onto us as we climbed out of the car.

'Fuck me,' said Seawoll, looking up. 'How long the fuck has this been here?'

Three more storeys rose above the ground floor, all the same blank white plastered masonry finish, with picture windows running the full width – bisected by the railings of a purely decorative balcony. I couldn't see it, but I knew it would have a flat roof with a parapet to ensure rainwater pooled and caused it to need replacing every ten years. It was a poem of volume and geometry without humanity – a little bit of Swiss megalomania come to the North.

As Bev says, I have views about the International Style.

The front door was made of frosted glass in a brushed aluminium frame and the doorbell was a palm-sized rectangle of pale blue plastic. When I pressed it we heard a low musical chime from somewhere above.

We waited a bit and then I rang again – three times.

Nothing – and it started to rain heavily again.

I was about to press again when we heard a strange breathy, hissing sound and footsteps getting closer. A tall shape loomed behind the frosted glass and then the door opened.

A very tall East African woman stood there, with her hair in convenience twists above big brown eyes and a crooked smile. She was dressed in a black cashmere jumper that looked very expensive, despite the definite animal hairs on her arms and shoulders.

'Hello, Peter,' she said in a low murmur. 'This is awkward.'

'Hello, Caroline,' I said, and would have said more except Caroline shushed me.

'You have to be quiet,' she whispered, 'or they'll wake up.'

I lowered my voice.

'Who will wake up?' I asked, but Caroline ignored me and turned to Seawoll.

'You I remember,' she said, and then, nodding to Danni, 'You're new. Is this an official visit?'

'Yes,' I said.

'Folly official or Old Bill official?'

'Yes,' I said, because you can't show weakness to posh people or they'll mercilessly take advantage. I think it's something they learn at school in between conversational French and practical condescension. Lady Caroline Elizabeth Louise Linden-Limmer may have been adopted into the gentry, but she'd picked up the attitude from an early age.

Seawoll obviously remembered her, too, so I introduced her, quietly, to Danni.

'You'd better come in, but keep it down,' she said. 'If you wake them up you can sing them back to sleep yourself.'

Inside was a cool white hallway with a floor of red terracotta tiles and a side door that, presumably, opened into the garage. At the far end was that most beloved of modernist deathtraps – a spiral staircase. This took us up, the steps creaking slightly under Seawoll's weight, to an open-plan lounge, dining room and kitchen which seemed to be furnished entirely with enormous beanbags in a variety of pastel shades – blue, pink and purple. There was a strange smell, and I saw that people were curled up asleep on the beanbags. One was close enough to the stairs for us to get a good look and I heard Danni stifle a 'Fuck'.

It was easy to see that the woman, dressed in loose shorts and a pink T-shirt, was covered in fur from head to feet. Large pointed ears rose from the sides of her head, and her mouth and nose were elongated into just enough of a muzzle to be clearly non-human. No whiskers, I noticed, but the fur was thick and slate-blue. Although I could see whitening around her face.

The first Faceless Man had made chimeras for his select clientele in the Strip Club of Dr Moreau. The ones we'd found had all been dead, except for Tiger Boy, who'd been shot by armed police on a Soho rooftop.

'Yes yes yes,' hissed Caroline, looking at us staring. 'Upstairs and we'll talk.'

The next floor had several rooms off a hallway – bedrooms and bathrooms. We kept climbing up into a stair tower with a door out onto a roof garden. Or possibly the upper ground floor, since the roof was level with the hillside and the garden extended back into a terrace. There was an empty swimming pool outside, with white concrete walls stained with old leaves and mould at the bottom. Next to it was a pool house with a raked skylight roof, to which Caroline led us and told us to make ourselves comfortable while she made coffee.

We hadn't asked for coffee but we all recognised a stalling tactic when we saw it.

One entire wall of the pool house was floor-to-ceiling patio doors, and rain rattled on the skylights to run in rivulets down the slope and into the guttering – which, in keeping with the International Style, had been designed for the south of France, not Derbyshire, and was overflowing, and probably responsible for the disfiguring damp patch on the south wall.

'When do you think this was built?' asked Seawoll, who was trying not to wallow in a pastel-coloured modular sofa unit. The rest of the furniture was definitely late seventies, from the Habitat catalogue and fitfully cared for since then. The corners were worn and the colours faded.

'Judging by the building materials,' I said, '1930s probably, maybe later.'

The garden showed echoes of old landscaping but had been allowed to run wild and the trees had encroached until they overshadowed the flat roof of the main house and the pool house. It was mature growth, too – thirty years' worth of trees, maybe more. It explained why the satellite view on Google Maps had failed to show anything. There was a path leading from the pool area into the trees and I could hear an intermittent clang coming from that direction. A ringing industrial sound – metal hitting metal.

'We're definitely in the right place,' I said.

Danni snorted and I looked over to see her staring at me and biting her lip. She had a lot of questions, starting with *WTF cat-girls?* and *WTF tall posh black woman?* But she knew better than to ask them until we were away from said posh woman. Seawoll knew about the chimera, and had met Caroline before when she and her mother had got involved in our hunt for Martin Chorley.

Who, incidentally, had inherited the title, the chimera and the casual cruelty from the first Faceless Man. We'd thought all the original cat-girls, the ones created to entertain the Faceless Man's select clientele, had died ages ago. That was one connection we were going to have sort out straight away. Also, there were things Danni would need to know – potential eavesdropping or not.

'Caroline is a practitioner,' I said. 'A good one from

a separate British magical tradition. You would have been briefed about them last week if we hadn't been distracted.'

'Not another local god, then?' said Danni, and I heard Caroline laughing in the kitchenette.

'Have you perfected flying yet?' I called.

'Not quite yet,' said Caroline, bringing in four mismatched mugs on a tin tray. 'There seems to be a rather strict time limit.'

She put the tray down on an oval glass-topped coffee table. Thoughtfully, she had provided a scattering of sugar packets with differing labels.

'How long?' I asked.

The fact you couldn't levitate yourself using magic had been a source of constant frustration to generations of practitioners.

Caroline pulled a face.

'That's the problem,' she said. 'The duration is variable, from as little as thirty seconds to as long as two minutes. So I try not to get too far off the ground.'

'Impressive, though,' I said.

'Not enough,' said Caroline.

'That's all very interesting,' said Seawoll. 'Would you like to tell me why you have a house full of illegal medical experiments?'

'Victims,' said Caroline sharply. 'Victims of illegal medical experiments. This is a shelter for them, and I think they've suffered enough without the authorities taking an interest.'

I wanted to say that we didn't care – we were pursuing a double murder inquiry, and what consenting adults chose to do with their time was none of our business. But the trouble with turning a blind eye is that people often take the opportunity to punch you in the face.

'Do you run this place?' I asked. 'Is your mum about?'

'Still back in Montgomeryshire,' said Caroline. 'Thank God.'

'So what's your involvement?' I said.

She explained she was there to keep an eye on the 'ladies', but others helped out. I didn't press on who the 'others' were, but I guessed that they were probably further practitioners – what the Folly had used to call hedge wizards or hedge witches. I supposed we'd better come up with a modern term, probably something like 'Unregistered Informal Practitioners'.

'They used to have a house on our grounds,' said Caroline. Her mum owned twenty hectares of ex-hill farm in Wales where she raised foster-kids and ran alternative therapy retreats for nervous rich people. 'But they were beginning to attract attention and this place became available. Mum still pops up to do medical checks.'

'How long were they at your mum's?' I asked.

'Since the eighties at least,' said Caroline. 'They used to babysit us when we were kids.'

'Who owns this place?' asked Seawoll.

'Technically, the IronFast Trust, which is famous for sponsoring apprenticeships in traditional country crafts with a focus on . . . guess what?'

'Smithing,' I said.

'And less famous for its property portfolio in Manchester, Leeds and Bradford,' said Caroline. 'And this place. It's all totally legal with a board of trustees of which, unsurprisingly, my mum is one. If you want more details you're going to have to ask her about it.'

Seawoll looked at me and I shrugged. This was something we could pursue later.

'Does that property portfolio include the Sons of Wayland's archive?' I asked.

'As it happens,' said Caroline, 'it does. But if you want to see inside you're going to need permission from the Grand Master.'

Seawoll sniggered.

'The Grand Master?' I asked.

'Traditional title of the leader of the Sons of Wayland,' she said. 'Didn't Nightingale tell you?'

'I think he assumed there wasn't one,' I said.

Caroline looked up at where rain was still pounding the skylights.

'Let me get an umbrella,' she said. 'And I'll take you to see her.'

Having procured a pink and yellow polka-dot umbrella from a stand by the door, Caroline led us away from the pool house down a path paved with tan concrete slabs. It had probably originally been intended to wind through an attractive terraced garden, which had subsequently been left to be overrun by the forest. As we threaded our way through the dripping trees, the clanging sound got louder and the rhythm of the hits became obvious – it was the sound of someone hammering metal. As we got closer I saw flashes of light radiating, like lens flare in a film, from a single point ahead. The path opened into a small clearing in front of an open-fronted Nissen hut made of rusty corrugated iron that extended back into the hillside.

There, sheltered from the rain, worked the Grand Master.

She was a short East Asian woman in her late twenties, dressed in jeans, sensible steel-toed work boots and a scarred leather apron over a long-sleeved grey cotton sweatshirt. She had an angular face with a dramatically pointed chin, a small mouth, snub nose and black hair pulled back into a ponytail. Behind her thick protective glasses her eyes were large and black.

Those eyes flicked up briefly to clock us arriving, but then it was back to work. The workspace looked like every other modern smithy I've been in. Shelves and workbenches, bundles of metal rods, sturdy metal and plastic containers full of useful bits and pieces, metal sinks, a water tank for quenching, racks for tools, gas tanks to drive the forge and a utilitarian cement floor with a drain. The Grand Master had two anvils – a standard farrier's type for dropping on cartoon characters, and a broader-topped one with no horn that she was currently using. A blade-maker's anvil.

If the weird lens flare flashes weren't a sufficient giveaway, as I got closer I could sense the spell she was using to enchant her workings. Too fast and concussive to get a read on her *signare*, but it was different. Not like mine or Nightingale's, or even the weird yin–yang thing Guleed was rocking these days.

'Hello,' I said. 'My name's Peter Grant.'

The Grand Master ignored me and continued hitting

the blade with a hammer. A leaf-bladed spearhead, I saw, with a long neck and flanges to stop it going in too deep.

'You know that's an illegal weapon, right?' I said – more to make conversation.

'Wait until she's finished,' said Caroline. 'Have you got no manners?'

The Grand Master gave the spear blade a last smack, held it up in front of her face and turned it left and right to examine it before laying it down on a stone-topped workbench to cool. I noticed that she only wore a glove on her left hand, which held the tongs – the right, in which she held the hammer, was bare.

Once she'd carefully placed her hammer in a rack, she turned to Caroline and started signing.

I'd learnt a bit of BSL in training, just enough to say 'yes/no', 'police', 'are you OK?' and 'please make your way to the nearest emergency exit.' All of which I realised I had completely forgotten.

Caroline signed back and the Grand Master signed again.

'This is Grace Yutani, Grand Master and current custodian of the archive of the Sons of Wayland,' said Caroline. Then, after another flurry of signing by Grace, 'And keeper of the *true* secret flame.'

Seawoll signed his own name, but Caroline had to introduce me and Danni.

I had a million questions, but when you don't know where to start you go with trivia to break the ice. I pointed at the spearhead cooling on the workbench.

'What's this for, then?' I asked, and Caroline signed.

Grace signed back.

'Dragon spear,' said Caroline, but I remembered to keep my eyes on Grace.

'Are you expecting to meet a dragon?' I asked, and remembered Brook had mentioned them, too. Perhaps dragons were a northern thing, like flat caps and an ingrained sense of grievance.

'I don't know,' signed Grace. 'But it'll work with fish as well.'

I wanted to touch it and see what *vestigia* it had, but I figured that would be a mistake and not just because I would burn my fingers.

'We heard you had a break-in?' said Seawoll. 'Somebody stole a lamp.'

Grace flinched when Caroline translated, and frowned at her friend, who then signed back. I didn't need a translation to know that Caroline was denying she was the source of that information.

She didn't want us to know, I thought. *I wonder why?*

'We had a break-in,' signed Grace, and then crossed her arms across her chest.

'But you didn't think to report it?' asked Seawoll.

Grace kept her arms crossed and glared at Caroline.

'You've seen who lives here,' said Caroline. 'Whom do you think I should have called?'

'You should have called Peter here,' said Seawoll. 'He likes cats.'

'We didn't think it was any of the Folly's concern.'

'Two people are fucking dead,' said Seawoll. 'Perhaps if you'd fucking reported this we might have got to them first.'

This, I thought, was highly unlikely, but it had its effect. After Caroline had signed her the gist, Grace uncrossed her arms.

'We had no reason to think it was a significant item,' she signed. 'We thought the thief had snatched it while running away from the ladies.'

Because, while sleeping, eating and watching soaps were the ladies' primary activity, a couple of them liked to go out at night and prowl around the forest.

'And do what?' asked Danni.

'We don't ask,' said Caroline. 'But they have to wash up before they're allowed indoors. Anyway, the screaming woke me and I ran out to see what was going on.'

'Who was screaming?' asked Seawoll.

Danni had her notebook out by then and was taking notes.

'The ladies,' said Caroline. 'They have a very distinctive scream but I didn't think it was anything important – sometimes they can be very cat. So I got up and went out to tell them to shut up.'

Seawoll asked Grace, through Caroline, where she'd been when the screaming started. When Caroline went to answer for her, she slapped her hand on the bench. They exchanged looks and Caroline dutifully signed the question. Grace signed back.

'She was fast asleep because nobody bothered to wake her,' said Caroline. 'We share the pool house, and the ladies are my responsibility so I didn't think it was worth ruining her beauty sleep.' She signed the last bit with more emphasis.

Grace signed again – also with emphasis.

'We're a couple,' said Caroline to us wearily, and then she signed something angrily back at Grace, who crossed her arms again.

Two monomaniacs and a litter of cat-women, I thought. *That's got to be an interesting family dynamic – not to mention the basis of an exciting new reality show.*

'Anyway, I saw someone dodging out of here carrying something heavy, with Mildred and Sophia in hot pursuit,' said Caroline. 'They were having a great time, by the way.'

That 'someone' looked like a woman, according to Caroline, but she was dressed in black or dark blue, 'with one of those tight hoods, like a hijab but not', so Caroline couldn't be sure.

That would have been Lesley, I thought, *in full ninja mode.*

Caroline had done what she called an 'assisted jump' to close down the distance.

'Nearly hit a tree, by the way,' she said. 'Which is why you shouldn't fly on instruments without instruments.' Grace laughed when Caroline signed that – a sort of breathy giggle like one of Abigail's foxes. 'Then I hit them with a tangle and down they went.'

I was dying to know what a tangle was, but knew I'd have to wait.

'My main concern was getting to them before Mildred and Sophia,' said Caroline. 'But I think she hit them with a serious *impello* and, the next thing I know, they're flying in my direction. So I had to catch them, didn't I?'

While she did that, Lesley used the time to regain her

feet and head down slope. She'd talked about having a bike close by, and looking at the map on my phone it looked like there were houses and cul-de-sacs. Plenty of places to stash a bike – had she meant a motor-bike rather than a pushbike? No, a pushbike would be silent, with no number plate to get caught on CCTV. A pushbike which she rides downhill to the outskirts of Manchester, where she has a car ready to go.

Only something happens.

'I got one last shot at her,' said Caroline. 'I could see movement at the bottom of the hill so I cast a *radiradi* at her. Given how far away she was, it didn't have any effect.'

A *radiradi* was one of her mother's spells, handed down to her from *her* mother.

'A couple of *formae* that you lot at the Folly don't use,' said Caroline. 'It creates a sort of thunderclap at a dis-tant point. Sometimes lightning, too, depending on the weather conditions. You can change the *inflectentes* to vary the effect but I was aiming for maximum bang.'

And maximum bang is what she got. And a flash of light.

And everything goes white and then black – Lesley.

I looked at Seawoll and Danni, who were both think-ing the same thing as me. Pushbike or motorbike, a loud bang might have drawn attention. Throw in an accurate time frame, and the fact that Lesley would have been desperate to escape vengeful cats, and we had a good chance of tracking her movement.

Better still, we had the location for where the Angel of the Lamp had escaped. Unless she spent her hours between hits hidden in hyperspace – a possibility I wasn't going to think about – then we might be able to track her movements as well.

So we divided up the tasks. As senior magic wrangler, I would go into the archive with Grace and see what we could find from the crime scene. Danni would go into the woods with Caroline and see if she could trace the route of the chase and look for clues. Seawoll would return to the pool house, where there was a phone signal, and extract some co-operation from the GMP and Derbyshire Constabulary.

'And what if the ladies wake up while you're gone?' he asked.

'Tea and biscuits,' said Caroline, over her shoulder as she headed out. 'And be charming. Oh, and ask about their knitting.'

Grace beckoned me to the back of the forge, where a double-width roll-up metal door opened into an equally wide rectangular corridor. This only went back five or six metres before making a right-angle turn to the right. The original single-bulb light fittings had been ripped out and their cables rerouted to power a single line of fluorescent tubes. In accordance with the iron law of creepy ambience, every third or fourth tube was either out or flickering fitfully. The walls were bare concrete and the floor cement. I recognised the style – this was either Second World War or early Cold War British engineering at its most functional. The original Quatermass would have had a bunker like this. I'd have suspected a nuclear shelter except that, etched into the massive steel doors that were embedded every five metres in the left-hand wall, was the hammer and anvil sigil of the Sons of Wayland.

This was no hurriedly repurposed command centre. It had been purpose-built to house the archive. Beneath the sigil, each door had interlocking circles scored into the surface at waist height. These I associated with the wards and defences on the vault door back at the Folly, but when I let my fingers brush against the steel of the doors there wasn't even a whisper of *vestigia*.

Built, but not finished then.

After a hundred metres we reached a spiral staircase constructed to exactly the same specification as the ones in the Tube. It even had the same railings and cross-hatched foot grips on the risers. Since an unfortunate incident where I was buried alive, I've developed a well-founded caution about cramped underground spaces, so I didn't really want to go down. But down we went.

To stop at a landing and enter another long corridor identical to the one above. How much stuff did the Sons of Wayland stash away before the war – and why? Grace stopped at the third door and pointed at the lock – or rather, the hole in the metal where the lock should have been.

I put my hand up to get her attention and mimed touching the lock – she nodded.

The *vestigia* was the same muddled set of impressions as the lock on Althea Moore's door back in London. Only now I knew who'd worked the spell, I could feel the tick-tock and razor strop of Lesley's *signare*. Grace motioned me inside and I saw that I'd overestimated the amount of stuff you could store here. The room was a cement cell three metres deep and two wide. Instead of the floor-to-ceiling shelves I'd expected, there were free-standing cabinets separated from each other by half a metre. One had had its doors ripped off, allowing me to see that the doors and walls were at least three centimetres thick and made of dense hardwood.

I pulled on my nitrile gloves and squatted down for a good look. I do have a full exhibits kit in a go bag in the boot of the Asbo, but that was back at the Folly. Something told me that Caroline and Grace would not welcome a full forensics team tramping over their nice secret magic stash – not to mention asking difficult questions like 'Are these your cat-women?' The interior of the cabinet was a metre high and after I mimed measuring the height of a missing object, Grace indicated that it had been seventy centimetres tall.

The lamp had been larger than I thought. This explained why Lesley had had trouble legging it down the hill. I wondered why she hadn't zapped one or more of the 'ladies'. Lesley was a murderer – had shot a man in the head in cold blood, right in front of me. But hardened killers, outside of war zones, are rarer than people think. It probably would have been a last resort. Still, between Caroline flinging mystical smoke ropes to tangle and Lesley putting up shields and possibly returning fire, they had triggered the lamp.

Wood is terrible at retaining *vestigia* – which presumably was why these cabinets were made of it – so I wasn't surprised to feel nothing inside. There was a shallow internal drawer at the top – with no metal fittings, I noticed – that looked suitable for storing documents.

I mimed opening it and Grace signed knocking twice with her right fist – 'yes' in BSL. I was glad to realise some of it was coming back.

Gingerly, and holding my head as far back as I could, because you never know, I opened the drawer and extracted yet another manila folder. Inside was another tissue-thin carbon copy of a typed letter – the faded letters read:

WARNING DANGEROUS. MAGICALLY ACTIVE.
HANDLE WITH CAUTION

ITEM: One (1) Iberian patterned lamp 30" tall with opaque fluting of faience in the Egyptian manner. Active containment intaglio in gold and silver around base and brass top cap. Hebrew lettering, also in silver, on cap and on the bottom of the base. Believed to be a containment vessel for a Class A malignancy. Formerly stored at Bevis Marks Synagogue, London – requested for special storage by Sir Leon Davies FSW as part of war contingency plans.

I knew the term 'malignancy' from the reading I've done as part of my training. From the Latin *malignus* – 'wicked, bad-natured' – another catch-all term like 'fae' that could mean anything. Except I didn't think 'Class A' indicated that it was top streamed at school.

'We need to find out where this came from,' I said, and then, remembering, pointed upwards.

11

Communication

Police work can be frustratingly slow at times – you're always hanging around waiting for backup or a prisoner van or forensics, or for a suspect to arrive home, or just sometimes waiting for a witness to calm down enough to give a statement. Police work out of your area can be even slower because you have to keep explaining things to senior officers who have never heard of you and have their own problems, thank you very much, without a bunch of Londoners turning up and telling them what to do. According to Caroline, Seawoll's accent grew noticeably more regional during these conversations, see-sawing between Glossop, Bolton and Stockport with occasional pure Manc when he was swearing. To be honest, it all sounded the same to me. But I'm a soft southerner so what do I know?

One thing you learn early on in your career is how to fit refs into your shift. Especially now that senior management have decided to reduce the influence of 'canteen culture' by closing all the canteens. I can live without the racism and the misogyny, but I miss the food – and the camaraderie, of course.

These days you can drop a copper anywhere and they will have sussed out the nearest and most economical takeaway, greasy spoon, kebab shop or, if all else fails, fake KFC establishment. Out here on the outskirts of Glossop, and far from civilisation, we were treated to a Grace Yutani special – which seemed to be pan-fried tofu in a teriyaki sauce with rice and steamed mini-broccolis.

'What about the ladies?' I asked, as I helped Caroline lay the table.

'They don't eat tofu,' said Caroline, 'and they're perfectly capable of feeding themselves.'

I immediately thought of soup bowls full of raw meat, and it must have shown on my face because Caroline laughed.

'They're not obligate carnivores and they definitely have to cook their food,' she said. 'The bastard didn't alter their biochemistry that far. The evil fucker was only interested in surface appearances anyway.'

We ate in silence so that Caroline and Grace could use both hands for eating. Before we'd finished, Seawoll got a call that the GMP were about to arrive at the bottom of the hill to start their evidence sweep and house-to-house inquiries. Pausing only to finish his rice, my rice and the leftovers in the pot, he left and took Danni with him.

This suited me because I wanted to talk to Grace and I didn't think she'd talk with Seawoll in the room. I wanted to know if she knew why the remaining leadership of the Sons of Wayland had kept their new archive secret from the Folly.

'There were plenty of senior practitioners left at the Folly in 1946,' I said. 'Ones that hadn't been on active duty. I'm guessing this was true of the Sons of Wayland, too.'

'Not so many Sons,' Grace signed. 'Many of the senior masters were killed when their headquarters was bombed.'

'I heard about that,' I said. 'Unlucky.'

'Maybe not luck,' signed Grace. 'Maybe treachery.'

'Treachery by who?' I asked, not liking where this was going.

Grace gave a complex shrug that Caroline didn't need to translate.

'There was always a rivalry,' signed Grace. 'Resentment at the skills of the smiths. And there's the whole north–south thing.'

'I'm sorry,' I said. 'You think someone at the Folly leaked the location of the Sons of Wayland's secret wartime HQ to the Nazis because they preferred rugby union to rugby league?'

Which got a blank look from Caroline even as she translated, and an equally blank look from Grace when she saw the signing.

'Never mind,' I said. 'What's your evidence?'

'There was a famous V1 raid on Christmas Eve 1944,' signed Grace. 'Two flights of Heinkel He 111s approached the coast of Yorkshire and launched forty-five . . .' There was another flurry of conversation as Caroline checked her translation . . . 'Cruise missiles aimed at Manchester.'

Fourteen fell into the sea and most of the rest fell onto open fields. Only a couple did proper damage, killing forty-two people and injuring just over a hundred more. One landed in Hollingwood, completely destroying the wartime headquarters of the Sons of Wayland.

'It's a puzzle,' signed Grace. 'The missiles came down from Spennymoor to Northamptonshire. Do you really think it's a coincidence that of the two that did real damage, one of them took out the headquarters?'

'Coincidences happen all the time,' I said. 'And if the VIs were that inaccurate, how would they aim it at one particular building? Especially one in a built-up area?'

'The Germans originally planned to use radio for terminal guidance,' signed Grace – I think she had to spell out *terminal*. 'But that proved impractical. I think for this particular attack they may have used magic.'

'How?' I asked, and Caroline opened her palms and banged them together.

'I've been up on the moors,' signed Grace, 'and found all the crash sites I could. You'd be surprised how much of a bomb survives its detonation. Most of the wreckage had been recovered after the war, but there was enough for me to determine that in at least three instances there had been significant enchantment associated with a missile. A definite *vestigium* associated with all three. The sense of a raven in flight.'

I thought of the ghost of the raven – a ghost that had responded to German commands, that had so confidently joined the other ghosts, the human ones, for their final departure. Could you train or enchant ravens to fly a VI? Weirder shit had happened during the Second World War, including gigantic Catherine wheels, anti-tank dogs and incendiary bats.

'That would be evidence that the *Ahnenerbe* were

experimenting with Vis,' I said. The *Ahnenerbe* being the mystical branch of the SS. The ones that had weaponised the pre-war German magical establishment and run the camp at Ettersberg. 'Not that somebody at the Folly betrayed the Sons of Wayland.'

'It doesn't matter if it's true,' signed Grace. 'The surviving masters thought it might be – that's why they kept this location secret.'

'Not from the Society of the Rose,' I said, which got a gratifying double take out of Caroline.

When the gentlemen of the Society of the Wise froze out the women, perhaps they imagined they would return to 'proper' feminine pursuits. Which just goes to show that the Society of the Wise was no such thing, because many female practitioners formed their own society. Although they never had a hope of getting royal patronage.

'When did you learn that name?' she said – which was a mistake, of course, because now my suspicions about her, her mum and the 'others' that helped out with the Ladies were confirmed. She'd have been better off pretending not to know what I was talking about.

I looked directly at Grace.

'This is not sustainable,' I said. 'We have to establish some form of co-operation between all the magical disciplines or people like Lesley are just going to walk all over us.'

Grace made that hissing laugh sound again and signed something, with unmistakable smugness, at Caroline, who hesitated before translating.

'Catch the thief, return the property – then we'll talk.'

Seawoll put me on the train back to London while he and Danni stayed to see if they couldn't track our escaped angel from the Manchester end.

'I don't want your missus coming after me,' he said. 'Plus I think the people this angel woman is after are probably all in London. You'd be better deployed as a counter there.'

I went back in economy class with a delay for engineering works, feeling a bit like a chess piece in somebody else's game.

I phoned Bev after the train left Stockport and was relieved that nobody seemed to be constructing anything in the background. Whatever the big diggy thing had been for, they weren't using it just yet.

'I missed you,' she said. 'How was the North?'

'Friendly, open and honest.' I said. 'Also strangely whippet-free.'

'You obviously went to the wrong bit,' she said. 'Are you going to have this case wrapped up soon?' There was a dangerous edge in her voice – the kind to make anybody living on a flood plain nervous.

'Hope so,' I said quickly.

'Only I don't think the twins are going to hold up much longer,' she said.

I promised that even if I didn't wrap up the case, paternity cover was in place.

'Poor Sahra,' said Beverley. 'You make sure you don't drop her in it.'

We chatted for a bit, but then I heard Abigail calling in the background and Beverley had to hang up. Feeling

I'd done my bit to keep flood insurance premiums in Beverley's catchment area down, I put my phone away and got to work.

Even standard investigations can get complex, which is what the whiteboard is for. It's all too easy to be lost in a welter of conflicting detail. There are thousands of pieces of information, some of which are firm facts, others are inferences from forensics reports or statements by unreliable witnesses, and some are total conjecture. Like your best guess at the theory of the crime. None of them come with reliable labels, or even a soundtrack where the music gives you a clue as to when you've discovered something significant.

This is why modern police have massive data mangles like HOLMES 2, whiteboards and digital displays in their offices and, occasionally, a nice clean pad of A4 and a pen.

I settled for my unofficial notebook and, blasphemously from a policing point of view, an HB pencil.

In 1989 Preston Carmichael found a nifty set of seven platinum puzzle rings inside a hollowed-out book at the Portico Library. Realising that what the library don't know it had, it wouldn't miss, he half-inched them and, possibly because even if he didn't know what it was he could sense their enchantment, he decided to hand them out to the members of his charismatic Bible group. After all, there'd been seven rings and seven of them, so it must have seemed practically ordained by a higher power.

Something happened later that year and the Bible group split up and went their separate ways. Flash forward to the start of this month and Preston Carmichael is tortured and then killed and his ring taken. We'd assumed that murderer and thief were the same person, but now Lesley had shown her hand we knew it was her who stole the ring. Did she sneak in and grab it off his corpse, or had she nicked it prior to his introduction to magical heart surgery?

That was a crucial question.

David Moore and Preston Carmichael were still in touch enough for Moore to have Carmichael's phone number. Had Carmichael been tortured to reveal Moore's details, and had he given up other future victims' names?

David Moore had given away his ring – obviously not so precious to him. At least not until he was suddenly desperate to get it back. Did he think it would protect him?

Dame Jocasta Hamilton had also been a member of the Manchester Bible study group and, unlike Moore, had kept her ring. This hadn't prevented our fiery Angel of Death marching up the stairs to her office. What would have happened if she'd reached Dame Jocasta? Would the ring have protected her?

Which led me to the next question.

Who the fuck was the Angel of Death?

Something – or someone – had been trapped in a 'containment device' or lamp that had originally been stored at the Bevis Marks Synagogue in London. I couldn't keep calling her the Angel of Death, so I decided on Zelda. Because Angela would have been too obvious.

Zelda had been trapped in the lamp for at least eighty years, since the time it was transferred to the Sons of Wayland archives, probably longer. We would have to see if the synagogue knew when it had come into their possession.

When I'd checked up with Nightingale, he'd remembered Leon Davies. He'd been a near contemporary, a graduate of wizard school, a merchant banker in the 1930s. And had been reported missing in action, presumed killed, in 1943. He'd been performing a clandestine mission in French-occupied Morocco. Nightingale didn't know the details.

He'd also been from a prominent Jewish family, which might explain the connection to Bevis Marks Synagogue. Nightingale had said Postmartin, who had contacts everywhere there might be even the possibility of interesting books, would be looking into that connection.

So . . . assume Zelda had been in the lamp for ages, sitting on a shelf in London. Then the lamp had been evacuated first to the Volcrepe factory in Glossop and then, after the war, to the Sons of Wayland's secret bunker. Likewise, a bunch of enchanted platinum astrolabe puzzle rings were hidden in a book and erroneously stored at the Portico Library. I was assuming they, too, were destined for secure storage, but had gone astray.

Somebody American – I decided to call them the Collector – had hired Lesley to tax the lamp. Did Lesley find it on her own, or was she briefed by the Collector? Did the Collector want the rings as well, or was that a side hustle by our favourite former colleague?

Were they even linked? That was a dangerous assumption. Certainly all of the victims so far had possessed rings, but they'd also been part of Preston Carmichael's Bible study group. Perhaps it had nothing to do with the rings – correlation does not equal causation, and all that.

But David Moore had thought the ring would protect him. Was desperate enough to get it back that he tried to rob the Silver Vaults with an Airsoft pistol.

And if the rings really could protect them from Zelda, could they be the key to making a capture and an arrest – if that was possible? Otherwise, what were the alternatives? Nobody had tried shooting her yet. I didn't like the idea, but if we couldn't stop her before she killed again, it might come to that.

We needed to know where Zelda had come from, and what she was doing in the lamp. We needed to know what had happened to the Bible study group in 1989. On the last bit we were in luck, because Guleed called me just after Milton Keynes to let me know that they'd located another individual in the picture – Alastair, the world-class groper.

Guleed picked me up at Euston in her dragon mobile, a second-hand BMW Series 2 convertible in fire engine red that she shared with her fiancé. As inconspicuous as a clown at a funeral, it didn't often get used for police work, but Guleed said that all the pool cars were taken.

'Jocasta Hamilton has left the country,' she said as I climbed into the nice clean leather seat.

'When?'

'Late last night,' said Guleed, pulling out onto the Euston Road with the confidence of a woman who has not only completed the Met's celebrated advanced driving course but can also arrest any fucker that cuts her off at a corner. 'She boarded a private jet at Biggin Hill and flew to the Canary Islands.'

'Are we going to warn the Spanish police?'

'And say what?'

Police forces don't have the resources to babysit people against vague potential threats – especially on a resort island filled with tax exiles, celebrity golfers and other international criminals.

'You're right,' I said.

'And we think we've traced Andrew Carpenter to the States,' said Guleed.

'Let's hope Zelda hasn't discovered air travel, then.'

'Who's Zelda?' asked Guleed.

Alastair McKay lived in three million quids' worth of ugly detached red-brick villa off a private road on the Moor Park Private Estate, just across the north-west boundary of London proper. It wasn't gated or nothing, but a discreet green sign made it quite clear that this was, in case we hadn't twigged yet, private land and CCTV was in operation.

'And, no doubt, minimum wage pretend police,' said Guleed, who had become ill-disposed towards Mr McKay when she discovered he wrote for *The Spectator*.

'And *The Times*, and the *Telegraph*,' I said.

'Don't,' she said. 'I may lose my objectivity.'

It wasn't even the biggest or the ugliest villa that

lurked behind the walls or the front lawns you could play tennis on. All of them were built in a strangely utilitarian style, like enormous council houses, with undecorated flat facades of red brick and PVC windows.

There was a horseshoe drive.

I was expecting a maid, a housekeeper or an au pair to answer the door, but a vigorous white man in his mid-fifties opened the door. His hair was still thick and curly with just a bit of grey, and the jaw was still strong, and the eyes, when they switched to Guleed, still leering.

'Mr Alastair McKay?' asked Guleed, showing her warrant card. 'My name is Detective Sergeant Sahra Guleed. This is my colleague Peter Grant. May we come in?'

He hesitated, which was sensible, I wouldn't let the police into my house straight away and I *am* the police.

'Is this about Preston and David?' he said.

'May we come in?' said Guleed.

He nodded and stepped aside to let us in. The hallway was spacious, with a modern steel-frame staircase leading up, doors to either side and a door at the end, through which I could see a black dining table with a pale blue mug steaming on it.

Alastair led us into a vast kitchen–dining-room–lounge combo that took up the entire width of the house. The decorator had obviously tried to fill it with expensive furniture, but had run out of budget and been forced to space everything out to make it look less empty. You could have raced a go-kart in a figure of eight around the dining table and the granite-topped island in the kitchen area. Although the polished white marble floor was probably a skid hazard.

When we eventually reached the piano-finish varnished mahogany dining table, Alastair picked up his mug, put it down again and offered us coffee or tea. Guleed said no thank you in her fake Cheltenham Ladies' College accent, and I realised that we were playing sophisticated attractive hijabi cop and lumpish cockney sidekick. I tried to cultivate my inner Neanderthal but I think it was a wasted effort. Alastair hardly noticed me – he could barely keep his eyes off Guleed.

'It's the forbidden fruit thing,' she'd explained the last time we'd played these roles. 'They fantasise about us being highly contained bundles of repressed sexuality. The bigger the lecher, the more uncontrolled the fantasy.'

Alastair McKay had his lechery under control – finding out that two old acquaintances had been brutally murdered can have that effect.

'Are you sure there's a connection?' he asked.

Guleed said there was, and explained about the potential attack on Jocasta Hamilton.

'Have you suffered any vandalism recently?' asked Guleed. 'Any damage to your property or signs of an attempted break-in?'

Alastair hesitated, and then admitted, yes, there had been.

'Somebody scratched my front door,' he said.

His door had looked pristine when we'd come in.

'So when did this happen?' I asked, putting a bit of Hollywood Brit-thug into my accent. Guleed suppressed a smile.

Alastair said three days previously. He had reported

it to the private security firm which covered the estate, and then had it repainted.

'You didn't report it to us?' I asked.

'It didn't seem worth the trouble,' he said.

His or ours? I wondered.

'Was there like a gang marking?' I said, and Guleed did a strange half-sneeze. 'Or was it just random, like?'

'There was definitely a pattern,' said Alastair.

When we asked if he could remember what it looked like, he went one better and showed us a photograph on his phone. It was almost identical to the design scratched into the door of David Moore's flat in Millwall.

'Mr McKay,' said Guleed. 'Do you own a platinum astrolabe ring?'

Alastair blinked.

'Yes,' he said. 'What has that—?' He looked up suddenly and then back at us – a look of sudden realisation on his face. 'You mean those rings? From Manchester?'

'Do you currently own one?' asked Guleed.

'What's going on?' he asked.

'We think there's a link between the rings, the Bible study group in Manchester and the recent attacks,' I said. In my proper voice, because however amusing Guleed was finding it, I didn't think the stupid cop thing was working.

He had a puzzled look on his face that slowly changed to apprehension. You could practically see his thoughts slowly passing behind his eyes. Guleed had run an IIP check on him as soon as she'd got his name and found he was a semi-journalist. What Stephanopoulos described as that weird breed of posh writers who move between public relations, think tanks and newspapers, and write think pieces before turning up on *The Moral Maze* to tell us how outraged they were.

Skimming his articles in *The Spectator*, *The Economist* and *The Times*, it was apparent that Alastair's particular concern was overpopulation, which he blamed on an overly generous welfare system encouraging the feckless to breed. Since he had six kids of his own, he obviously thought sprog overproduction was fine for the appropriately wealthy. Just the one mother, though, which was odd given what Jocasta had said about him. He hadn't been me-too'd either, but that could just be luck.

He'd gone to Radley College, which was an all-boys boarding school in Oxfordshire. We couldn't get his results and, like most journalists and PR people, his social media was carefully scrubbed to keep things like his exams and school record secret. Manchester University was an odd choice, though – posh kids that fail to reach Oxbridge generally go to Bristol, Edinburgh or, for the true walk of shame, Exeter.

'Why did you go to Manchester?' I asked, and again there was the same slow response to the change of tack. I wondered if he was stoned, or perhaps medicated.

'Girls,' he said suddenly. 'I went for the girls. I thought I'd have a better chance at Manchester than at . . . somewhere else.'

'Why did you think that?' asked Guleed.

'I honestly don't remember,' he said. 'You think lots of stupid things when you're young, don't you? To be honest, I went to an all-boys school, so it's safe to say

I was a bit ignorant of the actual practicalities. There were plenty of girls at Manchester so I was right about that.'

'But then you found religion?' asked Guleed.

Again the delay as Alastair processed. Then he laughed.

'Better to say that I was in love with Jackie,' he said.

'The Jackie who was in the Bible study group?' asked Guleed.

'Of course, of course,' said Alastair. 'In those days you wouldn't have caught me at a group like that otherwise.'

'Do you remember her full name?' I asked, since we hadn't managed to identify her yet.

'Jackie . . .? Jackie . . .?' said Alastair, and then, triumphantly, 'Jacqueline Spencer-Talbot.'

'Was it reciprocated?' asked Guleed, as I texted Jacqueline's full name to Stephanopoulos.

'Definitely reciprocated,' said Alastair. 'Providing I did a bit of praying with her first.'

For a moment a proper leer twisted his lips, although it did look more nostalgic than current. Maybe he was over forbidden fruit. He looked off to the left for a moment – lost in memory – and then back at Guleed.

'She was very convincing. That's why I joined. I do believe in God, though,' he said quickly. 'As in an ultimate creator. You believe in God, obviously. But it's different for me – I didn't have any reason to believe in anything until . . .'

He trailed off.

'Until?' asked Guleed.

'Do you know what the gifts of the Holy Spirit are?' he asked.

We said no just in case he meant something different, but his explanation of how the Holy Spirit gives gifts to good Christians in order to strengthen the Church – that these were essentially miracles for ordinary people – was pretty much the same as the one Dame Jocasta of the blessed Canary Islands had given us.

So, he said, there had been a lot of talking and discussing aspects of the Bible and the real meaning behind certain passages. I asked him which ones, but he couldn't remember.

'I did learn to sleep with my eyes open,' he said.

I remembered one of my mum's many new church experiments, from when I was still young enough to drag to services, had been a series of long and exceptionally dull passages read by members of the congregation. There's something to be said for a professional clergy – especially when they can put some oomph into a sermon. I wished I'd been able to sleep with my eyes open back then, too.

'I thought it was all nonsense, really,' said Alastair, 'until things really happened. And they didn't start happening until we had the rings. At first I thought it was a placebo thing, you know, to encourage us. Like Dumbo's magic feather. Things got a bit freaky after that.'

'Freaky how?' I asked.

Alastair gave a lopsided shrug.

'Do you know what *glossolalia* is?' he asked.

'Speaking in tongues,' said Guleed.

'That's the lay term for it, yes,' said Alastair, and I

could see he was a bit miffed that one of us had actually known what the term meant. 'The idea is that the Holy Spirit gives you a gift to preach the gospel beyond the limitations of your own language. It sounds like gibberish, but if you truly listen it makes sense. That's the theory, anyway.'

'And the practice?' said Guleed.

'It sounded like Spanish to me,' said Alastair. 'Or maybe Portuguese, and once I thought it might be Hebrew or Arabic. I still didn't understand any of it but that's what it sounded like.'

'Who was doing the speaking?' I asked.

'All of us,' said Alastair. 'At the same time.'

'Talk me through the process,' I said. 'And start with where the rings came from.'

He confirmed that Preston Carmichael had brought them with him one day and handed them out. He'd even made a joke about it being seven rings for seven dwarves. Although Alastair admitted that he hadn't got the joke until the first *Lord of the Rings* film came out.

'We sat in a circle with our new rings on, bowed our heads and Preston led us in prayer,' said Alastair. 'Just as he had many times before.'

Only this time it was different – it felt different. When I asked him if he could describe how, Alastair became agitated, waved his hands and expressed frustration and worry.

'This is going to sound like I'm mad,' he said.

'No,' said Guleed in a firm posh accent. 'On the contrary, we think you might have the key to the whole mystery.'

'I felt something flow between us,' said Alastair. 'A sort of power.'

'Can you describe this sensation?' I asked.

'Like the shade you get in hot countries like Italy,' said Alastair, 'where the landscape is all sunny but you're sitting on a terrace in the shade with a cold drink. And there was an animal smell, a living animal, and perfume. It smelled like Jackie's perfume as well. Sort of lemony.'

Nothing like the bell-like silence and the hymnal that I'd sensed around the Angel.

'Then what happened?' asked Guleed.

'Nothing,' he said. 'Until later that night. I'm shaken awake by this blonde girl who's yelling that I'm having a nightmare.'

The blonde girl, whose name Alastair couldn't remember, had been a hook-up at a party he'd gone to after the prayer meeting. She said he'd been shouting in his sleep. When he asked, 'Shouting what?', she'd said that it had sounded like Spanish.

'Six o'clock the next morning, we're all in a café opposite the campus talking about what the hell had just happened to us,' said Alastair.

He couldn't remember exactly what everyone said. Jackie, he was sure, had said she'd been dreaming in Hebrew. She knew because of the letters. The others had similar tales of waking up shouting, or dreaming in a foreign language.

'I think we tried to convince ourselves it was a sort of mass hallucination,' said Alastair. 'But at the same time we wanted to do it again.'

They'd literally marched over to Preston's house and demanded he lead another session. He said he'd be delighted, but they'd have to wait until the evening when he was finished at work.

'We really didn't want to wait,' said Alastair. 'We'd have done it morning, noon and night.'

And probably killed yourself with magic, I thought. *And what was left of your brains would have ended up in the Folly's frighteningly extensive brain collection to serve as an awful warning to future apprentices.*

'Why?' asked Guleed.

'It was exciting,' said Alastair. 'A revelation. That evening, when we prayed again, I could feel myself being . . .' He made grasping motions with his hands. 'Being filled up with the Holy Spirit. Becoming close to God. I've taken some drugs . . . this was better. Better than alcohol – better than sex, even.'

They held prayer meetings for three more days.

On the first night they found themselves talking to each other in tongues – or, at least, in foreign languages they didn't speak.

'And definitely some Latin,' said Alastair. 'Which I'd done at school, of course.'

'Of course,' I said.

'And had never really got the hang of it – all those declensions,' said Alastair. 'But that evening we sat in the pub afterwards and chatted away – in Latin! Like we'd been speaking it all our lives.'

'Hard *c* or soft *c*?' I asked.

'I beg your pardon?'

'Did you pronounce it wenee, widee, weeshee,' I said, ignoring Guleed's puzzled look, 'or weekee?'

'It's funny you should ask that,' said Alastair. 'Somebody else asked me the same question once. Why is it important?'

'It's not really that important, but it would be useful to narrow down what flavour of Latin you were speaking,' I said.

This threw Alastair into confusion and got me a definite bit of side-eye from Guleed – who has picked up some prejudices from Seawoll and Stephanopoulos.

Especially now I had a better and more important question to ask.

'So who asked the same question?'

'Some American guy I got talking to at Davos in January,' he said.

But he couldn't remember the man's name, or even what he was doing at the World Economic Forum – although he wasn't an economist, a journalist or even a friend of will.i.am.'s Nor could he remember what he looked like beyond tanned, fair-haired and middle-aged.

'Maybe West Coast,' said Alastair. 'Had that kind of smoothness.'

He'd asked a lot of bizarre questions about the Bible study group, but Alastair had been more interested in the American's companion.

'Very blonde, very fit. Had big blue eyes and cheekbones you could butter your toast with,' he said. 'Helga, that was her name – Helga from Sweden.'

'So what was your answer?' I asked.

'About what?' asked Alastair.

'The Latin,' I said.

'Suddenly I could speak Latin,' said Alastair. 'It was like something out of *The Matrix*. You know – I know Kung Fu – like that. I didn't notice if I was using a hard *c* or not.'

'You said you met three days in a row,' said Guleed, a little impatiently. 'What happened the next evening?'

'We went and healed the sick,' said Alastair.

12

Faith

They walked into a hospital and bestowed their blessings upon the sick.

'And you saw them get better?' asked Guleed.

'We *felt* them get better,' said Alastair. 'We felt the Holy Spirit, the power of God's love, flow through us and into the sick people. We must have saved the NHS millions that night.'

Although he couldn't say which hospital they'd blessed with their presence.

'Whichever is closest to Fallowfield,' he said airily.

Another follow-up for Seawoll and Danni, I thought, and asked him about the third and final session.

'Prophecy,' said Alastair. 'We saw the future.'

Both me and Guleed were actually struck dumb – which is not a good look in a pair of experienced police officers. Fortunately, Alastair was off with the fairies and so didn't notice, and thus was the much-vaunted mystique of the Metropolitan Police preserved.

Guleed recovered first.

'And what did you see?'

'Jocasta said there would be floods and famines – which I thought at the time was just stating the obvious. But, what with global warming, I think she might have

244

been on to something.' Alastair shook his hand from side to side to show that he kept an open mind. 'David spoke of war in the Middle East,' he said. 'And guess what happened in 1990? Right. I saw the dawning of a new age of understanding, but I'm an eternal optimist. Jessica said the towers would fall and they did, didn't they?'

There was more of this, and I was disappointed because it was exactly the sort of vague prognostication that you get with your daily star sign. Unless Danni reported a rash of medical miracles dating from 1989, then I was seriously doubtful that Alastair and his prayer circle were talking anything but gibberish.

And yet . . . I was sure something had happened over those three days. I suspected it was some of that pre-Newtonian ritual magic that Postmartin was so keen on. He always claimed that it formed the kernel of human religious belief.

'Why do all that chanting and fasting,' he'd said, 'if you don't get something tangible out of it?'

I was yet to be convinced – people did stupid things for stupid reasons all the time, and also a lot of singing and dancing was enjoyable, especially in a group. I was willing to bet that Postmartin had been a romantic bookworm as a youth. Even when he was on active duty in Malaya.

'What happened next?' asked Guleed.

'I went back to my digs and slept,' said Alastair. 'Alone, unfortunately.'

'I meant,' said Guleed, slowly, 'what happened with the group?'

Alastair seemed surprised at the question.

'We never met again,' he said. 'Preston cancelled the next meeting, and the next, and kept cancelling, until one day he wasn't there any more. Jocasta went all exam-mad and Jackie caught feminism and became a lesbian or something.'

'What about the others?' asked Guleed.

'We never saw Preston again,' he said, 'and, to be honest, I don't remember what happened to the rest.'

He remembered the women but not the men. At least he's consistent.

'You didn't think that was odd?' asked Guleed.

'You lose touch with people,' said Alastair. 'You move on.'

'No,' said Guleed. 'You were speaking in tongues and healing the sick. You said the Holy Spirit filled you up and brought you closer to God.' She leant forwards, fixing Alastair with her eyes. 'If I had been taken closer to God I wouldn't have just wandered off afterwards.'

'I think we all had the impression that that was our lot,' said Alastair. 'We had been given our gifts and now we had to go out and do good works. Also, it was . . .' He hesitated, and he winced as if remembering pain. 'Terrifying,' he said, and nodded to himself. 'Getting that close to God. Best not to be greedy.'

'So a close encounter with God,' I said. 'And then back to lectures the next day?'

'It did change me,' he said with some emphasis. 'I was a more serious person after that. If God puts his hand upon your shoulder it leaves a lasting impression.

And I have been blessed in my life. I have to assume it's for a reason.'

'Blessed in what way?' I ask.

'In little ways that add up,' said Alastair.

His first newspaper job, for example, after he'd graduated with a semi-respectable 2:1. An old school chum who had gone to Oxford called him out of the blue and asked if he could write a piece about life up North.

'Because you were at Manchester?' I asked.

'That,' said Alastair. 'And I grew up in Harrogate.'

One article led to another. His friend brought him on as a guest editor and networking did the rest.

'And you think that was down to God?' I asked.

'Either you believe God organises the universe or you don't,' said Alastair. 'And I met my wife when I moved to London.' The smile faded and he looked away. 'That was another blessing.'

I was more inclined to put it down to him being a posh boy with posh friends, the right accent and the right attitude. Still, I've been having my suspicions about the more subtle influence of the supernatural ever since my dad gave up heroin and cigarettes overnight. Just after I'd done Mama Thames a solid.

And that led me back to ritual magic and, of course, the rings.

'Do you still have the ring?' I asked.

'I lost it,' said Alastair, without looking back at us.

We waited, but he didn't elaborate – lost in some other memory.

I glanced at Guleed.

'Can you remember when and where you lost it?' she

asked, and Alastair immediately turned back to look at her.

'I think at Davos,' he said. 'At least I wasn't wearing it when I went through security at the airport. It always set off the metal detector, so I always automatically slipped it off and put it in the tray with my keys and wallet. When I got to security, I went to remove it and found it was missing.' He mimed taking the ring off. His little finger, I noticed. 'I assumed that I'd left it in my bag and went through. Getting on the plane was a scramble – it always is when it's filled with hacks – and I didn't think to check until I got home.'

'So you usually wore it?' I asked.

'Yes.'

'Even when you were asleep?'

'I always wore it,' he said. 'As a sign of God's favour. Also, if you don't take it off you can't lose it.'

'Except you lost it,' said Guleed.

'Yeah,' said Alastair.

Something about the confusion on his face reminded me of Althea Moore when we'd asked her about losing her own ring.

'Did you have companionship on the last night?' I asked.

'What?' said Alastair. 'Did I get laid? Definitely.'

'Was it Helga the impossibly blonde Swede?'

'As it happens,' said Alastair. 'You don't think . . .?'

'Do you remember the sex?'

'What?'

'Do you remember having sex – the positions, who did what to who?'

248

'I'm not . . .' started Alastair and then stopped, a look of horror on his face.

I couldn't help wondering whether that was because his ring had been stolen, or Helga the Swede might have escaped his room without putting out.

We didn't ask for details. Apart from anything else, while we weren't sure whether the rings were a real defence against Zelda of the burning spear, Alastair didn't even have that possible protection.

We told him it was better that he relocated for his own safety. When we asked where his wife and six kids were, he told us California. Something about the way he said it suggested that they might not be coming back. But, from our point of view, his family tragedy was our logistical simplification.

We suggested, strongly, that he book in to the Hotel Russell, which was conveniently located across the square from the Folly. We'd discussed this contingency with Nightingale and, while we weren't keen filling up the Folly with 'guests', it would be handy to have them close by – just in case.

While Alastair was upstairs packing a suitcase, Guleed asked me what all the business about the hard and soft *c*'s was about.

'Latin pronunciation changed over time and different parts of Europe,' I said. 'Ecclesiastical Latin has softer consonants than Classical Latin – I thought it might give us a clue to what time and space the ritual spell came from.'

'Time and space?'

'Region,' I said. 'What country it came from.'

'When do you find time to learn all this stuff?'

'It's like PACE,' I said. 'You learn the basics and pick up the details as and when you need them.'

'The healing and the prophecy didn't seem authentic to me,' she said. 'Why do you think the speaking in tongues is important?'

'Because they weren't speaking in tongues, were they?' I said. 'They were speaking actual languages, which could be connected to the rings, which are probably connected to Zelda, the Angel of Death,'

'Spanish, Latin and Hebrew,' said Guleed. 'But not Arabic. So probably Southern Spain after the reconquest.'

'Or a Jesuit mission in Mexico,' I said. 'Let's see if Postmartin has worked out where the lamp came from.'

Back in the days of the Old Republic, Oliver Cromwell, Lord Protector of England and 360-degree religious zealot, believed fervently in the Second Coming of Christ his Lord, and that one of the preconditions for this was supposed to be the conversion of the Jews to Christianity. The Spanish monarchy, inspired by the same prophecies, took a robust straightforward approach and offered their large Jewish population a simple proposition – convert, leave or die. Most converted, and the rest left, heading for Antwerp, Italy and the Ottoman Empire – anywhere they could find a place of refuge, however tenuous. This approach proved popular in Spain and Portugal, too, and in fact in most Christian countries where the rulers needed to write off some debts, keep the mob happy or curry favour with the Church.

Cromwell, in marked contrast to his approach to the Irish and other dissenting voices, felt that it would be better to convert the Jews by setting an example of how decent, lovely and God-fearing his branch of Christianity was.

His main problem was that all the Jews had been murdered or expelled from England in 1290 by Edward I, and you can't convert people who aren't there. His solution was to advocate readmitting the Jews so that they could be shown the benefits of the true religion. That this would give the English better access to the capital markets of Antwerp and the lucrative spice trade in the Far East probably never crossed his mind – honest.

Cromwell convened an advisory council and asked their advice and they said no. So he convened a grand council consisting of lawyers, merchants and some of the finest and most august theologians in the land, and put the proposition to them.

Their response was *fuck no*.

But Cromwell hadn't got where he was today, effective dictator of England, by letting other people tell him what to do. He invited the Jews back into England to inhabit a strange legal limbo whereby they weren't explicitly tolerated, but neither were they bound up in the sort of rules that circumscribed the lives of Jews in other European countries.

Meanwhile there were, living in London, quite a few 'Portuguese' merchants who were probably not as Christian as the Inquisition might have wished. These were the New Christians, the *Marranos*, descendants of Jews who had converted rather than face death or exile from Spain and Portugal. Unfortunately, merely being baptised and attending church on a regular basis was not enough to allay suspicions, and the Inquisition, first in Spain and then Portugal, persecuted them for fun and the greater glory of God.

Some families forwent the dappled sunlit hills and red-roofed towns of Iberia for the dreary, crowded and pestilential confines of sixteenth-century London. There they could practise the religion of their ancestors in peace – providing they didn't do it in public. When England went to war with Spain, again, these merchants went to court to prove that they were in fact Jewish, not Spanish, and so therefore shouldn't have their stuff nicked by the state. They won their case and the re-settlement of the Jews in England became a matter of common law.

These were the Sephardim, the Jews of the Southern Diaspora, and they built a great synagogue in Bevis Marks in Aldgate, which opened in 1701. There it has survived fire, riots and two rounds of bombing by the Germans and the IRA, to become the oldest synagogue in England still in use.

Shortly after its founding, a Sephardic family going by the name Alfonzo had deposited the lamp at the synagogue.

'Although, maddeningly, there's no mention of why,' said Postmartin, who I'd found in the reading room, sitting at a table covered in papers, books and the remains of a light supper. Toby had jumped on a chair next to him, the better to clean up any crumbs or crusts that might have been left over.

I'd barely managed to sit down before I got the potted history of the early modern Jewish diaspora – or at least the bits of it that related to our mysterious lamp.

'There's no mention of the rings,' said Postmartin. 'But I do have a name – Moses ben Abraham Alfonzo. We have records of the circumcision and bar mitzvahs of two sons, but no record of his death, although he donated a particularly fine silver menorah sent down from Manchester in 1735.'

Postmartin showed me a close-up photograph of the candelabrum revealing that it bore two hallmarks, one of which was the distinctive hammer and anvil of the Sons of Wayland. The other looked like a sideways *A*, which Postmartin identified as the Phoenician letter Aleph.

'Which was associated with a famous Manchester-based jeweller,' said Postmartin, 'whose name was Mordecai Alfonzo. One of Moses Alfonzo's sons, as recorded at Bevis Marks.'

Postmartin tapped the image of the hallmark and managed to put his phone into sleep mode.

'Blast,' he said, and found the picture again.

'A Mordecai Alfonzo is listed as master in the formal rolls of the Sons of Wayland,' he said, 'until his death in 1803. And that surname occurs twice more during the nineteenth century and never again.'

'So the family died out?' I said.

'The name may have changed instead, because the hallmark continued to be used by the firm of Davies and Company.'

'Any relation to Leon Davies?'

'I'm looking into that. But it seems likely, given Leon Davies was the one who committed the lamp into the care of the Sons of Wayland at the start of the war.'

'So Zelda could have been in the lamp for over three hundred years,' I said, and then had to explain who Zelda was.

'That would certainly explain her irritable nature,' said Postmartin, but I was thinking of the raven on the moor and my theory that it had been used as a guidance system for a VI cruise missile.

'Could Zelda be a weaponised ghost?' I asked. 'A variation on the way demon traps are made?'

'She seems a tad too corporeal for that,' said Postmartin. 'But she could be a human being, or even a fae that has been altered to serve as a weapon, and then trapped in a sort of pocket *allokosmos* in the lamp.'

'What – in case of emergency, break glass for Angel of Death?'

'You're making an assumption there, Peter,' said Postmartin, wagging his finger at me. 'You're assuming that whoever created Zelda . . . Ha! I see what you did there. You're assuming that the creator of the weapon was also the creator of the lamp. But perhaps the lamp's purpose was defensive – to trap Zelda before she could eliminate her target.'

'Assuming,' I said, 'that Moses Alfonzo made the lamp to trap Zelda, and assuming that Zelda's not a natural phenomenon or a messenger of a god or gods unknown, then who created her?'

'When you find her,' said Postmartin with a touching faith in our abilities, 'you can ask her.'

I went and found Nightingale in the now repurposed visitors' lounge and we had a group call to Stephanopoulos to brief her on what we found.

'It's all very interesting,' she said. 'But none of it gets us closer to apprehending Zelda.'

'Let's hope Alexander and Danni have more luck at the Manchester end,' said Nightingale.

I drew some lines and squiggles on our whiteboard to show willing while Nightingale set up shop in the atrium – the better to rush out and fight Zelda should she try to have a go at Alastair, now snugly ensconced in the slightly decaying splendour of the Hotel Russell.

'Go home, Peter,' said Nightingale.

And, never one to disobey a lawful order, home I went.

It was dark when I got back to Beverley Avenue, and heavy rain was drumming on the tarpaulin-shrouded shapes that took up the lower half of the garden.

'What are you doing?' I asked Beverley, who was standing on her patio in nothing but a pair of knickers.

'Shush,' she said. 'You'll break my concentration.'

But she turned and held out her hand towards me. I stepped back out into the rain, took her hand, and she wrapped my arm around her so that she could lean back against my chest. I slipped my other arm around the smooth curve of her bulge. I felt two kicks against my palm.

'Soon, babes,' she said. 'Not long now.'

'Tonight?'

'No.' Beverley nodded at the tarpaulin-shrouded

shadows at the end of the garden. 'Things aren't ready yet. But soon . . . Don't leave town again.'

'OK,' I said. 'But you should come in – you'll catch your death.'

She took my palm and kissed it.

'No I won't,' she said.

Beverley's back was warm against my chest, but the rain was beginning to soak through my jacket and shirt.

'Fine,' I said. 'I'll catch my death.'

'You'd better not,' she said. 'But I'll come in if you rub my feet.'

'Deal,' I said.

As she led me by the hand back into the house, all the rain evaporated off her in a cloud of sweet-smelling vapour.

Not off me, by the way – I had to strip off and get a towel.

Monday

An almost fanatical devotion . . .

13

Improvisation

There's nothing the modern copper loves more than attempting the arrest of an armed and dangerous suspect in a public space. Especially when you've had to organise it on the fly while driving to their last known location. But when we looked at the map, it was obvious that we were never going to get a better shot at nicking Zelda with the minimum of risk.

'I don't like it,' said Stephanopoulos, who, while Seawoll was in Manchester, was the senior officer and therefore responsible for everything that went wrong. 'But we don't dare let her evade us again.'

Because, notwithstanding the possible teleporting thing, Zelda was on a narrowboat at a mooring in Kensal Green, which meant she could shift location at any moment the old-fashioned way, by water. We knew she was heading east into the centre of London – so the collateral was only going to get denser.

So me and Guleed arrived at the Ladbroke Grove bridge over the Paddington Branch of the Grand Union Canal and started tooling up. We'd both dug out our uniform Metvests because the outer cover came with pockets and handy clips for attaching Airwaves, hand-cuffs and useful bits of police kit. Like our CS spray and the X-26 Tasers that Stephanopoulos had authorised us to use. Guleed had her extendable baton, but I had half a metre of iron-cored oak stave with a canvas handle at one end and a metal cap at the other. It was a genuine antique Second World War battle staff and I normally didn't get it out of its case, but I reckoned this was a special occasion.

Once we were suitably equipped, we checked on everyone else's status and found that our Sprinter van of TSG and the 'just in case' armed response unit were still ten minutes out. More importantly, Nightingale hadn't reached the Scrubs Lane Bridge, a kilometre and a bit down the canal to the west. Once he and his contingent of TSG were in place, the plan was to cautiously work our way along the towpath from both directions.

'And I mean *cautiously*,' said Stephanopoulos.

Me and Guleed leant against the parapet and stared gloomily towards where the low charcoal clouds brushed the top of the gas towers, and wondered if it was going to rain on us as well.

'It's true what they say about the Job,' said Guleed, hitching her utility belt into a more comfortable position. 'You really do never know what the day's work will bring.'

What it had brought that morning was the Danni report, just as I was pulling into the car park at Belgravia nick.

'We think we've found her,' she said. 'I'm texting you a picture now.'

So I stayed in the Asbo, which had a hands-free kit, and propped my phone on the dashboard.

The picture was of a wild-eyed young woman who I immediately recognised as Zelda. Only her name wasn't Zelda – it was Francisca.

'Spanish?' I asked.

'We think so,' said Danni. 'Or at least from a Spanish-speaking country.'

She'd been found wandering naked and in distress along Glossop High Street first thing in the morning following Lesley's theft of the lamp. An ambulance had been called and, worried by her obvious disorientation, the crew had taken her to Stepping Hill Hospital in Stockport, where she was treated for exposure, dehydration and anaemia. Fearing that she'd been a victim of a sexual assault who'd then been dumped on the moors, the staff called the police.

'That's where the picture comes from,' said Danni.

Francisca continued to present as confused and agitated, and appeared to be unable to speak, although she was clearly trying. The hospital decided to keep her overnight for observation. When she did start speaking the next morning, it was in a language which a Filipino nurse identified as Spanish. Although the nurse said that she had trouble understanding the dialect. They did get her name – Francisca Velasco.

'Apparently there's almost as many Spanishes as there are Englishes,' said Danni. 'You're going to like this bit. When they brought in a Spanish interpreter from the university, he said that while he could understand what she was saying and it was a little bit like Castilian, it was not a dialect he'd heard before. Also, GMP got on to the Spanish consulate, who couldn't find any reports of a missing Spanish citizen of that name. Ditto Argentina and Colombia and the others. A couple of close matches, but nobody who fits the description.'

Needless to say, the GMP were not happy that we'd dug up yet another weird case on their patch and must have been overjoyed to dump this mystery on Seawoll. You can get a lot of co-operation out of other forces if you offer to pick up the tab.

During the previous December, despite now being able to communicate, Francisca continued to present as disorientated and confused, so she was referred to the Mental Health Liaison Team for an assessment, who then admitted her to one of their mental health wards for an evaluation period.

'She was there for two weeks,' said Danni, 'appeared to get much better, and since they needed the beds they moved her to a halfway house. We haven't got her medical records yet but we have talked to the halfway house.'

Who described her as quiet, well-behaved, very clean, maybe obsessively so.

'Apparently she fell in love with the Hoover,' said Danni. 'Would offer to clean people's rooms when she'd finished with the communal areas.'

'Did she have any friends that weren't household appliances?' I asked.

Behind Danni I heard the unmistakable thunk of a car door closing and a distant rumble that I recognised as Seawoll talking to a third party.

'Yeah, one friend,' said Danni. 'A woman called Heather Chalk, born Chester 1986, on the PNC for shoplifting. I'll send you the details in a minute. Also treated as an in-patient for depression, which was why she was at the halfway house too. They got very friendly and she was the one who helped Francisca learn English. Which she did amazingly fast. Then early Feb, both of them walk out of the halfway house and never come back.'

'Just like that?'

'They were both there voluntarily. The staff were concerned but there wasn't anything anyone could do about it,' said Danni. 'It wasn't a police matter.'

Is now, I thought.

'The thing is,' Danni said, 'before she was in hospital Heather was living on a narrowboat on the Macclesfield Canal and that's gone. We asked around and they said Heather had a friend boat-sitting it. We found the friend about an hour ago and she says that Heather took possession again. Had a new friend with her – one that matched Francisca's description.'

Danni, Seawoll and a couple of bods from the GMP had been checking the canal banks either side of the old mooring.

'Can you sail a canal boat from Manchester to London?' I asked.

'Of course you can,' said Danni. 'That's what the canals were built for. But . . . get this. Canal boats have registrations, just like cars, and we have the registration for Heather's boat.'

And a description. Seawoll had already contacted Stephanopoulos to organise a search at the London end. Danni had some friends who lived on narrowboats and she said that the Canal Wardens monitored the boats.

263

'If you've got a cruiser licence you're only supposed to moor up for a maximum of fourteen days,' said Danni. 'So the wardens check registrations regularly.'

And kept surprisingly good records.

'You have to,' said the guy from the Canal and River Trust. 'Or some entitled bugger will squat the best moorings.'

Heather Chalk's boat had been recorded as tied up at the Kensal Green visitor mooring at 10.15 a.m. and we'd been scrambling ever since.

'You need to change your motto,' Stephanopoulos had said over the radio as we headed west for Kensal Rise. 'Knowledge is Power doesn't hack it – it should be *Solum stulti irruunt* – only fools rush in.'

'I rather believe you looked that up specially,' Nightingale had replied.

Me and Guleed stood on the bridge and looked west along the canal.

On the northern bank was a permanent mooring where affluent boaters could pay to enjoy the canal lifestyle without the faff of having to move every two weeks. On the southern bank was the towpath proper, modern flats, beyond them a red-brick mega-Sainsbury's with its own access to the path and a stop-and-shop mooring – maximum stay four hours. Two narrowboats were tied up there.

'There's an inlet just there,' said Guleed, pointing to where a channel cut under the modern flats. 'Leads to a water activity centre.'

Just before the canal turned out of sight, there was a humpback bridge over an inlet that no longer existed, we thought, and then a couple of hundred metres beyond that, out of sight around the bend, the public mooring where Heather Chalk's boat had been recorded the previous afternoon.

'We want to stage on the lump there,' said Guleed, pointing to the vestigial humpback bridge.

We would be between Francisca and the Sainsbury's. There the north bank was filled with nothing but the stone-studded expanse of Kensal Green Cemetery and, on the towpath side, a decommissioned gasworks that was now a storage site for scaffolding, and the mainline railway track.

'And an electrical substation,' said Guleed. 'What could possibly go wrong?'

'Better than a school,' I said. 'Or a market.'

Nightingale reported that he'd reached his bridge and was deploying. Our TSG contingent called to say they were still five minutes out – traffic being heavy. I was calling our armed response unit when Guleed banged me on the arm with the back of her hand.

'Two women,' she said. 'On the hump.'

I grabbed my binoculars from the Asbo and had a look.

Two white women. I didn't need to check the descriptions because I recognised one of them from Middlesex Street – although minus the burning halo.

'It's them,' I said, and Guleed called it in.

Both women were dressed in jeans, jumpers and waterproofs. Heather Chalk's jumper was cream-coloured and bulky, Francisca's was a mad mix of purple, blues, reds and oranges as if hand-knitted from multicoloured wool. It was the kind of jumper that white kids get for Christmas from eccentric grandmothers. Their waterproofs were zip-up cagoules in orange and navy blue. Sensible clothes for living on a boat in the middle of winter.

Francisca was pulling a canvas shopping trolley.

The two women were chatting as they came down the steep slope. Relaxed, companionable – routine.

'They're doing their shopping,' I said. 'Sainsbury's.'

'Fuck, fuck, fuck,' said Guleed – which was the most swearing I'd ever heard her do. 'We need to keep eyes on – with luck they'll come back the way they came.'

'It can't be me, she's seen me,' I said, but Guleed was already stripping off her kit and dumping it in the back of the Asbo.

'Don't let any of the TSG lot steal my vest,' she said. 'I've just had it adjusted.'

By the time the two women had turned into the supermarket's back gate, Guleed was sauntering down the towpath towards them. Stephanopoulos, who had a map in front of her, ordered me to take position at the gate as soon as they were out of sight.

The TSG would drive their Sprinter around and park in front of the Sainsbury's. People are used to seeing police vans parked up around the place, and as long as nobody did anything stupid – Stephanopoulos left a menacing pause after that phrase – our targets should ignore it.

The armed response unit were to park on the bridge and act as reserve.

Nightingale's team would advance up the towpath from their end, and secure the narrowboat while Nightingale took position on the humpback bridge thing.

'Everybody stay calm,' said Stephanopoulos. 'Guleed, don't get too close – we have a perimeter around the supermarket so we can always reacquire them when they leave.'

'They're going in through the main entrance,' Guleed said. 'Temporary loss, I'm following.'

In the background was the unmistakable clatter of shopping trolleys being shunted about.

I trotted over the raised section of the towpath and tucked myself in beside some bushes on the reverse slope, where I could keep an eye on the gate. Ahead, the two-storey-high brick and crinkly tin box of the supermarket stretched out along the towpath like a 1950s American caravan that had really let itself go. Its aluminium cladding managed to be an even duller grey than the sky. There was a scattering of uninspired tags sprayed on the walls, and I couldn't help thinking that more graffiti could only improve its looks.

I glanced back at the bridge and was pleased to see that the armed response officers were hidden from view. Armed police tend to cause consternation when they turn up at anywhere that's not an obvious terrorist target.

'I have eyeball on both subjects,' said Guleed over the radio. Oh, 'they've got Island Delight.' There was a pause. 'It would be suspicious if I didn't put things in my basket.'

'Grab some biscuits, then,' I said, because the

stake-out bag in the Asbo was getting bare dry. And then I thought of the canal. 'And some bananas.'

'Fair trade or ordinary?' said Guleed loudly, and then softer. 'Heather is checking her purse – I think money must be short.'

It started to drizzle and I started to wish I'd worn my hoody over my kit. I looked over at the humpback bridge and saw Nightingale standing by the parapet. In his good suit. And he should have stood out, but with a city gent's black umbrella unfurled over his head, he was strangely too incongruous to look out of place. A man gazing over the cemetery opposite and contemplating the infinite.

'We're in position,' he said over the radio.

'Good,' said Stephanopoulos. 'We have all the access points covered – everybody needs to hold position until I say so. I don't suppose Thomas has a plan for when they come back out.'

'Assuming they return through the back gate,' said Nightingale.

We probably should have set up Bronze, Silver and Gold command levels but since Nightingale would have been the obvious senior officer and we needed him to get up close and personal with the suspect, we opted to do without. This is what's known as operational flexibility, and definitely not making it up as you go along.

'When they emerge, and assuming that nobody else is in the way, we'll let them walk ten feet or so in my direction before Peter leaves cover. Guleed takes position at the gate, joins Peter as he passes, Uniform 235 –' the TSG mob in the car park – 'move to create a perimeter, likewise Trojan One –' the armed response officers – 'stop up the towpath at the bridge end. When we're ready, Peter calls out to get Francisca's attention – while she's distracted, I come down from my position and attempt to subdue her. Peter will assist me while Sahra captures Francisca's friend.'

Everybody else would move in to secure the area.

We had contingency plans for if they didn't come via the back gate, in which case we all pull back and let Guleed and some hastily de-uniformed TSG maintain surveillance until such time as they returned to the narrowboat.

But they came out the back gate and at first everything went according to plan.

'Francisca, Heather!' I called. 'Wait up!'

Looking back, I think using Francisca's name was probably a mistake. We learnt later that she'd hidden her real name from any casual acquaintances she and Heather had met on the journey down. Me knowing her name immediately marked me as official and/or potentially hostile.

Still, using people's real names as a de-escalation tactic had been ingrained into me in training, and it's such an obvious move. People hesitate when they hear their name – they take time to process whether or not you're friend or foe. That's the theory, anyway.

They'd been just where Nightingale had wanted them, beyond the stop-and-shop mooring and the tarnished silver bulk of the Sainsbury's, and a couple of metres short of the steep climb to the top of the humpback bridge. I was three metres behind them, with Guleed a couple of metres behind me, doing a convincing 'I'm an ordinary member of the public coming back from the shops' impression. Helped by the Sainsbury's bags she was carrying.

Heather and Francisca were dragging the – now obviously overstuffed – shopping trolley between them, each with one hand on the handle.

Francisca said something that made Heather laugh.

I called their names. Like I said – possibly a mistake.

They stopped and turned to look at me. Heather looked puzzled, but Francisca recognised me at once. She jumped forwards, lifting into the air and arching towards me as if she'd bounced off a trampoline. Obviously Caroline had not been the only practitioner to invent almost-flying.

As she flew towards me, wings of fire sprang from her back and white light blazed behind her head. Her face was contorted into an angry snarl and her eyes blazed – literally.

But I've been trained. Better, I've been trained by the man who held the rearguard at Ettersberg. And, practically without thought, I brought my staff up and raised a shield.

I felt the smooth rich honey hum of the staff as it gave up its power, but even so I staggered back when she collided with my shield. There was an almost comical look of surprise on her face, but then she scowled and the wings swept around to try and engulf me.

I shifted the focus of the shield, swinging it round and down like an invisible fly swatter. Francisca gave a satisfyingly un-angelic squawk as she was flipped onto her back. Light flared in her hand and suddenly the burning spear was there. The tip was too bright to look at, but even as Francisca used the butt to lever herself upright, I could see Nightingale closing the distance behind her.

She must have sensed him, because while she was still on her knees she swung the spear in an arc at my face.

The spear cut through my shield as if it wasn't there. I desperately threw myself backwards, and even so the burning tip passed close enough for me to feel heat – real heat this time.

I fell onto my back and rolled – expecting the spear point to kill me any moment. But as I came up I saw Francisca had turned to engage Nightingale. He didn't bother with a shield, but ducked under the wing aimed at him. His left hand thrust out and, with a sound like cloth being torn, a section of Francisca's burning wing was wrenched loose.

She bellowed in pain, but didn't even hesitate before whirling to swing her remaining wing at Nightingale. He dodged, but it was a feint and she thrust her spear at his chest. I saw him make a chopping motion with his left hand and the spear deflected down into the towpath. There was a bang and a geyser of pulverised concrete fountained out of the ground. Nightingale rolled to the side, perilously close to the edge of the canal.

Further up, I could see Guleed dragging Heather away. The woman was kicking and screaming, but Guleed was ignoring the blows landing around her face and shoulders. Her priority was to get the member of the public away from the mad fight in front of them.

Two TSG officers were dashing down from the inlet bridge to help.

Francisca reared up and spread her wings – the damaged one repairing as I watched. But I didn't watch too long. First I lobbed a glitter bomb at Francisca's feet and popped a blinder in front of her face to distract her. She shrieked in pain as the *lux* variant went off like an industrial-strength flashbulb, and Nightingale used the distraction to shift away from the canal. The glitter bomb exploded in a rush of freezing air but Francisca seemed to dance over the shock wave, and I threw myself aside as a wing swept towards me. I saw her look over to where Guleed and the two TSG officers were bodily carrying her friend away.

She started towards them, but Nightingale cut her off. His shield splashed with fire as Francisca's wings tried to bat him out of the way. She hesitated a moment, spear upraised, and then she turned and ran.

Across the canal.

I saw the soles of her trainers slapping the surface of the water as if there were a concrete causeway just below.

'Peter!' yelled Nightingale, running past me.

We sprinted for the bridge and across, but by the time we made it into the cemetery our angel was long gone.

14

Love

We arrested Heather Chalk for assisting an offender and took her home with us to the Folly, where we keep the least-used, nicest-smelling and best-catered PACE-compliant suite in the Metropolitan Police Service area in the basement.

More importantly, the suite here was magic-resistant – so long as we persuaded Foxglove to sleep in her own basement studio, so that her anti-magic field, or whatever it was, extended to the cells. Not that we were worried about Heather doing magic . . . but we weren't sure that Francisca wouldn't stage a rescue.

I remembered the comfortable way they'd walked together down the towpath and thought a rescue attempt a real possibility. Or so I hoped.

Meanwhile, we had to check Heather in with the custody sergeant and store her shopping safely so it could be returned to her in the event of her release. Since assisting an offender is a serious offence, we arranged to have a solicitor come in even before she asked for one. In response we got a posh white woman in her fifties, in a tailored black pinstripe skirt suit and a tooled leather briefcase. This was not what we were used to in the way of legal aid briefs, so I took a moment to make friends.

She turned out to be a senior partner in the local criminal law firm, who had heard so many weird stories about the Folly that she'd come to check them out. Her name was Cynthia Hoopercast.

Good for upholding the principle of legal protection for all – not so good for your working police.

'So where did you meet Francisca?' I asked.

'I don't have to answer that,' said Heather Chalk, and Ms Hoopercast nodded approval.

I was flying solo on this interview since Nightingale, Guleed and half of the Belgravia mob were trying to track down Jacqueline Spencer-Talbot, the remaining member of the Manchester Bible studies group unaccounted for, while my FBI contacts at least tried to confirm that Andrew Carpenter and Brian Packard were still safely in the States.

At least Danni and Seawoll were on their way back.

'I've stuck Barry' – one of his up-and-coming detective sergeants – 'with the follow-up with GMP and points in between,' Seawoll had said.

I think the rush to get back was to provide cover for Stephanopoulos because of our failure by the canal. Now, to the rest of the Met Stephanopoulos continues to be the single most terrifying police officer who ever put the fear of God into a subordinate, but to Seawoll she was still his bright-eyed protégée. Would probably still be when she was chief constable of some county force and he was living in the Sunshine Home for Retired Northern Detectives on the seafront at Scarborough.

If Scarborough has a seafront – I'd have to check.

'Don't you dare get our Miriam into any more trouble,'

he'd said, and then sent me everything he had on the Thelma and Louise of the Macclesfield Canal.

'We know you met at the halfway house in Stockport,' I told Heather.

'Then why did you ask?' she said.

'Because we need to know your side of the story,' I said.

'Like you care,' she said. 'Like you give a fuck about me.'

We did twenty minutes of the *woe is me nobody cares I'm just an insignificant nothing* until she cracked. Proper professional criminals can keep schtum indefinitely but ordinary people always want to explain themselves. However hard the Ms Hoopercasts of the world frown at them. You just need to stay calm and look sympathetic and eventually out it comes.

'What are you after her for, anyway?' she asked. This was a genuine question and my first real opening.

'We think she may have seriously hurt people,' I said.

'No,' said Heather, but the slight edge of desperation in her voice meant she knew something, at least. 'Not a chance, she's nice.'

'We're worried because we think she may be acting under duress,' I said, and Ms Hoopercast looked suddenly interested, as I was hoping she would. 'We think she may have been abused and conditioned to carry out a series of attacks.'

'Are you saying she's a terrorist?' said Heather before Ms Hoopercast could stop her.

'Why would you think she was a terrorist?' I asked.

Heather looked at Ms Hoopercast, who shook her head and then back at me.

'You said she was,' said Heather, causing a pained crease to appear between Ms Hoopercast's elegantly plucked eyebrows. 'Whatever else she is – she's not a terrorist. She's a beautiful soul.'

'In what way?' I asked.

'She was touched by the numinous,' said Heather.

'What's the numinous?' I asked.

'It's that feeling you get when you're in church,' said Heather. 'Or a bit stoned, but in a good way. You saw it, didn't you? You was there, weren't you? She's an angel. A real angel – from Heaven.'

'She has power,' I said. 'But we don't think she's a messenger from God.'

Ms Hoopercast stopped making notes and stared in amazement, first at me and then at her client, and then back at me – her eyes narrowing.

'Ah,' she said softly. 'So it's true.'

I ignored her and kept my eyes on Heather. Love is a terrible thing in an accomplice – you can't turn one suspect against another if they put the needs of the other ahead of their own.

You have to sneak in through the back door instead.

'We think she might be being forced to attack people,' I said.

'Against her will?' asked Heather.

Ah, I thought, *she knows something for sure.*

'We think so,' I said, even though she'd looked pretty enthusiastic to me. 'Did she say where she was from?'

'Seville,' said Heather. 'It's in Spain, but I think she was from somewhere a bit rural, if you know what I mean?'

'Why do you say that?' I asked.

Because Heather had had to teach her how to turn on a cooker, let alone use a phone. She'd been suspicious of the toilet, took really long baths and thought the Hoover was the best thing since sliced bread. She did know how to make bread, though, and she knew exactly how to use the wood and coal stove on the narrowboat.

It never seemed to occur to Heather that Francisca might be a refugee from the dim and distant past – not even when she fainted at her first sight of an airliner. I'd have sussed it on the first day – which just goes to show why more science fiction should be included in the National Curriculum.

'Was she religious?' I asked.

'In what way?'

'Did she go to church?'

Heather shook her head.

'Did she pray?'

'All the time to herself,' said Heather. 'In Spanish, I think.'

'Did you ever see her with the spear?' I asked.

Heather hesitated.

'What spear?' she said, and I had a sudden memory of the spear as it swung through the air towards me . . . Flames streaming from what I realised was a blunt tip. The flames had made it hard to see, but the top quarter of the weapon had been a narrow cylinder. Grey-green, roughly textured with organic swirls and dribbles.

Lightning glass, I thought, and realised that both Heather and Ms Hoopercast were staring at me.

'The burning spear,' I said.

'Don't know what you're talking about,' said Heather, but I could see that she did.

'OK,' I said. 'Tell me about the trip down on the canal – it must have been hard in winter.'

'It can get very cold,' said Heather. 'But if you're moving every day you're working locks, stopping at pubs, meeting new people – keeps you warm.'

There was a rhythm to it — wake up, stoke up the stove. Heather would check the boat and look at the map – if they had a decent signal she'd log on to the boating sites. Plan the day's move. Have breakfast while they were under way. Take it in turns to steer while the other warmed up in the cabin. Spend the evenings in a pub, or in the boat snuggled up in the bed together.

'So what was your relationship?' I asked – casually.

'What do you mean?'

'Friends, girlfriends, lovers?' I said

Heather actually blushed and, although she tried to hide it, smiled a shy smile.

'I swear neither of us were lezzies,' she said. 'Only she used to cry at night if she were in her own bunk and . . . one thing led to another. I'd never done it with a girl before, but obviously, you know it's not hard to work out, she didn't have a clue.' Heather was staring at her lap. 'Sexually speaking. She'd been treated like shit when she was young – I'm pretty certain of that.'

Tears had started to fall from Heather's eyes. She made no attempt to wipe them away, they just fell into her lap.

'I reckon she was an angel,' she said. 'A broken angel.'

Ms Hoopercast asked for a break at that point and I suspended the interview.

A broken angel.

'But a real person,' I said.

'Yes,' said Nightingale. 'Indoctrinated or compelled – it's hard to tell.'

We were sitting in the small but pristine medical examination room that sits next to the cells. Neither of us thought it wise to get too far from Heather, just in case her angelic friend Francisca came looking for her.

'Could you compel someone to kill another human being?' I asked.

Nightingale was silent for a long moment, and then he looked away from me.

'During the war,' he said. 'I've ordered men to shoot strangers and I was the moving force behind an air raid in Norway. I didn't give the order directly, but it was at my instigation.'

'I meant with magic,' I said.

'Oh,' said Nightingale. 'That. Possibly – I've never tried it. Certainly not in a way that would last for weeks and months, let alone span the centuries.'

I suspected that time had been suspended for Francisca while she'd been in the lamp, otherwise she'd be even weirder than she was.

'Could any of your contemporaries make someone kill?' I asked.

'I doubt it,' said Nightingale. 'Interfering directly with a man's free will was not encouraged at the Folly. David Mellenby, whose notebooks you have, was of the opinion that the main purpose of the Society of the Wise was to distract its members from such things. "Drowning our Mussolinis in brandy and cigar smoke", he called it.'

According to those notebooks, the body's own defences were constantly renewed so that even spells like *Vox Imperante* – that parade-ground bark that could make a room full of people sit down on the floor or drop their weapons – only work about fifty per cent of the time.

'What about an old-fashioned ritual spell, pre-Newtonian?' I said.

Ritual spells used non-practitioners to amplify their effect. These types of spells had been considered by the old buffers of the Folly as either déclassé, dangerously foreign, or like, totally Dark Ages, man.

'David did believe that if you could marshal enough participants and focus them sufficiently, you might overwhelm a man's innate defences,' said Nightingale.

'Did anyone try?' I asked.

'Lord, no,' said Nightingale. 'David was careful never to reveal that particular theory, especially during the early part of the war – when things were desperate. He only told me because he had to tell someone.'

'I haven't seen it in his notebooks,' I said.

'You won't,' said Nightingale. 'I believe he destroyed those notes before he died.'

Only David Mellenby hadn't just died. He'd committed suicide in the face of the horrors they'd discovered during the raid on Ettersberg. He'd done it while Nightingale was recovering from his war wounds – I don't think it helped his recovery at all.

'Assume for the moment that our angel Francisca dates back to the Middle Ages or something – probably

Spain,' I said. 'She's then sort of enchanted and turned into a super-assassin and further indoctrinated to kill a number of people. But this is hundreds of years ago, so whoever her original targets were, they're long gone. So what's the criteria for her current target selection?'

'Could they be the descendants of the original targets?' asked Nightingale.

'You might have to ask Dr Walid for details,' I said, 'but I'm pretty sure that after twenty generations, hundreds of thousands of people would be the biological descendants of anyone from back then. And even if it's some weird mystical direct line thing, it would be a bit of a coincidence that they all ended up in the same Bible study group in Manchester.'

'Unless it was divinely ordained,' said Nightingale.

'Do you believe that?'

'No,' said Nightingale. 'But we have to consider all the options – even divine providence.'

'Or it could be something more obvious,' I said.

'You think it might be the rings?' said Nightingale.

'Yes,' I said. 'But I don't know why. They're enchanted and so was the lamp. They were supposed to be stored with the Sons of Wayland, as the lamp was. The only trouble is platinum is a modern metal – it's mostly mined in South Africa and they didn't open up those mines until the 1900s.'

'I believe Harold may have made some headway on that mystery,' said Nightingale. 'He was sounding quite pleased with himself on the phone earlier.'

'Did he say why?'

'You know Harold,' said Nightingale. 'He likes to

make a performance of these things. In the meantime, it's always possible that Francisca shared her motivations with her lover.'

It took another hour to get Heather to admit that Francisca had talked to her about her mission.

'What mission was that?' I asked.

But Heather had clammed up again, and we circled around the question of whether she'd known that her girlfriend had been off murdering people.

'They had it coming,' she said suddenly, when I described David Moore's death in the Silver Vaults. 'They', I noticed – not 'he'.

'What had they done?'

'We should never have come south,' she said, and she crossed her arms. 'We was all right until we came south.'

'Why did you come south?' I asked.

Heather mumbled something like 'She wanted to.'

'Who wanted to?'

'Francisca wanted to,' said Heather.

I caught Ms Hoopercast's eye. Her job is to act in the best interest of her client, and shifting the guilt on to an associate is a classic. Ms Hoopercast didn't do anything as crass as suggest Heather incriminate her lover, but I knew the next time her client looked to her for guidance she'd get a nod, not a head-shake.

Sure enough, when I asked whether Heather knew why Francisca had wanted to come to London, Ms Hoopercast didn't object when Heather said it was to find the blasphemers.

'That's what she called them,' said Heather. 'She

called them *Marranos* as well – whatever that means. Definitely not a good word, though. I think she thought they were dead, but she saw one of them on YouTube.'

I remembered Preston Carmichael's relentless self-promotion on YouTube, but he wasn't that big an influencer. I wondered whether it was chance or the malign workings of the YouTube algorithm. Because you liked happy cat videos, you might also like to smite this man with furious vengeance.

'She knew how to use the internet, then?' I said.

'It's not like it's hard, is it?' said Heather. 'She did love YouTube, though, spent hours watching travelogues and that kind of shit.'

We'd be able to check exactly what she'd watched once our Digital Forensics Technician had finished sucking the guts out of Heather's laptop. I was thinking that, if I was right, then in 1989 Preston Carmichael and his merry band of God-botherers were experimenting with forces they didn't understand. Francisca had been stuck in a magic lamp in a box under a hill just outside Glossop. How would she know what Preston Carmichael or any of the others looked like?

I asked Heather that very question but I left out the lamp stuff.

'She saw them in a holy vision,' said Heather. 'She said that they stood before her, and the angel Camael whispered in her ear that they were the new blasphemers and descendants of the original *Marranos*.'

I made a note of the angel's name and asked whether this revelation happened while Francisca was on the boat, but Heather said no.

'Francisca said it happened when she was reborn into the new world,' she said.

Was this the Manchester group's 1989 experiment with the rings and ritual magic? If no proper time passed within the pocket dimension of the lamp, assuming that's what it was, then that implied two things. One: that the rings were magically connected to the lamp and/or Francisca, and two: that ritual had marked the Manchester group as legitimate targets for Francisca's murderous rage.

Which begged the question – who were her original targets and what had they done to deserve having Francisca set on them? Nightingale is fond of saying that there is nothing you can do with magic that isn't cheaper and quicker to do by mundane means. Fireballs are fun, but it takes months of training to gain basic proficiency, while you can train an ordinary person to fire a handgun accurately in less than a week. The Germans had made a concerted effort to militarise their magical base, probably the most advanced in Europe at the time, but had ended up being ground into dog food by the conventional Red Army and its allies in Europe.

The magical forces on all sides had cancelled themselves out and the outcome was decided by strategy and logistics, courage, bullets, pain and blood.

And DNA evidence will catch more killers than my ability to sense *vestigia* ever will.

Nevertheless, magic was very much at work here. We didn't have the details yet, but transforming what appeared to have been an ordinary woman into an ersatz angel of death must have cost enormous magical resources. Just who had the resources to do such a thing? And why had they thought it necessary?

'Did Francisca ever say who gave her this mission?' I asked.

'The Holy Father himself,' said Heather.

'The Pope authorised the hit?'

'I don't know if it was the Pope directly,' said Heather. 'But it was definitely a Monsignor somebody something Prado – I think. She said he did it in the name of the Pope.'

I circled back to clarify as many details as I could, but Heather was getting tired and sleep deprivation only works as a tactic if you don't care whether the suspect is telling the truth or just what they think you want to hear.

Francisca had often gone off by herself.

'She wasn't a child!'

Once they were in London, Heather had shown her how to use an Oyster Card and after that there was no stopping her.

I asked Heather where Francisca had visited but Heather didn't know for sure, although Francisca would occasionally bring her back presents. Sweets and chocolate mostly, although one time it was a bunch of yellow roses that she suspected Francisca had plucked from someone's garden or a park.

'The stems were all different lengths,' she said.

On one of these trips, Francisca was probably torturing poor Preston Carmichael to death – probably to get intelligence on the rest of the Manchester group. Efficient torture for information is not something you pick up from TV – not even HBO – so I wondered who had taught her that.

'I think I can hazard a guess,' said Postmartin, when we convened upstairs in the atrium for tea. Molly had placed a tiered silver cake stand in the middle of a coffee table and surrounded it with plates of daintily cut mustard and cress, cheese and pickle, salmon paste and . . .

'Cucumber sandwiches,' said Nightingale. 'Molly must be feeling traditional today.'

Toby, who had obviously learnt a trick or two from Molly, appeared as if by magic beside my chair and gave me a much-practised look of pitiable hunger. Across from me, Seawoll delicately plucked a cucumber sandwich and popped it into his mouth.

'Don't keep us in suspense,' I said.

Postmartin flourished his tablet at us and pulled up an enhanced picture of the scratches on David Moore's door. He cleared a space on the coffee table and laid it down. He reached down and retrieved a thick book bound in scuffed leather from a side table, opened it up to a bookmarked illustration plate, and laid it down beside the tablet. The picture in the book was a line illustration of a sigil – an upright oval containing a branch with leaves, a very knobbly cross in the centre and, on its right, a sword blade pointing upwards. Around the oval border were the words *Exurge domine et judica causum tuam – Psalm 73.*

Side by side, it was obvious that the scratches on the door were a crude reproduction of the sigil. You could even see where the scratcher had tried to do the oval, but given up halfway through when they couldn't get the curve right.

'*Exurge domine et judica causum tuam*,' said Nightingale. '"Arise, O God, judge thy own cause."'

'Psalm 73,' said Postmartin. 'The motto of the Spanish Inquisition.'

'Well, fuck me,' said Seawoll. 'I wasn't expecting them.'

'There's long been speculation,' said Postmartin, 'that there was a magical component to the Inquisition – particularly in Spain and Portugal. We know for a fact that there was a strong Islamic and Jewish magical tradition in Andalusia and Granada, even if we don't understand its underlying principles.'

The Newtonian synthesis – as Postmartin liked to call it – codified the 'forms and wisdoms' that underpinned European wizardry. But knowing how to do something doesn't mean you know why it works.

'Nor does it preclude,' Nightingale had said during my early training, 'the possibility that some other techniques might work – possibly just as well.'

Isaac Newton himself, like many of his contemporaries, had been interested in the Jewish esoteric practice known as Kabbalah. For all we knew, he might have drawn inspiration – or even whole techniques – from Jewish and Muslim practitioners. It's not like our boy Isaac was famous for sharing credit.

'Some of those practitioners must have converted,' I said.

Must have become 'New Christians', and thus fell

under the jurisdiction of the Inquisition whose purpose was to root out backsliding converts.

'They might have used their skills to mess with the Inquisition when it came after them,' I said.

'Hence the lamp,' said Postmartin. 'And it might well have been that the rings were part of the process of entrapping the angel that was sent after them.'

'But the rings are made of platinum,' I said. 'That's a modern metal – like aluminium.'

'Aha,' said Postmartin, who'd obviously waiting for his cue. 'There was platinum available in the Renaissance – it was found in the New World and brought back to Spain. They called it *platina*, the diminutive of *plata* – which is Spanish for silver. There was certainly enough circulating by the sixteenth century for a suitably motivated craftsman to fashion seven rings.'

'Don't tell me it was cursed,' said Seawoll.

'I doubt it,' said Postmartin. 'But it is exactly the sort of rare and exotic material that attracted pre-Newtonian practitioners.'

'If there was a magical opposition to the Inquisition,' I said, 'then there was bound to be pushback by the Inquisition. They'd have needed a way to deal with the resistance.'

'I've never heard of Monsignor something Prado,' said Postmartin, 'but the name sounds Spanish. Perhaps he was influential in Peter's hypothetical magical inquisition.'

'Good God,' said Nightingale. 'I think Leon all but told me.'

Back in the 1920s, when they'd all been young – or

at least that's how it felt – and drinking in the Lamb off Guildford Place to stay out of the way of the old bores that ran the Folly. Nightingale had mentioned to Leon and some other friends, over a pint, that he was planning to travel up to Manchester.

'I'm curious as to how the Sons do their enchantments,' he'd said.

'Did you put him up to this?' Leon had asked David Mellenby, who was already famous as one of the new breed of scientific practitioners.

'Good Lord, no,' David had said. 'I believe he's looking to make his own staff.'

'It's a total bore,' said Leon. 'Take it from me. My family have been silversmiths and enchanters since biblical times, and the best thing my father did was agree to send me to Casterbrook.'

David, of course, had been instantly interested and asked whether Leon's family had truly practised enhanced metallurgy . . .

'That was David's term for it,' Nightingale told us. 'I'm almost certain that he coined it himself. He wanted to know whether it really dated back to the ancient world. David had this notion that a great deal of wisdom had been lost with the fall of the Roman Empire and the Christianising of the East.'

Leon Davies had admitted that he didn't know whether his family's skills really dated back to the time of Abraham, but they'd definitely been famous as makers of amulets and cunning devices in Muslim Spain. Indeed, had been men of substance until they were driven out by the Spanish Inquisition.

'Being crafty made them particularly suspect in the eyes of the Church,' Leon had said, 'who weren't above employing their own sorcerers.'

'Did he say any more?' asked Postmartin eagerly.

'Not that I remember,' said Nightingale, and Seawoll sighed.

'Are you really saying that the Catholic Church had its own version of the Folly?' he asked.

'Might still have,' said Postmartin. 'For all we know.'

'But not the bloody C of E, I hope?'

'No,' said Nightingale. 'That was part of the post-war settlement.'

'Thank fuck for that,' said Seawoll.

Apart from anything else, Francisca being a weapon of the Spanish Inquisition would explain the archaic Castilian. But it still left the question of who Francisca was, or rather had been, before she was an instrument of divine justice. With this in mind, for the next interview we switched Heather to the Folly's very own Achieving Best Evidence suite, which is furnished with a comfortable leather sofa and matching overstuffed armchair salvaged from one of the unused lounges on the fourth floor. The shift in venue wasn't lost on Ms Hoopercast, who – no doubt rightly – surmised it marked a shift for her client from suspect and co-conspirator to member of the public caught up in events beyond her control. Practically a victim in her own right. A new status that would only be helped by full and enthusiastic co-operation with the forces of law and order. Just to make the point, we threw in a pot of tea and a round of tuna sandwiches. I think Ms Hoopercast was somewhat taken aback by the willow pattern china teapot, but she rallied and continued to glower at us for the rest of the interview in the approved manner.

'She was a skivvy,' said Heather, when I asked what she thought Francisca had done back in Seville. 'Like she should have gone to university, but never got the chance and had to do shit jobs for a living. She might have been one of those modern slaves you hear about, only I thought they were mostly Filipino or something.'

Weirdly, we'd done *being a servant in olden times* at school with Miss Redmayne, who was one of those dead-keen humanities teachers straight out of training and ready to dismantle patriarchal capitalism one lesson plan at a time. In fact, being a top-class servant in the late medieval period was a prime job because of access to the great and powerful – plus perks. But being a skivvy and a cleaner was every bit as shit as modern slavery.

A person might clutch at any opportunity to escape that.

Especially if that opportunity was blessed by the highest moral authority you know.

I asked whether Heather thought Francisca truly believed that the *blasphemers* deserved to die, and she said that she did.

'Besides,' said Heather, 'I don't think she thinks she's going to be free until they're dead.'

'Free from what?' I asked.

Heather shrugged. 'She promised,' she said. 'And she always keeps her promises.'

15

Earthworks

They were wrapping up at the Kensal Green moorings, so I popped in to look at a hole in the ground. I parked up in the Sainsbury's car park and showed my warrant card to the PCSO guarding the gate out onto the towpath. To keep our secure area manageable, we'd moved Heather's narrowboat along the canal to the Sainsbury's stop-and-shop mooring. Guleed was sitting on the roof with Danni and an armed response officer called Cecil.

A Crime Scene Examiner in a noddy suit was waiting by a small tent erected on the towpath.

'Are you the one doing the Falcon Assessment?' he asked.

I said I was and apologised for keeping them waiting.

The Crime Scene Examiner shrugged and said he was on overtime.

Usually these white and blue crime scene tents are a horror, because they use them to protect bodies and bits of bodies from the elements and the prying eyes of the media. But this time it was just the point on the towpath that Francisca had struck with her spear.

It was a big hole. I'd seen the geyser of earth and concrete when it hit but I was still surprised by its size. It also had a very clearly defined shape, as if it had been gouged out by an enormous ice cream scoop – the same as the wounds on Preston Carmichael and David Moore.

No wonder they'd found a film of vaporised blood and skin all over the Silver Vaults – I really hoped they'd invested in some deep cleaning afterwards.

And, like with the terrible wounds in Preston's and David's chests, there was a short tube of lightning glass left at the bottom. I reached out with a gloved hand and brushed it with my fingertips.

Now I was used to it, the bell-like silence was louder than ever, and I was starting to get undertones of orange blossom and incense. You have to be careful with this stuff or you begin to sound like a wine taster – with about the same amount of meaningless bollocks.

Definitely the same *vestigium* as on the lightning glass and in Preston Carmichael's flat.

I sat on my heels and thought it through.

I'd got good and close to the spear at our last encounter, close enough to see that the tip was made of a blunt tube of lightning glass. I would check later, but it looked to me that the section of glass in the crater before me was the same length as the sections left inside the previous victims' chest cavities.

If a section broke off from the spear each time she used it – would she eventually run out of spear? Using the broken section as a guide, I tried to estimate how much 'ammunition' she had left. Four or five more strikes, I thought – four, plus three confirmed strikes, would make seven. The number of people with rings – could that be a coincidence?

Assuming that the spear didn't merely regenerate itself every time it vanished into hyperspace.

We needed to break that spear.

Guleed was sceptical.

'And what if it does regenerate?' she asked.

'Then we'll learn something new,' I said.

Since I was Falcon Two and thus, technically, more dangerous than he was, Cecil had wandered off for refs and I took the opportunity to have a rummage around the narrowboat. A POLSA search team had given it a thorough once-over and, while they're trained to not be too disruptive, what had probably been a properly ship-shape interior looked a bit dishevelled. Especially since the POLSA team had had the decking up to check the bilges.

'You'd be amazed what people try to hide down there,' said Danni, and she reached down to chivvy a section of decking back into its proper place.

Canal boats sit low in the water, so once down the narrow stairs in the stern you're half under the surface level. The stern cabin seemed to be general storage, with waterproofs and coats hanging on hooks, cupboards and a fold-down table. Next was the shower and toilet – a composting toilet, the latest in eco-friendly loo design.

'Because we're half under water,' said Danni, 'the shower has to have a separate pump for drainage.'

I asked Danni why she knew so much about canal boats, and she admitted that a lot of her friends lived on the canals.

'The non-police ones, anyway,' she said.

The double bed was next, raised a metre off the deck in an alcove with storage underneath. The pale pink sheets and green duvet were rumpled and a 12 volt adaptor trailed a cable on the pillow.

'Laptop,' said Danni – now with the Digital Forensics techs.

There was a chunky crucifix mounted between the two square windows, both hung with yellow and blue flowery curtains.

It would have been cosy, I thought, lying here in the warm, with rain pounding on the roof and wind in the trees. Far away from car traffic or sirens or the sounds of the city. Your lover in your arms. For Heather it must have been heaven . . . Had Francisca felt the same way? Could she be persuaded that no mission or vengeance was worth abandoning this warm bolthole?

I touched the crucifix, not expecting anything, but the burst of *vestigium* was intense – the same soundless tone as in the spear tip. I took the crucifix down and found that while the Christ figure was silver-plated, the cross was plastic. It said *Made in China* on the back, so I doubted that this was another antique. And so it must have acquired its *vestigium* from Francisca. It was far too large for her to have been wearing it during our encounter in Middlesex Street, so it must have soaked up magic where it hung on the bulkhead.

Did Francisca leak magic when she was asleep?

Had that affected Heather? So far she hadn't shown any changes in gross physical form or displayed any strange powers. People and children who'd been exposed to faerie had occasionally picked up some weird talents – we'd have to check for that in the medium term.

Faerie, I thought, allokosmoi, *spare dimensions, boundary effects*.

Francisca must be getting power from somewhere – the flaming wings, halo and spear had to be sucking up megawatts at the very least. Not to mention the teleporting and the walking on water.

Danni called my name and I went to check the rest of the boat.

Just for a change, I got back home before dark and, to avoid being waylaid by foxes, cousins and other distractions, I went in through the side gate so I could get a good look at whatever Maksim was doing with a JCB in the back garden.

Which turned out to be digging a big rectangular-shaped hole in the lower garden – although it looked like he'd finished for the night. The hole was covered with Monarflex, yellow and black hazard tape had been strung across the width of the garden, and a tarpaulin had been thrown over the JCB.

'Can I go in now?' said a small voice.

Lifting the tarpaulin, I found a miserable-looking fox sitting in the cab of the JCB. It seemed smaller than the others and had dark grey fur shading to black on its throat and belly. It brightened up considerably when it saw me.

I asked it what it was doing.

'Guarding important diggy thing,' it said. And, then,

after some thought, 'Getting damp. Can I go in? I haven't seen any cats at all.'

'Off you go then,' I said and it shot off, not towards the house, as I'd expected, but over the fence into the recreation ground.

I looked back at the house and saw Beverley waiting for me in the covered section of the patio. She had a mug of something in her hand.

'I've decreed an upper limit on the number of foxes allowed in the house,' she said as I walked up and kissed her. She tasted of hot chocolate.

'Where do the surplus stay?' I asked.

Beverley passed the hot chocolate to me.

'They have a provisional field operations centre down by the river,' she said.

'Which is what in reality?'

'A big den lined with the lino offcuts Maksim had in his shed and equipped with Abigail's old sleeping bag,' she said.

I took a sip and handed the hot chocolate back. I saw Abigail through the kitchen window, unpacking Tupperware containers – she waved when saw me.

'Why is Maksim digging a hole in the back garden?' I asked. I thought I knew the answer, but it's dangerous to make assumptions.

'It's for the birthing pool,' said Beverley. 'It was in the birthing plan.'

'I thought we were going to Kingston,' I said. 'I distinctly remember that.'

'That pool isn't big enough,' said Beverley.

We'd been shown round the birthing pool at Kingston Hospital the last time we'd gone in for a check.
There were calming blue walls with a mural of a flower
with sparkles rising out of it. Lots of nice clean medical
bits and pieces within easy reach. The pool itself was the
size of a hot tub, white and lit from below. There was
room for Bev and a midwife, with me offering physical and moral support from the sides and other trained
medical personnel on hand for complications.

The midwife had had reservations about birthing
twins in a pool because twins can be tricky, but Beverley
had reassured her that all would be well. So that had
been the agreed birthing plan, as far as I knew, until the
last couple of days.

'Big enough for who?' I asked.

'Your mum, for one,' said Bev. 'And my mum, of
course.'

That explained it – having the Goddess of the Thames
turn up at Kingston Hospital would be massively disruptive. Things happened on account of her being a
goddess, wherever she goes – the sort of things that re-
quire advanced public order planning.

'Kingston nick will never know the favour we're doing
them,' I said.

We had Korean that night, courtesy of the Ree family,
who were amongst Beverley's earliest . . . let's say
acolytes, because worshippers would probably be over-
stating things.

'People believe in me,' Beverley had said once, 'because I don't make promises I can't deliver.'

'What do you promise?' I'd asked.

'Good irrigation, for one,' she'd said. 'You should see Eun-Ju's allotment.'

Certainly the cabbage in the kimchi was home-grown, although I suspected the grilled pig offal had come from a specialist butcher in New Malden. Even before I encountered Molly's frugal ways with random animal leftovers I'd been raised eating cow's foot and pepper soup, so the offal didn't bother me, but I steered Abigail in the direction of the barbecued beef.

Every so often we could hear a low keening sound from the foxes, who had been banished to the patio and were staring into the house like the poor starving waifs they definitely weren't.

Sung-Hoon asked me if I was looking forward to being a father and I said I was hoping to make a good job of it, which both the Rees seemed to find hilarious.

Afterwards I was helping Abigail with the washing-up when I got a text from Special Agent Kimberley Reynolds, who is the Folly's semi-official liaison at the FBI. She handles what she calls the 'basement files', which I assume is a reference to *The X-Files*, and we swap advice and information back and forth using Skype and our official e-mail accounts. Our assumption is that the shadowy forces of the surveillance state were probably monitoring us, but our attitude was that if they wanted us to stop they could bloody well ask us nicely.

'Good tradecraft,' Indigo the fox had said. 'Makes the opposition lazy and allows you to feed them disinformation while you continue through clandestine channels.'

Abigail says that the foxes think they are, or may actually even be in some way, spies. Which is why it didn't surprise me when one of them, whose name I thought might be Sugar Niner, popped up from under the desk in the side room full of unpacked boxes that Beverley laughingly calls my study.

'Can I sit on your lap?' asked Sugar Niner.

'There's raw chicken on the patio for you,' I said. 'And dumplings.'

'No thanks,' said Sugar Niner. 'I already ate. Had eggs and a mouse.'

'You can sit on the other chair over there,' I said. 'But observation only.'

Sugar Niner reluctantly climbed onto the spare plastic garden chair next to the desk and watched alertly as I set up the call to America.

We'd asked Reynolds to follow up on Andrew Carpenter and Brian Packard, so I'd decided not to wait until the morning. It would be the middle of the afternoon at Quantico, so she'd still be in her office.

'How's Beverley?' asked Reynolds once we were connected.

A thin white woman in her early thirties, with short auburn hair, she was wearing her work suit with her ID badge on a lanyard around her neck. A beige cubicle wall with a wall planner was visible behind her – if it hadn't been for the letters FBI on her ID she could have been an office drone anywhere in the world.

I gave the latest update on Beverley, the bulge, and the fact that the birth plan appeared to be going out the window.

'I wouldn't worry about that,' said Reynolds. 'You're strictly kibitzing on this one. Make sure you don't fall asleep, do what you're told and you'll be fine.'

We moved on to Carpenter and Packard.

'They're both naturalised US citizens now,' said Reynolds, 'Andrew Carpenter originally worked for Ogilvy & Mather, they're a New York ad agency, but moved on to MullenLowe U.S., another agency, after he became a citizen. He still lives in New York.'

Reynolds had called Carpenter and found him co-operative. He remembered the Bible study group, and was convincingly surprised and shocked at learning of David Moore's and Preston Carmichael's deaths.

'He said he hadn't had any contact with the other members since he left Manchester,' said Reynolds.

'Did you ask him about his ring?' I asked.

'Oh yes,' said Reynolds. 'He says he lost his this past January.'

'Did he say lost or stolen?'

'Definitely lost,' said Reynolds. 'He thinks he left it at a Vietnamese restaurant in the East Village. Took it off in the bathroom to wash his hands and forgot to put it back on again.'

'Sounds unlikely,' I said.

'That's what I thought,' said Reynolds. 'So I asked a couple of the oblique questions we discussed.'

We'd recently talked over some of the interview techniques me and Nightingale had developed as part of the Falcon Awareness Course. They seemed to have worked in this case.

'There was a definite sense of disconnection from events,' said Reynolds.

'So probably he came under the influence,' I said.

'That's the way it seems to me,' said Reynolds.

'Do you have a precise date?'

'Fifth of January,' said Reynolds.

The 46th World Economic Forum had run from the 20th or the 23rd, so plenty of time for Lesley to grab one ring from Andrew Carpenter before jetting over to Switzerland to *seducere* the other from Alastair McKay.

'But,' said Reynolds, when I proposed this, 'that implies that Lesley knew who at least two of the ringbearers were.'

'Ringbearers – really?' I said.

'Hey,' said Reynolds. 'If the name fits . . .'

'So did Lesley know about Brian Packard?' I said.

'That's where things get interesting,' said Reynolds. 'Brian Packard went to UCSD Health Sciences for both his master's and his doctorate.'

That made sense – according to Manchester University's records he'd graduated with a first in biochemistry. Reynolds confirmed that it wasn't unusual for foreign students to be recruited by the top research schools. Although she said his résumé must have been impressive, since University of California San Diego was in the top five globally of biomedical research centres.

'They sponsored him for a visa, too,' said Reynolds. 'He became an American citizen and joined the Life Sciences faculty at UCLA in 2007, and then in 2014 drops off the grid.'

It's not as hard to avoid Big Brother as people think it is, although it helps if you have a source of readies and pay in cash. Without a legitimate reason to open an official investigation, Reynolds could only make a casual data sweep – basically social media plus reported crimes and deaths.

'Could he have just opted for a quiet life?' I asked.

'It's hinky,' said Reynolds. 'One minute he's a happy man around Facebook, with a Twitter and an Instagram account, and the next day he stops posting. The accounts keep running but he's not posting any more.'

'Could he be dead?'

'An identified body would have turned up in my initial sweep,' said Reynolds.

And she said she'd reached out to the LA Office to do a more thorough search and see if there were any John Does that might match his description.

But what had really caught her attention was that in the six or so months running up to his abandonment of social media, he'd started interacting online with some real nutjobs.

'Flat-earthers or our kind of nutjobs?' I asked.

'Difficult to tell from a distance,' said Reynolds. 'But the individuals in question used some of the key words you told me to look out for. I managed to obtain some transcripts of exchanges that happened on one of the 4chan boards and Mr Packard was definitely looking for something.'

Reynolds got the strong impression that Brian Packard wasn't looking to drink the Kool-Aid, but instead searching for the real thing. And me and Agent Reynolds both knew that there were groups in California who knew where real magic could be found.

'I'll send you the transcripts and let you know if

anything else turns up,' said Reynolds, and after pleasantries we shut down the connection.

'Classic case of recruitment,' said Sugar Niner.

I looked over to where the young fox was still sitting on the chair and looking pleased with himself, and asked what he meant.

'What's it worth?' asked Sugar Niner.

'You know the rules,' I said. 'Information first, payment second.'

'What if you don't like the information?'

'Then you don't get paid.'

Sugar Niner gave such a huge and human sigh that I was certain it was put on for effect.

'It's a pattern of behaviour,' he said. 'The best agent you can have is a trusted member of the opposition, and that's the same for them, too. So you need to be able to spot someone on your own side who's been recruited.'

'Do foxes join the opposition?' I asked, even as I wondered who the opposition was.

'No, but we learn about it in training so we can keep an eye on our human allies.'

And Sugar Niner had been taught about Henry Busybody, who worked for the Department of Important Business and thus had access to war secrets.

'Which war are we talking about?' I asked.

'Not relevant,' said Sugar Niner. 'This is a training hypothetical.'

So the opposition has three main weapons to gain Henry Busybody's co-operation – money, sex and ideology, or, as Sugar Niner put it, 'Cheese puffs, mating and cat dependency.'

'You don't really mean cat dependency,' I said.

Sugar Niner admitted he'd gone off track a bit. Money and mating were useful, but ideology was better because your potential agent will be cheaper, self-motivated and more likely to neglect their own safety.

'But the thing is,' said Sugar Niner, 'nobody just wakes up in their den one morning and thinks that a long-haired Persian is the epitome of creation. First they have to engage with other cat lovers, to be exposed to the ideology of cat supremacy, until they are willing to put the interest of felines ahead of their own.'

'Are we still talking about Henry Busybody and the war?'

'Or that the National Socialist Party is the last hope for national salvation,' said Sugar Niner – a bit testily, I thought.

'Do you even know who the National Socialist Party were?' I asked.

Sugar Niner hesitated.

'No,' he said. 'But that's not important. There's a pattern – Henry Busybody takes an interest, meets a couple of cat fanciers . . .' Sugar Niner paused again and recalibrated. 'A couple of fascist sympathisers, reads some articles in the *Daily Mail* and thinks they might have some good ideas.'

It was obvious that Sugar Niner had no idea about the *Daily Mail*, fascism or probably World War Two – it was all Bible stories to him. I had this sudden vision of a classroom full of foxes being taught basic espionage techniques and each of them translating Henry

Busybody's flirtation with fascism into something more culturally appropriate.

'But the thing is, you can't have a useful agent if they have cat hairs all over them,' said Sugar Niner. 'They'd be spotted immediately.'

'Wait,' I said. 'Are you at war with the cats? Are they the opposition?'

Sugar Niner looked shifty.

'No,' he said. 'We don't know who or what the opposition is.'

'So what's all this business with cats?'

'Cats are dangerous, cruel and sneaky,' said Sugar Niner. 'They make good . . .' His brow creased as if he was translating some difficult fox concept in his head.

'Scapegoats?' I said.

'Yes,' said Sugar Niner delightedly. 'Excellent scapegoats.'

'What has this to do with Brian Packard?'

'He's obviously interested in magic in America, yes?'

'Yes,' I said.

'Then he drops out of sight,' said Sugar Niner. 'Because he found magic and he doesn't want anyone to know he has. Or . . .'

'Or?'

'He was eaten by cats,' said Sugar Niner. 'That's why they never found a body.'

'I think one is more likely than the other.'

'You're right,' said Sugar Niner. 'Is that worth a reward?'

I started to have a horrible feeling about Brian Packard's role in the whole case.

'Let's go see what's in the fridge,' I said.

Sugar Niner plumped for a couple of eggs because we were out of cheese puffs.

'Can I have an egg box,' he asked, and I found one at the top of the cardboard recycling box and, after slotting the eggs, put it on the kitchen floor.

Normal foxes crunch their eggs and I supposed Sugar Niner probably did, too, when he didn't have an egg box, but now he carefully bit the tops off the eggs and licked them out with his tongue.

'Makes them last longer,' he said when he caught me watching.

But I wasn't thinking of foxes. I was thinking of magic and siphons and fiery angel wings.

Later that night, when we were safely in bed and out of the prying eyes of minders, cousins and foxes, I asked Beverley to do something magical.

'Is not my mere existence enough any more?' she asked.

I thought very carefully before giving an answer.

'Of course it is,' I said. 'But I need something that affects the material domain beyond the confines of my heart.'

She put her Kindle on her bulge and gave me a suspicious look.

'Have you been reading Greek love poetry again?'

'No, I'm still working my way through Marcus Aurelius,' I said. 'I want to try something.'

'Like what?'

'There's a theory that some types of magical phenomena are in fact a type of boundary effect where an *allokosmos* intersects our reality,' I said.

'For example?' said Beverley.

'Do you remember the unicorns?'

'Yes.'

'We know they're really creatures of Faerie, which is a type of *allokosmos*, right?'

'Right.'

'Remember how they used to be invisible half the time?'

'Except when you were stupid enough to feed them magic,' she said.

'So which do you think is more plausible?' I said. 'That half a tonne of bone, muscle and killer spike could turn naturally transparent, or it was out of phase with our reality and thus invisible.'

'For one thing,' said Beverley, 'I'd say they weighed at least a thousand kilograms, and for another, you got the whole out of phase thing from *Star Trek*.'

'Just because it's in *Star Trek* doesn't mean it's not true,' I said.

'And just because I don't have an alternative working hypothesis doesn't mean the first bit of technobabble you come up with is true.'

'That's why I want to test it,' I said.

'I walked into that, didn't I?'

I wisely said nothing.

'Fine,' said Beverley.

She struggled into a more upright sitting position. Fortunately I have developed some skills in strategic pillow placement that have served me well during the later stages of pregnancy.

'What did you have in mind?' she asked.

308

'Do a water balloon . . . Not yet!' I said, as Beverley raised her hand. 'Let me get into position, count to ten and then do a water balloon.'

I lay down flat on the bed and closed my eyes.

'I'm not sure you're supposed to involve expectant mothers in science experiments,' said Beverley.

But I've learnt to reach a state of receptiveness while under combat stress, so Beverley talking wasn't going to disturb me. Had she kissed me, on the other hand, I would have been fucked.

The house, like most structures over fifty years old, had its own background bits of *vestigia* and, of course, Beverley had left her mark. Like the little splashing sounds and the smell of car wax and drying laundry. I wasn't sure where the Russian church music came from unless Maksim had been keeping secrets – that was something I could check later.

I let the background stuff wash away.

At first I thought I might be wrong. I've never 'heard' Beverley when she's being professionally goddess-like, but then I'd nearly always been distracted at the time. Then I felt a strange tickle and a flicker at the periphery of my mind. There was the catch at the edge of reality that I'd come to associate with certain kinds of magic.

There's a spell called *sīphōnem* that is used to defuse demon traps. Its key components are two formae – *flue* and *conmove* – which, along with a bunch of other modifiers and *inflectentes*, allows you to siphon away the power in the demon trap and disperse it harmlessly. Like letting the air out of a balloon without popping it.

Only considerably more dangerous.

If it worked on a demon trap, I wondered if a modified version might work on the power bleeding through a boundary. Like that which was, hopefully, creating a water balloon.

'Is it working?' asked Beverley.

I caught the hazy sense of streams running through fields, through culverts, of cars being washed on summer afternoons, net curtains and Sunday lunch. The sensations coalesced into a round shape above my head – the water balloon.

I tried the first couple of *formae* that composed the spell and felt them catch the edges of the balloon. But having proved that much of the theory, I wasn't about to experiment further on Beverley.

'Yes,' I said, and I opened my eyes to find a wobbling globe of water hovering a couple of centimetres above my nose. 'You can stop that if you like.'

'OK,' said Beverley.

I watched with relief as the globe floated to the ceiling and, without any fuss or lingering dampness, evaporated.

'Will it help?' she asked.

'Let's hope so,' I said.

Tuesday

Amongst our weapons . . .

16

Commitment

Since I couldn't experiment on Beverley, I needed something primed with stored magic. We didn't keep any demon traps at the Folly . . . but one thing I knew for a fact had stored magic in it was my staff.

I usually leave it in the Asbo, but I'd brought it into the Folly that morning and left it in the demonstration room. This lives at the back of the Folly, and was a small lecture theatre with raked seating where the amateur savants of the Society of the Wise could demonstrate their latest magic to their peers. There was even a segregated Ladies' Gallery halfway up the north wall, so that the weaker sex could watch and admire their menfolk without getting underfoot. Toby was currently up there, grumpily wearing his lead, which was attached to the railing.

He'd thought he was going for a walk but actually he was a vital part of the experiment.

Another reason I was using the lecture theatre was that it was lined with two and a half centimetres of cork to act as magical shielding. Apparently, back in the day some of those public demonstrations could get quite explosive. Which explained why the top of the huge oak table on the podium was streaked and scarred with burns and scratches. There was even a patch where a hole had been burnt right through, with a matching crater on the floor underneath.

I mounted the staff above the table with a pair of lab stands and went through the spell *forma* by *forma*. Then I stood back from the bench, cleared my mind and lined up the *formae* and ran through them, saying each one out loud.

It didn't work the first time, or the second, but the third time I felt the spell catch as if I'd turned a key in the ignition. Hugh Oswald's staffs had spent years soaking up magic from his weird granddaughter's beehives, and so the release came with the hum of thousands of wings and the sickly smell of raw honeycomb.

Toby started barking – a mad excited yapping.

I let go of the spell.

The air suddenly had a greasy feel and the smell of burnt copper.

I'd put a bit more magic into the environment than I meant to. Theoretically this should disperse naturally, but according to David Mellenby's notes a high level of magical saturation was definitely a health hazard.

As insidious as carbon monoxide, only far more unpredictable in its effects, he'd written in his notes.

Toby obviously thought so. He'd stopped barking and was pulling frantically at his lead.

I began to worry – I needed to burn off some of the magic in a controlled fashion, but there was a ridiculously high chance of any spell, even the most basic, backfiring. Then I thought maybe I could put the *sīphōnem* spell into reverse and lock the magic into something. I should have brought something I could have used as a magic sink. Why is it you always think of these things when it's too late . . .?

Toby stopped struggling and lay down with his head buried in his paws. He started to whine.

A red flower opened above the demonstration table. It started as a fist-sized globe, but unfurled petals of crimson light shot through with blue veins. It grew quickly and I jumped back to give it some room.

And then it evaporated, the petals dissolving into the air just like Beverley's water balloon had.

'I trust the rest of the experiment was a success,' said Nightingale.

He was leaning over the railing in the Ladies' Gallery and smiling sardonically. At his feet, Toby had perked right back up – although he paused in the adoration of his master long enough to give me an irritated snarl. Nightingale led him away, and as I waited for them to come downstairs I tidied up.

The staff was cold and inert beneath my hand now. I gave it a few experimental swings. I'll say this for old-style wizardry – if the magic failed you could always beat someone to death with your staff.

Nightingale entered through the main door – Toby did not follow him.

'Did it work?' he asked.

'Better than expected,' I said. 'It drained the staff completely.'

'So I noticed,' said Nightingale. 'Perhaps the next such experiment should be conducted outside. In fact, some distance away from a populated area.'

'If we try this on Francisca,' I said, 'you may have to follow up with whatever it was you just used. Does it have a name?'

'Not as such,' said Nightingale. 'David developed it so I could clean up after his experiments. I have to note that I'm also worried that draining a staff will not be the same as drawing off power from another universe.'

'It might not be another universe,' I said. 'It could be a different dimension or a tertiary subspace domain. And in any case I don't think we have any choice.'

'There's always a choice,' said Nightingale. 'But often we don't like either alternative.' He took the staff from me and rested it on his shoulder as if he was on parade. 'This was a heavy sacrifice,' he said, 'since we are still some way from fabricating our own staffs. And that's not taking into account your upcoming leave.'

'You forget,' I said. 'We're back in bed with the Sons of Wayland. Grace will make us new staffs.'

'What makes you think Grand Master Yutani will be so accommodating?'

'For one thing, makers got to make,' I said. 'And once they've made, they want to see what they've made put to use. And secondly, we can give them and the Society of the Rose the thing that, deep in their hearts, they secretly crave.'

'Which would be what?'

I gestured up at the Ladies Gallery.

'Recognition and a seat at the table.'

Nightingale gave me a strange appraising look.

'Sometimes, Peter,' he said, 'you quite terrify me.'

*

Somebody else who was currently terrified turned out to be Alastair McKay. At least, judging by how happy he was to see Guleed when she went over to the Hotel Russell to bring him in for another interview. She said that according to the reception desk Alastair hadn't left his room since he checked in.

She brought him in round the back way, where the metal gates, Portakabin and concrete prisoner access ramp gave the illusion of being a bog-standard police station. At least how they appear in gritty TV dramas. We didn't want him getting comfortable.

Me and Seawoll sat in the cramped remote-monitoring room next door, and watched as Guleed got Alastair settled and gave him the 'caution plus three'. This is your standard caution followed by the assurance that you aren't under arrest, you are entitled to legal advice and we totally won't make anything of it if you try to leave. Thanks to TV, nobody ever believes the last bit – which is all to the good.

Danni walked in with a manila folder and sat down to the right of Guleed, who introduced her.

'Straight to the chest,' said Seawoll as Alastair dragged his gaze up to Danni's face with a visible act of will.

Guleed explained that they needed Alastair to see if he could recognise a number of people, and Danni opened the folder and started extracting photographs. Actually they were hard copies run off on my crap inkjet printer, but they would do.

This was where having a modern twenty-first-century interview room without a table, the better to monitor the suspect's body language, had its main disadvantage.

Danni had to clumsily hold up each picture in turn, using the folder as backing.

'We need to get a folding table,' I said.

'That's what you get for fucking with tradition,' said Seawoll. 'And as for the folding table, you'd need to have it bolted down otherwise the next evil scrote will pick it up and twat you with it.'

The first set of pictures were blow-ups of the people from the 1989 Manchester group photograph, interspersed with pictures of the same individuals sourced from family and friends. True to form, Alastair remembered the women's full names but only had the first names for the men.

He confirmed that a Brian 'maybe his surname was Packard but I don't really remember' had taken the photograph.

Then we brought out contemporary pictures of the Manchester Bible study group. We had images of all of them, either cadged from relatives or taken off the internet, except for Jacqueline Spencer-Talbot, aka Jackie, who we still hadn't found.

'Look at Jocasta,' said Alastair when he saw her in a still from a magazine article about third way entrepreneurs. 'How many companies has she started? It used to be a struggle to get her to make the tea. Just goes to show you really can't judge how someone's going to turn out when they're young.'

He recognised the 2009 picture of Brian Packard that we'd taken off Facebook – it was the latest picture we could find. Brian at a colleague's leaving do in Los Angeles. Originally a group shot, he'd had his arm around the shoulders of a plump elderly white woman with curly brown hair. *Next stop Florida* was the caption. Both the retiree, his other colleagues and Brian were tagged by name on the Facebook page.

All of their names had now been duly entered into what me and Reynolds were, this year, calling the Unreality Files. A database of people that had come to our attention, tagged only by nationality, by which of us had entered them, and by a code word representing the reason they were in there. No personal details or case references were attached to the names, to avoid violating data privacy laws on both sides of the Atlantic. The photograph and the names of the people in it were all tagged as BANANAs, meaning they were associated with something or somebody 'hinky' and/or 'sus'.

The picture we showed Alastair wasn't marked with a name.

'That's him,' he said when he saw it. 'That's the guy from Davos who was with the blonde. Only he was different.'

When we asked in what way, Alastair got the slightly glazed and defensive look that I've come to associate with people who have been subject to the glamour. Once it's worn off, the victim can remember what happened but they don't understand why they acted the way they did. This can lead to cognitive dissonance and denial – although if you listen to my therapist, so does walking down the street.

So Brian Packard was, probably, the mysterious Collector that Lesley was collecting the rings and the lamp for. Which meant he'd known about the rings and the Manchester Bible study group from the start. Had he learnt of the lamp after he started collecting the rings? It would be a hell of a coincidence otherwise.

'That's not bloody likely now, is it?' said Seawoll when I discussed it with him.

I didn't wait, but fired off an email to Special Agent Reynolds straight away. Even if she didn't have enough to initiate an investigation of her own, she definitely needed to know about Brian Packard. It was possible he'd wanted the lamp for his mantelpiece, but I didn't think that was the way to bet.

These days Big Brother, or more precisely, your Bratty Techno Uncle, doesn't need an army of paid informers to keep tabs on you. Everybody seems dead keen to take personal responsibility for their own surveillance. So the problem with trying to keep a low profile is that sooner or later you'll have an involuntary encounter with someone who's dying to share your details with the world.

Not that Jacqueline Spencer-Talbot, aka Jackie, was trying to hide exactly, but she hadn't been making an effort to blow her own trumpet either. What she had been doing was running a very successful homeless charity in Southwark. She was accredited with helping loads of people break various cycles of addiction, debt, mental illness and deprivation and get off the streets. And some of her clients were so grateful that they recorded their selfies with her on social media and dutifully tagged her by name.

So finding her was only a matter of time. The real question was what we should do once we found her. She was the obvious next target. But there was always the risk that Lesley was using us to find the rings and that Francisca was using her to find her targets.

Or perhaps she had already tortured Ms Spencer-Talbot's location out of Preston Carmichael. In which case, any delay could get her killed.

In the end we took the risk – policing is all about being on the spot, being visible and being in a position to do something about it. Even when you're not sure what 'it' is. So once we'd persuaded Alastair McKay to stay in the Folly, me and Guleed headed for Southwark in the Asbo. Five minutes behind us were Nightingale and Danni in the Jag. Stephanopoulos headed out from Belgravia with a couple of Sprinters' worth of TSG in tow, while Seawoll stayed decanted in the Portakabin in the coach yard to provide a god-like overview.

Guleed was driving, fast, with the Asbo's light strips flashing but the siren off.

'I don't agree,' she said, when I said Lesley wasn't going to be stupid enough to try and acquire the ring while we were on scene. 'You overestimate Lesley, Peter – you always have done. You underestimate the freedom of movement being police gives us.'

And she proceeded to prove her point by whooping her siren and running a red light at the junction of Charterhouse Street and Farringdon Street. I offered a few conciliatory words to the Goddess of the River Fleet as we surged under the Holborn Viaduct – not a prayer exactly, but it pays to be respectful.

'So you planning to do some mock exam papers?' asked Guleed.

'Before I try any mocks I thought I'd get into General Police Duties and Roads Policing,' I said.

Guleed expressed her doubts about whether I would have any time to study with two newborns and Beverley prepping for her finals. All the while weaving in and out of traffic on Blackfriars Bridge, where the strange blue bulging shape of the skyscraper known as the Pregnant Nun marked the way into Southwark.

When we shot down The Cut, Guleed asked what was on at the Young Vic Theatre, but we went past too fast to see. I got on the Airwave and reported that we were less than five minutes out.

Much less than five – more like two – minutes later and we were pulling up outside the Cherry Tree Shelter. Surprisingly, this was housed in a beautiful 1920s art deco purpose-built garage, single-storey but high-roofed, with Bauhaus-style Crittall windows and white stucco-covered walls. It sat sandwiched between a bus depot and the backs of low-rise 1960s council housing. I was surprised it had survived Southwark's great leap forward into gentrification.

'It's Grade II listed,' said the man who opened the door for us. We hadn't even had a chance to introduce ourselves – he must have spotted us admiring its lines while we waited outside. 'It's driving the developers mad – that's how come we get to use it.' He looked me and Guleed up and down. 'You're not developers, are you?'

'Even worse, we're police,' I said, and we identified ourselves.

'What is it this time?' he asked.

'We need to speak to Jacqueline Spencer-Talbot,' said Guleed. 'It's very important.'

While she did this, I checked to see whether the Spanish Inquisition had tagged the garage door. Nothing – it was as unmarked as the pedestrian door. I was beginning to hope we'd got ahead of Francisca on this – maybe even Lesley, too.

The man, who introduced himself as Greg, finally let us in. Inside, it was not what either of us were expecting from a homeless shelter. However hard the volunteers work they usually reek of despair – and other things. Instead, the whitewashed brick walls of the ex-garage reflected daylight back from a skylight that ran the length of the building. A pool table and café tables and chairs were set amongst shrubs and dwarf trees set in planters and big wooden pots. The high roof was supported by square brick pillars with whitewashed cement facing. Hanging baskets full of flowers hung from cast-iron brackets.

'This is the indoor garden,' said Greg, who explained that they were a referral-only emergency night shelter. They took referrals from any London borough and provided, in the first instance, a place to stay the night and then immediate help.

'Help with what?' asked Guleed.

'With whatever they need,' said Greg.

The garden smelt the way fresh potpourri always promises but doesn't. Although underneath there was Dettol, sadness and a hum – like somebody being tunelessly happy. Throwing-out time was 8 a.m. and clients

323

weren't allowed back in until the late afternoon, which meant, thankfully, that the shelter was largely empty.

'Who was it?' called a voice from further inside.

'The police,' said Greg.

'Tell Sting we're booked up for the night,' said the voice.

'No, the real police,' said Greg.

We emerged into a canteen area with rectangular tables laid out in a grid. Next to it, separated by a serving counter, was a large, well-equipped kitchen. The sort my mum cleans in hotels and office cafeterias. A couple of people were doing just that, and another woman was sitting at one of the tables with a laptop and piles of folders spread around her. She was white, middle-aged, with long brown hair that was streaked with grey and hung down her back in a French plait. She wore an indigo blouse with silver flowers embroidered at the collar and cuffs. When she looked up as we approached, I recognised the round face, the widely spaced eyes and the long straight nose as belonging to the woman in the 1989 photograph. She looked better without the Lady Di haircut. The smile was ironic but not unfriendly.

'I suppose another reunion concert was too much to ask for,' she said.

While Guleed made the introductions, again, I opened the door at the back of the canteen and found a short narrow corridor blocked by a fire door at the end.

'Excuse me,' said Jacqueline Spencer-Talbot. 'Where do you think you're going?'

'Is there a back door?' I asked.

'Yes,' said Greg, the ever-helpful, and he named the street it came out on.

I called Danni on my Airwave and told her where the door was. She and Nightingale would cover the back way in. When I joined Guleed at the table with Spencer-Talbot, I made sure to angle my chair so I could keep an eye on both the kitchen and the way we'd come in.

There were two people cleaning the kitchen – two white women who looked to be in their forties. Both were dressed in stretchy mum jeans, T-shirts and aprons – one pink and one blue. Both of them were making heavy weather of the surfaces, so I guessed they weren't professionals. One, with brown hair and big specs, was having a go at the grill and the burners, while the other was buried head first in the cupboards under the sink. I tried to keep them and the indoor garden in view.

This bit of sensible paranoia was not lost on Spencer-Talbot.

'Are you expecting someone?' she asked.

'Ms Spencer-Talbot,' said Guleed. 'Are you aware of the deaths of David Moore and Preston Carmichael?'

'Preston's dead?'

Spencer-Talbot seemed genuinely shocked. The media coverage of David Moore's death had been muted due to the lack of sensationalism surrounding the case. Dr Walid's theory was that the news media and their consumers unconsciously shied away from events that didn't fall within the narrow band of their expectations. Shot by a jealous lover or stabbed by a hoody were narratives they could run with. Killed in an unspecified manner with no witnesses, no CCTV and no obvious motive probably piqued their curiosity, but would it get clicks or sell papers? More importantly, would it fit the news agenda their organisation worked to?

These days, journalists are mostly freelance and only crusade when they're on the clock.

Preston Carmichael's murder had been louder and splashier. That he'd been tortured (*evil gangsters!*), the body hadn't been discovered for a week (*societal breakdown!*), and the fact he'd been semi-famous on YouTube (*famous influencer!*) meant his death got wide coverage. Even if most of it was bollocks.

But the news seemed to have passed Spencer-Talbot by. Too busy dealing with the immediate needs of her clients or wrapped up in her own little world?

'I'm afraid so,' said Guleed.

My Airwave squawked and I put the earpiece in and clicked back.

'Uniform 523 and 525 are at the back,' said Seawoll. 'We're setting up the perimeter now.'

The TSG had arrived and were in position.

Spencer-Talbot looked at Greg, who'd sat down on the chair next to hers. He took her hand and, comforted, she looked back at Guleed, who asked her when was the last time she'd had contact with Preston Carmichael.

'Not since Manchester,' she said. 'Did you say David was dead?'

'Also in suspicious circumstances,' said Guleed – keeping it as neutral as she could. 'We believe the cases are linked.'

I heard Danni's voice in my earpiece.

'There's no Inquisition insignia on the back door either,' she said.

'Pull back and stand by,' said Seawoll.

'He phoned me,' said Spencer-Talbot.

'Who did?'

'David Moore – only last Tuesday.'

According to Postmartin, the standard operating procedure of the Spanish Inquisition was to tool up to a town and promulgate an *Edict of Grace* which gave everyone a month to make a declaration of faith and grass up their neighbours. After that the inquisitors moved in and, acting as judge and jury, decided whether someone was an evil secret Jew, a heretic, or a Muslim. If they were found guilty most were taken away and burnt.

Postmartin believed that the *Edict of Grace* had been promulgated at David Moore's flat – written on the wall above his bed. David Moore had painted over it just as he'd covered the sigil scratched into his front door.

'I suspect he panicked and tried to deny it ever happened,' Postmartin had said when I asked why the cover-up. 'The forensics boys could only recover part of the writing but it was definitely in Early Modern Castilian.'

Or at least the colleague at Queen's College he'd sent it to thought it was, and what they could read was consistent with existing historical examples.

'When exactly did he make the call?' asked Guleed.

'Oh, I don't know,' said Spencer-Talbot. 'We hadn't opened up, so I suppose about around two.'

The same day as he'd visited his ex-wife and asked for his ring back. We should have picked up a call like that during the initial investigation. David Moore must have used a phone he wasn't associated with.

'And what was the call about?' asked Guleed.

Frustratingly, the sequence of events still refused to make any sense to me. Francisca tortures and kills Preston Carmichael on the first of the month. She then visits David Moore's flat on the third, then again on the fourth, and the next day David is calling a Ms Spencer-Talbot and then desperately turning up at his ex's – asking for his ring back. It's not until the next morning, when he turns up at the Silver Vaults with his pathetic imitation gun, that Francisca appears out of nowhere and explodes his chest.

'He wasn't making a great deal of sense when he called,' said Spencer-Talbot. 'He seemed to feel that God wouldn't forgive him. Which is absurd, of course – God forgives everyone. Eventually, at any rate.'

'Did he say what he'd done that was so unforgivable?' asked Guleed.

David Moore had thought his ring would protect him, if only he could get it back, but Jocasta Hamilton had a ring and Francisca had still turned up at her office. If I hadn't run her off, would Jocasta now be missing her heart? On the other hand, Alastair McKay had sat alone for weeks in his house in Moor Park's not quite gated community, completely undefended, and nothing had happened.

Although I did get the impression that his marriage was disintegrating.

'He said that he'd been living a lie,' said Spencer-Talbot. 'That, secretly, all he'd ever wanted was things for himself.'

David Moore had been a social entrepreneur, a man who'd spent his career being noisily philanthropic. After his death we'd taken his life apart piece by piece and if he was hoarding 'things', they'd been kept really well hidden.

'He said that God had sent an angel to punish him,' said Spencer-Talbot.

'What did you say?' asked Guleed.

'I told him to pull himself together.' Spencer-Talbot made a wide gesture, taking in her immaculate homeless shelter and the less immaculate deprivation beyond. 'There's people with real problems that need help – not spoilt fat children.'

'Fat children?'

'He was a greedy boy when we were at uni,' said Spencer-Talbot. 'Always stuffing his face.'

'But someone did kill him,' said Guleed. 'That's why we're here.'

'Desperate people do desperate things,' said Spencer-Talbot. 'Perhaps if we all did more to make things less desperate, then perhaps there would be less violence.'

It was clear that, unlike herself, she felt we, the police, were personally lacking in the 'making life less desperate for people' stakes.

'We believe you may be the next target,' said Guleed.

A disturbing thought was growing in my mind. What if Francisca was homing in on the rings? Perhaps Alastair McKay hadn't been in any danger despite the sigil scratched into his door because Francisca needed, or maybe wanted, both a positive identification and the presence of a ring before she could act.

That would explain why she'd had to torture Preston Carmichael – to get the ringbearers' names. Postmartin had briefed us that the Pope had authorised the jolly Dominican friars who formed the bulk of the Inquisition to use torture for information only – not punishment. I'm sure that had been a comfort to the poor sods who were set on fire in the public piazza.

Heather had said that Francisca had been granted a holy vision, complete with a named biblical angel – one with their own Wikipedia page, at that. I didn't know where Camael, angel of strength, courage and war, had come from, but I was almost certain that the vision was linked to the ritual spell that the Manchester group had unwittingly taken part in.

The flaw in my presence-of-a-ring theory was that David Moore had never got hold of his lost ring. Francisca had speared him in the Silver Vaults while he was still searching for it.

One of the women cleaning the kitchen had obviously finished for the day and was taking off her apron. The other cleaner had moved on to the pots and was making equally heavy weather of scrubbing them. My mum would have been through that kitchen in less than half an hour, but people are just too cheap to bring in professionals.

The departing woman paused to give me and Guleed suspicious looks before exchanging farewells with Spencer-Talbot and heading out through the indoor garden. She was going to get a shock when she ran into the security perimeter, but that wasn't my problem.

The interruption in the flow of the interview did give me a chance to check whether Spencer-Talbot still had her ring.

'What ring is that?' asked Spencer-Talbot.

'The one Preston Carmichael gave you in 1989,' I said. 'In Manchester.'

'Why on earth do you want to know about the ring?' she asked.

'We think there may be a link between the rings and Preston Carmichael's and David Moore's deaths,' said Guleed.

For the first time doubt crossed Spencer-Talbot's face.

'Do you still have it?' I asked again.

'I don't see what business it is of yours,' she said.

But then she relented and, pulling on a leather thong that hung around her neck, she lifted the ring into view. I stood up and leant over the table as she held it towards me for a closer look. It had the same silver gleam and markings as the other rings.

'May I?' I asked.

But I didn't wait for permission before reaching out and touching the ring. In the instance before Spencer-Talbot snatched it away, I got a flash of a distant voice raised in prayer, lemon-scented dust and blood cast like a crimson net.

What if there really had been a ring at the Silver Vaults? What if Lesley had been tracking David Moore in the hope that he'd find it for her? Would Lesley risk carrying the rings around with her? Why not? She didn't know there was a risk, and they weren't the sort of thing you'd want to leave lying around.

'Why do you keep it?' asked Guleed.

'Keep what?' asked Spencer-Talbot – her ring had already vanished back down her blouse.

'That,' said Guleed. 'It's an object of pagan belief – wouldn't a crucifix be more appropriate?'

I looked over at the kitchen area and saw that the remaining cleaner was no longer visible. A nasty suspicion formed in my mind and I stood up.

'That comment is somewhat inappropriate,' said Spencer-Talbot. 'How I choose to sanctify my God is my business, not the police's.'

I reached the counter in three steps. I already had a spell ready, which was just as well as before I could look over the edge Lesley popped up. I had just enough time to note that she'd padded her clothes to make herself look plumper before she tried to smack me in the face with a frying pan.

I flinched back and felt a breeze as the frying pan fanned my face. I'd prepped an *impello-palma*, which I slammed down on Lesley's foot. People always forget how vulnerable their feet are. Lesley gave a gratifying yelp.

She tried to flick a blinder in my face, but I felt the *formae* building and ducked away when it went off. Behind me I heard Spencer-Talbot screaming and Guleed calling it in on her Airwave. I tried to go over the counter, but Lesley had followed up the blinder with another swing with the frying pan, which hit me on the shoulder with a comical *boing* sound.

It was a dull blow and, because I maintain it's always a good idea to disarm a suspect, I wrapped my left arm around her right, rabbit-punched her once in the face and grabbed her collar.

Lesley threw herself backwards and the loose sweatshirt slipped easily over her head. I might have managed a second grab, or at least to tangle her in the sleeves, but she hit me in the chest with her own *impello-palma* which knocked me flying backwards.

I hit a table, which broke and spilled me sideways amongst the chair legs while I thought that a bit of assistance from Guleed might be quite nice about now. I scrambled up and looked to see that Guleed had jumped up and was staring at something behind me.

I thought it was probably Lesley, but when I turned I found myself face to face with Francisca.

17

Teamwork

We never did figure out how she got in. All the other sudden appearances were heralded by a flash and that bell-like *vestigium* that seemed so loud it was almost a real sound. Not to mention the halo and the wings of fire.

Certainly it was unlikely she walked through our perimeter, although, truth be told, it did prove a bit more porous than we might have liked.

Our best guess was that she was having a lie-down in the shelter's women's dormitory, although Greg swore later that he'd double-checked for malingerers. Perhaps the open reveal of the ring had brought her out, or she'd just finished having a nap and the timing was a coincidence.

One day we may find out. But at that moment I had other things on my mind.

'Francisca,' I said. 'Hi.'

Behind me, I heard Spencer-Talbot yelling at Guleed to get off her – in our risk assessment it was decided that in this eventuality Guleed would grab any civilians while I tried to contain Francisca.

'How are you doing?' I asked.

Francisca cocked her head to one side and frowned as if seriously considering an answer.

'I'm OK,' she said.

'Good, good,' I said, hoping that Nightingale was on his way. 'Heather was asking after you.'

Her face twisted then. Concern? Pain? Anguish? It was hard to tell. Definitely a strong emotion, though.

'She was wondering whether you might come see her.' I said.

Francesca's face fell back into a puzzled frown, and I thought I might even be able to talk her down, when suddenly her gaze flicked over my shoulder. I had a choice then – keep talking or start the spell. I chose wrong.

'She misses you,' I said.

Behind me I felt, rather than heard, the distinctive ripping silk sound of Guleed letting loose and two thwacks in rapid succession. Then Lesley yelping in pain and Spencer-Talbot shouting in surprise.

Sīphōnem is a tricky spell at the best of times, and this was a modified version that I hadn't had a chance to practise more than once. Even as Francisca tensed and prepared to act, I was lining up the *formae*, but I was rushing it and tripped over one of the *inflectentes*. Luckily, all that happened was that the spell failed.

Unluckily, Francisca went full Angel of Vengeance mode.

It might have been because I was closer, or because this was not my first angelic manifestation, but this time I actually followed the sequence. And had I been slightly less terrified, I would have been amazed by its beauty. It unfolded like a rose, with petals of pink and white and the smell of incense and orange blossom.

More importantly, I could feel the edges – the boundary between the physical Francisca and the *allokosmos* that was driving her power. Plus there was a definite suction, as if gravity had twisted through ninety degrees, and if I let go I would plunge into the source of that colour, sensation and power.

I wondered what I would find there.

Fortunately, the sensible part of my brain concluded that it was foolish to stand there gawping and made the command decision for me to throw myself to one side. Unfortunately, I landed face down on a table I hadn't known was there, and went sliding across it and then head first off the edge.

I distinctly heard Spencer-Talbot shout 'Oh my God!' before I smacked into the rough cement floor. I managed to roll clumsily and, using a potted tree to pull myself up, I turned to make a tactical assessment.

Danni was pulling Greg towards the back door, but he was resisting and trying to get back to Spencer-Talbot. She was falling backwards after being pushed hard by Guleed with her left arm as she raised her extendable baton to fend off Lesley, who was trying to duck around her.

And Nightingale had advanced into the canteen area to block Francisca's advance on Spencer-Talbot.

Francisca herself was in a rage – wings of fire scattering salt and pepper shakers and napkins off the canteen tables, knocking plants out of their hanging baskets. But not – I noticed – setting things on fire.

I dodged through the tables, trying to take a position behind Francisca – on her blind side.

Nightingale had his left hand extended, palm out, towards Francisca, while his right was tucked into his chest as if he was limbering up for a boxing match. I could feel the tick-tick-tick of his *signare*, but whatever he was doing, it was too subtle for me to track.

Powerful, though – and complex.

Francisca froze in place, spear raised but not aimed, wings half-furled. For a moment, Nightingale had her, and I took a second to help out Guleed by flicking a water bomb at Lesley's head. I didn't wait to see if it landed, because Francisca shuddered and lurched towards Spencer-Talbot, who had crawled under the table and emerged into the clear space between it and the main fight.

She held up both her hands, palms out.

'I don't know who you are,' she said. 'But all are welcome here.'

For a moment Francisca hesitated – the burning spear raised.

Then the spear lunged forwards, striking at her chest.

But the hesitation had been long enough for Nightingale to pick up one of the trestle tables and *impello* it between Francisca and her victim. The tip of the spear struck the surface of the table and splinters of wood exploded backwards. I dropped to the floor in time to avoid the shrapnel, but I heard Francisca scream in pain.

The table split in half, but Nightingale held both pieces in place and then sent them flying towards

Francisca. I reckoned that since she was distracted, this was my cue to act. I didn't bother with a spell; instead I swivelled around on my back and kicked at her heel with both feet.

Francisca threw up her spear to guard her face as the table halves slammed into her. The timing couldn't have been better, as my heel connected with her ankle at exactly the right moment. She went over backwards and landed right on top of me. She was heavier than she looked and the impact knocked out my breath, but I still managed to lock my arms around her, pinning her own arms to her sides.

Francisca wriggled and grunted as she tried to break free. I could feel the power of her wings as a hot breath on my arms. Her physical body was hard and strong in the way some of my cousins, the ones who grew up on subsistence farms in Sierra Leone, were. I didn't think I could hold her for long, so I looked around for help.

There was a confused fight amongst the tables as Danni and Guleed tried to drag Spencer-Talbot out, while Lesley tried to grab the ring from around the poor woman's neck. Spencer-Talbot was struggling and yelling something incoherent about letting God help.

He certainly wasn't helping me as Francisca smacked her head back against my face, once, twice. I felt my grip around her body weakening.

'Peter, let go!' shouted Nightingale from the other side of the room.

I released Francisca and she was dragged feet first off my body and up towards the high ceiling. I caught a sense of the spell – there was the *aer forma*, which gives you a grip on bits of air, plus a complex mass of other *formae*, all swirling around too fast for me to clock.

I rolled over and came up on one knee. In front of me, Francisca was hoisted and wrapped in bands of what I learnt later were thickened air – visible only in the way the light refracted through them. She looked at the time like a Barbie doll trussed with Sellotape.

'Now!' shouted Nightingale.

I tried the *sīphōnem* variant again and this time it went smoothly, almost naturally, and I could feel it working. I felt the edges of the spell catch at something that was simultaneously both around and inside Francisca's body. I think she felt it, too, because she began to thrash, wriggling like a snake shedding its skin. I saw the barely visible bands that bound her suddenly shatter.

There was nothing I could do to speed things up – the spell was going at the speed it was going.

But I was almost there.

Francisca flipped like a cat and landed on her feet. With an angry snarl, she flung out an arm in Nightingale's direction and he disappeared in a blizzard of bits of table, plant pots, chairs and jangling stainless steel cutlery. A chalk menu board flew across the canteen and smacked into the far wall with a bang and a small cloud of chalk dust.

I was sure I had her – even as she turned her gaze on me and raised her spear.

I had the connection; the power was beginning to siphon out . . . although something was pulling me into the boundary. I had the weirdest idea that I had to let go

339

and allow myself to be sucked inside, as if an exchange was necessary for the spell to work.

That's the trouble with magic – it's unpredictable, and you never know what's going to happen until you try it.

Francisca reared up above me, wings spread, spear poised.

For a moment Francisca was framed in a peacock's tail of blue and green – like a stained glass window in full sunlight. And through it I felt the warmth of summer stone and the sound of running water.

I could feel a connection, as if part of Francisca stretched back into the unknown.

If I could just follow that thread . . .

Then something grabbed hold of the back of my belt and yanked me backwards.

The spear came down and the cement floor exploded as I skidded backwards. I heard Lesley shout, 'For fuck's sake, Peter! Get out of the fucking way!'

I slammed into an overturned table and before I could move, the spear came darting for my chest again. One thing was for certain. Francisca definitely had a thing about hearts.

A shield formed in front of me, a shimmer in the air with a tinge of blue. The spear struck it and slid upwards, so I went sideways. As I scrambled for safety I felt, rather than saw, Nightingale try the binding spell again.

Third time lucky, I thought, and tried to clear my mind. But before I could line up the spell, Francisca screamed. There was a brilliant light and she vanished.

Then there was one of those pauses that happen just before a disaster, and are just long enough for your realisation and too short for useful action.

I'd barely got to my knees when a concussion blew me over, tables and chairs splintered, and a nearby pillar cracked from one side to the other.

Not a real explosion, I thought as I got to my feet.

My ears were ringing, but they didn't hurt. But powerful enough to fill the air with cement dust and leaves and petals ripped off the plants of the indoor garden, as though by a gale.

There was a smell of burning grease coming from the kitchen.

I couldn't see Nightingale, Danni or Guleed.

But I could see Lesley standing nearby and calmly tying her hair back with a yellow scrunchie. The clothes she'd been wearing as a disguise were hanging in shreds to reveal a skintight blue and white lycra top. She must have heard me, because she looked over and smiled.

'That could have gone better,' she said, and bolted.

She went out through the back door, which was hanging off its hinges.

I hesitated – thinking that maybe I should check on the others first. But this was probably the best chance I was getting to get to nick Lesley, so I went after her instead.

The fire door at the end of the short corridor was still swinging closed as I shouldered through it. With the amount of magic we'd been flinging around, any operating phone or Airwave would have been dusted and I didn't have time to fish out my backup.

I'd just have to hope that Seawoll's perimeter would call it in for me.

There were a couple of members of that perimeter lying on their backs just outside the back door. I slowed, but the two TSG officers, in full protective gear including helmets, were swearing and clutching their knees.

'Left, left, left!' shouted one of them. 'She went left – over the wall!'

It was a courtyard surrounded on three sides by high Victorian red-brick walls. There was a closed double gate at the far end and stacks of pallets, industrial-sized silver bins and other catering cast-offs against the right-hand wall. The only thing on the left was a big chest freezer pushed up against the wall. I jumped up on it and, because this was Lesley we were talking about, cautiously looked over the top of the wall.

As a cheap alternative to barbed wire, broken bottles had been cemented along the top. A metre-wide gap had been blown to smithereens, leaving pulverised glass and cement dust behind. Beyond was the 521 bus depot, with ranks of single-deck buses lined up ready for use. I caught a flash of blue to the right and spotted Lesley sliding into the narrow gap between two buses.

'In the bus depot!' I shouted, in the hope that backup was just behind me, and I vaulted the wall.

It was a longer drop than I expected, and the shock jarred my ankles when I landed. I stumbled, and when I looked up Lesley was gone, but I'd marked her route.

It's always the same problem when chasing an armed suspect. Not only can they run flat out while you check round every corner first, but you've got to avoid bottling them up with unsuspecting members of the public. Still, I didn't think Lesley was going to start indiscriminately flinging magic around in a populated area, or blow my head off if I stuck it out.

Do something unpleasant, maybe. But not kill me.

And while she paused to do that, Nightingale would have time to catch up.

So I ran quickly down the narrow red canyon between the buses and didn't pause as I emerged out into the access road beyond.

Ahead, I felt the sudden ticking of a clock and the long scrape of a straight razor sliding down its strop. Lesley's *signare* again. And then a real-world sound like guitar strings snapping. Ahead of me was a line of double-deckers parked parallel to the access road. I ran through the short gap between two of the buses and ran into a brick wall. It was chest-high and topped with another two metres of chain-link fence. The buses were parked just far enough away from the wall to allow me to slide along to where a large hole had been melted in the fence. When I brushed my hand against the twisted ends of the wires, they were warm to the touch and resonated with the cry of a seagull.

On the other side of the wall was a 1950s council estate, six or so storeys, brick-built and solid in a way later estates aren't. A concrete access road ran left and right but there was no sign of Lesley.

I sighed and hauled myself over the wall and through the hole in the fence. At my feet, I found a pile of rags. I squatted down and had a look – they were the remains of Lesley's disguise. By now she would have grabbed a jacket from somewhere, changed her face and would be Jason Bourne-ing it off into the sunset.

If she knew what was good for her.

I heard running feet and looked left.

Nightingale was loping up the access road towards me. He slowed to a walk when he saw I wasn't chasing anyone any more.

'Do you think she went to ground in the flats?' he asked when he reached me.

I said it was possible but not likely.

'She knows how we work,' I said. 'She's counting on the fact that we're going to have to go door to door just to be on the safe side.'

'How many dwellings do you think that is?' he said.

There were two main blocks, plus a three-storey block that ran along the back.

'Over two hundred,' I said, and pointed out the other, bigger tower block over the road to the right and the even bigger high-rise to the left.

'I'm not sure that would be a good use of our time,' said Nightingale.

He was thinking that safely tackling Lesley would be a job for both of us, and even if we used Danni, Guleed and the TSG as beaters – Nightingale's analogy, not mine – chances are she could still evade us.

'And then, while we're otherwise occupied,' said Nightingale, 'she could be about her business.'

Which was, for some reason, collecting rings.

'She took a bit of a chance trying to grab it with us there,' I said. 'Not to mention Our Lady of the Radical Heart Transplant. She must want those rings quite badly.'

Nightingale's eyes had never stopped scanning the blocks in front of us.

'It appears so,' he said. 'Although she did act to save your life. Twice, in fact.'

'I did sort of notice that,' I said.

'I wouldn't count on her saving it a third time,' he said.

'Interesting, though, isn't it?' I said. 'First she warns us about the angel and then she saves my life. She could have gone after the last ring, but she shielded me instead.'

'Do have any idea why?' asked Nightingale.

'We were friends,' I said. 'Mates are like family sometimes. You don't always behave in your own best interest.'

'True,' said Nightingale. 'Combat is disorientating – soldiers often act on instinct rather than rational consideration. I'd rather you avoided such situations in the future.'

'I'll do my best,' I said.

'Yes,' said Nightingale. 'That's what worries me.'

Somebody was frying something in a nearby flat and my stomach rumbled. I was about to suggest that we went in search of a working phone when Danni and Guleed drove up in a commandeered response car.

Given that both Francisca and Lesley had escaped, they seemed in a good mood. Danni was practically bouncing up and down on her heels and Guleed had that particular shade of non-expression that I'd learnt to interpret as unbearable smugness.

'What?' I asked when they walked over and Danni grinned.

'Guess what we snatched off Lesley?' she said.

And she held up a yellow and black narrow-gauge bungee cord tied into a loop and strung with silver rings. Platinum rings, to be more precise, and there were five of them.

18

Command and Control

On the basis that we were already there, and that the place had already been trashed, we set up camp at the shelter. Although the indoor garden and kitchen were a mess, a surprising amount of the canteen area and the offices that led off it had survived intact. The fire brigade had given the remains of the kitchen and the structure the once-over and declared it safe, though they did turn off the mains gas just to be on the safe side.

Since the TSG often find themselves parked on stand-by for hours and hours, they can always be counted on to either have snacks or to know where the nearest refs can be found. Danni had gone off to 'liaise' with them while Guleed and Nightingale headed back to the Folly with Jacqueline Spencer-Talbot.

I sat at a table in a corner with a good view of both entrances. The rings were tucked into one of the pouches of my uniform MetVest.

'You're supposed to put that on *before* you get in a fight,' Danni had said as she headed out.

I wrote up my notes while waiting for coffee.

We'd tentatively formed a theory that Francisca only struck when both her intended victim and one or more rings were in the same locale. On the additional assumption that only Lesley was interested in the rings for themselves, I was keeping them in the hope she'd come back for a second try while Nightingale stashed Spencer-Talbot and Alastair McKay in the basement with Molly and Foxglove.

I thought of the alleged magical defences around the Folly – perhaps we'd get a chance to see how well they worked.

I was still waiting for coffee when I looked up to find Professor Postmartin picking his way through the debris to reach me. He was wearing what I think of as his action academic suit – thick tweed with leather re-inforcements at the elbow. The patches went with the battered green leather briefcase he'd brought with him.

'My, my, my,' he said. 'What a mess.'

'It's a circus,' I said.

'I do love the classics,' he said. 'Although somehow I missed out on the original TV series.'

He looked around what was left of the indoor garden and joined me at my corner table.

'This must have been very nice – before,' he said, not specifying before what. 'I came down because Nightin-gale said you'd probably go straight home from here.'

'Pretty much ordered me to,' I said. 'I think he's worried about me.'

'Should he be?'

'I don't know if we can stop this woman.'

'The *sīphōnem* spell didn't work?'

I talked him through my two failed attempts to put the spell on Francisca.

'She's too fast and destructive,' I said. 'We all piled in

348

and she nearly took us all to the cleaners, Nightingale included.'

Postmartin opened his briefcase and pulled out an A4 envelope folder made of clear rigid plastic.

'I don't know if this will help,' he said, opening the folder, 'but I think I've found your Inquisition practitioner.'

He removed a picture from the folder and put it on the table before me. It was an old-fashioned engraved portrait of a middle-aged white man with hooded eyes, a beaky nose and surprisingly fleshy lips. He wore a high collar with a minimalist ruff.

'Magister Cristoval Romano,' said Postmartin. 'Born 1581 in Carmona, which is near Seville, died . . . Well, nobody's that certain. We have no confirmed date of death but the last reference to his life was from 1623, when he was listed as a *calificador* for the Inquisition in Seville.'

A *calificador* was a consultant who assisted the Inquisition by assessing the evidence against the accused. What was unusual was that normally this post was taken by a theologian.

'Whereas the Magister was famous as an alchemist and a natural philosopher,' said Postmartin. 'Another unusual feature is that the Inquisition kept next to no records of the cases that he worked on.'

The Inquisition were famous for keeping records of every denunciation, confession, torture session and trial they participated in. So detailed were their ledgers, including meticulous record-keeping of goods seized from suspects' households, that social historians know more about the material culture of ordinary Spaniards of that period than anywhere else in the medieval period.

'It's an ill wind,' said Postmartin.

'Maybe the records were lost,' I said. 'You're always moaning about gaps in the historical record.'

'According to my friend at Queen's,' said Postmartin, 'and he can bore for England on the subject, we have good records from the Inquisition in Seville for that period. Their absence speaks to secrecy, rather than rising damp or rapacious mice.'

'You think he was part of an occult branch of the Inquisition?' I said.

'Or perhaps the whole of that branch,' said Postmartin. 'Or a mere consultant brought in on an ad-hoc basis. Whatever his official standing, I believe I have found his nemesis.'

Postmartin produced another A4 hard copy of an antique portrait. Judging by the flattened greyscale, this was a monochrome printing of a full-colour painting. This man was darker-skinned than the previous guy, younger, and his hair was cut long enough to show loose curls. His eyes were black, his nose what they call patrician, and his expression one of utter confidence. Even without colour I could see that his clothes – the embroidered doublet, the ruff, the silver chain around his neck – were not just richer but finer than those of the magister. He was practically smirking at the painter.

'Enrique Jorge Perez,' said Postmartin. 'Born 1570, also in Carmona, died 1656 in London at the ripe old age of 86, in bed and surrounded by the weeping and wailing of his family.' Postmartin winked at me. 'Now, that's the way I want to go, although I think I'm good for at least a century – don't you?'

I said, if anything, he seemed to be getting younger.

'Chance would be a fine thing,' he said. 'He was a *converso*, a New Christian whose family probably converted following the pogroms of 1391.'

When the synagogues of Seville had been converted to churches, the Jewish quarter was looted and Jewish property seized by the Church. Postmartin suspected that the Perez family had abandoned their original Jewish family name when they bowed to the inevitable.

'But possibly not the religion of their fathers,' said Postmartin. 'As evinced by later events. Because we don't know their original family name, we can't trace their activities prior to 1391, but given the speed with which they built a reputation as apothecaries, alchemists and natural philosophers, I suspect that they had been pre-Newtonian practitioners under the Almohad Caliphate.'

Who had been the Muslim rulers of Morocco and southern Spain until Charlton Heston turned up tied to his horse and drove them out. I admit I may have faded out a bit during that part of Postmartin's explanation. I tuned back in at 1478, when Seville became host to the first Spanish Tribunal of the Holy Office of the Inquisition. Three years later they held their first auto-da-fé, which is Latin for 'act of faith', in which sinners were helped to give penance for their sins by being set on fire in front of a festival crowd. Most of these sinners were new Christians who had been judged insufficiently Christian – or worse, secretly Jewish.

'Denunciation was a common way to settle scores or duck out of debts,' said Postmartin. 'So it probably isn't that surprising that a rich and powerful family like Enrique Perez's would be denounced. Still, they managed to stay out of trouble for over a century until Enrique was accused in 1622.'

The Inquisition locked Enrique up in the Castle of San Jorge by the River Guadalquivir that served as their HQ and jail. Just to be on the safe side, and because the Inquisition was nothing if not thorough, they locked up his wife, his children, his sisters, their husbands and their children. They seized all the family's property and did a very thorough assessment of their worth.

'It was the sheer amount of glassware, crucibles and metalworking gear,' said Postmartin, 'that allowed us to identify Enrique as an alchemist.'

There was no detailed account of any subsequent investigation or trial. Instead, there was only a sketchy report of a severe fire at the castle, which claimed a surprisingly large number of members of the Inquisition.

'It is the very next month that Magister Romano is enrolled as a *calificador*,' said Postmartin. 'It's possible that his name turns up in other records we haven't checked yet, but the last reference to him we have is the payment he received from the Bishop of Seville of a large sum in silver.'

Enough to build a small castle.

Postmartin pulled out some more prints to show me. A woodcut of the Castle of San Jorge, a map of Europe with arrows showing the Jews' escape routes from Spain and Portugal. And a portrait of what I realised was an older Enrique Perez.

'Antwerp, 1645,' said Postmartin, 'only now he is calling himself Rodrigo Alfonzo and claiming to be a Portuguese merchant.'

'The same Alfonzo family that left the lamp at Bevis Marks?' I asked.

'That seems likely,' said Postmartin.

Antwerp, while under Spanish control, was a cosmopolitan trading city. The Inquisition had yet to get a foothold there, and it became a well-known stop on the underground railway that was moving threatened Jews from Spain and Portugal to the relative safety of the Ottoman Empire. Going a very long way around – according to the map.

The alchemist formerly known as Enrique Perez had white hair, grown sparse and thin, but the artist had captured a great satisfaction in the eyes and the twist of his lips. This was a man who was obviously pleased with himself. He was resting his right hand on a cluttered bench – both he and the bench were illuminated by daylight streaming in through a window. Behind him, the shadows hinted at expensive wood panelling, portraits and furniture.

Postmartin passed me a blow-up detail of the workbench and grinned.

Next to the subject's right hand was a tall fluted glass lamp with gold and silver intaglio around its base and a brass cap – either Leon Davies's lamp or its twin. Next to that was a thick book, open to show pages that were blank except for a single line of Latin. Scattered across the pages, with deliberate casualness, were seven silver rings. The artist had taken care to ensure that his work was detailed enough to guarantee that the occult symbols on the rings were visible, and the writing legible.

Quoniam requirens sanguinem eorum recordatus est, I read. '"Because requiring their blood it is remembered"?'

'It's from the *Av HaRachamim*, a medieval Jewish prayer,' said Postmartin. 'The rest goes like this in English . . .

Why should the nations say, "Where is their God?"
Let it be known among the nations in our sight
that You avenge the spilled blood of Your servants.
And it says: "For He who exacts retribution for spilled
*   blood remembers them.*
He does not forget the cry of the humble."'

'He definitely wanted the world to know what he'd done,' I said.

'It gets even better,' said Postmartin, who was practically vibrating with excitement. 'This particular painting was part of the Cathedral collection in Seville. It may have been seized by the authorities in Antwerp, but I prefer to think that Enrique Perez sent it to the Church authorities himself. He didn't care about the rest of the world, but he definitely wanted the Inquisition to know he'd bested them.'

The painting had been sold as part of a job lot in the late 1970s to the J. Paul Getty Museum in Los Angeles. The details of the book, the rings and the lamp were obscured until the painting was restored in 2008 as part of a push to uncover hidden artistic gems. Which meant that somebody – possibly Brian Packard – could have spotted the lamp and rings at the gallery. There'd been a great deal of publicity surrounding the restoration, and a special exhibition of the restored works. The portrait and the close-up Postmartin had showed me had been featured in an online article.

'Sensibly, he didn't hang around for the Inquisition to catch up with him,' said Postmartin, getting back on track.

A certain Rodrigo Alfonzo was named amongst the 'Portuguese' merchants operating in London – the ones that went on in 1657 to legally change their status in the face of wartime confiscation. Although he died before the case was brought.

'Neither Alfonzo nor Rodrigo are exactly unusual names,' said Postmartin. 'But luckily we can work back from Leon Davies to the point where his family take an anglicized surname in 1897. Since we know Leon was in charge of the lamp, we can surmise that they are the same family.'

Which is why we knew that the alchemist formerly known as Enrique Jorge Perez died smugly of old age in bed.

'I don't suppose he left a handy treatise on how the rings and the lamp worked?' I asked.

Postmartin laughed and started to neatly pack hard copies back in their folder. In the same order as they'd come out, I noticed.

Danni arrived with some coffee and offered to do another run for Postmartin, who told her not to bother.

'I brought my own tea,' he said, and he pulled a vacuum flask from his briefcase. It was an antique

1950s model with a rounded stopper and a faded blue and green tartan pattern on its sides. 'I always pack my own refreshments,' he said. 'Got into the habit back before there was a coffee shop on every corner.'

Danni slipped out to join the perimeter while Postmartin popped the plastic cup off the top of the Thermos and poured black tea. Steam rose, and there was a citrus scent which weirdly reminded me of the orange smell I'd got from Francisca's boundary effect.

'I'm partial to milk and sugar,' said Postmartin. 'But black tea with lemon stays hotter longer.'

He lifted his cup and blew on the surface to cool it.

'OK,' I said. 'This is what I think happened. Our boy Enrique falls out of favour and is denounced, accused and arrested. But the Inquisition don't realise how powerful he is and he breaks out of prison, grabs all his family, extracts a bit of revenge and gets the fuck out of Spain.'

Postmartin nodded and sipped his tea.

'So the Inquisition is not having this and, not being stupid, they know they're outclassed,' I said. Suddenly I could see the whole bloody thing as if Mary Beard was narrating it to camera. 'So they bring in this Magister ... what was his name?'

'Cristoval Romano,' said Postmartin.

'They bring in Romano as their big gun and set him the task of dealing with Enrique.'

'Bring me the head of Enrique Perez,' said Postmartin with a straight face.

To that end, they recruited Francisca, gifted her with incredible powers and set her on Enrique's tail. I thought of the cat-women and the child soldiers and all the fanatical cannon fodder that had been drummed up by powerful men to suit their purposes, and felt suddenly sick.

'But our Enrique was too good and too clever,' I said. 'He fashioned the lamp and the rings and used them to trap Francisca. Then he had that painting done and I bet he was already halfway across the Channel before it had left for Seville.'

'Do you have an inkling as to how the rings worked?' asked Postmartin.

'No,' I said. 'But I think she's drawn to them. Whatever weird bollocks Preston Carmichael did in 1989 created a link between him, their wearers and Francisca. Once she has identified her victim, she needs them and the ring to be in the same location. I think Preston Carmichael was wearing his when she tortured him for information.'

'But David Moore was still looking for his ring when he was struck down in the Silver Vaults,' said Postmartin.

'Lesley slipped up,' I said. 'She knew that Francisca had been in angel form at the vaults. So how did she know?'

'Because she was there?' said Postmartin, and sipped his tea. 'But she didn't steal David Moore's ring until later.'

'Meaning that it doesn't have to be the owner's ring,' I said. 'Any of the seven rings will do. By then Lesley had the one she glamoured off Alastair McKay in Davos. She must have had it with her when she followed David Moore to the Silver Vaults. So it doesn't look like Francisca cares about the rings themselves per se.'

I patted the pouch on my MetVest.

'Interesting,' said Postmartin, and poured himself another cup. 'That implies that the rings form a gestalt – a collective linkage between the Manchester seven and the rings. Since they were obviously designed as a countermeasure to Magister Romano's magic, I doubt their purpose was to attract his angel of death.'

'Something obviously happened at that prayer meeting,' I said, and finished my coffee. 'But me and Nightingale have no idea what.'

'Prior to Newton,' said Postmartin, 'a great deal of weight was given to the notion of correspondence. The idea that one thing, either through resemblance or a symbolic connection, could be used to influence another thing.'

So the penis-shaped stinkhorn mushroom made a frequent appearance in folk recipes for curing impotence. Although given how they smelt, I couldn't see it helping with the foreplay part of the problem.

'So if Carmichael did, unwittingly, practise an effective ritual in Manchester,' said Postmartin, 'then I think it's entirely possible that the group may have created a bond with the rings and thus with Francisca.'

'It would be nice if we knew what they were for originally,' I said. 'They wouldn't be so prominent in the painting if Enrique hadn't thought they were important.'

'And they wouldn't have been included,' said Postmartin, 'if he hadn't been sure their significance would be obvious to the Inquisition in Seville. There's no point taunting your enemies if they don't understand the insult.'

'Perhaps not to the Inquisition at large,' I said. 'Maybe just the Magister.'

'That's a definite possibility,' said Postmartin.

'Have you reached out to Leon Davies's family?' I said, thinking it was too much to hope that they had a lost family journal lying around the house.

'I'm still waiting on a reply,' said Postmartin. 'Do you have a backup plan to deal with our troublesome Lady of Spain?'

There was a lump in my stomach that I wasn't used to.

'Nightingale does,' I said.

'I could not control her, nor bind her, and you saw what happened when I tried to knock her down,' he'd said. 'It's obvious that the *sīphōnem* variant you have developed will not work while she actively resists it.'

I'd pointed out that we really didn't have any alternative.

'Yes,' Nightingale had said quietly, 'we do. If we position snipers out of her immediate range, I'm confident that a suitably high-powered round will bring her down.'

'Ah,' said Postmartin when I told him. 'It does have the virtue of simplicity.'

I said nothing, He was right and so was Nightingale. Francisca had killed two already, and what's more, if we didn't deal with her she'd probably kill again. I've never had a moral problem about lethal force to save lives – in the abstract, anyway. But luring Francisca into an ambush and gunning her down seemed a bit premeditated to me. I didn't feel good about it at all.

*

I was still feeling queasy about our options when I arrived home to find my mum had moved in. She was in the kitchen; all four burners on the cooker were in use and the emergency backup rice cooker had been dragged out from its cupboard and was running in tandem with the main rice cooker.

The air smelt of cassava leaf, palm oil and fried fish – I wondered how many people she was catering for.

'So where's Dad?' I asked, because my mum never leaves my dad on his own overnight. He might be in his seventies but my mum still remembers that mad bad jazzman she married – and what that led to vis-à-vis addiction and self-neglect.

'*E dae na di Folly*,' she said in Krio. '*Thomas and Molly dae watch am for me.*'

'You can't just dump Dad on my boss,' I said, but of course she could. Mum was a world-class exponent of the *it's easier to beg forgiveness than ask permission* school of interpersonal relations. Not that she ever begged forgiveness, either.

'*E nor dae tay*,' she said, and then banged her ladle on the edge of one of the bubbling pots.

One of the foxes came running in and skidded to a halt in front of her, claws skittering on the tiles.

'Tell Abigail to lay the table,' said my mum.

'Yes, boss,' said the fox and, turning, scampered out.

My mum turned back to me.

'*You dae hep me for cook?*' she asked. 'No? Then why don't you go and see what Max has done in the garden – he's very proud.'

Apart from anything else, Maksim had laid the

360

groundwork for an occupying army. Half a dozen pop tents had been pitched next to the patio, their nylon fly-sheets glistening in the drizzle.

Beyond them, I found the man himself surveying his handiwork.

At least the JCB had been sent back to the rental agency – assuming Maksim hadn't just 'borrowed' it off a construction site. Maksim had been a professional criminal in both Russia and London, and he had the tattoos to prove it. Occasionally he forgot that he'd given all that up in favour of being Beverley's Mr Fixit.

'It was quite an easy job,' he said. 'You dig hole, pour in floor, concrete blocks for the walls and render on top. It should have taken longer because of drying but Beverley did her miracle thing and speeded it up. Then I put in the fittings, the pump, the drain and finally paint. What do you think?'

I thought it looked more like a slipway than a pool – although it was painted a nice sky blue. It ran twenty metres – half the length of the garden – and was six metres wide, not counting the flagstone border path. There were white Perspex dome lights fitted along the sides and textured navy non-slip tiles along the border. At the end nearest the house it had a gradual slope like a kid's pool, and the far end was open to the river. As a result, the water in the pool was full of algae, twigs and other unidentifiable bits of urban river debris.

'Don't worry,' said Maksim. 'We take care of that when the time come.'

'And afterwards?'

'We block off the end,' said Maksim, 'build sauna,

and next time it snows we can have a proper swimming party.'

I was almost certain he was joking about the winter swimming parties, but the sauna sounded like a good idea.

'Where is Bev?' I asked. Maksim always knew.

'She's bringing her sisters.' Even as he said it, spring arrived – sort of.

It had been late evening when I walked out of the kitchen, and under the low clouds it darkened quickly until the garden was lit only by the patio lamps and the muted glow of the underwater pool lights.

Then a very localised dawn broke at the point where the pool met the river. Pale sunlight filtered through deep water, as if the sun was coming up somewhere under Beverley Brook.

It only lasted a moment, and I wasn't even sure if it had been real light made from real photons, or some artefact my brain had conjured up in response to a magical stimulus. Two small shapes came shooting like seals up the pool towards us, slowing only when they reached the shallow end. Two black girls in expensive pink and yellow neoprene wetsuits broke the surface and came up the incline towards us. The youngest, Brent, who was seven, leapt into Maksim's arms. I was glad to see that even he staggered under the momentum.

'Uncle Max!' she yelled. 'Are we sleeping out?'

The other girl, Nicky – a too sensible twelve to show enthusiasm – gave me a wave and walked sedately out to join us. Behind her came Beverley in her specially adapted wetsuit. I stepped forwards to help her out

362

– chill water sloshing into my shoes. She kissed me; her lips were cool from the water. But she refused a hug.

'Your clothes,' she said. 'You idiot.'

She handed me a yellow waterproof holdall to carry back to the house. We walked hand in hand past where Maksim was showing Brent her pop tent while Nicky followed on, asking about supper.

What with Nicky, Brent, Abigail, Maksim, various hangers-on and my mum, we'd had to lay the extra gate-leg table and use a couple of folding garden chairs to get everyone seated. Not that Mum ever sat down for more than five minutes – instead, she bustled around dishing out rice and soup and making sure the less habituated, like Maksim, ate from the less spicy pot. This, I might add, means 'less spicy' by West African standards, so the big man's face went an interesting red colour at one point.

The sacrifices people will make for their religion, I thought, and felt a twist in my stomach. It must have shown on my face because I caught Mum giving me a strange look.

I caught her looking at me again when we were clearing up.

I don't like overloading the dishwasher, so I was doing the big pots and crockery by hand when I turned to grab the next dish and found Mum staring at me. This is unusual. Growing up, most of my interactions with my mum were done in the teeth of some other distraction – football, cooking, cleaning, family gossip, *EastEnders* . . . my dad. I'm not used to getting the full force of her regard. It was unsettling.

'Why are you upset?' she said. 'Is this not a beautiful home? Is Beverley not a beautiful woman? Are you not about to be a father?'

'What makes you think I'm upset?' I asked, but even as I said it I realised I was.

'Because you had that face when you were a boy,' said Mum.

'Well, that's hardly surprising, is it?' I said. 'It's my face. I only got the one.'

'You know what I mean,' she said. 'So what is the problem, hey? Is it this case? Or this?' She waved her hand to encompass a house full of relatives, foxes and shouting.

'I think I might have to kill someone,' I said.

Mum took an involuntary step backwards and her hand flew to her mouth.

'No,' she said. 'No – please say this is not true. *God nor wan mek you kill porsin.* You did not become a police-man to kill.' She stepped closer to me again and stared up at me. 'Who is this someone?'

'There's a woman who believes herself to be an angel of death,' I said. 'She's killed two already, and she has five more on her list.'

'Is she a witch?' asked Mum, who has pretty cultural-ly specific notions about right and wrong.

'No,' I said. 'She was made this way by wicked men. And I don't think I can stop her without killing her.'

'Let someone else do it,' said Mum. 'Let Thomas kill this woman. What would one more killing be in his life?'

364

The last straw, maybe, I thought, but Nightingale was not Mum's concern.

'It doesn't matter who pulls the trigger,' I said. 'It will be my responsibility either way.'

Mum shook her head.

'You must find another way,' she said.

'If I don't stop her, she *will* kill again.'

Mum picked up the mop and bucket and headed for the back door.

'Find another way,' she said, as if the issue was decided.

'Peter, love,' said Beverley as we were preparing for bed. 'You need to get a move on and either wrap up this case or hand it on.'

'I'm not sure I *can* hand it on,' I said.

'Of course you can, and you're going to do it tomorrow afternoon,' she said.

I took her hand and helped her into the bed – strategically placing pillows as she wriggled into a comfortable position.

'Really – tomorrow afternoon?' I said.

'At the latest,' she said. 'After that, I can't say for sure.'

We lay side by side in the darkness, while outside I could hear rain pattering on the pop tents and the sounds of Beverley's sisters definitely not settling down to sleep.

Lesley wanted the rings and we wanted Lesley.

Francisca wanted to poke out the hearts of the Manchester seven, but would only show up if both victim and at least one ring were in close proximity.

But there was no reason to believe it meant being in the same room.

Or even the same floor.

The *sīphōnem* spell had nearly worked, but I needed more time to find the connection back to the *allokosmos* that was driving Francisca's powers and sever it.

A restrained suspect was a safe suspect, but Nightingale couldn't do it on his own.

There was a mechanism to save Francisca; I was sure I had all the pieces. I just needed to figure out how to put them together.

I think I must have dozed off, because all was suddenly quiet when I realised I had a plan– one that would kill two birds with one stone. If it worked.

And if it didn't?

There was always Nightingale's alternative.

I got up and padded into the kitchen – the only part of the house devoid of relatives, friends or foxes – and phoned Nightingale.

He picked up on the second ring.

'Peter?' he said – sounding wide awake.

'The Folly's magical defences,' I said. 'Can we turn them off?'

Wednesday

I'll come back in again . . .

19

Hearts and Minds

I arrived back at the Folly at dawn the next morning, to the sound of trumpets.

The sky was lightening above the dome of the atrium as my father stood at its centre, playing 'The Night We Called It a Day' while Nightingale sat in one of the over-stuffed leather armchairs reading the *Telegraph*, legs folded, the toe of his shoe gently bobbing in time to the music, and Toby did a very good 'his master's voice' impression – no doubt in the hope of sausages.

I caught a glimpse of Molly drifting along the first floor balcony and, behind her, Foxglove, pirouetting.

I wondered if my dad had played the night before in the faint light of a crescent moon while the sisters danced around him. He wouldn't have noticed them, though. When my dad plays he goes somewhere else. You could set fire to the stage and he wouldn't notice.

Nightingale folded his paper, set it aside and rose to greet me.

'Are we ready?' I asked.

'Preparations are well under way,' he said. 'Although I do not care for our chances of success. I'm very much afraid that we may have to take the direct approach – given the alternatives.'

'Or I could be completely wrong,' I said. 'And then you're going to have to come up with another plan without me.'

'I could order you not to do this,' he said.

'Are you going to?' I asked.

'Perhaps we should swap roles.'

We'd gone over this earlier over the phone.

'I'm not skilled or fast enough to play your role,' I said. 'So that's a non-starter. Does Foxglove know what we need?'

'The explanation proved quite difficult, but in the end I drew her a picture,' he said. 'A comic strip, if you like.'

'This I have to see,' I said.

'I'm afraid Molly confiscated it,' he said.

'Pity.'

Guleed came in first, carrying with her her MetVest and officer safety gear in a sausage bag and my demagicked staff over her shoulder.

'I don't see how this is going to work,' she said.

'You do your bit,' I said, 'and everything will be much easier.'

'I don't mean that,' said Guleed. 'I mean their bit – what makes you think they'll be so helpful as to follow your plan?'

'The lure is irresistible,' I said. 'They'll be here.'

Molly arrived with coffee and tea but before we could settle down, the team from SCO19 arrived. Guleed took charge and led them upstairs, but not before scooping up a cup and the coffee jug.

A sudden worry caught me off guard.

'Where's Toby got to?' I asked.

'In the kitchen,' said Nightingale.

I realised that I was breathing fast and shallow – almost hyperventilating. The atrium went in and out of focus. I realised that I was terrified. Which seemed so absurd, given that I was having tea in the middle of the Folly, that I had to stop myself breaking into giggles.

'Deep breaths, Peter,' said Nightingale. 'In, hold, out.'

I followed his advice, taking long slow breaths as if I was preparing for a particularly tricky spell. My heart slowed, the panic subsided – although the fear remained.

'What the fuck was that?' I said.

'The responsibility of command,' said Nightingale. 'You're personally brave to the point of recklessness, Peter. But now you are waiting for the battle and you know, because you're not stupid, that you might have overlooked something or the enemy might have a capability you haven't considered. But you know it's too late. It's going to happen now, and if it goes wrong and people die, you will be responsible.'

'Cheers, boss,' I said. 'That was a morale-booster.'

'This is a workable plan,' said Nightingale. 'I wouldn't have approved it if I didn't think it had a chance.' He looked at his watch. 'We might want to take our start positions now, however.'

I watched him trot up the side stairs and went to find myself somewhere to hide.

Back in the Regency, when the Folly was built, the gentry were very clear about the role of servants in society. They were to be helpful, subservient and, above all, as invisible as possible. To this end, the Folly was built with a number of corridors and stairs to allow the maids and stewards to circulate unseen. They also had semi-secret doors into public areas, and these doors had spyholes to allow loyal servants to check the coast was clear before entering. That this allowed the lower classes to spy on their betters never seemed to occur to the latter.

I opened what looked like a normal stretch of oak panelling and slipped into the access corridor that led to the back stairs. I turned off the single 40-watt light that illuminated it and opened the spyhole.

And then, feeling sick, I waited to see how workable the plan really was.

As we reconstructed it later, Lesley had scouted the Folly in advance and picked out one of our analysts as a suitable mark. Whether she did this on the fly the evening before, which would have been fast work, or had done the recce and selected her target earlier in the week, we were never able to establish. Either way, she'd done it early on enough to have time to acquire a professional-quality Afro wig – not something they sell at TK Maxx.

In any case, that morning she turned up at Nathan Fairbright's front door in Norwood, talked her way in, put the glamour on him and then fed him some sleeping pills. Danni found him later, fast asleep on his *My Hero Academia* bedspread. Nathan was a clever choice because, despite being male, he was short and had a slight build. Better still, he walked around in baggy sweatshirts, cargo trousers and an enormous parka with a fur-lined hood.

The timing was clever, too – Lesley coming in with the tail end of the rest of the police staff, minimising the risk of an acquaintance talking to her while still using them as cover as she walked in the front door, bold as brass.

She probably thought her main risks were Molly and Toby – who both knew her by smell. But they were safely downstairs in the kitchen with Foxglove, with instructions to stay low until told otherwise. Once she was in the atrium, she could head for either of the two main staircases, or even the side stairs, and it would have been interesting to know where she would have searched first.

But when she was halfway across, I stepped out of the servants' corridor and called her name.

It was clever, coming as a man, because we were expecting a woman. I would love to say that it was something subtle, like the fact that Nathan always takes his parka off the moment he steps inside and never walks with his hands in his pockets. But really it was because she hadn't quite got his face right. Lips too thick and nose too wide – he looked like he'd stepped out of an early *Asterix* comic.

Subconscious racism, I thought – *it will fuck you up every time.*

She flinched and even from behind I could see that she was swearing. Then she turned to face me. I walked over and stopped a nice safe three metres away. She gave me a rueful grin – it was Lesley's smile on a cartoon character's lips.

'I see your security is still as shit as it ever was,' she said, and her face changed.

It wasn't the first time I'd seen it happen, but it wasn't getting any less weird to watch. The skin on her face rippling like some undersea creature settling into the seabed. The brown colour not so much fading as being squeezed out, as each fold rolled and merged, rolled and merged. It looked painful.

'We seem to have caught you,' I said.

'Only after I was all the way inside,' she said.

Then she paused, clocking the now-closed doors front and back, the absence of any civilian collateral and, more importantly, the fact that Molly had removed all the breakable *objets d'art*. Including our first edition copy of the second *Principia*.

'No . . .' She sounded almost impressed. 'You didn't?'

'Didn't what?' I asked.

'You sly fucker,' she said. 'You laid a trap. You knew I'd want the rings back and you knew that I still have access to the police network. I'm so stupid. Nice touch having Danni make the breach of security – new girl and all that? I was in two minds this morning until I read that text.'

Danni had put the location of the rings on CRIMINT that morning, in the hope that Lesley's contact in the Met would pass it on. Obviously they had, and equally obviously the Department of Professional Standards would try and trace who the leak was.

I really should have said three birds with one stone.

'How's she working out, by the way?' asked Lesley.

'Not bad,' I said. 'She's good with dogs and canal boats.'

Lesley was looking around the atrium, not bothering

374

to hide that she was checking the angles and looking for an escape route.

'Where's Thomas the tank eater?' she asked.

'That would be telling.'

'And Frank Caffrey and his merry bunch of part-time murderers?' She craned her head, checking the balconies for snipers.

'He's got the day off,' I said – lying.

'So, what next?' she said.

'I thought we might try a bit of de-escalation,' I said, thinking that one day it was going to work. 'We have tea and biscuits.'

Lesley laughed then – not a cynical laugh, but a genuine burst of good humour as if I'd done something that delighted her.

'I'm not redeemable, Peter,' she said. 'I know that, you know that, the Crown Prosecution Service knows it, too.'

'So do you have any weapons on you that I should know about?'

'Why don't you search me?' she said. 'That's what comes next, isn't it? Off to Belgravia and into the hands of the custody sergeant. If I'm not going to get a Molly breakfast, I might as well have something . . .' She stopped suddenly and made a half-amused, half-exasperated huffing sound. 'Wait, you're not actually—'

And suddenly the atrium was full of vengeful angel.

'You total cunt!' shouted Lesley, but she was proud of me – I could tell.

Francisca had arrived in full Samuel L. Jackson furious vengeance mode, wings of fire extended, a crown of light blazing behind her head and, of course, a burning spear tipped with lightning glass.

You can generally tell when and by whom a spell was perfected by the name it's given. Old Newton himself was crap at names, or more precisely didn't really give a shit. Thus we get *telescopium* for the telescope spell and *kisef* for a spell that is supposed to determine the purity of gold but really doesn't. In the period between Newton's publication of the second *Principia* and the founding of the Society of the Wise, the diverse bunch of quacks, ambitious apothecaries and dangerously independently minded women who were his immediate heirs named their spells however they liked. *Dancing Dog* does what it says on the tin, although you can use it on most mammals, not just dogs. Not that I've seen it in action, on account of ethical considerations, and Toby would probably bite me if I tried. I think the posh women that went on to become the Society of the Rose used ancient Greek for some reason, and then there are spells named things like *Shazorami!*, with an exclamation mark, which comes straight from the music hall.

The pedantically precise Latin of such spells as *clausafrange* come from that era when the newly formed Society of the Wise was clawing for respectability and royal patronage. By the first half of the twentieth century, the language opened up again but there is a marked difference between serious spells such as *aqua ex vestibus exi* and the *Treacle Foot* spell I threw at Lesley as she legged it across the atrium.

According to Nightingale, this was a spell that was passed around and down by the boys at Casterbrook

School for gentlemen wizards. It was considered a frivolous spell because it basically caused someone's shoes to stick to whatever they were standing on. Nightingale said it was used during rugby matches.

'Magic while playing was encouraged,' said Nightingale, when I asked whether this was cheating. 'But strictly forbidden to spectators and, of course, equally forbidden when playing against teams from mundane schools.'

So while the *serra obscura* and the narrow-gauge fireball officially called *lux bodkin* were perfectly adequate for chopping up your enemies and brewing up their tanks, for a peacetime copper *Treacle Foot* was as nice a non-lethal way to neutralise a suspect, and was just what the Officer Safety Policy Unit asked for.

Lesley, who'd sensibly been legging it for the side door, suddenly found the soles of her shoes sticking to the floor tiles. Her best bet would be to yank her feet out of her trainers, but I didn't have time to watch because Francisca was trying to kill me.

I ran to my pre-planned position at the north end of the atrium – my back to the entrance – and put up the best shield I could. This was the first test.

I saw the movement in her shoulder that telegraphed her strike. Even as the spear darted forwards, I was jumping back. Whatever else she might be – former housemaid, devout believer, angel of death – nobody had bothered to train her to use a spear. She overextended, so that when the tip hit my shield she was at full stretch and off balance.

'Now!' I shouted, but Guleed was already airborne.

She parkoured off the balcony onto one of the green overstuffed leather sofas and bounced in a way that Michelle Yeoh would have been proud of. In her hand was Hugh Oswald's battle staff, serving its country for the last time. It might have been drained of magic, but it was still a metre of solid oak around an iron core.

She struck, not at Francisca but at the spear – where the glass met the haft.

It broke, the lightning glass shattering, splinters spraying across the atrium to bounce off my shield. I heard Guleed shouting. Her vest and reinforced trousers took most of it, but a couple of shards struck her hand – even as she was vaulting for cover on the other side of the sofa. Lesley, I learnt later, had abandoned her trainers and ducked behind a pillar.

The wings of fire flared and Francisca reared back, blood from multiple cuts on her forehead and cheeks running down her face. She screamed in pain and something – we never did work out what – struck my shield with such force that I was driven backwards.

Then Nightingale stepped out of the eastern stairwell and bound her.

The same spell as last time, only the bonds were thick enough to show blue refracted light. They looped around Francisca, wings and all, and tightened.

I stepped forward to cast the *sīphōnem* spell. As I did, I noticed that Lesley was hiding behind that nearby pillar. She saw me moving and shook her head in exaggerated disbelief.

'Not again,' she said as I cast at Francisca.

Yes again – the same spray of colour behind Francisca

like a stained glass window, again the drag as if I could lean forwards and fall into the boundary between our world and the *allokosmos*.

And again the sheer power overwhelming Nightingale's binding spell. I felt it slipping, the bounds loosening.

'Lesley!' I shouted. 'Help!'

And this was the second test.

I was having to constantly reinforce the triggering *formae* and didn't dare look over but I felt, rather than heard, her long sigh of frustration. Then she swore and then I felt the tick-tock razor strop of her *signare* as she cast her own spell. I couldn't see what it did, but suddenly Francisca's struggles stopped. Nightingale's binding tightened.

And my spell caught.

I felt the gap opening in front of me and I let myself pitch forwards.

The third and final test.

I fell into somewhere else.

I've been to the stone memory of London, the singing crystal ghost palace of Chesham and the unicorn-infested wild lands of Faerie. I have looked into portals from strange *allokosmoi* and felt things staring back – so what happened next was terrifyingly familiar.

I found myself standing in a courtyard full of fruit trees. There was the scent of orange blossom and the gritty taste of dust. Above me the sky was cloudless and an impossible dark blue – the colour a sky goes at dusk when a storm is rising on the horizon. The flagstones beneath my feet were warm from the sun.

I looked down at myself – I was stark bollock naked.

The orange trees were arranged in ordered ranks, and the pattern of the flagstones drew me towards a fountain and beyond that a shadowy gothic arch rose two storeys high. The great wall it was set in was blurred and indistinct, like the surroundings of a dream. I could practically feel my mind trying to impose shapes and order on what I was looking at.

I felt the archway was the obvious way to go. I've done this kind of thing before, and sometimes your real, actual flesh-and-blood body is asphyxiating in slow motion. When I took a deep breath, the whole pulmonary gas exchange seemed to be working fine, but I thought it better not to take the chance.

The fountain was dry – the beautifully blue and white abstract tiles of the basin and rim dusty and bleached. Still, as I passed by I felt the caress of water on my face, my arms, my head and my feet. It was refreshing but I could have done with a drink as well.

As I approached the archway it stayed in darkness, while around it the angles and shadows shifted and changed. From abstractions to statues, to carvings of animals and mythical beasts. I saw a sad woman, eyes downcast; a young man holding aloft the head of Medusa; some were what I thought might be Roman gods, others saints or kings. My feet slapped on the steps leading up and I stepped into the shadows.

It was a cathedral nave, with stone pillars stretching upwards to an impossibly high vaulted roof lit by golden sunlight. The walls were shaded and elaborately carved with animals and gargoyles, saints and sinners.

I thought some may have moved as I walked past.

I was drawn forwards towards an arch that was too squat and plain to be part of a cathedral. As I stepped through, I smelt burning and could hear men shouting in fear and frustration.

If before had been the cathedral in Seville, then this must be the Castle of San Jorge that sat across the River Guadalquivir from the city. Judging by the scorch marks, the smoke and the shouting – some point after Enrique had busted himself and his family out.

Ahead was a plain square doorway from which candlelight spilled like a beacon. I became aware of the bell-like tone that I associated with the violent arrival of Francisca in her guise as an angel of vengeance. It grew louder as I reached the doorway, but softer, too – like a bell humming.

I'd heard those tones before – from the bell Martin Chorley and Lesley May had planned to summon Punch with. Was this the same magic, or was it an innate quality of bells?

I decided that these were questions for another day, and stepped through the doorway.

It was a chamber the size of my parents' living room, with white plastered walls and carpets laid over a flagstone floor. There was no fireplace, but a couple of dozen candles burned in five-branched candlesticks mounted on stands around the room.

A man sat on a high-backed chair with the window behind him. He was old, white and thin, with grey hair poking out from under a black skullcap. His eyes were dark, deep-set and fixed on mine as I approached.

He was dressed in brown robes with a comically large starched white collar, making him look like a wilting flower or a Time Lord.

Kneeling in front of him was a naked white woman with brown curly hair; she had broad shoulders and muscular arms and legs. On her back were pale lines – old scars left by the lash. Her head was bowed but her arms were outstretched, her hands resting in the palms of the seated man.

Behind the man was a workbench with the crucibles, alembics and assorted glassware of the late medieval alchemist. Books and papers were stacked untidily on a wooden writing desk under the window, where they could catch the daylight. The view through the window was of an impossibly blue sky fading into the mist below.

The man said something in Spanish or Portuguese. His voice had a rasping quality – as if he hadn't spoken for centuries, and his mouth was dry.

'*Salve, loquerisne Latine?*' I said, on the basis that any man of letters would be more familiar with Latin than I am with Spanish.

'*Esne mi salvator?*' he asked – Are you my saviour?

I was tempted to say 'yes' and claim the ultimate authority, but I reckoned that would be a bit presumptuous – even by my standards.

'*Non sum, sed nuntius de longe emissus,*' I said – claiming I was a messenger from a far land.

'Have you come to release me from this burden?'

His Latin was fluent, although he pronounced his *c*'s soft, which would have annoyed Nightingale and

Postmartin, who were adherents of the hard consonant school of classical Latin.

I crouched down beside the woman and checked that it was, as I'd suspected, Francisca. Or her avatar, or spirit, or whatever it was we were doing here. It was definitely her, her face serene, her eyes closed and her lips moving in silent prayer.

I looked back up at the man.

'What's your name?' I asked him.

'Cristoval Romano,' he said. 'Magister. Once called the wise.'

'Once called?'

'In an educated man, hubris is the worst sin of all,' he said, and gave a spluttering cough that I realised was a laugh.

'How long have you been here?' I asked.

'It seems an eternity,' he said. 'At first I steeled myself to patience, then I sought to amuse myself through games and the recitation of poetry. For a while I tried to lose myself in erotic thoughts, then in dreams of vengeance against those that had urged me to this foolish action. Particularly that venal dog de Pruda. More recently, I have found comfort in prayer.'

I had so many questions, but also a real sense that it was better to get the fuck out while I could. How he'd done it, I decided, was less important than why.

'This is a terrible work,' I said. 'Why did you do it?'

'The usual reasons,' said the Magister. 'I told myself it was piety and duty to the Church, but a thousand years of contemplation will batter down the doors of one's own delusions.'

But not your tendency towards tortured metaphors, I thought.

'In truth, it was a test of skills,' he said. 'We had always been rivals, Enrique and I, and I was eager to prove myself the better philosopher.'

I glanced at the naked avatar of Francisca, kneeling, head bowed, also trapped within this VR recreation of an Inquisition prison. A thousand years of contemplation didn't seem to have revealed the fucking awfulness of what he had done to her. Perhaps he needed another thousand years for that.

But I didn't see why Francisca had to do time with him.

'Perhaps it is time for you to let her go?' I said.

'Ah,' said Romano the no longer wise. 'I fear you have not properly comprehended my circumstances.'

He glanced down and I followed his gaze to his hands. Francisca's work-strong fingers had a tight grip on the Magister's wrists. It was she who was holding him.

'What will happen to you if she lets go?' I asked.

'Perhaps I will be set free,' he said. 'Perhaps I will fall into oblivion or Heaven or Purgatory or Hell – I no longer care.'

I thought of the airmen of the moors, and the eager way they had boarded the Glossop's cargo cult passenger plane. They hadn't seemed to care where they were going, as long as they went. And I thought of Heather's narrowboat, its journey down from the North, and its cosy double bunk.

I had to think carefully about the next question – my Latin isn't *that* good.

'Did you make a weapon of this woman?' I asked.

'For my sins,' said the Magister.

'What did you offer her in return?'

'Offer?' The Magister seemed genuinely puzzled by the question. 'Nothing. She was a servant, a woman – obedience to her master and to God was enough.'

Right, I thought, *let's hope my counter-offer is better.*

I shifted so that I could see Francisca's face and called her name.

At first, nothing, and then the slightest frown appeared upon her forehead.

'Francisca,' I said again, and then in English, 'Your work is done. It's time to go home.'

She turned her head to look at me.

'*A casa?*' she said.

'Yes,' I said. 'Heather is waiting.'

Francisca definitely reacted to Heather's name, but it seemed disconnected.

'You haven't finished unpacking the shopping from Sainsbury's yet,' I said.

Her frown deepened and became a real worry attached to a real problem. I put my hands on hers and gave an experimental tug. Her grip stayed firm.

'Some of that stuff is going to go off if we don't put it away,' I said.

Suddenly her hands slipped off the Magister's. I didn't hesitate, and used my grip to raise her up and turn her to face me.

'Heather needs you,' I said, and we turned and walked away hand in hand.

I heard the Magister's coughing laugh, and looked

back to see him turn into vapour and drift away. Exactly like Beverley's water balloon or Nightingale's crimson flower – then the bench and wall behind his chair did the same.

I resolutely faced forwards and tried to pick up the pace.

Back through the corridor of pain and smoke, the cathedral of stone and light.

The courtyard of water and orange blossom.

I opened my eyes to what was left of the atrium. Ahead of me, Francisca was standing and looking around with amazement. When I took a step forwards, something caught my foot and I nearly stumbled. I looked to see what I'd tripped on and saw that the black and white floor tiles had been rucked up in concentric circles centred on the spot where Francisca stood.

'Stay still,' said Nightingale.

He was standing to my left with his right hand raised above his head, palm facing upwards, his left across his chest and clenched into a fist. Above us, the air shimmered in a curve over our heads. Raindrops were splattering on the shield and running in rivulets off the sides. I looked up further and saw that the Victorian glass and cast-iron dome that roofed the atrium was mostly gone. As I watched, a final section of iron girder with some attached glass tumbled down to smash on Nightingale's shield. It slid down to join the ring of debris I saw surrounded us.

Oh God, that's going to make a dent in the budget, I thought. *Maybe we can get a Kickstarter going.*

'I trust that you have resolved the angelic aspect of the case,' said Nightingale.

'I think so,' I said. I glanced at Francisca, who had slumped down to sit on the floor. 'Was anyone hurt?' I said.

'Not that I know of,' said Nightingale. 'But I doubt Molly will be pleased.'

'Lesley?'

'She bolted when the roof fell down,' said Guleed, picking her way through the debris towards us. 'If she's sensible, she won't ever come back.'

'She will,' I said. 'She won't know why, but eventually she'll come back.'

Francisca looked up at us – the cuts on her face were going to need the paramedic who, according to the plan, should be parked up in the courtyard.

She looked at me, her eyes wide.

'Am I free?' she asked.

'Yes,' I said. 'And no.'

20

Reconstruction

Duress is not a defence in murder cases. But balance of the mind is. And with that, and a sympathetic judge, prison could be short and then out on licence. Back to Heather's narrowboat and the glamour of the open canal.

Which means we'd need to devise a new offender management set-up for Falcon cases.

Which meant I'd made more work for myself, but not that afternoon. Once Francisca had been reunited with Heather and introduced to our custody sergeant, I was sent packing by Nightingale.

Guleed drove me home.

'Done?' asked Beverley after I'd kissed her.

'All bar the paperwork,' I said.

'Good,' said Beverley. 'Get in the bath and tell me about it.'

So I soaked in our enormous tub while Beverley sat on the stool beside it, listening, eating a plate of rice and soup and occasionally reheating the water. I left out the bit where I deliberately threw myself into a trans-dimensional rift, but even so Bev had that deceptively calm look that told me she was shelving her complaints for a more convenient moment.

After lunch with Mum in the kitchen, I went into the bedroom and lay down for a quick nap.

I awoke to darkness and the sound of women's voices like the laughter of water tumbling over polished stones. I lay in that halfway state between dreams and reality and listened as they moved around me in whispers of silk and perfume.

'You want to get up now, babes,' said my beloved. 'Or you're going to miss the main event.'

I rolled out of bed and luckily I was still in my boxers, because I wasn't dreaming – the room was full of Beverley's eldest sisters. Lady Ty was there, in a white cotton shift tied at the waist with old rope. There was gold at her throat and wrists and threaded through the braids that were piled up on her head like a crown. She glanced at me and shook her head in resignation.

Effra was there, long and lean in an eye-wateringly psychedelic halter neck dress cinched at the waist with an iridescent scarf of green, gold and black. She'd taken out her normal extensions, and instead her hair was a magnificent puffball Afro with a single Bride of Frankenstein streak of electric blue above each temple. Her nails were long and decorated with flags and shields, lions and leopards, crosses and chevrons. She grinned when she saw me looking and gave me a mocking salute.

Fleet was there, all broad shoulders and narrow waist in blue Lycra gym shorts and matching crop top. Around her neck hung a compact digital stopwatch, and her hair was sensibly hidden beneath a bathing cap.

She gave me a curt nod and turned her attention to the stopwatch.

Standing amongst them was Beverley, huge and beautiful, vast and magnificent in a white linen undershirt with her dreads falling free down to her bum. She stood with her hands on the small of her back, spine slightly arched, eyes closed, cheeks puffing in and out.

'When did it start?' I asked, while desperately searching for my jeans, my work trousers, tracksuit bottoms – anything.

'Hours ago,' said Beverley. 'But you looked so sweet I didn't have the heart to wake you until I was ready to go.'

'Are you ready?'

Beverley grimaced suddenly and then relaxed.

'Oh, I'm beyond ready,' she said, and her sisters laughed, even Lady Ty, which was quite unsettling in and of itself.

I found a pair of swimming shorts under one of Beverley's wetsuits and dragged them on. I spotted a T-shirt under the bed, but when I grabbed it Beverley told me to leave it off.

'I need you with your shirt off,' she said, and then she tensed – her face screwing up.

I looked over at Effra, who shrugged and rolled her eyes – she didn't know why either.

Lady Ty clapped her hands to get our attention.

'If everybody's ready,' she said, 'then let's get this show on the road.'

She opened the French windows and, putting her finger to her lips, motioned us outside. Effra led the way and I took Beverley's arm and followed her out. Beverley was perfectly mobile, except when a contraction hit – at which point she grabbed hold of me and, breathing hard, waited for it to pass. We had to stay quiet because of the row of tents that had been pitched on the patio and the lawn beyond. Tents full of the younger Rivers and hangers-on. Their older sisters and cousins were in the spare bedrooms upstairs.

Counting them, it was obvious that more had arrived while I was asleep.

'Has everyone in the entire demi-monde decided to turn up?' I whispered.

'No,' Beverley whispered back. 'Miss Tefeidiad couldn't make it.'

The night was dark, overcast, and I could smell rain on the air. Not fifteen hundred metres away was a perfectly good birthing pool at Kingston Hospital that had figured prominently in the birth plan not two weeks earlier. A nice, small, uncomplicated birthing pool for a nice low-key birth.

I sighed, and Beverley laughed and intertwined her fingers with mine.

'I remember seeing you on the riverbank at Richmond,' she said. 'Staring out over the water with that same boggled expression on your face. And I thought, even then, there's a boy who will be easy to surprise.'

'That makes no sense,' I said.

'It does to me,' she said.

Given the size of the pool at Kingston, the original plan was that I would be kneeling outside the pool behind Beverley, offering support both moral and physical. But now I was wading into – surprisingly clean – river water. Beverley led me by the hand until the water reached my hips and then stopped. She started tugging at her shift, which was already sodden and heavy.

'Help me off with this,' she said, and we peeled it off together.

I wadded it up and threw onto the pool side, where one of Abigail's fox friends grabbed it and dragged it away. I turned to look and saw that Nicky, Brent and a couple of other junior river goddesses were piling out their tents and jumping up and down in excitement. Maksim shushed them before they could start making a noise and then opened a box full of sweets to bribe them to keep quiet. Standing on the patio, Abigail was chatting to Chelsea and Olympia.

Beverley had another contraction, and I slipped my arms under hers to support her. She blew out her cheeks and made a very strange whining sound which devolved rapidly into the much more familiar 'Fuckfuckfuckfuck.'

Fleet, Effra and Tyburn waded into the pool to join us. Tyburn passed me a net on a stick, the sort Beverley used to scoop up fishes and insects. Because my hands were full, Tyburn had to delicately trap it under my armpit.

'What's this for?' I asked.

'Floaters,' said Tyburn, and giggled.

Tyburn, as far as I knew, was the only one of Mama Thames's daughters to have actually given birth, so I assumed she knew what she was doing. We'd asked her advice a couple of months previously.

'Go to St Mary's,' she'd said. 'And make sure you ask for an epidural.'

392

The Lindo Wing of the private St Mary's Hospital was where the royals went to drop their sprogs, so I wasn't surprised. And Beverley wasn't keen. Besides, it didn't have anything that Kingston didn't have.

Listening to Beverley alternately puffing and swearing, I wondered if maybe she wasn't regretting our al fresco birthing pool. Even if the water was unnaturally warm.

'This is so undignified,' said Beverley as she gripped my arm.

'Anything worth doing usually ends up undignified,' I said, and Beverley gave me a harsh look.

'Peter, just so we're clear,' she said. 'Your role in this is strictly supportive.'

'Yes, my love.'

'Shut up,' she said, and turned her head to kiss me.

Fleet laughed and I heard Tyburn making gagging noises like a teenager.

'Heads up,' said Effra. 'Here comes Mama Grant.'

I looked back again to see my mum approaching from the house. Her hair was covered in a white wrap, and she, too, wore a white linen shift like a baptismal dress. Or maybe not linen, because as she stepped into the pool lights the material shimmered with glints of colour. She was looking down at us with a beatific smile that I'd only ever seen on her face when Dad was soloing, and I was even more shocked to see the tracks of tears down her cheeks.

God, African mothers . . . If you can't be a doctor, a lawyer or an engineer, knock out some sprogs and they will forgive you *all* your failures.

She hesitated short of the water and I was wondering why, when I heard the sharp cry of a seagull and suddenly the air smelt of the sea.

With just a hint of diesel and coal smoke.

The whispers and murmured conversations in the garden ceased; even the constant rumble of traffic on the Kingston Bypass faded into nothing. Fleet, Tyburn and Effra separated to leave a path.

Mama Thames rose from the river at the end of the pool and came gliding towards us as if she was carried along by an invisible current. She had black eyes set in a smooth round face, pinked at the corners like her daughters', broad shoulders, strong arms and wide hips. Her skin was as dark and as smooth as a young child's. She was dressed identically to my mum – the same iridescent headdress and shift with the colours rippling like wavelets across the fabric. The only difference was an old-fashioned nurse's watch pinned upside down to her breast.

'About fucking time,' said Beverley.

My mum waded past me and joined Mama Thames in front of Beverley, the senior sisters stepping in to form a half-circle.

Mama Thames took her daughter's hand.

'Whenever you feel ready,' she said.

'Actually,' said Bev, 'I think I could go for some breakfast – fuuuuuuuuuuuuuuuuck!'

There was a lot of panting and shouting and swearing, and I like to think I carried off my very minor role in a properly supportive manner. Literally supportive when the first twin crowned and Beverley flung herself back against me, her feet leaving the bottom of the pool.

It felt good to be doing something useful that didn't involve fishing out floaters.

Then Beverley gave a shudder that seemed to run down her body from head to hips. Mama Thames stooped to lift the first twin clear of the water. Then the baby cried and my mind went completely blank with the enormity of it all.

'Peter,' hissed Beverley, 'we're not finished yet.

Mama Thames held up the first twin and spoke in a voice loud enough to cause noise complaints across the neighbourhood.

'Taiwo,' she called. 'Mamasu Rose.' The last being my mum's two first names.

She passed the baby – umbilical still attached – to Tyburn, who looked down at her, then blew a raspberry and stuck out her tongue.

'Fuck!' shouted Beverley.

She tensed again, made a terrible face and then relaxed and slumped back against me. I heard another baby cry and Mama Thames held up another glistening, squirming infant.

'Kehinde,' she said, and then looked at me, the power of her regard fixing me in place. She raised an eyebrow.

'Beatrice,' I said.

'Beatrice?' asked Beverley.

'After Betty Carter.'

'Yes,' said Fleet. 'The one and only.'

'Yes,' said Mum.

'Yes,' breathed Mama Thames, and her affirmation was like the wind bellying out the sails of a clipper turning for home.

In films and television they always gloss over the messy bits that come next, the umbilical cord cutting and afterbirth disposal – the alarming pink cloud that briefly suffused our end of the pool.

And so will I.

All through the later stages of the pregnancy I'd imagined the twins as already sly and mischievous, but instead I was entrusted with a pair of wrinkly faced gnomes – albeit with curly mops of black hair and black eyes that pinked to the sides like a cat's.

'Yes,' I said, as I waded out of the pool with the twins in my arms. 'You are mine.'

'You've got that the wrong way round,' said Lady Ty behind me.

I woke the next morning to the sound of the foxes begging my mum for snacks and then running around yelping because they were too spicy. Beside me, Beverley stifled a laugh, but when we heard Abigail chasing after the foxes and trying to get them to eat white bread, she couldn't keep it in any more. The laugh woke the twins, who immediately wanted feeding.

I helped Beverley get into position for tandem feeding and watched as her face took on an expression of pained surprise as the twins clamped on.

'OK, girls,' she said, 'there's enough for everyone.'

About a minute after feeding, I got my first taste of nappy changing. I don't know what people complain about. I've cleaned up much worse than that. It didn't even smell that bad.

'That's because they're yours,' said Auntie Ty when

she visited that afternoon. 'For everyone else, the shit stinks just the same.'

Obviously, the world does not stop just because you're on paternity leave. Fortunately, between Bev, my mum, Maksim and, disconcertingly, Lady Ty, I managed to carve out enough time to finish up the paperwork. Nightingale, Guleed and Danni handled the inquests and the legal aftermath without me, although the DPS called me in for an interview. I took the twins with me, so it turned out to be quite short.

One thing I did early on was prepare an official briefing document for Special Agent Reynolds, and a definitely unofficial document for the secret branch of the New York Libraries that deals with dangerous magical artefacts. My hope was that they would send someone after Brian Packard and Lesley May to try and secure the lamp. To ginger them up, I may have exaggerated its significance as a magical artefact – just a tad.

'Is that wise?' asked Nightingale at the next weekly conference call. 'We hardly parted on good terms.'

'We're all too separated,' I said. 'And these informal links are OK, but what if something happens to me and you?'

'You think we should formalise our association with the FBI?' he asked.

'And with the Dutch,' I said, 'and the French, and anyone else who wants to talk. Magic has never been purely local, has it? We've just done a case from the Middle Ages which extended from Seville to Manchester.'

Nightingale agreed that greater formal co-operation was desirable, but added that the Home Office was still opposed to any such links, and we hadn't even broached the idea with the Foreign Office.

'We have potential allies with influence,' I said.

'You're thinking of Lady Ty,' he said. 'Not someone who has shown us much goodwill in the past.'

'Ah, but we've got family connections now,' I said. 'And baby diplomacy.'

Nightingale remained sceptical, but less than a week later Grace and Caroline came down from Glossop to visit.

I offered them a twin each to hold, but strangely they said no.

'Not everybody wants children, you know, Peter,' said Caroline.

'And it's hard to talk with your hands full,' signed Grace.

Since the twins were doing their rare impression of sleeping angels, I made coffee and put some biscuits out. Grace had taken the opportunity to nose around the living room, and when I got back she was having what looked like a heated discussion with Caroline. I was definitely going to have to pick up some British Sign Language soon – if only so I could eavesdrop on those two.

The discussion wound down and the two accepted coffee. Unfortunately, Beverley and Abigail had eaten all the Molly-supplied biscuits and we had to make do with the ones donated by the local Waitrose.

Grace and Caroline had brought a hanging mobile for the twins – carved wooden figures interspersed with moons and stars and capering kitchenware. The figures were traditional fairytale witches wearing pointy hats and riding brooms, although at least one of them was brandishing a hammer, and they had foxes as familiars, not cats.

The foxes puzzled me a bit, but before I could ask about them Grace presented me with another gift. This was a tooled leather smartphone case – the type with a flap that protected the screen.

'Thank you,' I said.

When I took it, it seemed to be much heavier than it needed to be. When I opened it I saw that gold threads had been inlaid into the leather in looping knots and curls. When I looked back at Grace and Caroline they wore identical grins.

'Magic-resistant,' signed Grace.

'Nice,' I said. 'Stay here a moment.'

I went and fetched an Airwave handset from my office and showed it to Grace.

'Could you make one for this?' I asked.

Grace's grin grew wider and slightly feral.

'What's it worth?' she signed.

'I don't know,' I said. 'What do you want?'

Less work-related, ironically, was a visit from Stephanopoulos and her wife Pam. They'd come for what Stephanopoulos jokingly called an 'infant assessment session'. They'd been thinking of either having their own kids or adopting, and the twins did their best to persuade them that they might prefer to adopt older children.

'Once they're past the screaming and pooing stage,' said Pam.

I did put them in touch with Stacy Carter and Tyrel Johnson, who fostered older 'difficult' kids and might be able to advise.

'You're a compulsive networker,' said Beverley when I told her.

'It seems to work,' I said, although my therapist constantly tried to convince me that the networking was a displacement activity to help me avoid dealing with my own emotional issues. She was having to work quite hard at the moment, because I've found I can happily talk about how much I love the twins for a whole hour, no problem. And unlike my other acquaintances, my therapist can't make excuses and run away.

Spring arrived, and by May, Maksim had remodelled the water feature into something a bit less like a slipway and a bit more like a swimming pool. To celebrate that, and some surprisingly good weather, we held Beverley's birthday party outside in the garden. Just to be on the safe side, we rigged an awning that extended over the patio in case it rained. Which, of course, it did. Fortunately, Fleet and Effra took it in turns to sit in the water and keep it warm enough for all the kids – river goddesses or not – to splash about in without contracting hypothermia. Since we weren't having a christening, the party also served to introduce the twins to a wider circle of friends and family. And Seawoll demanded that he be made a godparent.

'I've always wanted to be a disreputable uncle,' he said.

He'd brought presents, just in case – two pairs of

onesies with a picture of the Tardis on the front with SO MUCH BIGGER ON THE INSIDE printed beside it.

Because new parents crave sleep above all things, we wrapped up the party by the early evening, but Nightingale lingered. While Mum and Beverley settled the twins, Nightingale beckoned me out onto the patio and, sensing a lecture coming, I reluctantly joined him sitting at the white enamel garden table. Judging by the bottle of Kloud beer in front of him, this wasn't going to be an official lecture. I suspected something much worse. Friendly advice.

Before we got down to it, though, Nightingale turned and addressed the shadowed length of the garden.

'This is a top secret confidential discussion,' he said loudly. 'So you lot can all pop off back to your duty stations.'

The pool lights were still on, illuminating the water and the drizzle falling on it. Traffic rumbled on the main road and Mum was singing 'Stormy Weather' in the kitchen.

Nightingale lifted his hand in a vaguely threatening gesture and there was a sudden rustling amongst the bushes, as if half a dozen medium-sized quadrupeds were departing at some speed.

'Alone at last,' I said.

'I doubt it,' said Nightingale. 'Those were decoys. They'll have left at least one fox on station. Their hearing is really quite magnificent, as is their sense of smell, although Abigail thinks they may have traded some of that for greater intelligence.'

Nightingale seemed about as eager to give the friendly

advice as I was to receive it, and I didn't see any reason to spur him on.

'What do you know about them that you haven't told me?' I asked.

'It's what Abigail knows that she hasn't told either of us that interests me,' he said. 'But we can deal with that issue at a more appropriate time.'

Oh well, I thought. *It was worth a try.*

'Had you died, Peter,' said Nightingale without pre-amble, 'or vanished into some ghastly *allokosmos*, it would have been my duty to come here to notify Beverley of your death.' He tilted his head towards the house. 'I was spared that, thankfully. Not least because the consequences in terms of flood damage to south-west London could have been dire.'

We both managed weak smiles at the joke.

'I had hoped that incipient fatherhood would temper your recklessness,' he said. 'But we are what we are, aren't we? But being the people we are, we take our re-sponsibilities very seriously. So, in an effort to curb your enthusiasm somewhat, I plan to retire.'

I nearly dropped my beer, and six metres down the garden a squeaky fox voice went 'What?'

'But—' I said.

Nightingale smiled and raised his hand to stop me.

'Not just now, of course,' he said. 'But certainly within the next five years. You, in turn, will be required to take a more managerial role in the Folly. This way, you will be forced to put a higher value on your own life.'

Because, of course, I thought, *administrative duties have been such a feature of your tenure.*

I opened my mouth to . . . what? Object? Plead? Scream?

'When I first contemplated recruiting you,' said Nightingale, 'I spoke to your Team Inspector Francis Neblett.'

'He must have loved you,' I said.

Neblett had been so old-school uniform that I'd had to fight the urge to salute every time he walked past.

'I believe he would have preferred not to have recommended you,' said Nightingale. 'But he was far too upright a man to dissemble. He said you were prone to "overthinking" things and that you were easily distracted. But if I could engage your attention, you were capable of anything.'

'That is not the impression he gave me,' I said.

'Indeed,' said Nightingale, with a disturbing grin, 'he also warned me about you.'

'Warned you about what?'

'He said that you were surprisingly reckless and that I would age significantly with you under my command,' he said.

'And have you?' I asked.

'I've had moments of worry,' he said. 'And this is my solution.'

'But what are you going to do with yourself,' I said, 'if you retire?'

'Peter,' said Nightingale, 'there are so many things I would like to do. For one thing, I would like to see the mountains of Kashmir again.'

Oh, good, I thought, *a war zone. Now who's going to get white hair?*

'It would be nice to visit Germany and not be shot at,' he said. 'Or China, or Sierra Leone – places I've never been.'

The panic I was feeling must have shown on my face.

'Not all in a rush,' he said. 'Obviously. When I was younger even than you, the headmaster of Casterbrook suggested that I consider becoming a teacher. I was horrified at the time, of course, but now I think we should consider reopening the old place.'

'As a school?'

'More as a college and a training centre,' said Nightingale. 'After all, there's no point in my leaving you in charge if you have no underlings to order about.'

'A police training college?' I asked – the College of Policing would probably love that.

'We can start modestly right away,' said Nightingale. 'That much is in your operational plan already.'

'PIP level 1 Crime Scene Vestigia Awareness,' I said.

'Quite,' said Nightingale. 'Although I think in the long term we should pursue a wider curriculum.'

'Is that wise?' I asked.

'The wider the base, the greater the stability of the building,' said Nightingale. 'You taught me that.'

I thought of the future – which now had my daughters in it, and foxes, and mad Northern smiths, and whatever mischief Abigail was going to get herself into.

I raised my bottle.

'To the future,' I said. 'Whatever that is.'

THE END

Technical Notes

DCI Seawoll is probably too old to have played in the ruins of Volcrepe Mill, since it didn't stop production until 2003, but it made such an interesting scenario that I've decided to bend the laws of time and space. I'm sure Alexander wouldn't mind.

The aircraft crash sites on the moors are real, too, as was the V1 attack on Manchester.

The London Silver Vaults is a real place and well worth a visit. I spotted some very pretty foxes down there when I visited, and if you need silver, rings, plates, cutlery or just weird statues, it's definitely recommended. Also, it's one of those quirky bits of London's tapestry, like the sadly gone Whitechapel Bell Foundry, that we're going to lose if we don't support it.

Acknowledgements

Alas, my Latin and Early Modern Castilian is non-existent, so many thanks to Penny Goodman and Paul White from Classics at Leeds and Simon Doubleday from Hofstra University for their translations. Likewise Mary, for providing the Krio and the recipes that inconvenienced the foxes. I need to thank Andy Ryan for behind-the-scenes help and Clive Hall for architectural advice, as well as Thom Hetherington for a guided tour of Glossop. Thank you to everyone at the Portico Library and the London Silver Vaults. And doubleplusgood thank you to everyone on Twitter who answered my numerous questions no matter how bizarre they were.

Credits

Ben Aaronovitch and Orion Fiction would like to thank everyone at Orion who worked on the publication of *Amongst Our Weapons* in the UK.

Editorial
Emad Akhtar
Brendan Durkin
Celia Killen

Copy editor
Steve O'Gorman

Proof reader
John Garth

Editorial Management
Jane Hughes
Charlie Panayiotou
Tamara Morriss
Claire Boyle

Audio
Paul Stark

Jake Alderson
Georgina Cutler

Contracts
Anne Goddard
Ellie Bowker
Humayra Ahmed

Design
Nick Shah
Nick May
Joanna Ridley
Helen Ewing

Finance
Nick Gibson
Jasdip Nandra
Elizabeth Beaumont
Ibukun Ademefun

Afeera Ahmed
Sue Baker
Tom Costello

Inventory
Jo Jacobs
Dan Stevens

Marketing
Jen McMenemy
Brittany Sankey
Tom Noble

Production
Paul Hussey
Fiona McIntosh

Publicity
Stevie Finegan
Will O'Mullane
Leanne Oliver

Sales
Jen Wilson
Victoria Laws
Esther Waters
Frances Doyle
Ben Goddard
Jack Hallam
Anna Egelstaff
Inês Figueira

Barbara Ronan
Andrew Hally
Dominic Smith
Deborah Deyong
Lauren Buck
Maggy Park
Linda McGregor
Sinead White
Jemimah James
Rachael Jones
Jack Dennison
Nigel Andrews
Ian Williamson
Julia Benson
Declan Kyle
Robert Mackenzie
Megan Smith
Charlotte Clay
Rebecca Cobbold

Operations
Sharon Willis

Rights
Susan Howe
Krystyna Kujawinska
Jessica Purdue
Ayesha Kinley
Louise Henderson